OLIVIA RENNER

THE
BURDENED
ROSE

BOOK TWO

First edition
ISBN: 979-8-9923102-2-1
Cover art by: Miblart.
Edited by: Callie Rickard

For those who have ever felt as if they were a burden.
You were never too much.

Glossary

Seasons in the Realm of Nesrin:

Sprouting season - Spring

Flowering season - Summer

Harvest season - Autumn

Wither season - Winter

The deities:

Aeterna - goddess of the earth

Cordelia - goddess of the sea

Esen - god of the sky

Akuma - god of death

Content warnings can be found after the acknowledgments.

.

REALM OF

ESEN'S
SHRINE

◆ KELDOVAR

◆ NARTHIS

THE IRON THORN

◆ VELORAAN

EMERALD MOUNTAINS

◆ ELDRAVINE

THE IRON BORDER

THE STONE BORDER

WO

AETE
FA

THORNROSE

One

Chaos replaced the night's peaceful song. Screams echoed in the rocky cliffs, followed by trees whining until they snapped. Embers flickered against the once black sky, now an ominous shade of amber. It blurred in the tears that welled in my eyes. The only thing to break me out of my daze was familiar arms as they enveloped me, pulling my useless body off the ground.

The shift was harsh, and air hissed through my teeth. Casimir's gaze found mine, messy black waves damp to his forehead. His lips moved in what resembled a muttered apology. It was inaudible beneath the thrum of bodies as they moved along the shoreline.

My eyes slammed shut, and I tightened a fist around a ridge in Casimir's onyx armor whenever the movement jerked at my side. He didn't slow his pace—*couldn't* slow his pace. If we didn't leave, the shore would be swarming with the king's men, and it would be the end of our people. Our final days spent with our petals blooming only to be sheared among a useless garden.

"Captain!" A voice rang over the chaos, slowing Casimir.

His head turned, but he never released me.

Another reverberating crack shattered the night, and I grimaced, ducking deeper into Casimir's shoulder.

"I want you to get her on the first ship. Taryn and Galan will accompany you." *Valor*. He was close, at the edge of Casimir's shoulder.

Grief bubbled inside my chest at the thought of losing another parent in the carnage as King Lendorr's soldiers pursued us.

We stayed with the throng of bodies, never stopping. Any hesitation, and we could all be captured.

Casimir glanced over his shoulder as Valor continued toward the fight. "General, shouldn't you—"

"Go!"

Casimir's arms tensed at the command.

Wails of agony pierced the night, followed by the sound of blades clashing, the contact ringing across the shore. It echoed and threatened to split my skull.

My breathing quickened with Casimir's desperate pace. His hands clutched me tighter. One of my arms went across his chest, holding his shoulder. I peered behind him, the sight turning my stomach as Valor stalked through the crowd, his sword drawn.

Through the throng, the armor of the Iron Guard was a harsh contrast of glimmering scarlet.

When Valor plunged his blade through an Iron Guard, I ducked back into the safety of Casimir's armor, my vision nothing more than scattered threads of crimson and black. The sensation rolled through me with feverish heat.

My palm fell from his shoulder, pressing to the rough texture of his chest plate.

"Casimir." My voice was muffled, lost in the cacophony of screams, but I sensed his gaze; felt the rigidity of his limbs, the falter of his pace.

The earth moved beneath us, out of balance as the once solid surface changed. Casimir's boots hit hard on wood. I opened my eyes, and the frame of a black ship came into view. We ascended the ramp, swaying as the water pushed and pulled the hull. His unsteady stride tugged at me until my wound sparked with pain.

It turned into a frenzy. People shoved, pushed, and stumbled with no regard for each other. I felt it all as bodies fought to get on the ship, desperate to escape the guards who stormed the shoreline. The hair on my neck stood when I thought of Prince Talos pursuing us.

Somewhere on the ship, a woman barked orders to depart.

Casimir's breath was heavy and warm on my neck. The ragged rasp drowned out everything else, a lull of peace flitting beneath my skin when his palm brushed an exposed portion of my back where my tunic had rolled up. I didn't look again until the pressure of the crowd let up, followed by the release of Casimir's arms. The lack of touch took the sensation of peace with it.

He lowered me to the ship's deck, safe beside a crate further from the panicked crowd. The sight behind him reminded me of the visions that once haunted me. Embers kicked up into the air, burning the blackened trees, long ago turned to rot by Aeterna's curse.

The wound on the left side of my abdomen pulsated, and I winced, a shaky hand finding the bottom of my tunic. The fabric stuck to my skin, a small patch of blood discoloring the dirty ivory. A cruel reminder of what Ronin had done.

A quiet "oh" passed my lips, lost in the building noise. My fingers quivered as I rolled the hem of my tunic, exposing the jagged sutures a few inches above my left hip bone. The inflamed vertical line was popped open along the middle of the stitching. I swallowed and rested my head back on the crate.

Casimir knelt before me, sweat causing his messy hair to stick to his temples. Intensity clouded his scarlet eyes, turning them nearly black.

"Where's Taryn?" Casimir's voice carried enough to reach those around us, but no one stopped to answer him. Many of them scrambled to get below deck, the ship rocking violently in response to their desperation.

Casimir cursed as he glanced around, a hand pressed to my shin.

In the crowd, I spotted Galan ushering more people onto the ship. Beyond the ramp, the only person I recognized was Orin, his white hair difficult to miss. He retreated with more Roses, leading them toward another ship. I couldn't find Valor in the sea of bodies.

My breath hitched, and I sat straighter to survey the ship once more. When I found Taryn's fiery red hair, my heart wrenched.

She sat on her knees with a terrified Ulrik clinging to her torso, tears pouring down her face. She didn't make a sound. Her blank stare echoed a terror only a mother could understand. Taryn's hands gripped Ulrik tight, her knuckles white.

"Taryn." Casimir tried to get her attention. She didn't move. "The wounded, Taryn!"

Her pale orange gaze never left the sky. Tears continued to trickle down her cheeks as Ulrik burrowed his face into her hair.

"Damn it," Casimir muttered, facing me. He moved closer as he eyed the wound. "Don't move." He stood and scanned the ship as more people disappeared below deck.

The ramp rose, and not a moment after, the ship jerked. My head swam at the sensation. I watched in a daze as the sails dropped and smacked the mast. The sound was thunderous, silencing those who continued to weep.

It happened too quickly. Whoever controlled our ship didn't stall. The fiery cliffs shifted, growing farther when the sour wind caught the sails.

I barely noticed when Casimir returned to my side. He was panting, a leather pack in one hand.

In the distance, a swarm of soldiers painted the shores red as the final ship dropped its sails, arrows soaring from the archers in the mast.

The brush of Casimir's fingertips was enough to get me to face him. He studied my wound, his hands shaking, before he tore through the leather pack and returned with salves and sutures.

Everything became a dizzying spiral—Taryn's blank stare. Galan, as he searched through the crumpled bodies around the ship. People clung to each other. Hands tugged at ropes.

Someone grabbed Casimir's shoulder. "Captain, we need you!" Warm brown hair fell in cascading waves, ash clinging to the crown of the woman's head. Elrin didn't show the same fear as the others. Her face was resolute. No sneer in my direction. A soldier like Galan, like Casimir.

Casimir's head whipped in her direction, his hand holding the edge of my tunic. I watched him cast another glance at Taryn. She looked as though all the blood drained from her face as her mouth moved with inaudible words.

"Captain, the people need—"

"Taryn!" Casimir tried again.

Elrin's brow furrowed. "They need someone to reassure them. You're the captain of Everbloom, they need you."

Casimir's gaze locked with mine, the items still in one hand, his other keeping the fabric off the popped sutures.

My trembling fingers wrapped around his forearm and squeezed. "Don't leave. Please." It was just loud enough for him to hear—loud enough to banish his hesitation from existence.

Elrin shuffled behind him. "Casimir, you have a duty to these people."

"Hayes can help them far better than I can right now. Go." Casimir didn't spare Elrin another word. He made quick work of threading the sutures. The rock of the ship was not enough to deter him.

Elrin froze, bewildered.

Casimir wrapped an arm around my back, moving me further from the crate. My head rested on the deck, and the absence of his warmth pained me when he pulled back.

I grasped his wrist, desperate. The threat of Talos finding me twisted my insides with panic. "I can't go back to the Temple. They can't reach us."

Sadness etched Casimir's face. His eyes flickered to the sacrificial mark on my neck, no longer hidden by my hair after Ronin had sheared my petals. Talos's claim on me was bare for all to see.

Casimir reached up with blood-tinged fingers, and his palm rested on the curve of my neck, covering the scar. The weight of it brought me comfort. Beneath the warmth, prickling echoed in my skin.

"I've got you," he whispered.

The prickling turned into all-encompassing numbness, my limbs heavy. Abrupt peace rippled through my veins, and every flutter of my lashes slowed until I couldn't open my eyes.

Crashing waves whisked me away.

Two

Thirty-two days later

Ocean spray ricocheted off the hull of the ship. Waves rose and fell as the sails caught another sour wind. The cursed water foamed against the wood, frothy and the same shade as gray moss. I spent many days worried that it might rot the ships and sink us all, leaving us to whatever lurked in the depths below—if there was anything at all.

Gone were the days when creatures roamed the open waters. When Aeterna threw off the balance between the four deities, she destroyed Cordelia's domain along with her own, cursing the land and sea.

We left any sign of civilization behind us, and the only view we had was water as far as the eye could see. Despite how far we sailed from Orondal, my raven stayed with me. Calla spent much of her time on the mast or on my shoulder. She picked at grains and pieces of dried fruit, much to everyone's dismay. There wasn't much food to go around, but I spared some of mine to keep her close. She was all I had from my life before.

Three large boats trailed behind ours, two beside, and one massive ship that led the way. Valor manned that one, far from the ship I found myself on. It seemed deliberate, an easy way to avoid the questions that ate at me, desperate to be answered.

Many of the wounded accompanied us, with Taryn tending to all of them. Alba sailed on another ship, her own healer abilities hardly enough to keep up with how downtrodden the people of Everbloom were. It was better than nothing.

The only form of correspondence between the ships came through Casimir and his ability to dreamwalk. It'd been a collective relief when he confirmed most of the Roses escaped unscathed.

It was short-lived when he broke the news that ten people were killed in the retreat. Cut down without a second thought from the Iron Guard. Their deaths echoed in the soft cries that filled the sleeping quarters at night. Grief too heavy to hold in.

I grimaced as Taryn prodded beneath my rib cage at the wound that was reluctant to heal. Casimir had done what he could, a memory lost to me—but I was grateful I didn't have to experience the thread of a needle through my skin.

After two weeks, Taryn removed the redone sutures. The edges of my skin were still ragged and inflamed, despite the accelerated mending offered by Taryn's abilities.

The bruises on my ribs, remnants of when Casimir brought me back, were nearly faded, and only a hint of yellow remained. I was left with a torso that ached when I turned, and the echo of a plea too painful to recall.

Calla lifted from my shoulder the second the emotions swelled, and went for the mast.

Taryn muttered an apology as she pressed a shaky hand to my skin— dehydrated and worn down, as we all were. I pursed my lips and stared at the waves to block out the way it stung as the energy coursed through her palm into the tissue on my side.

The sun was low on the water, shimmering in a magnificent reflection that hid how putrid the cursed sea appeared. I tried to focus on the orange flicker of the sun. It was my second healing of the day. One in the morning, one before sunset, so Taryn still had plenty of light. We avoided the use of lanterns if we could help it.

Valor was able to follow the path of the stars, and Galan had assured me that my estranged father knew the voyage well and had sailed it many times himself. Despite how careful we were, or how quickly our ships sailed, I still had a pit in my gut every time I glanced out behind us to see if we were being followed.

It wasn't a matter of if King Lendorr and Prince Talos would come, only when. They'd search the ends of the realm to find the Roses that escaped. It wasn't in their nature to allow us freedom.

After another grueling few minutes, Taryn removed her hand from my side. "How does that feel?" She asked the same question every time, and each time, it felt no different to me. I lied for her benefit.

"It feels better than yesterday," I muttered while I fixed my tunic. I winced at the way the skin pulled.

Taryn's lips pressed into a thin line, and she sat straighter. Her hair was pulled into a tight twist, the red curls poking out at the edges of her face. "You can tell me if it still hurts. If it isn't healing properly, I need to know. I can only feel so much with my palms."

I met her pale orange gaze, pulled back to the first night on the ship for a moment. She didn't talk for the first four days. She healed me without a word, Ulrik at her side, before she hid away with him. It wasn't until we lost sight of land that she ventured to the upper deck.

The memory of her terror continued to haunt me.

I sighed and pulled my leather vest back on, leaving the ties undone. "It's truly not as bad as it was. Day to day, it's hard to feel a difference."

She nodded and closed her healing supplies. "Try to get some rest. If anything feels off, let me know. Got it?"

I offered a small smile and stood from the crate. My boots slapped the deck of the ship as I left her behind, though there weren't many places to go.

The sun melted into a pale red sky, painting the clouds an ominous color. Bodies swayed and trudged around the ship, adjusting sails, checking supplies, and the ropes. I moved past them, not paying them any mind. The busyness of it all had become normal to me, and their routine hardly ever changed.

As I made my way back to the sleeping quarters, I spotted Casimir emerge from below deck, his eyes sunken as dark circles threatened to swallow them. His eyes met mine, but within an instant, he averted his gaze. I bit the inside of my cheek and tried to ignore the way his avoidance stung.

Part of me felt that I deserved it. The threat to turn over Everbloom to follow Ronin back to the Iron Thorn was a terrible reminder. My foolish behavior cost lives in Everbloom and stole their safety. I knew all too well what that was like. Casimir had every right to resent me and avoid speaking to me. It didn't stop it from feeling akin to a knife in my chest.

I watched him walk to the top deck, taking the spot he always did near the ship's captain as the sun disappeared. He remained below during the day, and I had accepted the sole purpose was to avoid me.

He didn't spare me another glance as I trudged to the lower deck. I ducked to avoid hitting my head on the narrow entrance down the steps and pushed through the group of people who chatted while they organized the supply crates. The ship was much too crowded, and it made it difficult to navigate the cramped space. Each day spent at sea with unfamiliar faces and an abundance of voices and sounds, it often felt as if my head might burst.

My life before had been quiet. The only sounds were the soft chatter of Eldravine as I strolled through the markets or hunted in the woods with my father. Most of my days were spent with my head ducked low, and no obligation to speak with others. With no company outside of Casimir, I only had my father to speak to. My social ineptitude made the time on the ship more difficult.

Kind strangers took the time to help me as I became accustomed to sea travel, learning the many things I needed to in order to be of help on the ship. I couldn't be more grateful for their kindness, yet the hollowness never eased. Despite how Elrin offered me help the entire first week, taking shifts with Taryn to help me change wound dressings. And the way Galan helped lift me into my hammock each night until I could do it myself. Or the times a quiet man with somber eyes always took the heavier supplies from me when I helped with the upper deck tasks.

Each person I began to feel comfortable with morphed into something sinister—a sneer hidden in their expression.

It was torture.

I reached the end of the ship, finding the familiar cabin door propped open with Galan lying in the lower of the two thin brown hammocks. My brow quirked.

"I thought we agreed I could have the bottom hammock," I said, watching as he scrambled in the fabric, half asleep.

"My apologies, Elita," he said, sitting straight.

Guilt racked me within an instant, and I shook my head, chuckling. I hadn't gotten used to him using my first name. Some days, he still used my family name, which I found strangely comforting. A piece of them, forever tied to me.

"I was only joking. My wound is healing well. It shouldn't be a problem."

He shook his head and clambered out of the hammock. "Ms. Taryn does not seem to think so."

I shrugged, avoiding his look of concern, and hoisted myself into the bottom hammock. My stomach twisted with discomfort as the fabric swayed with my weight and the ship's constant motion.

Galan did his best to gracefully climb into the upper hammock, but he nearly fell every time he got into it—his long limbs struggled to fit in the tight quarters. Most people took issue with the suffocating cabins of the ship.

I couldn't bring myself to agree with the complaints. Not when my sleep remained free from visions of rot and death. And there was no need for the ghost in my dreams when he walked among the ship. I sometimes wondered if the act of being sheared—of *dying*—had brought me the peace I longed for all those years.

Ronin's snarl didn't follow me in my dreams. Instead, I saw him when I was awake in the faces of everyone on the ship.

Memories of him plagued me anytime I let my guard down. It acted as a lesson and a warning against ever opening myself up again. Especially when the people from Everbloom had been prepared to let Valor lock me away. They didn't protest Valor's plan to kill Ronin. No one could have known his true intentions, and they intended to let him die.

The people I thought I could trust from Everbloom proved to have their own sinister intentions and beliefs, but beyond that, I had betrayed them, too, when I threatened their sanctuary. It pained me to remember their shared looks of horror. There was no way to escape how I was willing to trade their lives for a single man who doomed the entire realm.

My thoughts spiraled too far, and I tried to push back the visions of Ronin's hand trembling as he hesitated—his resolve split as he grieved and burned with hatred. None of it was truly for me, but for the realm in its entirety. The disdain cost his life, and the memory of him dead in the grass was one I longed to forget. But no matter how hard I tried, I couldn't escape the sound of Casimir ending Ronin's life.

I pinched the space between my thumb and finger, trying to bring myself out of the cycle of torment.

"Galan?" I cut through the quiet.

"Hmm?" He sounded half asleep, but Casimir continued to appear more exhausted by the day. He didn't look well, and I needed to know if he was okay, despite everything pointing to the opposite.

"Has Casimir talked to you at all? About what happened?"

Galan sighed in response, shuffling in the hammock above me. "I hardly see him, I'm afraid. Have you tried speaking with him about your concerns?"

"We still haven't spoken."

"Perhaps you should—"

"He won't let me, Galan. He hides all day. The moment I get near him, he goes the opposite way." My anxious gaze flickered over Galan's hammock. "I worry he'll continue to avoid others."

When silence followed my words, Casimir's plea for me to breathe bounced around my skull. Every inch of me coiled in response.

Galan shifted again. "I will try my best to speak with him. I feel your company may be of more help, though. Something of that magnitude is easier to speak about with those who shared the experience."

"Yes. I know," I whispered.

Rolling in my hammock, I faced the dark wood of the ship.

The loneliness that followed Casimir's cold shoulder reminded me of that truth each passing day. He was the only one who knew how long my death had haunted me. How many times I had been in that clearing in my nightmares. It had never been clear before, but the eyes in my nightmares were *his*. A piece of him died that day, and I worried he would continue to carry the burden alone.

I sighed, shaky and exhausted. The shorter hairs flattened in an oily mess at my shoulders when I lay on my back, my vision strained by fatigue. I pulled the wool blanket over me, blocking the chill that swept through the cabin.

No matter how much I hated the gods, I gave them my gratitude for the reprieve during my sleep.

Casimir's begging couldn't haunt me there. Not in the blissful nothingness. The only time my past didn't torment me was when my eyes finally closed—no more nightmares or ghosts to haunt me.

Three

A *pulse like thunder echoed through the clearing. Heavy, desperate. His presence became another pulse in the earth. It brought nothing but agony. A visceral ache bloomed in my chest.*

In the blur of black trees, soft emerald eyes watched, flickering to black and gold with every thud of the rapid heartbeat.

The figure moved with elegance, gliding over the rotten earth. His face was hauntingly familiar, only for a split second before it switched again; gold and black eyes beneath golden hair. The suffocating weight of sorrow blocked out the streaks of light that slithered through skin and bone until grief outweighed it all.

The warmth evaporated, leaving me hollow.

Ruby eyes gazed back at me, drowning in pools of black until the irises seemed to glow.

Thick dark hair cascaded down either side of the figure's face, hiding all but the glowing irises that bore into mine. The hammock beneath me was solid, though a bit thin. It swayed with the ship, and above me, Galan's soft snores told me I was awake.

In the inky darkness, I tried to speak. My mouth opened, but no words left my lips. Every bone in my body turned rigid, and I tried to move them, to reach out and jostle Galan awake. They refused my attempts, and

I stared over the side of the hammock, unable to look away from the eyes that watched me.

The figure approached, though it made no sound. Not a pad of a foot, nor the soft shift of breath. It moved as though it were floating on water until it closed the space between us. My panicked heart hammered in my rib cage like a trapped bird when the figure raised its hand. A faint glow thrummed in swirls inside its skin, the only way to track its slow, taunting movement. Claw-like fingers dragged across my throat, then my cheek. They continued their fiery path until it wrapped around a severed curl. I whimpered, the only sound I could make.

I willed my body to move, to jolt upright. But my efforts were wasted, and left my breathing ragged as I watched helplessly while the figure placed a palm on my chest.

Flashes of bloodshed blinded me. Swords locked in battle, spatters of blood painting the earth. Onyx vines slithered over eviscerated bodies, leaving more carnage in their wake.

Pain radiated through the back of my skull, and I tried to shake my head to rid myself of the awful sight.

A strangled sob forced its way past the block, and not a moment after, Galan scrambled out of his hammock, half asleep and thumping onto the floor. The figure and visions vanished in his wake. A puff of smoke in the night.

"What's happened?" Galan's voice came from the floor before he stood, his frame almost lost to the low light.

I inhaled as my body began to shake. Sensation rushed back into my limbs, and I sat upright in the hammock, unsteady with the sway of the ship, accompanied by the fear that coursed through my veins.

Flames came to life as Galan lit a candle. It remained close to the hammocks in case they were needed, and I was grateful when it illuminated the cabin. It didn't ease the dismay when I noted the lack of another person. The door hadn't been disturbed, and there was no sign anyone had been there.

I ran a shaky hand through my hair and slipped my legs over the side of the hammock. "Sorry. I must have been dreaming."

His brow creased, and he offered me a hand. I gave him a look of gratitude and took it. My legs shook when my feet found the floor.

"You've not had trouble sleeping since Orondal," he said while he set the candle on the small table.

I shrugged and tucked loose curls behind my ears. "It's okay. I need to walk for a bit, I think." I wasn't willing to tell him that it wasn't actually a dream. The only explanation I could conjure was that we had been on the sea too long, and I'd lost my mind.

"Are you sure?" he asked, concerned.

I offered him a small smile. "Yes, I'm sure."

Galan's features were weighed down by exhaustion, and it didn't take much for him to climb back into his hammock.

I left the cabin and took the candle with me. The ship carried an eerie silence as many of the Roses still slept. It was peaceful, and it helped settle my pulse. I was reminded of the walks I used to take with Aedric, the father who raised me. They had saved me from many nightmares.

When I trudged up the steps, I was greeted by the warm sun on the horizon. I stared for a moment, captivated by the sight. It wasn't often that I went above deck so early. No longer needing it, I set the candle on a nearby rail and hoped I would remember to bring it back to the cabin.

"Elita!" Taryn's voice startled me, and I glanced to the right. She waved and started toward me. I almost darted the opposite way to avoid another healing, but the flutter of multiple wings stopped me.

I noted birds overhead—their squawking almost inaudible over the shouts and chaos that rang throughout the busy deck.

The presence of birds was uncommon on the cursed seas. We'd been too far from land to see any in weeks. The only bird around was Calla. I was grateful for the distraction from the figure, but the remnants of the horrible vision clung to me.

Taryn strode to me with a grin. "Beautiful, aren't they? Although I've seen three people take a shit to the shoulder. I'd not stand under them," she said, hands on her hips.

I grimaced and dropped my gaze. "Maybe being up here isn't the best choice," I grumbled, fiddling with the edge of my tunic.

Taryn watched as I fidgeted. "Any pain today, white bloom?"

It took great effort not to recoil. The title was a horrible reminder of what I lost and what I had done to the realm.

I shoved the guilt back. "No. Just sore." For once, pain wasn't the reason I was awake so early. Goosebumps crept up my arms when I thought of the eyes that watched me. I cleared my throat. "What are birds doing this far out?"

Taryn rocked on her heels, excitement in her eyes. "Captain says we're close. We'll be there within a day."

At that, I perked up and scanned the horizon for any sign of land. I longed to feel the solid ground beneath my feet.

Any hope of relief disappeared when I thought of the state Mistvalle may be in by the time we arrived. I imagined a dead and barren land and the people there ready to demand my head.

Taryn noticed the shift in my mood and she placed a hand on my shoulder. "Don't worry. Good things to come. I can feel it."

Hope was foreign, but I clung to any fragments of it I found.

Taryn sighed after a moment, and she gave me a serious look. "Something bothering you?"

"Bad dream." The answer was a short lie, and it was clear she picked up on it by her expression.

"Wanna tell me about it while I heal?" Taryn patted my back with a stern hand. "Pesky wound is pissing me off," she said, the worry barely hidden underneath her light tone.

"I mean, it's a miracle in itself that I'm alive. Maybe we can accept that and leave the rest to chance?"

She gave me a pointed look.

"Fine," I muttered.

She clapped a hand on my back again, pushing me toward the same place we always found ourselves. I planted myself on the crate, resolving to keep the hallucination to myself.

I raised the edge of my tunic to expose the wound. As always, her expression fell. The infection was relentless the first week on the ship, and Taryn struggled to combat it for a while. It was finally on the mend, thanks to her abilities, but it still appeared irritated. It likely didn't help that I trained with Galan most days, using light weapons—despite Taryn telling me not to.

Taryn shook her head as she brought a hand to my side. Her eyes darted from side to side, as they always did. The sensation rippled through my skin, cold at first, before it melted into prickling heat the deeper her abilities worked.

In truth, I hated the sensation of her hand on my skin and the way she looked over my hair. There were no records of any Roses surviving a shear, and she suspected there wasn't hope for me to bloom again.

The sound of a child whining worked as a distraction, and I looked over at the steps to see Casimir and Ulrik leave the lower deck, his wide green eyes searching for Taryn. Out of everyone on the ship, Taryn only trusted Galan and Casimir to guard Ulrik's room when she did her early healings. Rather than sleep through them like he was meant to, he dragged Casimir along with him. When Ulrik caught sight of us, he left Casimir's side and scurried our way, his legs still wobbly on the ship.

I patted the crate next to me, and he hopped up, kicking his feet while his arm looped with one of mine. Casimir didn't join us, though I didn't expect him to. He went back down the steps and disappeared just in time for Ulrik to begin his morning commentary.

"That looks gross." He pointed to my scar, and I bit back a laugh.

"Ulrik," Taryn scolded. "What did I say about mocking Elita's appearance?" She winked at me and pulled her hand back.

I scoffed and straightened my tunic. "Most people tune out what you say. I'm sure Ulrik is an expert at it."

Ulrik giggled and covered his mouth with a dirty hand. He spent a lot of his time playing below deck, where it was perpetually unclean. The damp, slimy wood offered little room for good hygiene.

When Taryn moved back, I stood from the crate. Ulrik remained seated, dangling his feet.

"Any different?" Taryn bumped my shoulder.

"Not really. Sorry. I know that doesn't help."

She sighed. "Telling me it *doesn't* feel better actually helps me. Maybe someone in Mistvalle can give me pointers. I've got minimal training. I'm okay, at best."

"Don't sell yourself short. You brought me back, didn't you?"

She clicked her tongue. "Vanmore did that. I mean, I did what I could with my ability to stop the blood loss. Repair some cells. But had he not acted so quickly…well, you'd be as dead as what's-his-face."

I flinched.

"Yeah, my bad. That was in poor taste." She raised her hands. "I promise, if you give yourself permission to forget that brute, you'll feel much better. Healer's orders."

A pit formed in my chest. "You make it sound easy."

Taryn offered me a more solemn look. "It can be. With time. And some ale. Possibly the stronger herbs." Taryn elbowed me.

It sounded too simple.

The hollowness never dissipated. Whenever I believed I had escaped its hold, memories pulled me back. A hook embedded in my mind, sinking deeper the further I secluded myself. Something would remind me of him, and I would prickle with a cold sweat.

I didn't talk to Taryn about it. They were all aware of my struggles after the events with Ronin. And unwilling to be forgotten, the scars left by Talos—always somewhere in the back of my mind. A snarl and pale green eyes. Burning tinctures and a blade through the skin on my neck.

Goosebumps prickled my arms, propelling me further down the deck with little more than a glance back. I waved goodbye to Taryn and Ulrik over my head, though they were never out of eyesight for long during the day.

None of those on the ship were. It was much too small for how many bodies it held. There was no other choice, though, and it surprised me that Alba had meant what she said about Valor. He got everyone on despite how he threatened to leave the wounded behind. Meaning me. Meaning all the others Taryn cared for on the ship we were on.

Another parent who would abandon me for being an inconvenience. My mother's callousness followed me on the cursed sea. It echoed in Valor's cold shoulder and his avoidance of me.

Nothing compared to the quiet truth that lingered in the back of my mind. A harsh reality that the Roses would have sacrificed my bloom had I stayed in Everbloom. Where Ronin was seen as cruel for shearing me, they had intended for me to fulfill the prophecy.

All those years Casimir and Valor never came back for me, they knew where that led me. A shearing in the sacrificial garden. Nothing more than the salvation promised to them.

The bitterness took root deep in my soul. It matched the anger at the realm, my mother, the deities.

The crash of the waves, decay in the air, lack of fresh water—none of it was enough of a distraction. I longed to have the father who raised me back. A guide through the grief and the festering rage.

I wondered then if he ever knew I wasn't really his. Had my mother told him? The thoughts plagued me. It boiled under the surface. Buried beneath the foam that racked the side of the ship.

Salt burned my nose when I inhaled, and I braced my hands on the railing. I didn't realize I had gone so far until the soft spray of the ocean dusted my hands. The regret would come later when the cursed water caused unbearable itching. For a moment, it brought me out of another spiral.

My knuckles went white as I squeezed the rails. Wood pricked at my skin and left behind more splinters. The subtle sting blocked more of the racing thoughts out.

Another breath. More salt. The space behind my eyes stung. I hadn't cried since we left Orondal. The tears never came. No matter how heavy things were, the numbness consumed it all. It wiped away the sensation of tears—evaporated like the froth when the ship barreled through it.

Winds slapped in the sails, and they collided with the mast in a thunderous crack.

I stared out into the water until everything else fell away. The shouts of the crew. The waves crashing. Boots on hollow wood. Ropes tugging. It disappeared, and my heart thudded in my ears.

I hoped for land. I hoped for something better in Mistvalle.

The moment I wished for it, I felt the desire turn into a curse.

Four

I once thought nothing could be more chaotic than when we departed from the shores of Orondal. Until we dropped anchor near Mistvalle. Long docks stretched from the shore, barely visible as the sun dipped low in the sky. Everyone clambered to get close to the ramp, eager to be off the ship after over a month at sea. I shared the sentiment, but kept my distance when I caught a few people in the crowd glaring in my direction. The blame for Everbloom's fall rested on my shoulders.

The moment the ramp lowered, the sounds that erupted in the late afternoon were almost loud enough to be heard throughout the entire realm. There were two guards posted at each of the separate docks, their armor pure white and glistening in the dying light.

Soldiers of Mistvalle.

I joined the group of spectators at the railing as they marveled at the view of the mountains, their peaks and valleys a sight to behold in the distance. It appeared ashen, with rocky edges and expansive cliffs stretching out as far as I could see.

White willows, silver pine, and red trees dotted up and down the mountains. The sight left me speechless, unlike anything I had ever seen. The stunning fall and rise of the land was more magnificent than the mountains of the Iron Thorn or Orondal. They loomed in the distance, the red and white like a beacon of light drawing us toward the shore.

The sour bite in the air remained, but as we neared Mistvalle, it lost its overwhelming nature, no longer able to burn inside my nose. The breeze was refreshing, and it rustled the black linen dress I wore, lifting the cloak off my body until I shivered at the lack of its warmth. I tugged the long sleeves down, though it wasn't quite my size, and they stopped a few inches above my wrist. It'd be a relief to have better clothing than the little available on the ship.

More birds dotted the sky, little blurs of black swooping close to the ship, welcoming us to shore. Their wings carried them high and with ease.

A grin tugged at my lips when Calla perched on the railing before she took off, flying to shore.

In the thrall of awe, I hadn't noticed Casimir stop at my side. When he did, some of the excitement vanished. The way he stood, rigid and uncomfortable, I suspected my trip off the ship wouldn't be as easy as those who sprinted down the docks, unsteady on their sea legs.

I sighed. A goodbye to the moment of peace. "Do I play the part of prisoner here, too?" I asked, the question almost lost to the breeze.

"General Valor has asked us to escort you to the leader of Mistvalle for a formal greeting." The familiar smooth, deep tone of Casimir's voice was one I had missed; the formality, however, tainted it. Some of the first words he'd spoken to me since we left Orondal, and they felt like an exchange between strangers.

Finally, I faced him, looking up into the stoic expression he took to. "I don't want to meet another leader. I want a meal and a bath. Is that too much to ask for?"

Casimir exhaled, sounding exasperated. "It's only a greeting. What you do from there is your choice."

I almost scoffed at him. Every person I had met since leaving the cottage sought to gain something from me. Whether it was Ronin's need for revenge, or everyone in Everbloom seeking to fulfill the prophecy through my bloom. It seemed unlikely that the leader of Mistvalle didn't want something as well.

I faced the docks and adjusted my cloak. "Well, good luck getting me there willingly. I'll get lost finding somewhere to bathe, if I have to."

"Stubborn as ever." Taryn's voice came from behind us, and I peered over my shoulder to watch Ulrik drag her our way, a wide grin on his face.

"I'm not—"

"Oh, come off it. I've been helping you for over a month now. You're stubborn. Don't think I didn't notice those sneaky training sessions with Galan, too." Taryn gave me a pointed look, to which I ignored. The moment the infection had calmed down, I practically forced Galan to help me learn how to wield a short sword. It caused many setbacks with my healing, but I never mentioned it to Taryn. Clearly, I hadn't been as cunning as I thought.

Taryn and Ulrik paused beside us, much to Ulrik's dismay. A frown replaced his grin.

"Speaking of healing, I want you to find me later. Have this guy help you if need be." She gestured to Casimir. "Ulrik is ready to run about," Taryn said, smiling softly at her son.

I bristled and cast a sideways glance at Casimir. "You won't walk with us?" I asked, hoping she'd say yes.

She gave me a look that said she wouldn't be a buffer for Casimir's standoffish behavior. "Bub needs a good meal and a bath. He's become a grimy little thing. We don't want to get held up with the greeting." Taryn winked at me, and before I got another word in, Ulrik tugged her down the ramp.

Uncomfortable silence lingered after their departure, and another gust of wind swept in from the sea, brushing the short curls in front of my face, a constant bother. Taryn had tried to help me shape it into something less ragged. There wasn't much hope of salvaging hair that was sheared in haste by a blade.

I didn't mind the look of it, only the memories it carried.

Without a word, we started down the ramp. The boat rocked beneath us, and the sensation, the man beside me, brought me back to when we first boarded the ship. Before Casimir's resentment for my choices led us to stiff silence. I blamed the odd separation for the awful visions. It was unbearable to lose the connection with him once more.

The docks were high over the water that lapped at the posts. I hoped that once we made it further from the cursed sea, the smell might finally dissipate.

At the end of the docks stood a man I had hoped to avoid.

Valor waited for us, his demeanor that of a general. The similarities in our appearance were uncanny. I'd grown used to thinking the curse was why I didn't look like my mother or the father who raised me. Now, I realized many of my features mirrored Valor's.

Heaviness settled in my soul, and I pushed the melancholic thoughts from my mind as we neared Valor. He appeared as if he hadn't suffered the same month at sea. He moved with far too much grace for such a hardened exterior. A dark scarlet cloak adorned his shoulders, and he wore a sword at his hip, the pommel fit with a ruby.

Valor dipped his head in greeting when we stopped before him, our feet finding land. There wasn't even a moment to enjoy it.

"The leader of Mistvalle awaits our arrival. It's an hour-long trek through the woods to the palace. Lady Estelle has requested a word with you, Blackthorne," Valor said, his focus on me.

"If the intention is to find some way to use me, despite the absence of my petals, I decline." My voice was even, despite how my stomach twisted in knots.

Valor sighed, exasperated, and stood straighter. The slight slump in his shoulders was the only sign he was affected by the journey. "Lady Estelle has no intention of using you. And despite your lack of popularity among the people of Everbloom, she has no opinion of you, yet," he said, the implication there that it could change.

"That's all very interesting, but I've just spent a month at sea and I'd like to make it to our destination before the sun sets."

Beneath his eye twitched, the first sign of his frustration with me. "There are things to discuss. We need to prepare for the likely event that King Lendorr will pursue us."

Any dignity I had dwindled when the blood drained from my face, eyes gone wide. My first concern wasn't the king. No, the fear came from the thought of Talos finding me, and I recoiled from Valor.

I tried to hide my fear. "Even so, I would like to change and eat something before people start requesting things of me."

Valor seemed to weigh whether there was any point in pushing back. "Very well," he agreed, reluctant. "Vanmore will accompany you. But there *will* be a conversation with Lady Estelle. There is no way around it." He gave a nod of acknowledgment to Casimir before he left.

With his departure, I watched the herd of people as they disappeared into the woods. Casimir trailed close as Valor commanded. Dutiful and never too far, and with the added glares I encountered in the crowd, his presence became a comfort.

No matter how distant he had become, I could walk alongside a crowd of people who despised me without fear, knowing Casimir would keep me safe.

Burgundy, white, and silver trees dotted the path through the forest. The colors contrasted against the ivory of the bark, a stunning sight. Every stone of the path was placed in an intricate display, easy to follow as it twisted and turned, despite the darkness that fell.

The ashen appearance of the stones became illuminated as the moon peered through scattered clouds.

When we made it over the top of the hill, the sight made me stumble.

Bathed in moonlight, a palace stood in the rocky valley below, luminescent and breathtaking—its structure carved meticulously from the white stones that illuminated our path. The spiral towers stretched high to the sky, appearing like iridescent spikes. A line of colors surrounded it, the same stunning shades of red and silver. A few white willows dipped near the water's edge. A long, pearlescent wall separated the palace from a rushing river. From the cliffs behind it, a waterfall roared. I noted an abundance of ruins and structures throughout the rocky mountains, small homes burrowed into the cliffsides. The expanse of it sent my mind reeling.

The excitement intensified as we traversed the white stone bridge that spanned the river, leading to the courtyard before the palace.

We neared the stone gates, and I noticed people coming and going, their attire different from those of Everbloom or the Iron Thorn. Where the voyage was obvious in our wares, the people of Mistvalle walked with a purpose, their clothing pristine.

Many of them paused to smile or wave, not a cruel face in their crowd. Though something was unsettling about that, too. There was no look of apprehension in them.

Valor led the way until we were at the end of the bridge. Everbloom's population flooded the area.

"It is at this time I ask you all to follow the guides from Mistvalle. They have made preparations for our arrival, and I know many of you are exhausted from the journey. They will show you to the feasting hall and the camp our people will occupy." Valor's voice carried in the courtyard.

I wasn't able to focus on anything but the idea of a warm meal, a bath, and somewhere solid to sleep. It barely registered with me when Calla landed on my shoulder, already back from her first flight on land.

Everyone murmured excitedly as members of Mistvalle orchestrated people into groups. They wore white armor, no cloaks to be seen, despite the cold bite in the air. Many of them had the same red gaze, though a few were different. I spotted brown, green, and blue eyes among some of their guards.

Not all of them are Roses.

The crowd shuffled into pairs as the guards took them in different directions. I waited to be pulled into a group, only to be one of the last few in the crowd. The few who remained were Valor, Orin, and Casimir.

I nearly groaned my frustration out loud. Calla screeched on my shoulder when she picked up the shift of my mood. I focused my anger on

Valor. "Do I not get the same courtesy as everyone else? Can I not eat and sleep?" I snapped.

Valor's nostrils flared. "You are a guest here, and should Lady Estelle wish to speak with you, she will—"

"You always were too uptight, Valor." A voice came from the top of the steps, interrupting Valor.

A woman stood at the top of the pearlescent stairs. She wore a flowing scarlet gown that rippled over the steps like waves as she descended. There was a golden diadem laid across her forehead, the warm color stunning against her ebony skin. She descended the stairs, each step with natural elegance, pausing above Valor and Orin, enough to still tower over them.

"I hope you haven't terrified your poor daughter. She is welcome here, as any Rose should be." Her vibrant red gaze fixed on mine, and she offered a kind smile.

To be called his daughter felt wrong. Our blood relation didn't change his years of absence. Calla bristled on my shoulder and, without warning, took off. I watched her go over the palace until she disappeared into the night sky.

Valor gave a small bow at the waist. "Lady Estelle, we didn't intend to make you seek us out. My apologies for not hurrying the crowd along." When Valor groveled, I had to hold back a chuckle.

With an airy wave of her hand, Lady Estelle dismissed his apologies. "Your people have only just left the horrible sway of a ship, and after a month, no less. They needn't hurry on my account. We have plenty of time to discuss any pressing matters in the morning, after your people and the white bloom have had a feast and some rest," Estelle said.

Despite her kind demeanor, I recoiled. Casimir took note, his worried gaze finding mine when I nearly bumped into him.

Casimir spoke on my behalf. "Lady Estelle, Elita no longer carries the white bloom."

Estelle's attention snapped to Casimir before she looked me over. She beckoned me forward, the sleeves of her dress like scarlet waterfalls. I swallowed the apprehension and approached her, far too aware of the way Casimir tensed, though he stayed rooted to the spot.

Estelle kept her hand extended to me, and when I reached her, I put mine in her palm, my dirty fingers and nails a stark contrast to how well-groomed she was.

She looked me over, her eyes bouncing in a familiar way.

After a moment, she pulled back, her gaze wide. "Who is your healer?" she demanded, catching everyone off guard. From her tone, I hoped no one gave Taryn by name.

"She is not present at the moment. She is with her son getting settled," Valor answered her with as little information as possible.

"This woman's wounds are not healing well. She will need our healers to tend her from this point on, if there is any hope of restoring a bloom."

I stumbled back, nearly falling down the stairs. The thought of blooming again caused my skin to prickle with unease. It was all too fresh. I never had the chance to finish a full bloom, and I expected to never experience one again. By everyone's shared confusion, I wasn't the only one who made that assumption.

Valor's brow knitted together as he stared up at us. "Did Vanmore not relay with his abilities that her bloom had been sheared? There is no hope of a bloom returning. Not for her."

"Of course, he informed us," she said. "Although I cannot find it within myself to believe the white bloom ends at the hands of a shearing. With the right healers and adequate abilities, we may have hope for the prophesized bloom."

The dreaded words followed me throughout the realm. A prophecy I wanted no part of. My vision tunneled, and I fought the urge to bolt down the stairs.

"Then you would be asking me to give my life," I said, bewildered. The realization sent a shock up my spine, a bitter reminder of how Valor had intended to still use my bloom to save the Roses. They would've carried out the same wicked deeds Ronin had, a reality I viciously tried to ignore.

I moved backward, careful on the steps as I looked to Valor. "I knew you only saved me for selfish gain. You should never have claimed me as your blood. What a horrible truth to make me aware of, then turn around and use me." The sting caused by his callousness was evident in the crack of my voice. I glanced back at Estelle. "I didn't come here to be studied and fuel your hope. If that's why you granted me passage here, I kindly decline."

After a long pause, Estelle smiled, her shoulders releasing some tension. "Dear girl, we will not force you to do anything against your will. You are safe here. I was under the impression you knew," she said, her attention going to Valor. "However, we have time to discuss things. No choices must be made now. Regardless of your decision, you are free to stay here as any other Rose."

Though every part of me knew not to trust the words of strangers, I gave a nod and whirled around to hide the way my hands shook.

When I reached Casimir's side, Estelle clasped her hands in front of her gown. "I do apologize if our intentions felt intrusive. Please, I implore you to join the others at the feast, have a bath, and rest well. There is much to discover here in Mistvalle, and our people are eager to help you all settle in."

The promise of finding peace became tainted by lies that I feared would never release me.

I can't trust any of them.

Five

When Estelle mentioned a feast, it didn't prepare me for the sight of Mistvalle's magnificent banquet hall. It was massive, built from marble, and the ceiling above was made of glass, giving a wondrous view of the stars that dotted the night sky. It was a dome, the walls rounded as they met with the glass, held up by alabaster wood beams.

The space overflowed with an abundance of tables and chairs, fitting where they could inside the spherical room. There were delicacies piled high on trays. Full of bread, meat, fruits, and vegetables.

I froze, unsure of where to start. Across the hall, I saw Galan for the first time since the anchor dropped. He had been one of the first few off, and he sat with Alba, Taryn, and Ulrik. Alba's face lit with joy as he spoke to her. She took hold of his arm, leaning over to tell him something.

The sight warmed me, though I longed to join them. I stared at the full table, surrounded by people they knew from Everbloom. Their companions from before.

It stung for a moment, realizing that I'd only known them for such a short time. After a month of separation, they were reunited with people they had missed. They shared a closeness that I couldn't understand. The people of Everbloom spent their lives together. A bond I envied. They took care of each other, put each other first.

There was no one like that for me. Not anymore.

Emotions stirred in my chest, and I set my sights on the tables piled with food.

I gravitated toward it, my shoes tapping the slick marble floor. Casimir stayed with me, silent but never going to find others in the crowd. He was only doing what his general asked of him, guarding me until I was somewhere safe. It was wrong of me and brought more pain, but I chose to pretend it was by choice.

The aroma of food was a decent distraction, and I took a larger helping of stew than was necessary. It'd been so long since I had fresh food, let alone beef. The spices and cut vegetables floated among the broth, and I rushed to a table, two slices of bread in one hand while the other cradled the bowl. The linen dress swished at my calves when I took a seat and scooted closer to the weathered oak tabletop. Beneath the table, cool air nipped at my skin, and I pulled the emerald cloak tighter around my body.

Casimir's plate was stacked with various meats and a decent helping of seasonal vegetables. He skipped the bread and made up for it with a side of berries. He sat across from me, never meeting my gaze.

We ate in silence. I may as well have been alone.

His disconnect became a constant reminder of what I had done to deserve it. The price they all had to pay on my account.

The only reprieve was sleep free of nightmares—my escape from every face that haunted me. And for a fleeting moment, the green cloak on my back felt heavier. It felt cursed.

I made a vow to burn it and hope it could turn some of the memories to ash.

Many of the Everbloom guards paused by our table to talk to Casimir. It was a blur of muttered words about training or the occasional smiling face who let him know they missed sparring. Most of them I didn't recognize, though Elrin followed along with one of them, the same question about when and where they were meant to train.

Casimir spoke low, his tone without any emotion. The conversations were dismissed quickly, and though he wasn't speaking to me directly, the sound of his voice brought me comfort I wanted to force away.

Midway through our meal, Alba found our table. There hadn't been a moment to swallow my mouthful of food before she wrapped her arms around my shoulders from behind, squealing in my ear.

"Oh, I missed you!" She squeezed tighter. "You have no idea how boring Valor's ship was."

I grinned up at her, watching as Galan approached. "I started to think we'd never reach land," Alba said as she straightened, a hand resting on my shoulder. "Anyway, you look well!" She beamed at me, though I watched some of her smile fall as she looked over my curls. "Now, you," she pointed at Casimir, "look like you're on your way to Akuma. When's the last time you slept?" she teased.

Though the question was lighthearted, when I saw the expression on Casimir's face, my heart dropped. I wondered then if he had nightmares after what happened. If the month on the ship was spent being tormented by his own mind, while he shut himself away.

I opened my mouth to say something, but Alba already changed the subject as she carried on about finding the bathhouse. After her tangent on hygiene ended, she gave me an excited grin. "Galan told me about the training you did on the ship. A short sword? I always thought you were more of a dagger kind of girl," she mused.

"I'm hoping I'll have the chance to train more while we're here. Maybe I can test that theory," I said, eager to really start training. I spent much of my life locked away, and after feeling helpless against Ronin, I wanted to do whatever I could to feel strong.

Alba gave me another quick squeeze. "That's what I like to hear. I'll find you tomorrow, and we can spar?" she asked as she backed away, almost bumping into Galan. His hands gripped her waist to steady her, and I had to cover my mouth to stop myself from saying something that would embarrass the two.

"Sounds perfect." I wanted to say more, but kept my musings to myself as the two parted as quickly as they appeared.

The silence returned when they left, and when I finished my food, I stood. It was the cue Casimir needed to leave the table. He gestured to the exit of the feasting hall.

My brow furrowed, and he noted my hesitation.

"Are you finished eating?" he asked.

It made the confusion worse. "Yes, but—"

"I'll escort you to the camp set up for Everbloom." He spoke to me the way a guard would. I opened my mouth to protest, but seeing the exhaustion on his face, I didn't press for an explanation.

We left the feasting hall behind and walked out into the night. Wind tangled through my hair, and I ducked further into the cloak, shielding myself from the chill.

Lanterns dotted the pathway we followed, and Casimir led the way. Mistvalle was a massive sight to behold, with every corner and rocky cliff holding fortresses and homes—burrow-like structures carved into the side of the cliffs.

To the east of the palace, there was a quiet market. From the elevated path we followed along the cliffs, I had a bird's-eye view of the market below. The sight was nauseating. Only stone pillars and a short wall of stacked rocks separated the path from a perilous fall.

Moss covered some of the stonework as we found ourselves in thicker foliage. The stone walls became unnecessary the farther we went as the path twisted into the depths of the forest.

I surveyed the treeline, waiting to glimpse the striking contrast between the white stone houses and the dense forest.

The homes never appeared.

I gazed at the tall overreaching tents woven through the trees, and a pang of longing stole the awe. The canvas fabric was a rich blue, adorned with silver embroidery at the edges, which glimmered in the moonlight.

The path stretched between the many tents, creating a long, winding line of stone. Among the space, I spotted people from Everbloom around a bonfire, laughing and filling the night with chatter.

It was different yet painfully similar to Everbloom. I hadn't expected to see anything like it again, and the sight made me miss the underground forest.

Casimir led me down the path until we reached a small tent. The canvas fabric was thick, blocking out the chill. Inside, it was more crowded than what I'd seen in Everbloom. It ran in a tight circle, raised to a point to create a more spacious roof. The compact size was fit for one person. There was a single bed and a black wooden chest to match, tucked in the right corner. A small white shelf sat to the left, empty. A woven rug that swirled with white and blue adorned the dark stone floor, giving it a more homey feel.

Casimir never came closer. When he dipped his head at me, my stomach sank. "You won't require guards here. Lady Estelle will want to speak with you in the morning at the palace."

I faltered, unsure what to say. "What—"

"Goodnight." It was a dismissal from a captain, and it turned my insides as I watched the drapes fall together in his absence, isolating me.

The vision came back with harsh intensity, his body limp across from me. It chilled my spine, and it took all my willpower not to sprint out of the drapes after him.

For the first time in a month, I stood in the quiet, utterly alone. No splash of the waves or the shouts of a crew. It was absent of children's laughter, or Galan's snoring and poorly executed jokes.

I hadn't been truly alone since I found Casimir.

The silence wasn't the relief I expected—it was suffocating, and I wrapped my arms around my torso, a heavy exhale leaving my lungs.

In the dark of my tent, fear crept in, and I hoped I wouldn't wake to the figure that appeared on the ship. I almost asked Casimir to stay. To guard my tent the way he did in Everbloom.

But I pushed past the fear and clambered into the bed. Exhausted and hoping for rest.

There were no nightmares, no memories of what transpired in the clearing. But the moment I awoke, the sun still not fully risen, the figure stood beside my bed. It watched me, its eyes a void. When it reached out for me, its arms covered in scars that were dark as midnight, my breathing quickened.

I couldn't move. Couldn't scream.

Its fingers were cold, the touch real. It echoed through my skin, an icy thrum. The sensation tore through me until I had to shut my eyes, begging for it to make the figure vanish. But its touch didn't leave, and visions flashed through my head, a swirl of chaos. None of it made sense to me, yet the pain that crept through my veins was real, tangible.

It melted over into sorrow, and every vision that flashed through my mind held another image of golden hair and skin that cracked like marble. At the will of the stone-like hand, symbols were carved into the ground, the trees, and through skin.

I gasped, and it all fell away.

When my eyes opened, the figure was gone. It left me with a tremor in my hands, and the hollow ache of betrayal in my bones.

The moment I could move again, I stumbled out of bed and strode out of the drapes, determined to forget the figure and the visions. The forest was a decent distraction, and I was enamored by the sunlight that dappled through the trees. It made the silver embroidery on the tents glisten. The sight was enough to brush away the remnants of the visions.

Faces from Everbloom crowded the camp as they left their own sleeping quarters and poured out to the stone path. Among the crowd was a flame of red hair on its way toward me. I both had a swell of joy and dismay knowing Taryn needed to do another healing, but pleased to see her friendly face.

When Taryn reached me, she grinned. "Someone looks well rested," she said. Ulrik stayed close to her side, peering up at me. He offered a smile and a quick wave.

"Their beds here are so comfortable, it's sinful," I said with a chuckle. "If not for the blinding sun, I may have slept the entire day away." A pit sat in my stomach when I spoke. It'd do me no good to mention the figure. Not when I'd had enough mental breaks after what took place in the clearing. And I couldn't ignore what Casimir said about meeting with Lady Estelle after the first meal, no matter how much I wanted to avoid it.

Taryn didn't notice my shift in mood; her focus was on the crowd headed down the cliffs. "It's so inconvenient we're this high up," she grumbled. I nodded in agreement.

Reluctantly, my gaze shifted toward Taryn as I asked, "Where do we go for today's healing?"

She glanced at me with an out-of-place somber smile. "The general told me not to worry about it anymore. They have more skilled healers here in Mistvalle."

My heart sank when I recalled what Estelle said, and suddenly, a healing with Taryn didn't sound bad. I hated the thought of a stranger prodding at my side.

I ran a hand down my face. "That man pisses me off," I said.

Taryn laughed and clapped a hand on my shoulder. "He has that effect on everyone he meets. Try not to take it too personally." She stood straighter, making her height more noticeable. She was taller than me, and taller than many of the men from Everbloom.

Ulrik tugged on her arm, and she glanced down with a kind smile reserved for him. "Yes?" she asked, her voice softer.

"I'm hungry," he complained.

Taryn chuckled and patted his hand. "We're off to the feasting hall if you want to join us."

Not wanting to be alone anymore, I nodded.

We started down the path and followed the throng of people. My attention shifted to the striking cliffs and the way the colors popped against the white stone in the daylight. It looked even more magnificent than the night before.

When we reached the bottom of the walkway, far from the cliff's edge, I spotted Estelle, her flowy dress replaced with white light armor and a burgundy cloak, and her hair pulled into intricate braids.

She approached us eagerly, smiling as she spoke. "I must apologize for the sleeping quarters. We had little time to prepare."

Taryn came to a stop beside us.

"It's no trouble, Lady Estelle. Your hospitality means a lot to the people of Everbloom," I replied.

"And who is it that accompanies you today?" she inquired, glancing at Taryn and Ulrik.

"I'm Taryn, and this is my son, Ulrik. Sorry to cut out, but we were heading to eat," Taryn said, an apologetic grin on her face. I realized it wasn't the best idea to inform Estelle that she was my previous healer. Her hesitation made me think Valor must have already explained how upset Estelle was.

Taryn left with Ulrik. I longed to go with them as my stomach twisted with hunger, but my feet stayed planted.

"I meant to grab you after the first meal. However, we have found ourselves short on time this morning," Estelle said.

"Of course." I gave an understanding smile. "The beds here are quite comfortable. I didn't mean to sleep so late." In reality, I couldn't have made it on time if I tried. Much of the morning was spent unable to move.

She waved a hand. "There is no need to explain. Now, if you feel up for it, I would like you to accompany me to meet our healers. You will eat soon after, I promise." She winked.

Estelle led me toward the market area that was flooded with people who browsed the many shops. The structures worked their way into the nature around them. It left the trees preserved in patches of dirt encircled by stone. Many of the buildings were small, though some stood tall, their roofs pointed, reminiscent of structures in Eldravine.

They were a mix of soft colors, pastel blues and greens. They stood out among the shops that were made of the same pale marble or ivory wood. It was endearing, and the different paths caught my eye, going farther back until I lost sight of the scattered buildings.

The main square was filled with light chatter, and I found myself distracted and pulled into the energy that thrummed around me. In the center of the square, a large willow tree towered over everything else, much taller than I'd ever seen them grow. White wisps caught in the breeze, and children laughed beneath the tree as they danced through the swaying branches.

Another circle of stones gave the willow a large berth of space; the gray rocks shimmered when the sun caught on the crystals that shone through the cracks.

I narrowly avoided bumping into bodies dressed in silk. Many of them skipped a cloak altogether, despite the cold. They didn't pause to gawk at the scenery, no, it was home for them.

Our trek led us to another towering white structure, which appeared to be made of pure marble. The spire at the center of it stretched high and caught the light. We ascended the steps to the expansive, wide-open doors.

People scurried around inside. They all wore black tunics as they carted things around the room or paused to jot something down.

Estelle cleared her throat to get the attention of a few people who I assumed were healers. When they caught sight of us, they halted their activities. One of them approached us.

"Lady Estelle." A man with straight, silky blonde hair stopped a few feet away. He bowed his head in Estelle's direction.

"Halburn, this is Elita Blackthorne. She is the daughter of General Valor, and she is in need of our best healers." Estelle rested a hand on my shoulder, the touch featherlight.

He eyed my disheveled appearance. "Fascinating. The general's own?" he inquired, a brow raised.

Estelle looked like she wanted to slap him. "Mind your manners, Halburn," she chided, and he immediately muttered an apology. "Elita is also the white bloom."

The words stopped the man's stammering and he observed me with more intensity. "We will have our best healers study her, my lady."

The implication made me tense.

Estelle shook her head. "She does not desire observation. She merely needs two healings a day until she's recovered. That will be all."

The words did little to soothe my nerves, and my hands fiddled with the edge of my tunic.

Halburn appeared surprised, but he didn't voice it.

Satisfied, Estelle nodded. "Well, I have things to tend to. The healers here will take good care of you, Elita, and then you may be on your way to eat. There are many shops overfilled with clothing and anything else you may need. And do not fret about cost, it's been handled. I do hope you'll feel at home here soon." Estelle smiled and turned without another word, leaving me alone with the healer.

Halburn cleared his throat to draw my attention. One of his hands gestured toward the beds set up in lines throughout the main area. It was organized, clean. The sunlight poured in from above, another glass ceiling. It cast shadows that shimmered on some of the floors.

Ivory shelves lined much of the space, filled with herbs, tinctures, and books. The center of the building had many untouched beds, made with care. Charcoal-colored curtains near each bed were drawn back, ready to be pulled for privacy. It stretched on for what appeared to be fifty beds long on each side, ending at a large hearth meant to warm the healing center.

On either side of the long stretch of beds, there were double doors. A few healers darted in and out of them, carrying supplies.

It was beautiful, like everything in Mistvalle. The amount of tinctures, herbs, and other healing supplies was more than I had ever seen. Taryn would have been fascinated, and it upset me how Valor treated her as if she weren't an adequate healer. She had saved my life alongside Casimir. It wasn't an easy feat.

I followed the healer until he stopped at a bed, the frame made of the same ivory wood I'd seen throughout Mistvalle. I sat down on the soft linens, and my legs dangled over the edge.

He pulled a wooden cart closer and grabbed a few things from it. Herbs I didn't recognize, and a jar that looked as if it had a salve inside.

"Well, let's see what's causing such a fuss," he said gruffly, his bedside manner poor.

No part of me wanted to raise my tunic.

Hesitantly, I undid the leather vest and let it hang open before barely lifting the side of my tunic.

When the dirty fabric was out of the way, his eyes went wide. "And a healer was caring for this?" he asked in disbelief.

I fought the urge to snap at him.

Without warning, he moved his hand to my side, and I came close to slapping it away. He noticed me recoil and gave me a frustrated look, which only made the wrinkles in his face deepen.

"May I begin?" he asked.

I hesitated, uncomfortable that he didn't think to ask before touching me. "Yes." The word came out harsh, my displeasure clear.

The only hands to heal the wound had been Taryn's. She knew to be gentle. She understood the way it was numb in certain areas, and the way it still stung in others.

Halburn didn't even ask for more information about it. His palm lay flat against the scarred tissue, and air hissed through my teeth. Similar to Taryn, his eyes darted back and forth as he held his hand against the jagged skin. It burned in a strange way, not at all how Taryn's ability felt, and I gasped, standing from the cot as my tunic fell.

He stared at me, bewildered. "Blackthorne—"

"What was that?" I snapped.

He appeared perplexed. "I was healing your wounds," he said, as if the answer was simple.

"It isn't supposed to feel that way," I said, unsure how to explain. From his expression, it seemed he gathered what I meant.

Rather than try to touch me, he grabbed the jar and opened the lid. "Will you sit?" he asked, tone cautious.

I clenched my jaw but sat, anyway.

"The healing, it's supposed to burn," he explained. "There are many internal intricacies. Things the eye can't see, and untrained hands can't sense. It's why your healer wasn't too effective tending this wound."

Despite my unease, I exposed my scar again and let him apply the salve.

"Our healers are born here. Trained from the moment they show a knack for healing. For some, that's as early as five," he said, not stopping even as I flinched. "I doubt your healer had that kind of training. Don't hold it against 'em." Halburn closed the jar. "I won't do another healing right now. But it'll be important that you return each morning and night for healing. The sooner you allow us to do our work, the sooner you'll be as good as new." He offered a tight-lipped smile.

I stood and redid the ties on my leather vest. "Thank you," I said under my breath.

Halburn returned to putting his supplies away, then rubbed his hands on a black cloth. I didn't linger a second more.

Once outside, I leisurely strolled, my attention roaming over the different shops, trying to distinguish what each of them held. It wasn't hard to pinpoint where the clothes were sold, as they spilled out into the street in the form of wooden racks laden with fabric and cloaks alike.

I hadn't worn clothes of my own since I left the cottage. Something I owned, and only me. The excitement was impossible to contain as I weaved through the crowd and rummaged through the different colors. Most of it didn't seem practical, and I settled for a few pairs of black leather trousers, an array of tunics, vests, and a black cloak. I added three dresses for good measure, their style a reminder of the ones I used to wear at the cottage.

I stuffed my arms full with the items and set a pair of new boots on top of all of it. It occurred to me that Estelle was likely trying to buy my favor, but I didn't mind.

When I waddled up to the man at the desk, he gave me a strange look.

"Elita Blackthorne." I introduced myself, peering behind the pile in my arms. A knowing look flashed across his face, and he grinned.

"Need a sack for all that?" he asked in a thick accent.

"Yes, please."

He pulled one out and slung it over the counter, holding it open.

I shoved it all into the bag, eager to be out of the clothes that still carried the faint scent of the cursed seas.

With a wave goodbye and the pack slung over my shoulder, I walked out of the shop, giddy as I made my way toward the bathhouse.

Seven

I reveled in the newfound cleanliness. A slate wiped clean and the sting of salt long gone, replaced by the delicate scent of flowers and honey that clung to my skin, courtesy of the soaps in the bathhouse.

When I got there, the women who tended the room were quick to add boiled water to a porcelain tub, mixing it with the cold spring water. It was refreshing and quick, alone in a steam-filled room, no bite in the air to rush me along.

I walked down the path, relishing the snug fit of the new boots on my feet. I decided on a green tunic, paired with black leathers, and a black cloak to match. For the first time in months, I felt like my old self. A young woman without the weight of a prophecy on my shoulders or the clothes of a traitor on my back.

Short, springy hair tore that vision away with a swift blow of the wind, tangling wet curls in my line of sight. I grunted and pushed them out of my face, tucking the hairs as far behind my ears as I could. Some still managed to escape.

Before I fought with the short hairs again, Alba appeared from around the bathhouse. She caught sight of me and jogged over, a grin on her face.

"Are you coming from the bathhouse?" she asked eagerly, skidding to a stop. She took in my appearance and the wetness of my hair. "It's lovely, isn't it? The most relaxing bath I've had in ages!" Alba's hair dusted along the path, but the rest of her curls looked refreshed.

"I feel much better, although I haven't had a bite to eat today, and I'm dreading lugging this back up the hill," I said, gesturing to the pack on my shoulder.

She rolled her eyes and took it from me. I envied her strength.

Alba led the way to the feasting hall, my pack flung over her shoulder. I considered telling her we could take it up first, but the aroma of food stopped me short. The distinct scent of stew wafted through the feasting hall. I ogled the spread of food as I filled a plate, Alba no longer a concern to me as I both stuffed my plate and my face—not waiting to sit at a table before I dug into a thick slice of meat.

When I finished eating, Alba sprang up from her seat, not waiting for me to chew the rest of my last bite before she tried to pull me up from the chair.

"Give me a second," I said around a mouthful of buttered bread.

"Oh, come on, I've been waiting all morning for your lazy butt to get a move on. I have severely missed sparring, and I *need* a partner today. Galan wasn't interested."

I almost made a joke about Galan's interest, but thought better of it. A smile tugged at my face, anyway. It was thwarted the moment I thought about how my scar got irritated last time I sparred on the ship.

She noticed the change. "Sorry, I forgot about your wound," she blurted.

I shook my head. "No, it's fine. I want to spar." The words were true despite my hesitation. "I need to hone my abilities, I've not been able to conjure them again since—" The words caught in my throat.

"You conjured them? When?" she asked, missing the way I paled.

"Ronin." The name burned my tongue.

Her face fell, and she gave me a knowing look. "Oh. I see." She didn't prod further. Alba had a good sense for when I needed to gather myself, and I was grateful for it. I may have fallen apart if she tried. I had blocked out the memory of my vines wrapping around Ronin.

I ran a hand through my curls, letting them fall back to my shoulders. "Let's go."

Halfway through the walk to the training grounds, Alba handed off my sack of clothes to a poor, unassuming Mistvalle guard and requested he return it to my tent at the top of the hill.

It was comical how quickly he obliged when she mentioned I was Valor's daughter.

We made our way farther from the feasting hall, and every twisting stone walkway appeared similar. If not for Alba's guidance, I wouldn't have the slightest idea where to go.

We entered the training grounds, which were much more uniform than what they had in Everbloom. The entire field was laid with stone and high walls that were adorned with weapon racks.

Many Roses stood throughout in a sparring stance, taking turns throwing punches or vines at their opponent. Some guards sat to the side and sharpened swords or used wooden models to practice their swing.

A familiar head of messy black hair caught my eye, and I watched as Casimir dodged beneath Orin's arm, a strange pair as they fought in the center of the training grounds. Orin looked amused, his hair pulled into a long white braid behind him.

Everyone continued, none of them noticing our arrival, to my relief. The mishap in Everbloom with Novian was enough humiliation to last me a lifetime, and to my dismay, he was present on the field, a smirk on his face while he watched Casimir and Orin spar.

Alba grabbed my wrist and pulled me over to a less crowded corner, one that lacked any stonework on the ground. It was a rectangle carved through the stone, filled with dirt and a few big rocks.

A grin split her face, and she began to stretch. Hands over her head, behind her back, and eventually she leaned forward and placed both hands to the ground. A practice I remembered well.

I sighed and shrugged off the heat of humiliation, then put my hands to the dirt across from her and closed my eyes.

Without even reaching, the pulse thrummed through my hand, familiar despite the month at sea spent detached from it. The life beneath the ground moved, and I smiled despite the doubt that plagued me. After everything, my body didn't forget what it had learned. It jumped back in with ease; the sensation made my pulse flutter.

I opened my eyes and glanced up, seeing Alba already peeking at me from where she was bent over, her hands in the dirt. "I told you, once you feel it, it's second nature."

My grin matched hers, and we both stood.

"We can start with something easy, if you'd like. Dodging? Countering?" She offered as she took a moment to pull her long hair in front of her, twisting it into a quick and long braid. I envied her ability to braid her hair and dreaded trying to spar with mine like it was.

"I want to work on countering attacks. I'm not very good at it." My tone was light despite the reason I chose to practice countering.

She nodded, then her expression fell into the serious mask she wore when she sparred. It wasn't like Alba to be stone-faced, but she looked frightening every time she went on the offense.

The weeks of training with Galan helped me find a comfortable stance easily. Though he doubted his own skill, he was a good teacher. I hoped the training was enough for me to counter Alba.

The thrum of the earth and rush of blood in my ears helped me tune out my surroundings. I waited for her to move first. It'd be difficult to outmaneuver her with the skills I had, so I needed to work with what my body knew best. If I figured out her patterns early on, it would help me counter her moves.

I observed as she inhaled, her nostrils flaring. Every twitch of her face was a signal, and I anticipated her advance before she moved, her braid flailing behind her as she sprinted toward me.

My muscles braced. I solidified my stance, waiting.

Alba didn't hold back a grin as she closed in.

With a tumble to the left, I dodged her, dirt clinging to my fresh clothes as I rolled, moving quickly until I jumped back up.

My fingers tugged at the clasp of my cloak, and I tossed it to the side, not wanting it to get in my way. I ignored the tightness around my scar. We'd barely started, and I refused to call it quits because of discomfort.

Alba's face was back into a stern expression, not waiting as I adjusted my vest before she charged toward me again. I pursed my lips, feeling the tension build as I waited. She would expect me to roll or dodge. I didn't want to be predictable.

My arms flew up and blocked her kick that flew close to my face. I was unsure of every move I made, but I couldn't hesitate.

One of my hands grabbed her ankle before her foot could fall back to the ground, and I used the leverage to throw her off balance, watching her flounder for a moment.

She barely missed a beat.

With a jerk of her other foot, she caught my waist, pulling me sideways with her into the dirt.

I couldn't help but cackle.

We both scrambled up, and she wagged a finger at me. "A soldier doesn't laugh in battle. A guard doesn't chuckle when she's been disarmed," she chided.

I rolled my eyes and dusted my black leathers off, discarding the vest to the side, leaving me in a tight tunic and trousers for easier movement.

Alba didn't need the lighter clothing to have an advantage. Her speed, strength, and smarts were going to win her the spar. But she was training me, and it was clear she was taking it easy—for the time being. I wanted to reach the point where she no longer had to. I wanted to be strong on my own.

The smile fell from my face, and I resumed my stance, forearms covered in a layer of dirt.

If there weren't so many people present, I might have removed my boots to feel the earth beneath my feet. But I refrained from removing them, and took the time to call to it without physical touch.

Alba watched me, analyzing what I was doing. She smirked.

Kicking up dust, she sprinted for me, vines tearing up through the ground behind her as she charged, her face manic.

Despite how much I begged it to, the earth didn't move for me. I rolled again and dodged rather than countered.

"You need to allow the sensation to consume you. Feel the earth until it's no longer a separate entity; rather, you two operate as one. Then block me with vines," she said, as if it were simple.

Under the surface, frustration simmered and grew. I wanted to be further in my training than I was. To conjure the earth without a struggle. The feeling of being constrained overwhelmed me, as if I were operating at only half capacity.

On cue, the scar tissue on my abdomen throbbed, breaking my train of thought and pulling me back to the present.

Alba waited, watching me.

I exhaled and relieved some of the tension in my limbs. The rigidity didn't serve me, and it prevented me from conjuring the vines. I splayed my hands wide as they hovered over the ground. The thrum of the earth still echoed with my pulse. A quiet whisper without my skin flat to the dirt, but it was enough.

A strange sensation bloomed in my body. I found the thrum of the coiling vines, the twisting roots. Their life had a unique pulse, and my mind followed them, attempting to pull them up from the earth.

My muscles strained, the veins in my arms somewhat protruding the harder I tried. I sensed the pulse of the vines grow more distant and I groaned in frustration, but tried to focus my energy more.

With a flex of my hand, my fingers came open, trembling as I tried to finish it, to pull the vines from the earth. Heat rippled through my palms. The vines withered, the thrum dying in my veins.

"Damn it!" I shouted, sweat beading on my brow.

Alba sighed as she made her way over to me. "It's okay. It takes time."

I shot her a glare and she froze, letting me seethe for a moment. I hated it, but part of me didn't want to conjure the vines. The memory of Ronin screaming and thrashing against them made me ill. Panic rose in my throat the longer the images lingered. My grief pulled me away from the thrum of the earth swiftly. The anger doubled and killed the pulse.

I heard snickering and looked up, full of fury as I found a group of the Everbloom guardsmen watching me.

Humiliation and frustration both licked up my skin, a bout of heat that turned my face and neck red. If I could conjure the vines, I'd slap every one of them.

Among the laughing faces was Orin, and amusement flamed in his gaze as he watched me. Beside him stood Casimir, arms crossed over, his expression emotionless.

Alba saw the rage flare and went to grab my arm, but I was already stalking across the training grounds, ready to unleash my anger in the form of words if I was unable to force the earth to display it for me.

Casimir's expression changed into restrained curiosity when he noticed my approach.

Orin only snickered more when I stalked up to him, glaring.

"Is my training amusing to you?" I hissed, stepping closer than I meant to. His height threatened to make me shrink back.

Orin sneered. "You won't ever match the skill of the guards here. It *is* quite amusing," he taunted.

My gaze fell to each chuckling face on the guards. "Was my ineptitude amusing when I almost died because of it?" The words landed hard, and Casimir winced. His palm rested on my shoulder, jarring as he moved me further from Orin, who glowered, looking as though he'd swing at me.

I took a step back and shrugged Casimir's hand off.

His brow creased, and he crossed his arms. "The situation would have never reached that point if you had kept the deal with General Valor. Our guard tried to keep you somewhere that was safe," Casimir replied, calm and even—like a captain. A poor attempt at diffusing the tension.

"You mean be held captive again? How is it any better that everyone in Everbloom was content with using my bloom?"

Orin took a step toward me, mouth opened as if he were going to add something. Casimir threw his hand up and signaled the guard to disperse. Orin looked as though he would pull rank, but puffed his chest and walked off as if it were his idea to leave.

Casimir searched my face, something broken in his eyes when he lingered on my neck. "We tried to keep you safe for the remainder of your bloom. There was only so much we could do." The words displayed more emotion than he had shown me in over a month. The change was almost intoxicating. The need for him to say something, *anything*, made me irrational.

I shook my head and clung to the intensity he spoke with. The air of indifference was gone. He couldn't hide forever. "That doesn't mean much coming from someone who lied to me, and has barely spoken to me in a month." The words came out confused and broken.

Casimir went rigid, the pent-up frustration plain on his face. Red and bewildered, his irises lit like flames. "I was dreamwalking *every night*, Elita. I was beside your cot in Orondal while you slept for days, in case you started screaming again," he said in a low breath to prevent the words from carrying. "From the refuge cliffs to the cabin of the ship. Any nightmare that tried to take root in your sleep...I'm the only one who can dreamwalk. I was the only one who could help you."

The words hung in the open, and a heavy wave of guilt swelled as I stared at him. The exhaustion was obvious in his features. Every flick of his gaze betrayed how bone-tired he was.

"Why would you—why didn't you say anything?"

Some of his anger melted, giving way to a look of shame. He swallowed. "I felt your ribs crack under my hands; covered in Ronin's blood and yours as you bled to death. I just—" He looked away, surprising me as his voice cracked. "I meant it all those years ago when I said I didn't want to hurt you. I couldn't keep my word. Had I not convinced you to cross the Forge, none of that would've happened."

I struggled for the words that lumped in my throat, impossible to get out. He wasn't to blame for my choices. He wasn't the one to put me in harm's way, no, I had done that myself. My fingers twitched at my side, longing to reach out to him—to grasp his arm and give him a thanks I didn't know I owed him.

I thought I had earned peace. Never did it occur to me that it came at a price; written on Casimir's face and body as he stared at me without the mask he usually hid behind. His emotions were bare for all to see. It made my stomach twist in knots that I put him through so much torment without even knowing it.

"Casimir…" It was barely a whisper. The shame was impossible to speak over.

He sighed and released his tense shoulders, closing his eyes for a moment. When they opened, the walls were back tenfold. He looked at me with indifference as he straightened his posture—a stoic captain.

"You didn't know. It doesn't matter," he said coolly.

"You don't have to anymore," I blurted, desperate to offer him some kind of relief. He appeared wounded, the mask slipping for a second more. He pursed his lips and turned his back to me.

"Consider me relieved."

I almost didn't hear him as he walked back to Orin and the others. I had to fight the urge to stalk after him. Both asking him for forgiveness and scolding him for not telling me. I didn't want him to suffer for my benefit. He needed the kind of rest he wouldn't get if he continued to fight off my nightmares.

I cursed myself and ran my dirt-covered hands over my face. Every gaze in the training field fell on me. They at least had the sense to turn their heads when I noticed their stares.

Only Alba held my gaze. She didn't say a word about Casimir. She moved closer and placed a hand on my shoulder to draw my attention from Casimir's retreating form.

Alba gave my arm a slight tug, and I sighed, facing her. I rounded my shoulders and settled back into a sparring stance.

"Again."

ight

Alba and I trained until sweat drenched my new tunic and the dust clinging to me turned my trousers from black to tan, even coloring some of my short strands of hair.

I tried to spar and forget what Casimir said. No amount of training could erase the guilt of causing his tortured appearance.

Why did he do that?

Under the guilt, I couldn't understand why he took on that responsibility. Or why he didn't tell me. But the answer was obvious, he'd implied it himself. His own internal struggle and guilt over what happened made him avoid me.

I bit the inside of my cheek and sighed, wishing I could take back my harsh words.

Alba gave me an empathetic look. "You did good today," she said, trying to cheer me up.

My fists furled at my sides. "The vines are pissing me off."

"Yeah, those can be hard to figure out. But once you do—"

"It'll be like second nature." I dismissed with a wave of my hand, not needing more encouragement. I didn't plan to stop until I mastered the ability to summon them at will.

I wouldn't let Ronin steal anything more from me.

Alba and I had trained for hours, and the afternoon meal already passed. I wasn't hungry enough to care. My gut remained in knots after Casimir confessed to dreamwalking.

The realization hit me that my peaceful sleep, the lack of nightmares, would end the moment I lay down that night.

Regardless, I refused to let him continue to exhaust himself on my account. That didn't stop the fear that began to fester when I thought about sleeping. I didn't want the memories to haunt me.

Alba and I parted ways, and in a panic, I sprinted through the markets until I found myself back at the healing center. The steps barely registered with me as dread clawed through my head, accompanied by the fatigue in my body that followed the disappearance of the sun.

The doors pushed in beneath my palms, and I scanned the room. Blonde hair caught my eye, and I hurried inside.

Halburn startled when I tapped his shoulder. "Blackthorne, is there something I can help you with?" He sounded bewildered.

"Do you have something to help with sleep?" I inquired, not beating around the bush. Fear made me desperate.

Halburn raised a brow before releasing a sigh. "Well, there's a system here. I'm afraid I can't give a sleep aid to someone who hasn't had a proper examination."

"Then do one," I said, practically pleading. I tried to reel it in, but the prospect of nightmares returning was enough to drive me mad.

Halburn eyed me curiously. "Are you feeling ill? Do you need me to get someone from your group?" His concern was genuine.

I shook my head. "Herbs for tea, a tincture, anything to help with sleep. That's all I need."

Halburn hummed in understanding, then ushered me out of the growing crowd of stares and over to one of the first beds in the room.

"The general briefed us on your condition. Physical as well as mental," he hesitated. "Unfortunately, herbs do not erase trauma."

I grimaced, hating the word and loathing the way it settled in my bones. For the first time since Orondal, I'd have nightmares of Ronin's torn expression and his hands ripping at my hair, a blade glinting against the sun. It was too much. I wasn't ready to be thrust back into the clearing.

Halburn surveyed my expression until he caved, scratching his neck. "Well, I suppose we have a blend of herbs that can be used in tea. But I'd have to advise against using it as a crutch. It'll affect your sleep if it is overused."

A sigh of relief left me nearly empty of air.

He moved over to one of the shelves, grabbed a jar of loose-leaf herbs, and brought it back to me.

"An hour before you decide to rest. No more than three times a week," he warned, the jar outside of my reach despite my greedy fingers grabbing for it.

"Hour before bed. Three times a week," I repeated, smiling when he handed me the jar.

Halburn took note of it in a piece of parchment nearby. I thanked him for the herbs, agreed to a quick healing, and darted out the doors as soon as it was done, my skin tingling as I sprinted toward the hill.

The herbs stuffed easily into a sachet, which I dunked into the boiling kettle I had outside my tent, a small fire crackling beneath the iron.

Daylight faded fast and left me with desperation that gnawed at my insides. If I weren't intent on being stubborn, I may have asked someone to at least stay in my tent with me.

As the steam swirled from the kettle and into the black sky, I tried to remind myself of the truths that could bring me solace: It was a month's journey from Orondal. Ronin was dead. The king and the prince were nowhere near.

The realm is still dying.

I shook my head.

When the kettle began its soft whistle, I pulled it before it could disturb the silent camp. Outside of a select few who roamed or chatted in hushed voices, most people had already retired for the night.

I doused the fire, kicking dirt and rocks over it, then watched the smoke billow to the sky.

The handle of the kettle was hot in my hand, and I ducked into my tent, pouring the tea into a mug I had grabbed from the feasting hall.

After pouring the tea, I eased myself onto the bed and relished in the sensation of the pure wool stuffing beneath me. It was the most comfortable cushion I'd ever sat on.

Nestled in the covers, I crossed my legs and cradled the hot mug in my hands. I blew a gentle breath on it, hoping to cool it quicker.

When the steam dissipated, I took a careful sip. It burned all the way down, the flavor a mix of licorice, lavender, and spearmint. It was soothing, and I settled against the bed frame, finishing it in a hurry as it chilled.

With the mug emptied, I set it on the floor, off the rug. It made a soft clatter as it toppled on the uneven rocks. I paid it no mind and sank into the thick blanket, shaking as I pulled it to my chin.

It didn't take long for a strange sensation to fill my body. I tried not to panic as it relaxed me.

My heart raced even as my limbs melted into the cushion, becoming one with the bed. My breathing grew shallow, my chest weighed by the pull to sleep. It happened too quickly, but the worry had no place in my body as the herbs pushed it away. As I drifted toward sleep, the sensation of hands pulling me down took me off guard. There wasn't a chance to open my eyes.

Darkness consumed everything.

The trees around me twisted, whining as flames climbed their trunks. They burned through the bark, leaving behind symbols that glowed from the heat of the fire. I watched as they shifted, thudding to the beat of my frantic heart.

In the carnage, the sound of weeping broke my chest open. Wings brushed the earth, lingering among the flames as the man held onto the limp frame of a veiled woman. His sorrow burned everything in its wake.

Screams of torment echoed, bouncing around in my head until it felt as if my skull split open. It pulled my attention off the figures, and I trembled as the scene shifted, giving way to a crumbled kingdom, devoured by Aeterna's curse. Bodies blurred beside me, their faces blank.

Across the battlefield, Casimir stood tall, his blade quick to cut through the blurred bodies. Until it wasn't enough, and an arrow soared past me, catching a curl before it burrowed into his chest.

"No! Please!"

Symbols thrummed in the earth beneath my feet. They held me there, and I wept as blood pooled beneath Casimir's body.

The scene changed once more, and the earth swallowed his body whole. A vibrant, lush forest appeared—a stone platform in the center of it. The symbols had a pulse, red as they shimmered. In the absence of Casimir's body, the winged figure crept out of the trees, its eyes golden but somehow cold.

Wails of agony tore through the woods, leaving nothing but death in its wake.

The figure hovered above me, its hair falling in tendrils of black onto the bed. It watched me, unblinking, as my mouth opened to scream. No sounds escaped, only a weak groan while I tried to will my body to move.

It reached out, its fingertips blackened as if they were covered in charcoal. It inched closer, and I felt the scrape of its nail, the chill of its skin—the type of cold that told me it wasn't alive.

"You continue to run." Its voice caressed me like a wither breeze. Its hand pressed to my chest, creating an icy thrum beneath my skin. *"Do not fight it."*

The sound of a boot scraping outside the tent made its head snap toward the drapes. The break in eye contact caused it to evaporate into nothing. It left me with ice in my veins and air searing into my lungs.

I gasped as I sat up, my hands fumbling over the blankets in a desperate attempt to find something to ground me.

Ringing echoed in my ears and my fingers shook as I ripped the fabric off my body. Coils of hair stuck to the side of my face and the back of my neck. I shook it, ridding the way it tickled my skin. Every blink of my lashes brought the figure and symbols flashing across my eyelids. The glow of the runes tugged at something inside me.

Darkness filled the tent. It pushed and pulled at me, threatening to tear me apart.

My hands continued to tremble as I threw open the drapes and let them flutter to the sides as I stepped out into the dark camp. It bore no resemblance to the dead forest in my dreams, yet the vision clung to me with a wicked grip.

Casimir...

A soft flutter disrupted the night, and I expected a familiar blur of black. Instead, a white raven landed on a tree nearby, watching me. I stared at it, my pulse erratic.

Past the pale raven, I caught sight of someone heading for a tent at the edge of the woods. The burly frame told me it was a man, and he hurried through the dead, silent camp, somewhat familiar. I recognized him as one of the people who sailed on the same ship I did.

The white raven watched him go, its head turned at a strange angle.

When the man ducked into his tent, leaving me to allow the panic to settle, I drank in a heavy gulp of the cold air and tried to calm down. I pressed a palm to my chest and closed my eyes to shut out the unsettling stare from the pale raven, only to be met with visions of the figure's shadowed face.

"Trouble sleeping?"

I yelped as my eyes flew open.

The raven lifted into the air, its white wings vibrant in the night as it flew away.

Surprise replaced the fear when I spotted Valor. He wore his full armor still, sword at his hip. He was a few feet down the path from me, returning from the cliffs. Though he spoke to me, his attention was on the tent where I'd seen the man disappear.

His gaze found mine, a mirror to my own. It never failed to catch me off guard. I disliked Valor for irrational reasons, but his company soothed my nerves somewhat. It was better than being alone.

"The healer gave me a fake sleep aid, I think," I said, trying to hide how breathless I was, lest he try to prod. Valor was the last person I would tell about the figure that followed me from the ships.

Valor observed me, perplexed, but didn't press for a better explanation. He continued his approach and came to a stop at the edge of my tent. "It isn't wise to be out at this hour alone."

I had to stop myself from laughing outright. "You're out, aren't you?" I countered.

"Not a soul in Everbloom nor Mistvalle would approach me with ill intent," he said, the answer nonchalant. "The white bloom, however, is a different story. Especially among the people of Everbloom."

I scoffed, hating it more every time someone uttered the dreaded title I still carried. "Well, I guess it's lucky they have healers here who view themselves as goddess-chosen."

Valor stared as if he were trying to figure me out. The scrutiny made me uneasy. "Taryn is an adequate healer," he started, speaking with caution. "However, she had only been living in Everbloom for four years before your arrival. That's hardly enough time to become a skilled healer."

My shoulders tensed. "She saved my life."

"*Vanmore* saved your life, Elita," he corrected.

Despite how much I wanted to shrink away, I stood straighter. Meeting his gaze, I said, "Taryn has fought off infections in my side for a month now. Not like you would know. You sailed ahead of the rest of us, not caring if the wounded made it to shore or not." I watched Valor's expression harden. I was too aware of how I owed my life and my previous peace to Casimir. It added to the shame I already carried, and I didn't need Valor's reminder.

"I care for my people," Valor replied.

I shook my head. "Is that why, before we left Orondal, you said the wounded would adapt or die? Do you feel any remorse for the fact you intended to use my bloom? Or have you somehow justified your intentions to shear me?" I enjoyed the way my words caught him off guard.

He steeled his composure and stood taller. "Return to your tent for the night, Blackthorne."

"You aren't the leader here, and I'm not a member of your guard. Your orders mean nothing to me," I retorted.

His face twitched, but he kept his composure. "No, but I am the last remaining family you have. And I am telling you, return to your sleeping quarters."

My blood boiled, and my nails bit into my palms. "So you make a claim on me when it serves you? You are not my family," I seethed. "I am a grown woman, and I will do as I please."

Anger flashed in Valor's expression, and he took a step closer. "Then act like it," he snapped. "Your selfish and naive decisions sent us here. Had you let my guard do as they were meant to, that man would have been gone before he turned over the location of Everbloom or sheared your bloom. You brought this on my people, and you're lucky I allowed you to remain with us. You have your mother to thank for that."

My mother's face flashed through my mind, too painful a wound to reopen. "How dare you invoke her memory?" I said, voice low. "You left us both there to die. Don't ever speak of her in my presence again." The fury replaced the panic that followed the nightmares and the appearance of the figure. Valor was there, and he was infuriating. It made it easy to release the pent-up frustration. "She spent her last breath in my arms. A death *you* could have prevented had you come for us."

The words wounded him. I saw it in a flash of his expression, despite how he tried to hold on to his composure. He cared for her.

The realization was jarring.

If only it'd been enough for him to keep her safe.

Before the shock could soften my resolve to hate him, I turned to my tent. I paused at the drapes and looked over my shoulder.

"She lived every day of my life in fear. My mother never could find it in herself to love me. She was too scared to." The memory stung, even as I chuckled, numb to her indifference. "It could have been different if you had helped us." I gulped down the emotions. "But I'm glad you never came for us. I would trade you in an instant to have my father back."

I didn't stay to see how the words landed. I ducked into the tent, knowing there was no hope for peace.

Nine

Y ou've been summoned to Lady Estelle's council." I rubbed at my sore neck after tossing and turning all night. The Mistvalle guard stood outside the drapes, stoic and unaware of how close I was to screaming at her to leave. Too much light filtered into the small tent, and ached in the space behind my eyes.

The exhaustion would turn me into a walking manifestation of rage. Since the poor woman was only doing her duty, I refrained from taking it out on her.

I yawned and ran a hand through my messy curls. "Where can I find her?" I asked.

The guard eyed my attire and gestured out of the tent. "I have been charged with getting you there safely." She paused and did another once over my sleep clothes. "And in a timely manner."

"By the gods," I grumbled. "The sun has barely risen. Why wasn't I informed last night?" I thought of Valor and how he could've told me. The fact that he didn't shouldn't have been a shock. He kept many things from me to make my life more inconvenient.

Worry pulled the guard's brow together. "An urgent matter has come to their attention. It is in regard to the King of the Iron Thorn."

My frustration drained. Any mention of Lendorr or Talos had the same effect as pouring ice down my tunic.

"Of course. I'll get changed."

The guard dipped her head and stepped out of the tent.

I tied the drapes and went for the chest. The latch was a challenge to get open while my hands trembled.

"He's not here. He can't find me," I whispered, sounding insane.

When we left the shores of Orondal, I had hoped it'd help me forget what happened among the Temple cells. But it all followed me then, and sweat beaded at my brow. Talos wasn't the kind of man to let go of a grudge.

It took me longer than I intended to get dressed. I shook from my shoulders to my feet, and putting on leather armor proved to be a challenge. I wouldn't show up to Estelle's council looking unprepared.

The armor was all black, and I threw a new emerald cloak over my shoulders to break up the bleakness.

I left the drapes and joined the guard. We didn't try to converse. The threat of the king pursuing the Rose people was sobering.

The walk down the mountain was silent, and the guard led me into the palace with haste. It was busy with guards. The sounds hit me all at once, and I gulped. Chaos didn't help with how ill I felt. I couldn't focus on my surroundings, and it all became a blur of white at the edge of my vision.

We entered the council room, and it was a stark contrast to the noise in the rest of the palace. The higher-ranked guards of Mistvalle all sat at a long and wide table. Estelle stood at the head of it, wearing armor.

The room was larger than it needed to be, and the scattered decor didn't look quite right. Shelves stood in odd places along the walls, the blackened wood jarring among the ivory.

Like the feasting hall, windows let light in from overhead and made the lanterns that lined the walls useless in the daytime.

On the other side of the full table, four pillars stood evenly on either side of the room, with silver vines twisting up them until they reached the glass above. The sun on them was harsh and stung my eyes.

I scanned the people at the table and spotted Casimir, Valor, and Orin. The guard led me over to the table and gestured at an empty seat. I bowed my head in thanks and sat. My legs relentlessly bounced beneath the table, and I hoped no one could tell how afraid I was.

Estelle cleared her throat when the door shut. Everyone turned their attention to her.

"I thank you all for being here on such short notice. We have learned of concerning news regarding Lendorr of the Iron Thorn."

I noted the way she didn't speak of him as a king.

"We suspect they are gathering forces to pursue the Roses who escaped his grasp." She looked at me, then Valor. "There is some concern over maps he may have acquired after Everbloom's rushed departure. General Valor will share more with you all now." She dipped her head at him, and he stood.

Valor's focus on me was unnerving. "When our people left Orondal, we did not have the proper time to vacate. As many of you recall, it was a surprise assault."

I shifted, and my hands knotted together in my lap. Despite not wanting to, I held Valor's stare.

"We left many things behind, and this includes a map to Mistvalle. We are fortunate enough not to have put Thornrose or the Emerald Mountain at risk. We only kept out the maps necessary to make our voyage here. The journey was much longer than it needed to be, but this had been intentional. The charts of the voyage are difficult to understand, and it took us further out to prevent anyone from following closely. That said, it is not hard for one to see a map of this land and find access from Tyvolia."

Murmurs erupted among the council, and I tried to drown out how many of the people zeroed in on me: the Rose at fault for undoing centuries of secrecy.

My hands in my lap became the most interesting thing in the room, and I watched my thumbs twirl in an anxious dance.

Valor continued, "There are reports of the prince putting together a plan to cross the land of Tyvolia. The Roses who have been gathering information from villages near the borders have had a difficult time getting solid details. They've relayed much of it through Captain Vanmore."

I couldn't stop myself from glancing at Casimir.

His abilities. The perfect way to quickly share information. But I knew what it cost him to dreamwalk, and it added another layer of guilt. He couldn't escape the aftermath of my choices, not when he dreamwalked for me on the ship or used his abilities to keep an eye on what transpired after we left.

"The prince seeks the Rose who escaped the Temple, in particular." Valor's tone was heavy with malice.

When Valor didn't elaborate, Estelle stood again.

"The white bloom, is that who you speak of?" she clarified.

Valor nodded. "Yes. If you recall, she had been at their Temple for a short time."

My skin burned with the sensation of everyone's attention on me.

"We will not let Lendorr nor Talos reach our people. And though the news of them seeking us out is distressing, it is vital that we keep our wits about us." She clasped her hands in front of her silver armor. "Until we know more, we will do all we can to prepare. Rigorous training for the guards, and making sure we have enough armor and weapons."

Estelle turned her attention to a woman beside her. "It may be wise to prepare the stronghold for those who would not be able to fight. Make note of it, as well as increasing security throughout Mistvalle. Have scouts take shifts at the border as well, Moria."

Moria nodded in response and began to jot things down on parchment. Many of the people started to speak to one another, flipping through books, and pointing at places on the maps before them. Two women brought up the topic of stronger armor materials. Orin chimed in, though they didn't appear to appreciate his input.

Estelle walked around the table until she was at my side, and my head whipped in her direction.

Timidly, she placed a hand on my shoulder. "When you have time, I would like to inquire about your days in the Temple. If there was anything that could be of use—"

I recoiled, instantly embarrassed by the reaction. "Of course. My apologies, my lady."

Estelle's face flickered with knowing, and it nearly made tears spring to my eyes.

"Do not apologize, dear girl. We can discuss it when you feel ready. I can't begin to imagine what you endured." She patted my shoulder. "You may leave, if you wish."

Her smile was soft, not a hint of frustration. It gave me a sense of relief to know she wouldn't force me to recount things I wished to forget. Had there been anything I thought might be of use, I would have told her then. But I spent most of my days in the Temple hallucinating.

Estelle went to Valor's side, and they began to look over papers on the table. I took the moment to stand. The room suffocated me, and I couldn't listen to one more person mutter Talos's name as they began their preparations. No one had tried to speak of him since the last conversation I had with Casimir regarding my time in the cells. Before the nightmares returned, I had shoved it all down and chose to avoid going back to those memories.

It didn't matter how much I wanted to erase my time there. It came back, and I walked a little too fast out of the room. The muscles in my shoulders and chest ached with the quickening of my breath.

When a hand pulled me to a stop, I nearly screamed.

Casimir stood closer to me than he had in a long time. He held my arm for a moment before releasing me. I could tell that he didn't know what to say.

"I'm okay," I said softly, no longer willing to hold the stubborn silence. I saw his struggle, and I refused to make things harder for him.

Casimir pursed his lips, hesitating, before he said, "You've never been a good liar."

A somber smile tugged at my cheeks. "I don't think I have any other choice but to be fine." It sounded forced, and to speak to Casimir with so many unresolved issues weighing on us made me feel more alone.

Behind Casimir, Valor exited the council room. He glanced around until he caught sight of us.

"Captain, your presence is required," Valor said. Outside of the council room, he didn't meet my gaze. I had dealt a low blow the night before, and I wouldn't blame him if he chose to never speak to me again.

I had a habit of driving people to that point.

Casimir glanced over his shoulder, then back at me. It caused a physical ache to be so close to him, yet I felt further from him than ever before.

"Of course, General," Casimir replied, still focused on me.

I dipped my head at him—too formal and out of place—then turned to leave before the tension shattered me.

Being alone was the wrong choice. For three days, after the talk of Talos and Lendorr's potential pursuit, I avoided anyone who knew me. Nightmares plagued me, and despite my hope that the sleep paralysis would end, the figure visited me as well. It was too much, and I couldn't bear to have people ask how I was doing. It was harder to talk about the fear, and I quietly trained in the woods alone.

I pushed the memories of Talos down and continued to practice with a short sword. The poor tree I chose as a target had cuts on every inch that I could reach with the blade. It caught in the bark once more, and anger tore through me. I cried out and yanked the sword from the tree and stumbled backwards. The frustration boiled over and I swung again, cutting through another chunk of white wood.

My shoulders heaved with heavy gasps as I relentlessly slashed through the bark. Too reckless and quick, blinded by rage.

The anger turned into hysteria and I swung too sharp, missing the tree. The edge of the blade skimmed my shin as the force drove it back toward me.

"Fuck!" I dropped the sword and sat in the grass, staring at the cut through my trousers. Bright blood bubbled to the surface of my skin. It shimmered in the streaks of dappled sunlight.

I bunched my knees closer to my torso and ducked my head between them. I tried to settle myself with slow and controlled breaths. I barely noticed when Calla swooped in. Her talons rested on my shoulder, careful. The top of her silky head bumped my cheek, and the comfort of my raven eased some of the tension in my body.

The rustle of leaves made me tip my head up, and watching from a tree, the white raven had returned, its unnerving stare locked on me. My only company shifted to winged creatures. They followed me everywhere, even if they remained at a distance.

Calla's presence brought me the most comfort, even as it had me longing for home.

Twigs snapped nearby, and I looked up to find Taryn coming my way. Calla stayed, but the other raven left, a flicker of white among the red leaves before it disappeared above the trees.

Taryn had on Mistvalle clothing, which appeared too extravagant. The matching trousers and blouse were white with silver embroidery on the sleeves and neckline.

"Come out here to scream at the gods?" she asked.

I sighed. "That loud, huh?"

"Be glad most of the camp is busy today. I'm sure a group of guards would've sprinted this way at the sound." Taryn noted the sword discarded on the ground. "Solo training?"

"I didn't feel up to training with anyone."

When Taryn found the cut in my pants, her eyes widened. "By Cordelia's sea, what have you done to yourself?" she chided, dropping to a knee next to me.

"I swung wrong. It's fine." I didn't mean for my tone to come out so clipped, but I noticed how Taryn paused.

"Elita…" It wasn't normal for her to use my name, and I bristled, not ready for the emotions that came to the surface. "Why are you training alone?"

I bit the inside of my cheek and stared at the sea of red and white trees.

When I didn't reply, Taryn shuffled closer, kneeling in the grass. "Can I work on healing this?" she asked.

My throat felt like it closed over, but I choked out a quiet, "Yes."

Her hand rested on my shin, not worried about the blood. The sensation didn't take me off guard anymore. If anything, Taryn's abilities were a comfort. The way she healed was different, and it didn't sting as badly.

Calla stayed on my shoulder and watched Taryn work on my wound.

Some time passed before Taryn spoke again. "I heard the general say something about the king and prince pursuing the Roses."

I met her orange gaze, unable to respond.

"Thought I'd try to find you. It's not good to be alone with something so heavy. You don't have to talk to me about it. Believe me, I understand." She shook her head and fiery curls brushed her cheeks. "But sitting in silence by yourself is no way to deal with the fear."

My lips pursed and I nodded in agreement.

Taryn pulled her hand back and wiped it on the white trousers.

"Taryn—"

"Don't worry about that. I hate these clothes." She shrugged.

At that, a timid smile pulled at my lips. "Very impractical for life in the forest," I said, voice shaky.

Taryn gave me a somber look. "You're right about that. Now, this leg will need some patching up. Follow me back to camp so I can help? That way we can keep that uptight healer from scolding you." She winked.

I went to stand, letting Calla lift from my shoulder. She flew in the same direction as the pale raven, and when she was out of sight, I retrieved my sword. "Thank you, Taryn," I said.

She shook her head. "It's a little healing. No big deal."

"No, not that. Although I'm grateful for that as well." I hesitated, then said, "Thanks for coming to find me."

Taryn's brow knitted together and she pulled me into a tight hug. It was jarring when I thought of how long it'd been since someone had embraced me in such a way. I shut my eyes and forced back the sensation of tears.

Despite all the bad that had befallen me since I left the cottage, I chose to focus on where those circumstances brought me. A life with friends who cared for me, and people who noticed my absence.

Ten

After Taryn patched me up and went to get Ulrik, I made my way out of the Everbloom camp for the first time in three days. My time spent training in the woods had kept me secluded, but it was nice to stroll through the markets again.

Everyone in Mistvalle appeared friendly, not a glare in sight. It was still novel to me to be able to look others in the eye without having to avert my gaze or worry guards would come for me.

It was a decent distraction from impending war with the Iron Thorn. Made easier by how I was free to hold my head high, engage in conversation with the merchants, and enjoy the warm shift in the weather.

It was a pleasant place to wait out the end of the realm.

When the thought crossed my mind, the dread came back.

The novelty of everything made it easy to push thoughts of the realm aside. Although if someone were to look hard enough, they could see the signs, even in Mistvalle.

It wasn't unusual for leaves to wilt and fall during the harvest, but the subtle difference was there. It showed itself in the way the leaves seemed to gray in spots rather than turn their usual brown. Bark chipped off the trunks of trees, and the weather went from one extreme to the next. Everything felt off balance.

I pushed past the sense of dread and made my way through the bustling shops and vendors until I found myself at the luminescent palace.

There was much of the area I had yet to explore, and after not being allowed to see the castle in Keldovar, getting to walk into the palace of Mistvalle gave me a rush of excitement.

The steep, blinding steps brought me to the wide-open doors. White roses dotted the doorway. Sunlight reflected off every surface, and I had to squint until I walked inside.

It bustled with people from Mistvalle. It made me want to turn around when I noticed I was the only one from Everbloom, but I walked further into the palace, despite my hesitation. The foyer was enough to draw my attention.

The main foyer was expansive. High ceilings and open floors allowed for me to easily scan the room. Through an archway across the entrance, I spotted a room filled with bookshelves. It immediately piqued my interest, and I made my way toward it.

People from Mistvalle passed me without a second glance. It differed from the stares I always received from those of Everbloom in our camp. Or on the ship, where it had been sharp glares and people who quickly averted their attention from me.

I welcomed the indifference. They didn't know me as the woman who betrayed Everbloom. Many of them likely didn't know I carried the weight of losing the white bloom. It gave me more confidence as I moved through the palace. The room of books tugged at me until I walked under the archway, gasping when I took in how massive it was.

Bookshelves reached until the high, arched ceilings. Books filled them in an assortment of colors, disrupting the white of the room. Ladders stretched to the top shelves, and only a few people scurried quietly through the library.

Settees made a comfortable circle in the center of the library, and there were books stacked on the floor until they reached the soft peach colored fabric on the arms.

I walked past the settee and ran a hand over the satin fabric. It was cool to the touch, even as the sun came in through two arched windows that oversaw the sitting area.

Tea sat alone on a table beside one of the settees, and steam swirled from it. Still hot, and I smelled notes of turmeric, vanilla, and cinnamon. A warm blend which made my mouth water.

I had to find out where it came from, and make a cup for myself.

Leaving the cozy area behind, I made my way to a bookshelf that held their older books. The spines were worn and nearly faded from years of being cracked open and read.

The gold and silver paint which once told the titles of the books had brushed away, but the etched markings remained. I ran my hand over a few of them and read their titles.

'The Battle of the Gods.'

'Nesrin's Reign: the History of the Realm.'

'Herbs and Tinctures for Wound Healing.'

'Aeterna's Fall.'

'Process of a Bloom.'

Many of the titles didn't appeal to me. Two about the battle and Aeterna I had already read from my father's library long ago. *Aeterna's Fall* was one I had read more than most. Her story brought back memories from many nights ago with Casimir in the dreamspace as he retold it for me, shaping the scene to match the tale.

It caused a pang of sadness—the pull too intense.

I paused with my hand hovering over the book. It had become a comfort for me back in the cottage. Familiar, and I knew the ending. No more surprises. Simply a story of a goddess who let her rage destroy the realm. A sentiment I realized Ronin shared.

"'And her anger seethed until her tears poisoned the seas, and her fury scorched the earth.'"

I jumped and turned to see Estelle close by, the cup of tea I had seen now in her delicate hands. She wore a ruffled burgundy blouse tucked into a flowing black skirt. Her hair fell in a display of stunning onyx coils.

"I hadn't meant to startle you," Estelle said, the corners of her lips pulled in a soft smile.

"That's okay," I replied, drawing a finger over the spine of it once more. "Aeterna's story used to be my favorite to read." I moved my fingers to the top of the book and pulled it out. The cover was familiar, and it brought a spark of grief to my hollow chest.

Estelle tapped her nails on her teacup. "Both a lovely and tragic story, that one. Have you only encountered the version from the Iron Thorn?"

Out of curiosity, I turned the book over and glanced at the width. It was subtle, but it may have a hundred extra pages than the one I grew up reading.

My fingertips brushed the frayed edges of it. "Why does the Iron Thorn have a different version?" The question was easy to guess before Estelle answered. King Lendorr.

The people of the kingdom had no knowledge of a Rose who was prophesized to be the last sacrifice. They erased the prophecy from their books and clung to it. A secret I didn't understand, but hoped Mistvalle might have more answers to.

Estelle put her hand out for the book, and I placed it in her palm.

"The Iron Thorn spreads many falsehoods. Stories of a goddess who blessed mankind with a means to save their realm. A race meant to be their sacrifice. They left out many key pieces, and turned her into something she was not." She stopped and shuffled through the pages.

I watched as she muttered to herself. The pages fluttered as she searched. It took her a moment, but when she got close to the end, she handed me the book.

Her slender finger pointed to the line at the top of the page. "From this point on, Lendorr had it changed. I marked inside much of this copy," she chuckled. "Rather than the fury of a selfish goddess cursing this realm, it speaks of her grief and a love that was forbidden. It is quite a heavy read, actually. If you so desire, take it. Mark the differences you find."

I looked at the first line of the page. *'Aeterna's fall started with a simple choice that would soon throw the realm out of balance. A curse born of mourning for a love that could not be.'*

The book my father had in his study had left out anything similar to that. It didn't speak of love or grief, only her rage. Goosebumps echoed across my skin, and I shut the book, pulling it close. It would be a good distraction.

"Thank you, my lady."

"Please, you may call me Estelle. Now, this—" She moved a few spaces back until her hand swiped the table where her tea had been. A pale yellow paper crinkled when she retrieved it. "I'm afraid it isn't as fascinating. I have been told you haven't seen the prophecy for yourself. I thought it may give you some peace."

The paper seemed as if it would turn into dust in my hand. It looked ancient, though I suspected it was merely a copy of the true prophecy.

"Read it on your own time, if you would like. Now, I must return to my duties for the day. I hope to see you again soon, Elita." She grinned and tipped her head when she went to leave.

"Estelle?" I stopped her before she even crossed the room.

"Yes?" Her voice chimed like a bell, and she turned slightly.

"Since coming here—since losing my bloom…" I couldn't bring myself to finish what I meant to say. She didn't need me to.

"You feel listless?" She guessed. I nodded, and she crossed the room, her skirt billowing. Her hands took mine, careful not to crinkle the paper or knock the book away. "Lucky for you, we have an abundance of things to do here. Walk with me?"

I smiled softly, and she led the way out of the library. We walked in silence through the palace. Friendly faces grinned at Estelle as we made our way outside.

The cobblestone streets moved in an easy flow of bodies. They all made their way about the markets and courtyard with purpose. A healer barreled through with a cart full of supplies. A seamstress ducked into her shop with an abundance of fabric draped over her shoulder.

Somewhere in the crowd, soft music thrummed. The people in Mistvalle had a unique type of freedom. More so than Everbloom. They were much farther from the king's clutches. Their secret sanctuary seemed impossible to reach.

Their joy overflowed with chortling children who skipped in the street. Not all of them were Roses, unlike in Everbloom. The only person in Everbloom who hadn't been a Rose was Ulrik.

Mistvalle was different, and the norm children who had grown into adults still strolled the streets without a sideways glance at any of the Roses. Many of the younger generations appeared to be a balance of Rose and norm. An oddity, yet proof the realm could be different if the Iron Thorn allowed it to be.

Estelle's skirt swished at her ankles as she led us further from the center of Mistvalle.

"So, Elita, what is it you found yourself involved in before you showed up here? Talents you'd like to share? Oh! Do you bake? We're short on bakers lately."

I glanced over my shoulder, and nowhere in the markets called to me. "Gardening, actually. I tended the gardens with my father most days. Foraging. Hunting. Simple things."

Estelle beamed. "I have just the task for you. It's not too far from here." She waved for me to go faster as she picked up her pace.

I followed, the paper and book still clutched to my chest as we left the sight of the palace behind. The trees were cleared from the area, and a smoother path of light round stones led the way.

Short rock walls shaped the path, leading us as it curved. Flowers adorned the top of the stones. White gardenias took up most of the space, with a few clusters of gypsophila popping up throughout.

The intricacy in which every flower was planted surpassed the Iron Thorn. White flowers overpowered any of the other colors, drenching us in a strange mute scenery. The contrast of the red trees was enough to leave me breathless.

In the Iron Thorn, the leaves still changed into vibrant colors when the seasons shifted. Orange, yellow, but never red. The white bark of the trees added another layer to the whimsical sight.

Estelle led me through the path until the stone wall ended when a white fence cut through. It was tall, and the archway in the center twisted like pearlescent vines. An assortment of red flowers poked out of holes in the archway. I stared, enthralled as we walked beneath it.

The other side of the fence carried the awe another step further. Gardens stretched on as far as the eye could see. Seasonal plants grew among uniform lines of planters.

I sensed Estelle watching me, and I looked at her. She appeared pleased. "A few of our gardeners are out for the season, and we could use the extra help. Or, well, Sol could. Don't allow her antics to deter you."

That didn't bode well. Nevertheless, I followed Estelle deeper into the gardens.

"Does Sol manage all of this alone?" I asked, trying to keep up with Estelle's hurried pace.

She waved a hand over her shoulder. "This would be too much for one gardener. She, however, would be delighted to tend it alone. There are three other gardeners you will meet as well. Just not today."

My mouth pressed into a tight line. Damp soil squashed beneath my boots as we moved through the muddy dirt path. Far outside the confines of the garden, the rocky mountain cliffs made a display of white and gray. The wine-colored leaves like a flag in the distance as the trees blew in the breeze. One wide and one thin waterfall jutted from the rocky cliffs.

Somewhere nearby, chickens clucked. A sound I hadn't heard since the morning before my parents died. The last time I had ever plucked items from our garden.

I forced the grief into a tiny box and focused on the different vegetation throughout the garden. Pumpkins grew in a small patch of vibrant green and orange. Corn grew on tall stalks, appearing ripe for picking. A few apple trees seemed to be finished for the season. More squashes filled planters, and their colors made a lovely cascade of life among all the white and red.

Estelle brought us to a stop near the corn stalks. She searched around for a moment before she sighed. "Surely our best gardener hasn't already quit for the day."

Silence.

Then the shuffle of footsteps. No reply came from the corn field, but a figure walked out—a basket in one arm, full from picking.

The woman stood taller than either of us, and her short, straight blonde hair made a sharp cut at her jawline. Pale pink eyes blinked back at us with abhorrence.

"Not this one," the woman, Sol, said.

She looked to be only a year or two older than me. Her clothes were blotched with dirt, and the emerald tunic made her complexion appear more pale. Her mouth pulled into a frown, which accentuated the slightly crooked shape of her nose. She was both beautiful and intimidating.

Estelle shook her head and pushed me forward. "Elita is new here, and we will greet her with eagerness. She will be helping you in the garden for the remainder of the picking season."

Sol surveyed me from head to toe, and when she finished, she looked even more disappointed. "Looks weak."

Nerves pooled in my stomach. "I'm not—"

Estelle patted my arm. "Elita is healing from a shear. You will give her grace, and you will teach her the ropes." She left no room for Sol to argue, and yet she opened her mouth as if she wanted to.

Sol seemed to think better of it. She closed her mouth, pulled the basket tighter, and jerked her head to the side.

"Wonderful!" Estelle clapped her hands softly. "Now, I must be off. I am needed elsewhere, and this detour has me scrambling for time. Elita, I'll come find you later. Don't let Sol scare you off."

Estelle winked and left, hurrying out of the gardens.

When I turned to ask a question, Sol was already disappearing into the cornstalks.

"Oh—uh, wait." I scrambled after her and pushed past the rustling vegetation. Sol didn't look back.

"Baskets are back there." She pointed to a group of them on the ground. "Picking in the mornings."

I stumbled on a fallen cob, and caught myself before I lost my footing or my book and paper. I tried to keep up with her as I stuffed the delicate parchment into the front cover of the book. It would be a shame to lose the prophecy before I had a chance to read it.

I eyed the many stalks, in awe at the amount. "How often do you pick? Is it daily? How do the plants produce enough for—"

I ran into Sol's back when she stopped.

"Oh, sorry—"

"Don't talk."

"But—"

"No."

I floundered, unsure how to interact with Sol.

Rather than prod further, I kept quiet and followed her as she led me deeper into the field of corn. She didn't speak again. Even when I watched close by or when I fumbled with my book while trying to search through the corn stalks for some ready to pick.

I never grabbed a basket.

Corn rested on top of my book. Time ticked by in the quiet until she faced me. No words. Her hands plucked the corn from my arms and put them in her basket.

I sighed and slumped down among the stalks. She paid me no mind and continued her task a few feet in front of me. She had gloves tucked into the waistband of her trousers, and moved with familiarity through the stalks.

Rather than try to speak to her, only to be shut down once more, I opened the book and retrieved the frayed parchment. It was thin and soft in my fingertips, and I unfurled it carefully. It rested on the cover of the book, and I scanned over the ink, which was somewhat faded.

The words were difficult to make out, and I squinted against the sun that poured through the stalks.

"When decay comes forth to devour the realm, a pure bloom, white as snow emerges, breathing new life into the earth. ▪▪▪▪ the white bloom. They will serve as the ultimate offering. The fate of the realm hangs in the balance. Should they fail, no bloom nor god will save you."

My fingers trembled. Ice poured down the knots of my spine until my body became so rigid, I worried if someone touched me, I would shatter. The pad of my finger brushed over the words distorted with ink—smeared to the point it became illegible.

My entire soul crumbled. The loss was greater than I had imagined. The words were definite and damning. No god or goddess would deliver us. We would die the way Ronin intended. He had won, and I was a fool to think I could escape the grief or the horrifying truths.

"Hey. Girl. Help or leave."

I glanced from the paper to Sol. She stood with a stuffed basket—to the point some of it fell out.

"Right. Sorry." My legs shook when I stood.

The paper tucked back into the cover of the book, and I wished I could erase it from existence.

Eleven

ours passed in the garden, silently following Sol. We went from the corn stalks to the other planters, where she checked their progress. She didn't explain her process to me, but I gathered she was gauging what would be ready for collecting next. From how most of them looked, they'd need another couple weeks to be ready.

Quiet company became a curse, and the prophecy burned a hole in my chest, pressed between me and the book. My hands were dirty from picking the corn, and my darkened nails clung to Aeterna's story.

Sol's presence offered me too much time to linger on the damning words.

When Estelle returned to the gardens, she approached us, observing Sol and I. She looked pleased with whatever she gathered, probably the fact Sol hadn't abandoned me in the corn field.

A soft grin tugged at her lips when she stopped beside me, watching Sol inspect the leaves on another squash. Estelle exchanged the flowing skirt and blouse for an entirely black light armor set and a deep burgundy cloak, embroidered with gold thread in a design of intricate vines. It was stunning when it caught the sunlight.

Estelle glanced at me from the corner of her eye, noting the book cradled to my chest. Some of her grin fell, turning somber.

"Did you have a chance to read it?" she asked, not needing to clarify what she meant.

My hands gripped the book so tightly, they cramped. "Why is it blurred by ink?" I kept my voice low, both of us focusing on Sol as she moved to another row of squash and muttered to herself.

Estelle sighed. "I wish I had the answer for you. I'm afraid no one knows what the kings erased. It makes things a bit more complicated."

I hummed in agreement. "There have been many times I've worried the prophecy wasn't clear. That my death didn't have to be certain. I wish this had given me more answers."

"Perhaps in Aeterna's story you will find enlightenment." She smiled at me, and I returned the expression.

"I hope so."

"Now, has Sol caused you any trouble?" The question was lighthearted, and from the field of vegetation, Sol scoffed.

"Wouldn't dream of it, my lady," Sol grumbled, leaving behind the plants. Though she was finished with gardening, she slid on her gloves, ducking her dirt covered fingers into the leather. She hadn't worn them the entirety of our picking, and I wondered why she chose to wear them then.

Estelle appeared satisfied with what Sol said, and brought her attention back to me. "If you're not too tired after gardening, would you accompany me for a walk?" she asked.

There was no obligation in her tone. It was a simple request, not a demand. The freedom to decide in Mistvalle brought me relief after years having someone else control my whereabouts. Though my father implied I had a choice, that didn't change his disappointment every time I did something that wasn't agreed upon.

"Of course, my lady," I said, turning to Sol for a moment. "Thank you, Sol. Do I return at the same time tomorrow?"

Sol's lip curled slightly. "Earlier. Sunrise."

It was clear she'd prefer to tend the garden alone, but I was grateful she'd give me the chance to help again. I smiled at her and dipped my head. "Sunrise. Got it," I repeated, whirling around to face Estelle.

"Splendid!" Estelle chimed. Her delight was contagious, and I was grateful for her presence. It eased some of the dread left over from reading the prophecy. It helped that she had read it before, and she shared my sentiments.

Estelle and I left the gardens, walking through the calm markets. Many people cleared out, already at the final meal of the day. The dirt that coated my palms reminded me I'd need a bath before I went to the feasting hall. For once, I wasn't in a hurry.

The company I typically found at night was familiar, but it always pulled me toward conversations I didn't want to have. Their muttered grief over the differences between Mistvalle and Everbloom. The comforts they missed. It added to the weight of guilt I carried.

In Estelle's presence, I may have been the white bloom, but I wasn't the one responsible for taking their sanctuary. They were safe, unburdened by the same fate that had befallen Everbloom.

We made our way through the markets, and people paused to greet Estelle with joyful expressions. It wasn't like the Iron Thorn or even Everbloom. She had their loyalty and trust. They didn't follow her out of fear, rather by choice.

Once we were out of hearing distance of the crowd, she slowed her pace. "Valor tells me your abilities never activated after your bloom. Is this true?"

The question made me rigid. I took a moment to breathe, allowing the clean air to soothe me. "I've been able to activate them only once. When I tried to escape the man who sheared me."

I saw the way Estelle glanced at me, eyeing my short and choppy hair, that rested at my shoulders.

"I see… Have you not told him?" she prodded.

"I avoid talking to him." The answer came out bitter, and I tried to rein in the unnecessary frustration.

When Estelle chuckled, I slowed, looking at her with wide eyes. She paused when she noticed my confusion.

"Oh, I apologize. I've known Valor for many years. He may not show it, but he cares for you. You are his daughter, after all." She continued on the path, her pace unhurried. "He's stubborn, but he'll come around. If given time."

I bit back a reply, frustrated that I had to give him time. As though he didn't have almost twenty-two years to come to accept that he had a child. Not only that, but the many years he could've come to help us. He abandoned me, and I resented him for it—to the point I considered never giving him a chance to mend things.

That resolve waned each time I thought of my mother. I wondered if that was why she never could bring herself to look at me for too long. I was nothing more than a reminder of a man she assumed dead.

"If you don't mind me asking," Estelle began, pulling me out of my thoughts, "how did your abilities present?"

"I was able to conjure vines."

"No enhanced strength, poisonous touch?"

Flashes of fending off Ronin, too weak to escape his burly frame, made my heart drop. "Only the vines. Should it have been more?" I asked, steering the conversation in another direction.

"Not exactly. With so much missing from Aeterna's story and the prophecy, I'm simply trying to unravel the threads. Your bloom was white though, yes?"

"It was." Sadness leaked into my voice.

She froze, staring at the sky for a moment. "The strands that held them, how did they present?"

I brought a hand to my hair, running it through the wild curls. "When the buds appeared, the strands with buds were strong, like thick thread. I don't know what's considered normal, that's something my father couldn't explain, but they thrummed with life. I felt their pulse, like a vein ran through them."

Estelle surveyed my hair, her head tilted. "That sounds perfectly normal to me. Can you think of anything, an echo of abilities, odd sensations in your body?"

I thought for a moment, recalling what I could. The blur of red leaves in my peripheral vision became a vibrant reminder.

"There are times I see…I don't know what to call it. It's almost like tendrils of smoke. Black and red at the corner of my eyes. When I conjured the vines, it devoured all the light. I've seen it before while having visions as well."

"Visions?" Estelle faced me, pulled to a complete stop.

"At least, I think that's what they are. Long before my shearing happened, I had visions of it. Sometimes there was a voice, too." I almost told her about the symbols I saw in the trees, but something I couldn't explain made me hold back that piece of information—not a choice made of my own accord.

"Aeterna speaks to you?" She acted astounded, the words breathless. "I wonder what the alterations to your sight could mean as well. How fascinating," she said. "Although I assure you, we will only take what information you freely wish to share. I hope my questions haven't felt intrusive."

"Not at all. I actually haven't had the chance to discuss my abilities or visions with anyone. Not since coming here." Talk of the visions brought my thoughts to Casimir. He was the only person who really understood them. After the clearing, I didn't have another one. Only nightmares.

Not even my father understood the visions. Since they first began, he explained them away as nightmares. Nothing to fret over. His comfort was well intended, but eventually, I stopped telling him what the deities showed me. The rot that consumed the realm. The petals slick with blood. It was easier to bury it.

My mother had been worse. Where my father was indifferent, when the visions began, a noticeable shift happened for her. I'd only been eight at the time, and I could remember the rapid change. There was no softness in her gaze. Though my presence always deterred her, it was worse after the voice appeared. She was frightened of me.

Estelle and I passed beneath an archway, the stone consumed by vines that lost their color for the season.

My steps slowed, and I glanced at the trees that loomed overhead. "In my visions," I started, hesitant, "the figure never did show me a realm bursting with life." The words lumped in my throat, and I avoided Estelle's gaze. "Every vision held nothing but desolation and bloodshed. Even their warnings were grim." Goosebumps prickled across my skin, and I couldn't shake the fear that crept in when I thought of the visions of Casimir among a battlefield, too far for me to reach him in time.

I swallowed, finally meeting Estelle's stare. "What if the prophecy was mistaken? What if I'm meant to usher in the end of this realm?"

Estelle's expression hardened, not one of judgment or anger, but of steadfast faith. "Dear girl, Aeterna gave us this hope. She gave us *you*. Do not let fear blind you. Have you ever considered that the visions were not from her? Rather the same deities who cast her out?"

A shiver ran up my spine.

"Esen and Cordelia?" Though I hadn't read through Mistvalle's copy of Aeterna's story, the one in the Iron Thorn spoke of the two and their valiant efforts to end Aeterna's reign. Akuma had turned away, not willing to take part in their conflict.

Estelle nodded. "Esen is held in high regard by the Iron Thorn. Why do you think that is?"

Leaves dusted the path, their scarlet hue reminiscent of bloodshed.

Lendorr took great pride in the gifts granted to the kingdom by Esen. The very deity they honored when they marked our people. The god they built their shrine for.

When the leaves kicked up, swirling off the path, I shook my head. "Why him, though? Why not Cordelia as well? They both carried out Aeterna's punishment. They're both responsible for her silence." The words sparked in my chest, a rage that was new to me. I rubbed at my breastbone, the heaviness of a memory living within bone and marrow. A vision long forgotten, but it was the first one that made Casimir falter. I could still sense the figure's palm pressed to my chest.

"Now that, I'm not sure. The history books regard Cordelia with much indifference. She followed Esen, but it was he who set out to stop Aeterna. He is as much to blame for the unbalance as she is. It was their love that broke her, after all."

I thought back to my father. He was one of few in the kingdom that shared the sentiment Estelle spoke of. He never believed Aeterna was the only one responsible for the downfall of the realm. His memory pulled me out of the moment, and I wished more than anything he was there to help me unravel it all.

Estelle and I fell into comfortable silence, my mind drifting back to a life I would never return to. The contrast in Mistvalle became another agonizing reminder that I wouldn't ever see my family again. The quiet life I once had was one I took for granted.

We continued on the same cobblestone path until it wove into thin trees, leading toward what appeared to be stables. They were tall, extravagant, and made from the white wood that surrounded Mistvalle. It was close to the healing center, and I was surprised I hadn't noticed it before.

Estelle saw me staring. "Would you like to see them?" she asked, gesturing at the massive stables.

I nodded eagerly, glad to have a distraction from the prophecy and deities.

When we entered the stables, the smells bit at my nose, hay and livestock. It reminded me of home, and my eyes scanned the many stalls, noting the horses among them. It stretched far, over fifty stalls, by the look of it.

My family's tiny stable didn't hold a candle to how massive Mistvalle's was. It was roomy, the roof high overhead. Few lanterns flickered in glass casings, stopping embers from finding the loose dry straw.

The day the cottage burned down, there wasn't time to check on Mora. There had been no point in asking anyone at the Temple what became of her. I grieved for her then, missing how it felt to ride through the forests as trees blurred past me, wind tousling my hair.

A horse peered its head out, its black coat shimmering in the lantern light. The resemblance to Mora was staggering, and I walked deeper into the stables and stopped at her stall.

Estelle followed, silent, observing.

I reached out to the horse, noting the small differences. This horse was taller, trained for much more rigorous riding. The horse didn't turn from my hand, and I ran a palm down the curve of its neck.

"Did you have horses?" Estelle asked, standing beside me with her arms clasped behind her back.

"My family had two. Mine was a black mare, a lot like this one." My hand froze, and I pulled it back. The last time I rode Mora was the day I hunted with my father. I would never see either of them again.

We didn't stay long, and another night ended with a healing done by Halburn, and few answers to the questions regarding Aeterna's story. Every mention of Esen brought an odd hollowness to my chest, but I kept it to myself and let the walk with Estelle and her musings ease the sense of dread over how little time left we had to unravel the truths of the realm.

Fretting over it couldn't change the outcome.

I worried with my bloom gone, nothing would.

Twelve

Aeterna's story followed me everywhere. The spine stayed cracked open when I read it during my meals. It tucked into the pack around my waist when I went out to the garden. I read it by lantern light when the nightmares didn't let me sleep.

Five days passed since I grabbed it from the library, and I continued to take my time, marking pages that stood out. Like the stories of realms burned and rebuilt in Aeterna's name. The creation of the Rose people. Or the pieces that were left out of the Iron Thorn version.

It never made things clearer. I tried to keep in mind what Estelle said about the story still missing pieces. The true histories were lost.

Near the middle of the book, the differences were more noticeable. It spoke of a bitterness that almost devoured the realm. One that stemmed from forbidden love. Esen's name was scrawled close to hers often—how their abilities spoke to one another. It was meant to be balanced, the sun and rain he ruled over bringing life to the earth she maintained. But she took it too far, and it destroyed the balance.

Aeterna's fury over the loss of choice ravaged our realm. Her anger forced out Cordelia, cursing the seas—not even her domain. Esen disappeared when Cordelia did.

In their absence, Aeterna ruled over the land, and she tore it to pieces, killed entire pockets of life, and as an apology, sent the Rose people to fix what she broke. Only that piece seemed falsified. The goddess blessed her own people with gifts, and sent them to die for a realm she despised and people she resented.

The other gods sat back and watched her destroy everything, and didn't step in until it was too late. Esen and Cordelia allowed Aeterna to curse their domain. Ever the watchful eye, Akuma didn't intervene, even when the others finally did.

Reading became less of an escape than I had hoped, but it continued to work as a bandage on a bleeding wound, trying to stop the emotions that fought to hemorrhage in Casimir's continued absence.

I spent another morning with the book open in my lap, already in my clothes for gardening; a teal and golden floral vest paired nicely over my cream long-sleeve tunic. After finding supplies in the markets, I embroidered it whenever there was time— half of the vest remained unfinished. Between reading, gardening, and training with Alba or Galan, I was busier than I'd been in a long time.

Calla perched on my shoulder. Her presence brought me a sense of peace, another piece from my home. After everything that transpired with Ronin, I realized she was also a protector.

Alba sat across from me in the grass, Astoria resting in her lap. Taryn and Ulrik ran through the open field not far off, and the sound of their laughter was always welcome while I skimmed the book.

Water lapped softly at the edge of the lake a few feet away, another calming sound that practically had me face first in the book, asleep.

From the corner of my eye, I saw Alba wave a pastry at me. "Hello, Elita," she trilled. "Do you intend to eat? Maybe the book itself?"

"Very funny," I said, taking the pastry from her. I shoved half of it into my mouth and grinned. "Happy?" It came out muffled by the sweet pastry.

Alba swatted at me. "No manners."

I chuckled and glanced down at the pages. Calla pecked at her wings on my shoulder when I went back to reading.

"I'm convinced she grew up in a barn," Taryn chimed in. "No manners to that one. You should've seen her on the ship. Stunk to Esen and back."

"Not fair. There wasn't enough water for daily baths."

"Ulrik and I never smelled that strong. Double late bloomer, maybe?"

I rolled my eyes and threw the remainder of my pastry at her.

"Don't be wasteful!" Alba scolded.

Astoria jumped from her lap and went for the pastry before any of us could stop her. Ulrik giggled when the cat dragged it away.

My attention went back to the book as Taryn tried to chase after Ulrik, who seemed intent on getting the pastry from Astoria. Alba never left. She watched, amused.

Ulrik ran on unsteady legs through the grass. "A white one!" he squealed, pointing out the white raven who continued to appear whenever Calla did.

I stared at it for a moment before my attention went back to the book, the pages soft against my fingertips when I turned the page.

Fatigue pulled at me the longer I read but I couldn't put the book down. I hadn't slept without a nightmare since arguing with Casimir, and each day that passed, I missed his company, wishing to share with him the things that weighed on me. The questions that had no answers.

I hadn't read the prophecy again after that day in the garden. The words haunted me, and it was easier to bury myself in Aeterna's story. I hoped perhaps it would give me more insight into my bloom.

It never did.

After going through three more pages, I shut the book. Taryn and Ulrik stood close to the lakeshore, skipping rocks.

I looked at the churning clouds and sighed. "I should probably head to the gardens."

Alba glanced at me. "I thought you didn't like garden duty. What, do we bore you?"

I elbowed her. "It's Sol I'm not fond of. Gardening, however, I enjoy. And as far as you being boring…"

Alba put a hand to her chest, feigning hurt. "We'll have to speak about lessons in manners with Lady Estelle. Now, away with you, heathen. Before Sol bites your head off."

I stood, tucked the book into the leather pack at my hip, and waved to them as I left.

It was my fifth time helping Sol. She did little to no talking and spent none of her time showing me where things were. Another gardener had to show me where shovels, watering cans, and baskets were kept.

Clouds blocked out the sun. A small reprieve. Though, days in the garden had burned my arms enough for me to learn better and keep on a long-sleeved tunic, regardless.

Halburn didn't need another reason to scold me. He already did anytime I trained. The people of Mistvalle were crafty, though, and had more salves than I had previously known to exist, which had healed my burns, for the most part.

The basket that was looped around my arm stuck to the fabric of my sleeve, and I fiddled with it for another time. It was an irksome combination, and I wished I had chosen a different top.

Sol walked out of a group of stalks and eyed me as I struggled. "You're slacking."

Coils of black fell in front of my face. The curls blocked my vision and tickled at my damp temples. I blew at the hairs to make them move.

"Yeah, thanks for pointing that out. It's just as helpful as the last few times." The curls drooped into my face again, and I huffed, dropping the basket to the ground when I went to adjust my hair.

To my surprise, Sol plucked my basket from the ground and offered it to me. She stared expectantly until I took it from her.

"Thanks," I said. After working with Sol for a few days, she had seen me overreact more times than I could count. It left me with a sense of shame. Patience eluded me, and my anger often sparked at the drop of a hat.

Sol went back to picking a stalk nearby. I returned to the one I had been picking, my back turned to Sol's indifference.

Fibers tore. Shucks landed in the basket with a soft thud. Pick, drop, repeat. The redundancy was enough to make the time pass quickly. In the garden, I would spend days in silence, performing many tasks I had mastered long ago with my father.

Their stash of different seeds fascinated me, though they were holding off on planting any new vegetation. Much of what we picked would be stored away for the wither, and we had to hope they would last.

It was easy to get lost in the task, and I tore through the stalks until many of them were bare. A few stalks back, I spotted one I missed, and without thinking, I twisted and stretched for it.

The uncomfortable stretch of the scar on my abdomen caused me to lose my grip on the basket again as the sensation triggered another spiral of memories.

I pressed a hand to the scar and kicked the basket. "Bothersome fucking corn." I sat in the dirt and let my legs rest out in front of me.

Silence followed my outburst, and I glanced over to see Sol giving me a quizzical expression. A shuck of corn rested in her hand as she surveyed me. After a moment, she set her basket down and looked as if she'd vomit.

"They say you were sheared by some norm."

The question took me off guard and explained the sick look on her face. Conversation was clearly not her favorite.

My hands shook in response to her question. It would have been preferable to have the tears. They still wouldn't come even as more time passed. I worried one day they would drown me.

I inhaled through my nose. "It's not my favorite topic of conversation."

Sol huffed. "Forget it."

I bit the inside of my cheek, then relaxed my hands. "It was someone I trusted. He…well, I *thought* he saved me. He wanted to shear my bloom." The words stuck in my throat and I didn't look at Sol when I spoke. "I'm the reason the realm is dying. Because I tried to save him in return." It poured out, and I couldn't control myself. "The healers here have done their best to fix some of my wounds. It's frustrating that they still bother me after this long."

To my surprise, Sol sat in the dirt beside me. Most of the stalks had begun to turn brown, and we likely didn't have many days left of harvesting.

Sol didn't speak. Her silence somehow became exactly what I needed. There was no prodding. When I overreacted in front of anyone else, it turned into them digging for answers. They wanted to help, and I was glad they cared. But there was no help they could give me. None that erased what Ronin did.

I pressed my hands into the dirt and let the soft thrum of the earth ground me. It breathed beneath my palms. A pulse which remained in the back of my mind ever since I first felt it. I tuned in to it, noting the sensation of the dying plants. When I gave them more of my focus, I felt life thrum through them, and I wondered if that was how Alba and others managed the accelerated growth.

After a while, Sol shifted. "Ready to work?"

I looked at her, shocked to see empathy make a crack in her demeanor. Most people treated me with disdain after learning what I had brought upon the realm.

Despite my hesitation, I asked, "That doesn't bother you?"

She stood. "Not my business. Mistakes happen."

I copied her and clambered to my feet. Collecting my basket with one hand, I used the other to dust off my trousers. "Realm damning mistakes?"

Sol shrugged. "I almost killed my father. When my ability activated."

My eyes widened, and I tried to give her the same understanding she offered me. It was the most she had ever said in regards to her personal life. I didn't want her to think I judged her harshly for it.

I cleared my throat. "How? If you don't mind me asking."

"I do mind."

"Oh."

Sol scratched at her cheek. "Halburn. He's my father."

The moment she said it, I saw the resemblance. The pale, nearly pink hue of her eyes matched Halburn's exactly. Pin-straight blonde hair, and even some of her facial features. Her nose and tight lip line.

"Your father is nice. He's a good healer." I didn't know how to hold a conversation with Sol, and it showed when her expression soured.

"Don't speak of him."

"Noted." I pursed my lips, unsure what else to say.

The conversation, as always, died out. I was comfortable with the silence while we finished picking. Soon, the gardens would be empty, and I hoped in the coming days there would be another task lined up for me.

I feared that when I finished reading Aeterna's story and completed my tasks, the darkness would force its way back in. The nightmares plagued me, regardless, but I had some reprieve from the memories when I focused on my tasks in the garden.

For the time being, I chose not to worry about it, and picked the last stalk of the day.

Thirteen

For three weeks, every day consisted of training until I was drenched in sweat, meeting with Halburn, gardening, and hours spent in the feasting hall with Galan, Alba, and Taryn. After many attempts to convince her, Sol quietly joined our group. The days in the garden were often spent in silence, but it didn't take me long to appreciate the contrast of her company.

Most of the others from Everbloom avoided me, and it seemed Sol had the same effect on those of Mistvalle. She didn't act bothered by the seclusion, but after much of my life was spent in isolation, I knew how lonely it could be, so I invited her to eat with me after every gardening session. Eventually, I didn't have to ask anymore, and she followed me to the feasting hall at the end of the day, exchanging very few words, and never prodding about my shear.

It was a nice change, and I was grateful she seemed to warm up to me. After a day in the gardens, followed by combat training, we all spent another night at a small round table, staying later than anyone else, as Galan and Alba made quips at each other.

Galan's face went a vibrant shade of red when Alba giggled at another one of his jokes, as if she didn't know the hold she had on him. His eyes twinkled when she laughed.

My own chuckles joined in when Astoria jumped onto the table, the black cat quick as it grabbed a helping of chicken from a plate, too fast for anyone to stop her.

Sol grimaced and turned her head in disgust. "Dirty paws," she muttered, moving her plate off the table.

Alba waved her hands around, shooing Astoria with a loving grin. Her familiar was never too far, even in the new land.

I was glad Calla had better sense than to swoop into the mess hall. Sol would have a fit if a bird pecked at the food on the table. She already wasn't keen on the amount of company I had. It was a feat to get her to come to the hall with me at all.

When Astoria was out of sight, my attention went back to the company at the table. Taryn sat quietly with Ulrik asleep in her lap, trying to stifle a chortle, lest she wake him. It was late for a child to be up, but Taryn never did go anywhere without Ulrik, unless her mother, Nora, kept him in the Everbloom camp. Even still, it was clear she preferred him close.

I yawned while I watched Taryn kiss the top of Ulrik's messy curls. Exhaustion pulled at me every hour of the day. Nearly a month passed with nightmares each night, and each time, I awoke to the figure standing in my tent. There was no respite. I spent much of the late hours in a cold sweat, scrambling out of the black of my tent when I could move again. I became the walking corpse of my companions—and for another night, I continued the conversation at the table each time it lulled, hoping they'd stay a little longer.

"It truly isn't so bad," Galan continued, explaining how the tent setup worked for the guard. "For the most part, it is quite peaceful. It's only Lyleen and Abner who are loud."

Alba chuckled, covering her mouth. "Oh, I'm sure. The two were separated for a month," she said between her giggles.

The implication made Galan's face redden.

As the two conversed, my attention drifted, and I noticed Casimir slip out of the hall. He walked with Orin, the two seemingly in an argument. Despite his visible annoyance, Casimir appeared rested, his eyes no longer sunken. It made my exhaustion not as bad—even as we swapped places, and the constant questions poured in from everyone who encountered me, asking if I was ill. Alba was the sole person not to ask.

Since he stopped dreamwalking, the nightmares continued a horrific rotation. More death, rot, and screams that pierced my ears. Symbols were carved into the skin of my parents, Ronin, and Casimir. I shivered as the images came back to me.

Alba glanced my way, her laughter ceased. "Elita?" Her tone was gentle as she rested a hand over mine on the cluttered oak table.

"I'm fine," I said, and gave her the most convincing smile I could muster. Everyone at the table turned their attention to me.

"Have you talked to Halburn again?" Alba asked, quiet so that the conversation wouldn't carry.

I ran a hand through my hair. "There's no point asking. He's given me nearly every herb in the book," I said, tone sour.

Alba didn't press any further.

Taryn gave me a mischievous look as she leaned forward, slow and cautious so didn't wake Ulrik. "*All* the herbs? Because I know of a few that'd do the trick."

Alba rolled her eyes at Taryn and shook her head.

Chuckling, Taryn leaned back. "Just saying. I doubt he's used the stronger herbs if the poor girl hasn't slept yet."

"What are you all on about?" Galan asked, his tone much more serious than usual.

We all stared in shock, not used to him speaking bluntly.

My hands fiddled with my tunic. "Galan—"

"Half the conversations you've had in the past few weeks have made little sense. And I do apologize, Elita, but you appear ill."

I tried not to take offense.

Alba sighed and gave me an apologetic look before she said, "Elita confronted Casimir over why he was avoiding her. It turns out, he was dreamwalking every night on the ship because of her—" She glanced at me, checking to see if she could say more. I nodded for her to continue. "Her nightmares. He had to after everything that happened." She struggled with the words, unsure of what to say.

Everyone's focus fell on me once more. I didn't miss Sol's confused expression. Dreamwalking was an ability which belonged to Casimir and his mother. According to Galan, no one in Mistvalle had ever encountered it. I didn't have the energy to explain it to her.

Galan stared at me in shock. "Was Captain Vanmore in our cabin every night?"

I shrugged and stopped picking at my tunic. It would fall to pieces if I didn't quit. "He used to dreamwalk from Everbloom to Eldravine. Who's to say he was in our cabin?"

"That's reassuring," he muttered, pushing the leftover food around on his plate.

"It's okay, I still think you're a good guard. Even if Casimir stood in our cabin without you noticing." I tried to lighten the mood. It didn't help, and the shame continued to eat at me the more I thought of how Casimir sacrificed his sleep to give me peace.

Alba stretched her arms over her head, her blue tunic sleeves slipping past her elbows. "I hate to leave now that this has been brought up, but I'm exhausted after today's training. And you," she jabbed a finger in my direction, "need some sleep. As much as you can manage."

Alba knew as well as I did I wouldn't get more than an hour, if that. It surprised me that I hadn't lost all ability to function yet. I was grateful for Mistvalle's healers. They took pride in their years of training, and it showed in how I hadn't lost my mind yet.

Galan stood from his chair first and offered a hand to Alba. She smiled at him and took it. From the look on Taryn's face, she was seconds from saying what no one else would. But she just grinned at their tender exchange and adjusted Ulrik in her arms as she stood.

I followed suit, fastening my cloak over my shoulders. Sol was the last to stand, and the first to leave. Under her breath, I caught her mutter about the gardens to me.

The four of us walked together back up the hill toward the Everbloom camp. I grew accustomed to having to stalk up the long, inclining path. Alba still complained about it. She was convinced they put us that high so we'd suffer. I chuckled when she went on another tangent. Galan was content to listen to her speak, and agreed with whatever she said. The two made quite the pair.

Taryn kept light on her feet, attempting not to jostle Ulrik. The boy slept through Alba's rant and the long trudge to the camp. I tried to enjoy the moment of peace before I returned to the quiet loneliness of my tent.

When we reached the top of the cliffs, Taryn parted ways and went for the family tents. She waved at us with one hand and ducked into her tent with Ulrik.

Everyone from Everbloom bustled around the area, getting in last-minute conversations before most of them retired for the night. The camp buzzed with chatter as stories of new discoveries inside Mistvalle circulated. I envied their energy to explore. I had little time to spare after training all afternoon with Alba and gardening with Sol in the mornings.

My training was especially important to me, though. And I was getting stronger and better every day. The thrill I got from my skills improving helped fend off the fatigue for a short while.

Until the sun disappeared and I felt as if I would crumble and become one with the dying earth.

Alba grabbed my wrist and stopped me before we fully entered the camp. "Please, *please,* get some sleep. I know you do your best. But we need to work on your vine technique tomorrow, and it takes a lot out of you when you're just getting started."

"I'll try," I assured her, knowing it was an empty reassurance.

She sighed, not convinced. "Well, if it comes down to it, I'll slap some sense into Casimir and make him help you get a good night's sleep."

Galan let out a boyish chuckle, and Alba scolded him. "You boys and your piggish minds." She backhanded his forearm, and he straightened, trying to stifle his laughter.

I didn't find it amusing in the slightest.

We didn't make it far into the camp before Galan went to the cluster of guard tents at the entrance of the camp. I tried not to focus on it, but my eyes searched anyway, catching sight of Casimir as he ducked into a tent near Galan's.

The two gave a brief nod of acknowledgment before disappearing into their separate spaces. I couldn't help but take a mental note of Casimir's.

One of the closest to the path. The drapes fluttered closed behind him, and I tore my gaze away.

Alba and I carried on without Galan. She fiddled with a strand of her hair as we walked, and I noticed how nervous she appeared. It wasn't like her to act so distressed.

"Everything okay, Alba?"

Alba paused, giving me a grateful expression. "I love him," she blurted, the words falling out as she stared at me with wide eyes.

I stifled a chuckle. "I'm surprised it took you this long to say something."

Alba elbowed me. "Elita, this is serious."

Clearing my throat, I tried to wipe the grin from my face. "Of course. Sorry."

Alba glanced back at the guard tents. "I've never done this before...I don't know what to do."

"You could try telling him."

She rolled her eyes. "Ha ha, very funny." Alba hesitated, then lowered her voice. "I've been fond of him for such a long time, but that time away from him on the ship...I really think I love him. I don't know what to do with that. What should I do?" Her eyes pleaded with me, and my smile disappeared.

I didn't have any advice for her. Though I was nearly four years older, I had less life experience than she did. I had never loved someone romantically. Even my time, my kiss, with Ronin; it caught me off guard, and I hadn't felt for him that way.

Alba loved Galan, and it was evident in her face.

The answer was so simple. There was no telling how much time the realm had left, and they deserved to spend it together.

"I promise that I don't mean to sound unhelpful. You should tell him," I said.

Alba looked horrified. "I'm serious," she deadpanned.

I chuckled and shook my head. "I am too. You won't be disappointed with his response. Truly." I reached out and gave her arm a gentle squeeze.

She sighed, her shoulders falling a bit. "I'll tell him…if you get a full night's sleep," she said, holding me to the impossible.

I nodded anyway and offered a smile. If I had to, I'd lie. They deserved happiness, and I didn't want to prevent that. Although I was certain Galan would be liable to faint when she told him. I hoped I would be present when it happened.

We parted ways, Alba waving over her head as she ran off to her tent, her hair trailing every footstep.

My tent stood close by, no longer somewhere that brought me peace. Dread pooled in my exhausted limbs. The herbs were no use. The gentle tapping on my temples, like Halburn suggested, didn't help. Nothing would.

I entered my tent anyway, praying to the gods for relief.

Black and icy blue eyes watched me from the shore.

Water lapped against me, cradling my body on the surface of the inky lake, limbs sprawled and suspended. It chilled me to the core until my chin quivered and I grew stiff. The weight of my stone-like body pulled me deeper into the water, and I opened my mouth to plead for the figure to help. It only let the thick black waves pour down my throat.

I couldn't move. The stiffness slithered through my veins, freezing my blood. I begged for tears.

Before I drowned, a hand wrapped around my wrist and pulled me from the water onto the shimmering sapphire shore.

The figure released me, and its strange eyes pulled me back in.

"You are not meant to be here, Elita." It was a man's voice. Soft and disarming.

My body relaxed into the ground, akin to an embrace. Warmer than the water, but not quite right.

The moment I relaxed, a heavy weight pressed on my chest. The sharp sting in my ribs caused me to cry out.

"Please, make it stop," I whispered, icy tears trailing my temples.

A face took shape beneath the black cloak, though the skin was as onyx as the fabric. I found comfort in his company, and wished he would pull me further from the water.

The figure stroked my hair. "Why did you not heed the warnings?" he asked. Not scolding. His voice was smooth and sweet like honey.

"I didn't know—" More weight pressed into me; an inferno in my bones. "Please," I rasped.

In the echo of waves, I heard Casimir's voice. Weak and begging. My ribcage shattered as he pleaded with me to stay.

The figure tilted his head, and my confusion turned into knowing.

"Akuma." It left my lips in a weak whisper.

The name had been scrawled from many history books. His existence was nothing more than grief and loss manifested.

In his presence, I felt at home.

Akuma hummed in response and offered me his hand. There was a soft shimmer woven throughout his skin. Like a midnight sky filled with scattered stars.

"I can end your pain, but you must be certain this is what you desire." His voice wrapped around me. A silky blanket of comfort.

The agony spilled over and drowned out the fire in my bones. I could escape the memory of Ronin, Talos, the death of my parents...the burden of being a sacrifice would no longer be mine.

Tears dried on my cheeks, and I reached for Akuma's hand, fingers shaking. When our skin touched, he pulled back, the black of his eyes more visible as they widened.

"Something stirs within you," he breathed. A misplaced fondness softened his sharp features, and strands of white hair slipped beneath the cloak. His immortality left him frozen, and he appeared younger than I had envisioned the god of death.

Before questions spilled from my lips, the sapphire shores began to turn black with rot. The same horrid vines that had followed me for months in my sleep.

Akuma's gaze turned pained. "Your fractured soul has no place here. You must leave." The words weren't meant for me.

He stared over my shoulder, and when I went to turn my head, black and crimson devoured my vision. The vines pulled me back into the water, drowning me.

The voice clawed inside my head: "Wake up."

It all fell away at the command, and in its wake, I switched places with Casimir, my hands stained as I reached out for his limp body. Thick blood pooled around him, and I cried out his name, begging, pleading.

He didn't move. Didn't stir. His lifeless eyes turned into endless voids. They pulled me in, and all I felt was despair.

I fought back a scream when my eyes snapped open. The vision was too real, tainted by death and Casimir's cries for me to come back. My ribcage ached in response as if the memories held my very bones together.

My body trembled as I stared at the top of the tent, afraid to move before the feeling passed. I ignored the haunting eyes in the corner of the tent, knowing I'd find nothing more than a figure made of shadow. I didn't need the added panic.

Minutes ticked by as I caught sight of new tears at the top of the tent, moonlight pouring through them.

Casimir's not dead. He's okay.

When I could move my limbs again, I sat. The hairs on my arms stood, and a cold sweat clung to my skin as the panic tried to find a way out. I couldn't take another moment of it. I had to see him.

Swinging my legs over the side of the bed, I exhaled and tried to ground myself. My hands shook while I threw my cloak around my shoulders and stood, forgoing my boots as I walked to the tied drapes of my tent. I loosened them and the night air met with my damp skin, cooling it where the cloak didn't cover.

Frost from the grass clung to my feet while I stumbled through the darkness, not letting it deter me as I moved through the trees instead of the stone path.

Tents passed like waves of the black sea as I made my way through the cluster of them. Everyone was peacefully asleep, their lanterns put out long ago. I envied their ability to sleep.

It was only a passing moment I saw him dart into his tent, but my mind held onto the sight. Noting the differences, the placement among the trees. My memory led my way to the furthest tent among the guards, alone at the edge of the woods, a few feet from the path down the cliffs.

The fabric shuddered in the breeze and a sense of urgency carried me along quicker as I approached the tied knots of the tent, ready to undo them in desperation—when a familiar pair of hands beat me there, pulling it loose in one swift tug from the inside.

Casimir stood on the other side, his hair disheveled from sleep. The sight of him sent a jolt through me, and I dropped my hands, trying to hide the way they shook.

He's okay. He's here.

"Nightmare?" It wasn't a question, more a statement.

I nodded in reply, my eyes searching his, still afraid he'd disappear with the swell of my emotions. But it wasn't a dream—and his hand beckoned me to enter his tent, despite us not speaking in so long. I stumbled in and left the darkness behind. A small lantern flickered beside his bed and illuminated the tent, the size identical to mine, and much too crowded. He worked at tying a knot in the drapes as I wavered on my feet.

My eyelids drooped, too heavy from the lack of sleep. Seeing him unharmed killed the adrenaline, and my body nearly slumped to the floor.

"When you told me I no longer needed to dreamwalk, I half expected the connection to be broken. Not so much—" Casimir turned and stopped. His brow furrowed, and he moved closer. "Are you alright?"

Swaying, I took a shaky breath. "I'm sorry. I can go."

Casimir took in my appearance. The lack of footwear, and still in my sleep clothes. I didn't want to know what my face looked like after weeks with only a few hours of sleep each night. Whatever had held me up before, it finally crumbled, and the tent tilted while my vision became unfocused.

Casimir grabbed my arm. The touch was jarring, and I glanced at him to be met with a shroud of concern.

"Do you need to lie down?" he asked.

The warmth from his hand eased more of the panic.

I ran a trembling hand through my hair. "I can't sleep. Or, I haven't. Not in a while—not blaming you. Sorry. I think it might be causing issues." The incoherence didn't help.

Casimir's grip on my arm gave gentle pressure. "El..."

My skin prickled with strange goosebumps. It felt like ages since he last called me that. Tears left my vision fuzzy, never falling over the rim. The exhaustion threatened to swallow me.

The crease in Casimir's brow deepened. "Do you need me to dreamwalk?"

"No." Panic filled my voice. "Please, I just need—" I glanced around the space that belonged to him, and insecurity overcame me. I couldn't remember why I went to his tent. I needed sleep, but the last thing I wanted was for him to dreamwalk. It was wrong to ask. But I couldn't be alone with the visions and the figure that followed me.

After a pause, my eyes closed. "I need sleep."

Casimir sighed. "Lie down. Try to rest."

I looked at him through slitted eyelids. "Don't dreamwalk?"

"I won't."

Softly, I shrugged his hand off and turned toward his bed, eyeing it. I hated how hard it was to be alone. But his offer made me feel safe for the first time in so long.

"Will you be fine?" I turned to ask, my hair moving too much as I did, the shorter locks twisting easily at my shoulders. Casimir watched me, his focus on my unruly hair. A flash of sadness overcame his expression, and I had to look away, not wanting his pity.

Without an answer from him, I clambered onto the bed and pulled my cloak over my body as much as I could, facing my back to him. I heard him sigh, then a second later, he blew out the lantern, followed by the sound of his feet shuffling closer to the bed. I felt him lower next to the frame, sitting on the ground with his back to mine. He leaned against the bed enough to support himself without touching me.

The sound of his breathing soothed me in a way I didn't know I needed, and only darkness filled my sleep, the nightmares chased away by a ghost.

Fourteen

Sun pooled over the fabric of the tent, causing me to stir awake. For the first time in three weeks, the only visions to visit me in my sleep were of flowers and ocean spray.

I rolled in the bed, startled when I noticed Casimir's head tilted back, resting on the frame, his lips parted as he slept. It looked uncomfortable, and I wondered how he fell asleep in such a way.

It didn't take long for the guilt to set in.

I sat up slowly to avoid waking him. I pulled my knees to my chest before I slid a leg over the edge of the bed to find the stone floor. Once my skin made contact with the cold, hard ground, I knew he would be sore the entire day.

There wasn't any way to take back my interruption of his sleep, but I tried to stay silent so as not to disturb him further. I shuffled over the cushion, and a gap in the edge of the bed frame caught my other foot, causing me to stumble forward.

I grabbed Casimir's shoulder to prevent myself from falling face-first into the stone, and a strangled gasp caught in my throat.

He jolted upright as if under attack.

I grunted and tried to maneuver myself in a way to prevent hurting him, but it only made it worse. His hands fumbled to grab me, trying to steady my still sleepy body as he struggled with his own lingering slumber.

The way he grabbed me pulled my body awkwardly into his lap, one of my arms pressed to my chest while the other still grasped his shoulder. He steadied me, a hand snaking around my waist.

Casimir's face was inches from mine. The sight of his wide eyes nearly caused me to topple over, yet again.

Curly strands of hair fell into my face as I gulped. "I didn't mean to fall on you. Sorry."

His gaze flickered over my face, and I saw a glint of amusement in his eye. "So, that assault was unintentional? Good to know," he replied. A sleepy grin tugged at his lips.

A ferocious blush crept up my cheeks. "I've disturbed your sleep again. I should go." I released his shoulder and scrambled up. I didn't know how to act around him after our confrontation, and even less after I took the liberty to use his bed.

The offer to let me sleep in his tent was more than I'd expected. It humiliated me that, in my exhaustion, I inconvenienced him once more. To my surprise, Casimir's expression implied he was over the confrontation as he eased back into his normal demeanor. The lingering sleep made him vulnerable.

He stood, and his face twitched when he did. I couldn't help the swell of guilt that he slept on the unforgiving stone floor all night.

Worry crept in, and I searched his sleepy features. "You didn't dreamwalk, did you?" I asked.

Casimir shook his head. "You asked me not to." He shrugged.

The phenomenon was absurd, but it had happened in Everbloom, too, when he stayed guard over my tent. All the sleep he missed on the ship, and there could've been a better solution. Although asking him to sleep in my cabin wouldn't have felt like an option then. Not when he avoided me.

But it was a relief to be free of the nightmares and the figure. It was as I thought, merely fear manifesting itself in horrible ways. Being close to Casimir was all it took to be free of them.

For a long, uncomfortable pause, we stared at each other. He broke first, rubbing at the back of his neck.

"I need to change for training," he said.

"Oh! Sorry again. I didn't mean to wake you last night. Or this morning. Sorry." I went to leave.

"El?"

My skin prickled. "Hmm?" I hummed, still untying the drapes.

"Did you sleep okay? Any nightmares?" he asked, hesitant. For some awful reason, my face burned with more heat.

"It was fine." My fingers trembled when the last tie fell away. The morning air rushed into the tent. Despite how much I knew I shouldn't, I looked back at him and offered a small smile. "Best sleep I've had in weeks. Thank you."

Casimir appeared flustered. "Anytime," he said, clearing his throat.

I went to leave when the sound of someone running broke through the trees, right as the voice followed.

"Casimir! Elita is missing, and her tent is empty—" Alba sprinted into view, out of breath as she watched us both for a moment. It took only a second for a mischievous smile to spread across her face.

"Morning, Alba." Casimir greeted her from behind me. I buried my head, unable to prevent the shrill noises that followed.

"What?!" she squealed, giggling like a child. "I was only joking when I said that to you last night." Alba's grin grew, and I nearly burst into flames.

"What was it you said, Alba?" Casimir inquired.

My head snapped up, and I pointed at her. "Don't. I only needed sleep. Casimir…helped." I hated speaking. I resented it. "He slept on the floor," I clarified, unable to look back at Casimir.

Alba bent at the waist with bounds of laughter. "That bad, huh?"

If looks could kill, she would have been dead.

Alba pursed her lips when she noted my expression.

Casimir scoffed. "Don't be childish."

It only made her burst into laughter again. "You two are bunking!" Her voice carried.

I had to bite my tongue to stop myself from saying something I'd regret, and walked over to her.

"Please, stop," I pleaded. "Nothing like that. At all. Ever."

She gathered herself, nodded, and pretended to lock her lips. I rolled my eyes, knowing she was going to blow it out of proportion.

Without turning, I waved at Casimir, unable to meet his stare. "Thanks again," I muttered, practically dragging Alba away from the tent while she giggled the entire way.

We got out of earshot and I gave her another glare. "And you told Galan he had a piggish mind." There was a joking hiss in my tone. She rolled her eyes, and I said, "It truly wasn't anything like that. The nightmares were too much."

Her smile fell and she gave an understanding nod. "I didn't mean to poke fun. It surprised me, that's all. I didn't mean to assume."

"He just started acting somewhat normal today. You've probably set us back another three weeks of cold shoulder."

"I think you'll survive," she said, her expression turning grim as she grabbed my shoulder. "But I won't. You slept, and now I have to talk to Galan."

We avoided the first meal. And the second. Alba continued to stall, and I found it both hilarious and infuriating. Rather than speak to Galan, she dragged me straight to the training grounds after I finished getting ready, and we didn't wait for Galan like we normally did.

To my astonishment, he hadn't shown up yet to make us both feel bad for leaving him behind.

Alba and I stood among the circle of dirt not far from the other sparring grounds. It was a warmer day than usual, the sun bright and unforgiving, no clouds to dot the sky. Sol would be upset I missed the morning garden duties, but Alba insisted on not being alone.

Sweat rolled down my spine while my hands hovered over the ground, my focus on finding the vines. Despite Alba being a good teacher, nothing seemed to get me out of my block.

I sensed the plants, and a few of the limp ones, I could focus energy into them to get them to perk up. But never move them. The vines remained dormant, unwilling to bend to my hands.

We went on for hours with no success.

Galan joined us hours after the second meal, his expression wounded. "Why was I not asked to join?" He sounded upset, and I glanced over at Alba, leaving her to stand on her own.

"Elita," she hissed and shot a glare at me.

I shooed her away. I wouldn't help her stall. It was pure luck they'd have to speak while I was there. I didn't have it in me to offer them the privacy they deserved.

But I saw the apprehension on Alba's face, and it was clear she wouldn't tell him—not as more people filled the training grounds.

Any opportunity for them to speak diminished. Even more so when Casimir approached us from across the field. He had on light leather armor, ready for sparring.

"Lazy," Casimir chided as he observed us three. "You won't get any better standing there."

Alba sighed. The conversation would have to happen another time. I put away my disappointment regarding the anticlimactic nature of their talk, and let myself feel a weight lifted. Casimir was acting like a friend again, a smirk on his face.

Alba took it upon herself to grab the weapons we'd been using for the past three weeks. She handed me a sheathed dagger, slapping it into my palm while she retrieved her own.

She gave Casimir a grateful look, which he didn't seem to understand. Galan appeared bewildered, unsure of what to say after his question went unanswered.

"Have fun with your guard stuff, then. We'll get back to our training," Alba said hurriedly.

Casimir chuckled and shook his head. "No guard training today, only personal. I figured Galan and I could join you both. Switch it up."

Alba blushed and snuck a glance at Galan.

"Well, I won't force you to spar with me, Alba," Galan said, his voice gentle.

It brought a scoff from her. She was always quick to accept a challenge, never one to turn down a spar.

"I'll take it easy on you this time," she teased, going to his side.

It created a berth of space between us and them. I watched Galan pick his weapon of choice, a short sword, grinning at something Alba said while she twirled her dagger.

A glint of light in the corner of my eye stole my focus.

Casimir watched me, a blade in one hand, and his expression lit with amusement. "Spar with me."

I rolled my eyes. "I'm not going to spar you."

"Come on, show me that all of Alba's teaching hasn't been useless. Just disarm me." He smirked, and heat crept up my cheeks.

Galan and Alba chuckled on the sidelines as they watched our back and forth, their chatter halted.

"Don't taunt her," Alba nagged as she worked her hair into a braid.

My heart raced, and I swallowed hard, my eyes fixated on the gleaming, curved blade in my hand. It was sturdy, the hilt worn to my calloused hand.

After a pause, I gripped it tighter, liking the way it felt in my hand. There were many things I continued to lack in my training, but I was quick with the slim and light blade, and I couldn't let Casimir have the satisfaction of me refusing to spar.

I took a steadying inhale, sheathed my blade for sparring, and moved my feet into a ready stance without a word to him.

Casimir grinned, showing teeth.

My heart hammered as we stared off. While Casimir was amused, I couldn't find it within myself to smile. After so much silence from him, it was misplaced to stand across from him then, as if nothing had happened. I was glad he was speaking to me, but the unsaid things threatened to make me run out of the field.

My nerves steadily increased while I waited for Alba to start the match —since she held off on starting her own to watch us.

The word rang in my ears as she belted it. "Begin!"

There was no time to hesitate.

Casimir didn't wait for me to attack first. He lunged at me, kicking up dust when he sprinted. He wasn't one to let someone else take the lead; he wanted the first blow. Impulsive and predictable.

I dodged him with a roll through the dirt, my hair sprawling as I did so, a nuisance. Jumping back, I regained my balance on the balls of my feet.

Casimir turned toward me, maintained his menacing grin, and lunged again, this time aiming for my left. A dirty move. I continued to be weaker on that side.

My body recoiled on instinct, barely dodging his practice blade.

Adrenaline burned through my veins and I didn't wait for him to round on me again. I spun, my blade arcing through the air, narrowly missing a lock of his hair as he ducked down. His legs swept for mine to knock them out from under me.

I yelped and jumped, landing in a mess, my legs shaky.

He let out a thunderous laugh and lunged again, his free fist swinging, though I knew he wouldn't let it make contact.

Swiftly I grabbed it and twisted myself under his outstretched arm to land a hit on his knee with my elbow. Taken aback, he let out a grunt of surprise as he moved backward.

"There, I'm done." I panted, resuming a protective stance when he prowled around me.

"I said disarm, not poke," he taunted.

My hand worked at the hilt of my blade and I bit the inside of my cheek. A crowd grew as others watched. They whispered and pointed, seemingly taking bets. My mouth pressed into a firm line and I raised my blade again with a heavy sigh.

This time I lunged first, going low to take advantage of our height difference. He smirked again and moved out of the way with a graceful side-step, practically mocking me.

I huffed and watched him switch the hand his blade was in. He charged at me, blade tucked close to his side.

Once more, I barely dodged, sweat beading on my brow. I had done many sessions of training with Alba and Galan. I knew the proper moves for countering, dodging, and disarming. Alba had burned them into my memory. But sparring with Casimir was different, and rather than stick to his strategy from before, he already changed his combat style. It wasn't feasible for me to win a spar against the captain of Everbloom.

Still, I wouldn't let him win so easily.

When he barreled toward me again, I ducked under his hand as he went to grab me, and I jumped at his back, trying to use the momentum to twist around him. My hands grabbed his arm that held his blade, my thighs tight around his torso.

But his strength outdid mine, and the realm turned on itself as he grabbed my arms and pulled until I slid over his shoulder.

I landed on the ground with a thud, his blade raised above me.

The air evaporated from my lungs.

A sick feeling spread through me, and I gasped, tears burning at the rim of my eyes. He noticed immediately and dropped the blade.

"Elita—" He went to help me up.

I pushed his hand away and fought the way my eyes stung with tears. I wouldn't let them fall. Not in front of so many people.

I stood, not glancing back at him as I stalked off. People in the crowd cheered for Casimir, their whoops of joy like ice down my spine.

Visions of Ronin's snarl above me—his dagger raised to shear my petals—made me sick to my stomach. The panic and bile rose in my throat, but I tried to fight it back to where I'd locked it all away.

I dug my nails into my palms and left the crowd of watchers behind, ignoring Casimir and Galan when they yelled after me.

Fifteen

The courtyard near the edge of the markets sat vacant. Everyone attended meals or final tasks of the day. The peace helped as I tried to shake off the awful sensation in my body.

I sat on the ground a few feet from the fountain in the center of the courtyard and let the water's rhythm settle my racing heart. It wasn't enough to erase the images from my mind.

Fear threatened to suffocate me. Before it consumed me entirely, I stared until my vision distorted. There and not. Nerves in my temples began to prickle, the sensation trailing to my chin, causing it to quiver. The day was warmer than most, but my teeth chattered as a cold sweat dampened my palms.

Footsteps approached, and I fought the urge to flinch.

It isn't him. He's dead.

"El?" Casimir's voice broke me out of my daze, but I continued to stare at the fountain as water sputtered from it. Crystal clear and shimmering where the sun's rays bounced off its surface. I wished it was enough to make me forget.

Casimir sat next to me on the ground, his boots flattening the tiny weeds that had poked through the stonework. Their resilience squished within a matter of seconds.

I sighed and felt for their thrum in the earth. Absentmindedly, I ran a hand over the ground, watching as some weeds perked up. If only I could've made them wrap him up and send him away.

The stillness lingered, giving me a moment more to breathe before Casimir spoke.

"I didn't hurt you, did I?" he asked.

I glanced at him, seeing the concern, and shook my head.

"Well, good…because that wasn't my intention. I tried to be gentle. I hadn't meant to pull you so quickly."

"You were trying to be gentle while we sparred? What am I, a child? Give me more credit than that. I can spar like anyone else."

"I know you can."

"Then why even ask? Why be more gentle with me than you would be with Alba or Galan?" I snapped.

Casimir recoiled and focused on the fountain, his usual mask of indifference gone. "Did it remind you of Ronin?" He hesitated to ask.

I gave a single nod, and turned my face to prevent him from noticing the tears in my eyes.

"I wasn't thinking of how you might feel," he said. "You know I would never hurt you."

"Of course I know that." I couldn't hide the tremble in my voice. "I just wish I could forget what happened. What he did—" Tears choked me, and I cleared my throat.

The water roared in the courtyard, warring with my attempt at peace, and my breath started to come in huffs. I desperately tried to rein in the anger that threatened to overflow as grief burned over into a rage that I worried would consume me if I didn't get control of it.

"I'm sorry I let you go after him," Casimir said.

Although he wasn't at fault, I turned on him, fuming. "It isn't your burden to bear. I damned this entire realm because I wanted—" I stood, desperate to move, to flee. Anything to escape the pain. "Because I was foolish. I wanted freedom from my fate, and to feel like someone had finally seen *me*. You aren't at fault here." I trembled as anger tore through me.

Casimir's brow furrowed as his face fell into a frown.

Tears escaped, coating my cheeks, unable to stay in any longer. It was relief and torture in equal measure.

"I shouldn't have left the Temple. I should have died like I was destined to. If I would've gone to the king long ago, my parents would still be alive, and I wouldn't have the blood of everyone in this realm on my hands!" A strangled sob ripped through me and I almost collapsed, if not for how quickly Casimir stood and grabbed my arms.

The walls crumbled and I gasped as my legs buckled beneath me. The weight was too much to bear. Agony rippled, and every shred of anger burned away in its wake. Grief shook my bones, and I clung to Casimir's light armor, my knuckles white as I gripped the leather in my hands, desperate for something to ground me.

It had been nearly two months since I cried over the loss. The pent-up emotions released tenfold in the courtyard. A horrible sensation as it ate at me.

Casimir pulled me into his arms and his grip tightened. He held my head to his chest with one hand, resting the other on my lower back. Tears saturated his armor, causing it to adhere to my cheek as I buried my face against his chest. My body shook while I wept, and he held me tighter.

We stood in the courtyard for a long span of time, my tears staining his armor, my weeping the only sound to be heard, until the tears dried.

Embarrassment lit my cheeks red when I pulled back from Casimir, afraid to meet his gaze. He didn't prod. He let me gain my composure, which I was thankful for.

With a shaky inhale, I braved a look at him. Concern and apprehension overtook his features.

Cautiously, he inched closer and brought his hand to my face. A gentle swipe of his fingers across my tear covered cheek brought goosebumps prickling over my skin, and the air caught in my throat.

"Don't carry that guilt anymore," he said, voice gentle. The warmth from his touch lingered even as he pulled back.

My heart skipped, strange and sudden. I looked at the ground, unable to hold his intense stare any longer.

We stood in the silence, the trickle of water filling the muted space. A breeze swept through, sprawling red leaves across the cobblestone, dusting both of our boots. I watched, too aware of how close Casimir stood. His soft sigh caused the messy curls that framed my face to tremble.

I could feel his gaze on me. I saw the hesitation when his hand clenched then unfurled. He shifted, his warmth palpable.

When I braved a glance at him, the torn emotions on display made my heart wrench. It was a vulnerability I hadn't seen from him before, no walls to hide behind.

Casimir's brow creased, dimming the scarlet in his eyes. "I'm sorry, El." I opened my mouth to speak, but the sad smile on his mouth gave me pause. He swallowed, his shoulders tense. "I thought staying away, being indifferent, would be better. That it'd protect you." He searched my face, close enough for my eyes to trace the small scar on his jaw. "I didn't intend to let you grieve alone. But you don't have to carry it on your own."

My lip quivered, his explanation a relief, though it didn't erase how the loneliness hurt. Other well-meaning people had offered their ear, their time. But speaking with them didn't offer solace. They didn't understand the depth of it all. The only person who did was Casimir, after the years of talking me down when I had another vision of my death. He was the only other person in the clearing when I lost my bloom.

I took a shaky breath. "Casimir…" His name was a whisper, the emotions stuck in my throat. "Don't think for a second that I blame you for what happened. Or that you caused it. I made the choice to go over the Forge, and despite everything, I'm so glad I did," I said, smiling softly at him.

I watched the tension melt in his limbs, the clench of his jaw softening, his eyes no longer shadowed by a crease in his brow. For the first time since Everbloom, it felt different. Lighter. He was more like the man who haunted me all those years, and he didn't look at me as though I were someone wounded.

The shift made pleasant nerves erupt in my stomach.

A soft grin tugged at the corners of his lips. "So, you're saying that almost dying was worth it because you found me?" The joke was halfhearted, mirth never quite finding his gaze.

His ability to bury emotions wasn't new to me, yet it made the truth of his guilt feel heavier.

Mortified by my own emotional outburst, I shoved the grief back to where it had been buried, and I gave him a teasing smile. "Actually, I was going to say because I met Orin. But I guess finding you, too."

He scoffed and ran a hand through his hair. "I'll be sure to tell him that. He'd be thrilled."

I chuckled, the sound strained after crying. "Hmm, I'm sure he would be." I shuffled back a step, eyeing the crowd that moved outside the courtyard. "I'm supposed to meet everyone for the last meal. I've not eaten all day." While it wasn't a lie, it was also a way to avoid talking about things I wished to forget.

Casimir raised a brow at me. "Are you actually hungry or simply trying to deflect?" he prodded.

"You're the one who made light of what I said. I'd say it's *you* that's deflecting. Still haven't learned how to talk about feelings, have we?"

Casimir paused, searching my face. He could read me better than anyone, and his expression fell the longer he observed me. "You don't have to pretend with me. Not that you're fine or coping. I'm here, and I know I should have been there for you sooner, and I've been a complete ass. But I'm not going anywhere. You can fall apart with me, if that's what you need."

Warmth spread through me, an abrupt feeling I'd only experienced once before—months ago when he first reappeared in my dreams after years of absence.

I swallowed the lump in my throat. "And if I offered you the same, to be someone you could be vulnerable with, would you? Because I know what it's like to hold onto what happened. In that clearing, we both—"

"This isn't about me," he cut in, trying to shrug it off. The way his entire body tensed showed that he was still haunted by what happened.

I deflated. "Casimir—"

"There's nothing for me to talk about. I'm fine." The vulnerability from moments before shut away, burying his grief.

I opened my mouth to speak, but before I could get in another word, he turned and gestured to the path. What I wanted to tell him was that I didn't need to simply fall apart. I needed to know if he was okay or if he had nightmares of ending Ronin's life, if he couldn't erase the image of blood on his hands. Because those very memories swallowed me whole, and I worried I would never find my way back out.

If he couldn't escape them, what hope did I have?

Upon entering the feasting hall, the cacophony of voices engulfed us. Despite the crowded tables, I was eager to fill my plate since I hadn't eaten yet.

In the crowd, I spotted Taryn and Ulrik sitting at a different table alongside one of the healers I had seen during a few of my trips to their healing center.

The people from Everbloom had started to integrate with those from Mistvalle. Many of the people I had grown used to seeing on the ship, the same ones who often cast glares in my direction, no longer paid me any mind.

I saw Elrin in the line for food, and it was a relief that she had stopped glowering at me. If anything, she was one of the people on the ship who helped me the most. Then there were a few others, the ones who still looked at me as though I were a curse—one of them had tried to get Valor to send me back to the Temple when the king sought them out after Everbloom fell. And to my dismay, Novian sat at a table not far from the entrance, with what appeared to be ale in his hand. Two months had passed since we left Everbloom, and as his bulging eyes locked onto me entering the feasting hall, a wave of unease still managed to wash over me.

I rushed further into the hall with Casimir close behind as I darted out of Novian's line of sight.

We spotted Sol, Alba, and Galan at a table, accompanied by two more who appeared to be from Mistvalle, their clothing different from those that the people from Everbloom wore.

Before sitting down, I filled a plate, Casimir never too far as he did the same. It took great effort not to watch him from the corner of my eye. I wondered if he spoke to anyone about what he went through. Considering his company consisted of Orin and Galan, I doubted it. He, like me, didn't willingly share.

We approached the table with Alba, Sol, and Galan, nodding to the unfamiliar faces who sat across from us.

"Glad you two could join us," Alba said, her tone coy.

I glared at her. "You quit that," I hissed before I took a bite of the meat from my plate, which was too hot. Alba chuckled when I sputtered, waving my frustration off.

Sol eyed me and Casimir, then shook her head. "Alba overshared." She stabbed a fork into the roasted squash on her plate and quirked a brow at us. "Interesting."

I shot Alba a glare, my face heated.

"Damn it, Alba. Do you think before you speak?" Casimir grumbled.

Alba feigned hurt, a palm to her chest, but a smirk on her face.

I was seconds from repaying her with a reminder about talking to Galan. Rather than embarrass her in front of everyone, I picked at the food on my plate, starved after training all day.

Galan's conversation caught my attention, an awful sensation sweeping through me as one of the people from Mistvalle said, "They didn't tell us much. Lady Estelle only said your people needed someplace safe. Never why you had to leave."

I nearly choked. Everyone looked at me as I covered my mouth, coughing.

Galan cleared his throat. "Someone discovered our location and gave it to the king's guard. We had to leave in haste." Galan didn't mention the pieces of the story that included Ronin or the part I played in bringing the king's guard on the people of Everbloom.

I needed to remember to thank him later.

"How does that even happen? A traitor?" the man from Mistvalle asked, shocked.

"A bad set of circumstances. Not much more to it," Galan said quickly, causing a few raised brows.

Sol rolled her eyes at the person next to her. "Nose out of people's business, Laken."

My appetite was gone, the food on my plate untouched as the topic continued to unfold. Next to me, Casimir stopped eating as well. I sensed his gaze, but refused to look at him.

The room blurred as the voices built on each other, every conversation too loud in the stone hall. Cutlery scraped on plates, glasses smacked the tables, and chairs screeched against the stone.

I sank deeper into my seat, mindlessly moving the food on my plate around, trying to tune it all out.

When something bumped into my chair, I jolted upright, my peace slipping away despite my desperate need for it.

I turned to see who it was, and my anger doubled.

Novian stood behind me, an obnoxious smirk on his face. "Gods, my apologies. Didn't notice the white bloom was sittin' here," he said. His gaze flickered to the other faces at the table before it settled on Casimir. "And never too far, her bunking partner." He winked.

I looked Alba's way, fuming. Her squeals from the morning practically announced to the entire camp I had slept in Casimir's tent.

"Go away, Novian. No one likes you," Alba snapped, pointing her fork at him.

He chortled, his burly frame shaking with every crude chuckle.

I shook my head and focused back on my plate.

"Careful who you trust, white bloom. Would hate for another one of your admirers to try to kill you."

My chair scraped hard on the stone, falling to the floor.

I felt Novian's skin move against my fist before the pain radiated to my elbow. His head snapped to the side with a resounding crack, my full strength behind the punch as it found its mark.

He sputtered and stumbled back into people who idly chatted close by. Novian's eyes were wide with shock. The corner of his lip split with a smear of blood, his cheek scarlet where my fist had met.

It barely registered with me.

I stared down at him while my lungs heaved. A hand grabbed my wrist, brushing over my knuckles and hand. Every person that spoke around me sounded as if they were underwater.

Alba came into my sight, waving in front of my face while I returned Novian's shocked expression.

The anger dissipated quickly and I sucked in a breath, glancing down at the hand Casimir held in his, already searching it for any damage as the pain spread beneath my skin.

"Elita?" Alba whispered as she rested a hand on my arm.

The people Novian had fallen into helped him up, their eyes fixed on me in confusion and disgust. To my right, Sol appeared to stifle a laugh. The contrast made my head swim.

Noises rushed back to me and I pulled my hand out of Casimir's, going for the exit as fast as my legs would carry me. The crowd continued to grow as I left, scrambling to see what the commotion was, and I couldn't take another judgmental stare.

I sensed Casimir follow me out of the feasting hall. His stride was longer, and he caught up with me, walking shoulder to shoulder.

While we trudged past more people who made their way down the hill, the sky transformed into a mesmerizing display of pink, orange, and blue. A joyful mix of colors in contrast to the anger and sadness that swirled in my body.

My hand ached, but beneath the shock, a twisted emotion tugged at me. I couldn't help but feel a swell of pride. It took long enough, but Novian had his payback for coloring my teeth red with blood after he slammed me to the ground.

The stone pillars passed by in a flash as I stalked up the hill, quick with how accustomed to the incline my muscles had become. Regardless, I couldn't lose Casimir. He didn't have it in himself to let me gain much distance, and it made me irrationally upset.

At the top of the cliffs, just inside the camp, Casimir grabbed my arm and pulled me to the left. We stalked through the trees to the tent I had woken up in. I started to protest, but he gestured to the drapes and I caved, ducking inside.

I waited for him to say something, but he didn't at first. He moved around the small tent, and it didn't take him long to gather what he'd been searching for.

With his hands full of an assortment of items, he tilted his head to the bed. "Sit," he ordered, using the captain tone he spoke with while training.

Despite my desire to refuse, I sat on the cushion. The blankets were a mess at the edge of the bed, unused by me or Casimir after I used my cloak and he slept on the floor.

It was so absurd, I nearly laughed.

He didn't seem in a joking mood.

"Give me your hand," he said, crouched in front of me after he set the items on the bed beside my thigh.

I eyed them, and noted salves, bandages, among other healing things. I scoffed. "They have healers here for that, you know," I grumbled, reluctantly offering him my hand.

"You'll be lucky if any of them want to help you after that." He shook his head. My hand rested in his, and he brushed a thumb over my sore knuckles, gentle not to irritate them.

"Oh, come on. It was Novian. No one likes him. Alba even said so." I chuckled, but he didn't find it amusing.

Casimir scanned over my hand. My knuckles were red, but there was no blood or broken skin. Closing my fist made it spark with pain, but it wasn't anything I couldn't handle. After a moment, Casimir grabbed a cloth from beside me and poured water from a waterskin over it. With a cautious touch, he pressed it to my sore knuckles.

"At least you didn't break a thumb," he mused.

"My father taught me how to defend myself. Not tucking my thumb when punching someone was one of the first things he showed me."

Casimir held the cloth to my skin, and the moisture felt nice, soothing the way my knuckles throbbed. "I apologize for the months of silence." His abrupt apology took me off guard.

"Why—"

"I'm worried about you," he said, blotting my knuckles with the cloth. "Has anyone talked about how to handle your grief? Have you even *tried* to handle it? Because the Elita I knew wouldn't have ever punched someone—"

I pulled my hand out of his and stood so quickly, he almost toppled over in front of me.

He stood as well once he got his bearings, bewildered.

"That's the problem," I said, going for the drapes and leaving him behind before the tears fell once more.

The truth under the surface broke me, and I couldn't bear to have Casimir say that I wasn't who I used to be.

A heavy, melancholic ache settled deep in my bones.

Without turning to look at him, I paused at the drapes. "I'm not her anymore. I have no idea who I am."

Sixteen

My feet carried me far from the camp. I didn't know where to go, but everything inside me screamed to flee. Nothing felt right. There was no resemblance to who I was before and I was stripped down to someone I no longer recognized.

The last time I experienced any semblance of normalcy was before my parents' death. My desperation to escape the weight of my bloom had made me dart out of the cottage, barely a moment spared with them. And now I wouldn't ever see them again.

I longed for the mundane life. The time spent in the garden with the sun on my face while the chickens clucked close by. The repetition of getting my horse, Mora, ready for a ride or hunt. The rainy days where I sat near the stone hearth, a book about plants in hand, chatting about what I read with my father.

It hurt to think about it all after I pushed the thoughts away. When I shut out the torment of Ronin's betrayal, I numbed myself to everything else. Closing the door on my grief and sadness coincidentally took the happiness, too. Memories with my parents, lost to me when I forced myself not to wallow in the torment.

I didn't want it, and despite my efforts to flee it, the grief latched on to me, following me far from Eldravine; far from the Iron Thorn. A heavy weight settled on my shoulders, and tears welled up as the feeling of being trapped enveloped me. I yearned to be free.

Free from what?

My body ached with rigidity as I stopped among the trees. I was freer than I'd ever been in the cottage. More free than when the white bloom became my destiny. There was no sacrifice to be made, not after what Ronin did.

But there was no freedom from the memories that haunted me from the cell walls. My screams echoed back in my mind, blurring with the sobs that left my throat raw while Ronin sheared my hair.

There was no freedom from them.

Once more, my legs carried me onward and to an opening in the trees that led to a lookout. The cliffs of Mistvalle rose and dipped in a wondrous display of white and gray stone.

Below the cliffs, lights flickered. The only sign of the bustling life. From where I stood, the lanterns scattered around resembled a constellation of stars.

The stillness was reminiscent of my nights in the woods with Ronin, his presence never too far. Regardless of my obliviousness when I was with him, I now understood why that was. He didn't stray too far because it may have ruined his chance for retribution.

Ronin let the woman in Woolfolk die to prevent the guards from taking me. He told me to run that night because he didn't want them to reap the benefits of my bloom. Every moment I thought he was protecting me, he was protecting his revenge.

A sudden and harsh wind twisted my hair across my face. When I closed my eyes, I was back in the forest while Ronin unraveled before me.

Biting the inside of my cheek, I tried to hold back the tears that threatened to spill.

I have to let go of who I thought he was.

Even as he brought the dagger down, my body and mind had struggled to accept it. I didn't want to believe he was capable of something so cruel. He had been my friend, a comfort through the grief.

"It was a lie," I whispered into the night. Something about saying it out loud was cathartic.

Though the weight persisted, I had no desire to willingly let it drown me. I refused to carry the pain from his choices. As tears burned at my eyes, my chin quivered with a heavy breath. I couldn't hold on to the pain anymore. It didn't serve me.

A chill ran down my spine as I felt the intensity of surviving his betrayal. He wouldn't have power over me anymore. There was no way to change his choice. I couldn't change who he was—too far gone to be saved. He let his own grief suffocate him, twisting his heart into something evil. I wouldn't allow the same to happen to me.

When a broken cry tore from my throat, I swore to live in spite of the weight, too heavy for my shoulders to bear alone.

I would never be who I was before he betrayed me. That person was gone. But I found power in that, too. There was a chance for me to be so much more. Refined from the torment, no longer held captive by the memories which plagued me.

Someone different.

A bloom that could grow even in the darkness.

The early rays of sun blinded me, a stark contrast to the darkness I had become accustomed to. It illuminated the training grounds as a thin layer of fog lingered among the stone walls.

My hands, calloused and gritty, were desperate to summon vines or roots from the earth. Every muscle ached as I tried again, my palms shaking and covered in sweat, which turned the dirt damp. It didn't bother me in the slightest. All I could concentrate on was the exertion required to perform the one task that many other Roses excelled at.

I longed for that power. I needed to conjure them again.

But the block remained, even as I tried to let go of the thoughts that had haunted me. They were far from my mind, my shoulders lighter than they had been in two months. Eager to try again, I had sprinted down the pathway at the cliffs during the night hours, hope carrying my feet.

The vines still didn't move.

Frustrated, I groaned and eased the tension in my muscles. My arms hung by my sides, my knuckles grazing the ground.

As the fog dispersed and the sanctuary outside of the walls began to bustle with people, Casimir joined me.

From the corner of my eye, I watched him approach, not dressed for sparring or training. He wore linen trousers, which appeared suited for sleeping, and his tunic was old and worn.

Casimir's attire took me off guard and I turned to him, sitting down in the dirt. "You look as though you've just stumbled out of bed," I mused, my voice carrying in the empty grounds.

He didn't look amused. "I hope you've at least had that hand looked at by someone before coming out here to train." He stood over me, his hands tucked into his trouser pockets.

"Seems pointless, after the most well-trained healer tended to it last night." I stared through slitted eyes, barely able to see his face with the sun behind him.

"I've punched enough people while sparring to know how to help sore knuckles," he replied, nonchalant.

I quirked a brow at him and raised a hand to block out the light. "And yet you scolded me last night as if I hit a child and not Novian," I chided and shook my head.

Casimir chuckled and sat next to me. I watched as he crushed the little plants in his wake like he had in the courtyard.

"I'll admit, it took me off guard when you hit him. But I was mostly envious that I didn't do it myself," he said, glancing over at me. He looked unsure as tension after our conversation the night before still lingered.

My focus went anywhere but him. "Despite how good it felt to see the shock on his face, I didn't mean to lash out. But what he said—" I shook my head, hating that his words caused me to react in such a way.

"You don't ever talk about him. Ronin, I mean."

The name made me flinch.

After a long pause, I shrugged. "Not much to say."

"Elita…"

I tucked my hair behind my ear. Still cropped in odd places. Still clinging to the memory of him tearing through it.

"I don't enjoy talking about him. I don't *want* to talk about him. What is there to even say?" My tone bit, but Casimir didn't retreat.

"I mean, you were willing to turn Everbloom over to save him. I feel that's significant."

The topic took a turn, filling me with dismay. It felt easier to bury the guilt. And while I apologized to Taryn and Alba before leaving Orondal, I never made amends with anyone else.

It took me a moment to speak again; the guilt was heavy and hard to push past. "When I said that, I was being selfish. I hadn't thought about what that would mean for you or anyone else in Everbloom. But he was a friend, and I was desperate to save him." I paused and looked at my dirty hands. "It doesn't excuse how I acted. I panicked, and didn't try to think of another solution. And I'm sorry, Casimir. I never wanted to hurt any of you." Tears burned in the corner of my eyes.

When I met Casimir's gaze, the lingering hurt was written on his face. "It probably didn't make it any easier when you felt we betrayed your trust —that *I* betrayed your trust. If we could go back, I would've done things differently," he said.

I gave him a sad smile. "It does little good to linger on things we can't change. Saying that for myself, too. There are many things I would've done differently, like not leaving the Temple with Ronin…but I wouldn't have found any of you. Regardless of those things, I'm sorry I put Ronin above you all."

Casimir bristled and tore his gaze from me. "Did you love him?"

The question took me off guard, but the answer was simple, instant. "No."

Ronin had been my friend. Someone to share my grief with. But I never had romantic feelings for him, even when he took things further and kissed me.

A few minutes passed before Casimir shifted beside me, pulling my attention. "I don't need to tell you this, but you have every right to be angry, to feel resentful, after what Ronin did. I just don't want you to become shaped by the pain people cause you."

I opened my mouth, but shut it quickly. What I wanted to say was that burying the anger, forcing myself to turn a blind eye, caused a visceral ache. The discomfort burrowed in my chest, begging for retribution. But I feared what he would think of me, and I couldn't bear to let him see that part of me.

My focus moved back to the tiny plants Casimir flattened, some of their stems snapped. One of my hands hovered over it and a small smile curved my lips when they stood back up. While not on the same scale as moving roots and vines, it was something.

"What did you just do?" Casimir's question caught me off guard and I looked at him, confused.

"What do you mean?" My gaze fixed back on the plants.

"How did you mend them?" He seemed astounded, his wide gaze on the plants. Casimir ran a hand over them, before he crushed them once more, tearing a few.

"Hey!" I shooed his hand away and repeated the same motion to make them perk up, their damaged stems mending. The plants stood tall again, despite Casimir trying to snuff them out.

Casimir jolted up, his face a mixture of confusion and awe. I watched him, bewildered by his reaction.

"You mended the plants," he said in disbelief.

"Yes?" I stood.

Casimir ran a hand through his hair and stared at me. "We need to speak with General Valor and Lady Estelle."

Apprehension settled in my stomach like a rock. "Why? I thought those who tend the gardens could do the same."

A smirk tugged at his lips. "No, El. Other Roses can't mend like that." Pride swelled in his gaze, easing some of my reservation. "They can only accelerate the growth of existing plants. The vines and roots, they pull those from the ground. You mended that plant, gave it *life*, from nothing."

Casimir grinned wider and took a few steps closer. "We need to find the general." Despite the urgency, I heard the excitement in his voice. Seeing him full of such enthusiasm was a welcome change to the heaviness of the day before.

Casimir grabbed my discarded cloak from the ground, tossing it to me. "Let's go."

The crowded market swallowed us. It was the busiest hour of the day, and bodies pushed and shoved past us. A few shoulders brushed mine, with only whispered apologies as they moved in a hurry.

It proved difficult to follow Casimir through the masses while it continued to swell with more people. The crowd from the Everbloom camp left the cliffs, and overfilled the bustling courtyard.

When another person bumped into me, I almost lost my balance. Casimir glanced back at me as more people pushed past us, creating more distance between me and him.

Wordlessly, he reached back, and heat devoured my face when he softly took my hand in his. My heart rate quickened, becoming an erratic flutter in my ears. I stared at his back, pulled into a memory long forgotten. A quiet night many moons ago, the silence in the dreamspace heavier than normal after a difficult day with my mother. It was the first time he shaped the space into something else. And it was one of the last times he visited before his disappearance.

A walk through an imagined forest, his hand like smoke in mine. The touch, there and not, had done something to our connection, and turned his abrupt absence into agony. A tug to a ghost that left me alone and hollow.

I had never told him nor did I show it in front of my parents, but I had shed many silent tears following his disappearance. It had been easier to pretend it was relief rather than unexplained grief. Now, he held my hand, solid and warm as he led me through the swarm of people.

Trepidation built as we ascended the steps. Casimir's hand released mine when the crowd dissipated, and I stamped out the disappointment that followed.

The pearlescent white burned my eyes with the sun high overhead. Four guards stood watch, holding the wide doors open. They wore armor made of silver that shimmered in the sun. It made them look much less menacing. They gave a nod to Casimir. His captain privileges followed him even there.

The great hall was mostly empty, and we made our way across it in a hurry, turning left to go down a hall.

Casimir seemed sure of his whereabouts, and I stayed close on his heels until he came to a sudden stop. Casimir didn't knock or wait. He pushed open the door, striding in as if he'd been called upon. I hesitated, not as confident as my gaze fell on those in the room.

Valor, Estelle, Orin, and many others who wore armor and the Mistvalle guard insignia all sat at a long table. It was littered with papers, books, and maps. Compared to everyone in the room, I didn't belong.

From the look of it, they were still deep in preparation for the potential fight if Lendorr followed through.

The sleep clothes Casimir wore had no effect on how he fit in. He carried the air of a captain, his shoulders squared, his footsteps sure. It gave me the courage to walk in, following him, with my clothes covered in dirt from training all night.

Their conversation halted as we made our way in, and they watched with curiosity. I tried to avoid Valor's gaze. I hadn't spoken to him after he found me outside of my tent, and seeing him then, guilt crept in over what I said to him. Ever the serious general, Valor's face held no emotion. There was no sign my words meant anything to him. It wouldn't surprise me if he forgot I said anything at all.

Lady Estelle stood first, her armor replaced by another flowing gown. It was scarlet, and the fabric appeared lightweight. It swayed with her every move and brought out the bright scarlet in her eyes.

She offered a soft smile. "What a surprise this is, Elita, Captain Vanmore." She nodded to us both. "What brings you here at this hour?"

Casimir cast a glance at me, mirth brightening his grin. "May I request an audience with General Valor and Lady Estelle?" he asked, causing a few mutters and eyebrows to raise.

Valor's focus fell to me when he said, "Clear the room."

The order led to the scrape of chairs and half bows at the waist to him and Estelle as the others left, including Orin. When everyone cleared, Casimir strode across the room and stood before the two leaders. With timid footsteps, I followed, standing at his side.

"Well, Vanmore, out with it," Valor said impatiently.

Casimir gave a nod of recognition to Valor before he straightened his posture, his hands behind his back, taking on the appearance of a soldier.

"Elita activated her abilities." Casimir's tone laced with his enthusiasm.

Lady Estelle was unimpressed. "Yes, Captain, we were already aware," she deadpanned.

Casimir quickly went from excited to serious. "It isn't vines I speak of. She can mend snapped plants, my lady. She also conjured vines from ability alone, without communing with the earth." His explanation was to the point, and from their shocked expressions, it was clear that was out of the ordinary, as if there'd been a reason to doubt Casimir.

Valor stood beside Estelle, looking at me. "That isn't possible," he said, his disbelief plain.

I opened my mouth to speak, but Casimir beat me to it. "With all due respect, sir, I saw it with my own eyes. I split the plant in two, and without more than a wave of her hand, she mended it. I don't know how, but she did." He looked at me, still beaming.

Warmth bloomed beneath my ribs at the sight, and I turned my gaze back to Estelle and Valor.

Estelle clasped her hands together, her eyes lit with excitement. "We must see it."

Seventeen

Estelle wasted no time. Everyone moved in a hurried fashion, and within mere moments, they had me at the nearest form of plant life to observe how I mended. Casimir never left my side, and Valor became a looming presence over my shoulder. It didn't take them long to be enthralled, already whispering among themselves, hope sparking like a wildfire.

I tried not to let it add unbearable pressure. But the day ended with them explaining that I am to be at the training grounds first thing in the morning, and soon, I was pulled away from Casimir, dragged to see Halburn for observation, and ushered to my tent as though I were royalty.

It was strange, and I tried not to diminish their hope, despite how uneasy it made me. I found myself back in my tent, alone in the deep blue fabric, swallowed by the weight of the realm. It settled like an uncomfortable cloak on my shoulders, too large and overbearing for one person to take on. One would think I had grown used to it, but it left me with an ache behind my eyes, and a spirit too withered to even bother with making tea.

I worried that sleep wouldn't come easily with the pressure looming over me like a dark storm cloud. I considered returning to Casimir's tent, but it felt wrong to ask that of him. Especially with Estelle walking me to my tent, along with Valor, Orin, and two other generals, Isebel and Moria. I wouldn't dare imply I had any business near Casimir's space. Plus, I had imposed on his peace enough, and I would hate to disturb his sleep once more.

In the late hour, my boots thudded onto the stone floor, lazily discarded near the woven rug. Then I tossed my cloak, not concerned with where it landed. All I wanted was to shut my eyes and block out the familiar bitter weight of responsibility.

The pillow caressed my cheek, and within a matter of minutes, I was too exhausted to stay awake. After training all night and being observed throughout the day, it caught up to me, and I burrowed my face deeper into the pillow.

Panic clawed up the back of my skull when crimson slithered behind my shut eyelids. It pulsated, thrumming with tangible energy until it felt as though hands wrapped around my head, pulling me through a black abyss.

Fingertips brushed against the stems of withered flowers. It was slow, deliberate, and with the spark of power, pure white vines swirled over the woman's forearms, dotting them with small, delicate, white flowers. The vines beneath the skin pulsated with a red glow, and in turn, the flower burst to life, the petals unfurling as though it hadn't been dead moments before.

Her hand pulled away, the color disappearing until all that remained were white vines carved into her skin. The woman straightened, billowing black fabric whipping around her body. The edges of the flowing gown moved over the tall flower field as though it were water, gliding with elegant grace.

Every flower that had withered, the woman's hand found it, giving it life once more. The field was an array of stunning hues, rising and falling with the hills as far as the eye could see. The woman moved like a swan over the surface of a lake before she halted at the only space without flowers. A large white stone surface made a circle in the field of flowers, and when she hovered over it like a wisp of fog, symbols thrummed in response, like garnets catching the sunlight.

A sense of pride rippled off the woman, and the flowers shuddered in response. Her hand reached down, the threads of black fabric dusting the stone, and she put a palm flat to the surface. A blissful sigh filled the air, and in response, the vines on the woman's arms began to creep with black energy, painting her fingers like charcoal. The sigh became a hiss of pain —only a hint—before it melted into a gentle thrum of power.

"How reckless. Was it not I who warned you against such a placement?" The voice was gentle, full of warmth that made the woman's shoulders fall with relief.

"Have you not learned? I never do listen," she replied, her voice like a soft melody.

When she lifted her gaze, a man stood before her, his white cloak thin, resting on his shoulders with an ethereal weightlessness. Brilliant golden hair curled at his ears, some slipping to brush his cheek when he knelt, his head bowing.

"Only you would be brave enough to come into my domain." Her voice spoke with a tenderness that made the flowers gently sway.

The man lifted his gaze, the black and gold shimmering with reverence. "I only brave such a thing as you allow me." He stood and moved to her, his hand outstretched, dipping into the thin black veil that covered her head.

He held her cheek in his palm, and as she leaned against him, tendrils of black curls slipped beneath the veil.

The sunlight shimmered in his warm golden irises as he memorized every inch of the goddess before him. "What an honor it is to be in your presence," he whispered.

Her chuckle trilled like a melody, and behind the man, the flowers opened, basking in the sun as her mirth echoed in the field. When he inched closer onto the stone with her, the symbols were drained of their color, and the vines on the woman's arms began to turn golden. He knelt, taking both sides of her face into his hands. His forehead pressed to hers, and onyx and ruby eyes opened to meet his gaze.

The touch echoed in my entire being. Warmth lit my veins until the light devoured everything.

"Elita!" Alba's chipper voice pulled me out of the depths, and I gasped as though I'd been drowning, the blankets damp against my skin.

I sat upright and rubbed furiously at my eyes. They ached after I tossed and turned all night. The vision didn't echo with death and decay, but it left me restless, nonetheless.

Alba stood inside the drapes, her hands on her hips. "You sleep like a log, woman," she said, shaking her head. I rolled my eyes and tossed my pillow at her. "Estelle is moments from stalking up here to pull your butt out of bed. Let's get a move on!"

"Please, Alba, morning voice," I mumbled, sliding out from the sweat-covered blankets. I was grateful my sleep clothes were black, otherwise Alba would have mocked the embarrassing display.

When I stood from the bed, my hands trembled, a strange thrum echoing through my veins. I tried to quell it, avoiding Alba's exasperated expression as I went over to my chest of clothing, which overflowed. A sliver of guilt crept in over the amount of clothes I gathered from the shops, but the people were so kind, and whoever it was that took care of the cost, I wished I could thank them. I wasn't certain it was Estelle, but it wouldn't hurt to ask.

Sensing Alba's impatience, I pulled out black trousers, form-fitting but stretchy, perfect for training. Then I brought out a soft emerald tunic and a black vest to go with it. It would be light and comfortable for whatever Estelle and Valor intended to have me do.

I whirled around and gave Alba an expectant look. "Privacy, please?"

"Oh! I'll leave you to it. But don't take long. I think I see Casimir heading this way." She wiggled her brows, and I huffed, pulling the drapes closed in her face. The canvas fabric couldn't drown out her amused giggles.

Hastily, I swapped my sleep clothes, pulling on the trousers first, then the tunic. I slid the vest on, bothered by the ties that ran up the back of it. To my dismay, I'd need Alba's help. Before leaving the tent, I pulled on gray leather boots. I left my cloak behind, ran my hands through my mess of curls, then opened the drapes.

Casimir and Galan were both near Alba, muttering between themselves. It was Casimir who spotted me first, his gaze finding mine the moment the drapes relaxed behind me. In turn, Alba and Galan faced me. When they all gave me a strange look, I nearly burst into flames from the embarrassment.

"I can't exactly contort my arms enough to tie the vest. Stop staring," I muttered, ignoring the smirk that tugged at Casimir's cheek. "Alba?" I glanced at her, gesturing to the ties.

She smiled, coming over to me in a rush to tie the back of the vest. "You know, I was eyeing this vest days ago," she mused. "Taking advantage of Valor's silly attempts at being a father, are we?"

The words stiffened my spine. She didn't speak in a cruel way, merely in a typical offhanded sense. It wasn't out of the ordinary for Alba, but the fact that it had been Valor that took on the cost...

Oh gods, I had overdone it more than once. Not to mention the thread for embroidery that I didn't have to spare any expense for. If I could force myself to speak with him, I'd have to offer him my thanks.

Casimir chuckled and stepped closer. "The look on your face would imply you didn't know," he said, eyeing the vest. "Although I would argue that he owes you after the years of absence."

I grimaced. "Could we not delve into all of this right now? As if I'm not nervous enough."

It was Galan who nodded in agreement, his hands clasped behind his back. "Her parentage seems inappropriate for light conversation, does it not?"

I could practically hear Alba roll her eyes as she pulled the vest tight.

"Oh, come on. None of us got to say a word about it back in Everbloom, it's an interesting dynamic, is all."

My stomach dropped, and I glanced at my boots, unwilling to meet Galan or Casimir's gaze. Time still hadn't erased that betrayal, and it stung to have her speak of it so flippantly. Things could have been different had Casimir told me long ago who my father was. Even when I first got to Everbloom. That well-kept secret had been a precursor to all the pain that transpired, and it was difficult to push past that.

Alba finished the ties, and noting the silence, she began to scramble. "Oh goddess…I wasn't thinking. I'm clearly an idiot. Ignore me." She patted my arm, apologetic.

I ignored the weight of Casimir's stare and started down the path. "Well, better get to the training grounds before anyone comes to drag me down there." I kept my tone even and desperately tried to forget that the ones I considered my friends had been so quick to betray my trust.

It acted as another reminder to guard my heart, and I trudged down the path, silent as they talked about mundane things. Casimir never joined the conversation, but Alba spoke of her days helping a seamstress in the markets, and Galan rambled on about his time baking. It kept my mind full enough, and I chose to ignore the layer of pain too thick to peel away.

When we reached the training grounds, it was, to my horror, full. Members of the guard lazed about the grounds, some sitting on the stone, their faces turned toward the sun. Others chatted in tight circles, eagerness thrumming through them all.

I froze at the entrance as Alba and Galan walked beneath the large stone archway, still deep in conversation. It was Casimir who stopped at my side, peering over at me.

"I apologize for what Alba said." His voice was low, the words not carrying past the arch.

Tension pulled at my shoulders as the bitterness rose back to the surface. I tried to quell it. "There are days I let myself forget. But it's never far from my mind, and I know it falls on Valor. But all those years…" I trailed off, unwilling to get into such a heavy topic right before I was meant to train in front of so many people.

Casimir bristled at the meaning in my words. He was the only one I knew before Everbloom.

"I should have told you the truth." His body turned toward mine, not shying from the heavy conversation. We faced each other, the rumble of voices fading somewhat. I couldn't bring myself to meet his intensity. "But I promise," he reached forward, gently brushing a knuckle beneath my chin to get me to meet his gaze, "I won't ever keep anything from you again." The gesture was small, yet the comfortable touch—the one built on years of knowing—caused a rapid flutter beneath my ribs.

I smiled, reminded of the days in our adolescence when things were much less serious. "No more secrets?" I whispered, searching his eyes.

His features softened, a grin tugging at his cheek. "No secrets."

"Blackthorne!"

I spun on my heel to face the training grounds, and to my horror, everyone was looking at us. I pursed my lips and hurried to the center of the field. I didn't look to see if Casimir followed; I heard the soft chuckle of amusement behind me.

When I stopped near the group of leaders, Estelle grabbed my arm, and brought me further from Casimir and the others. "I apologize, we're short on time. Though I assure you, today will be simple. We are testing your abilities in an attempt to see what skills you possess. Are you ready?" she asked, an eager smile on her lips.

I gave her a nod, though the idea of trying to activate any abilities made me uneasy. To the side, I watched Casimir join Galan and Alba. Further off, Sol stood near two Mistvalle soldiers.

"We start with strength," Estelle chimed, gesturing to my left. I stared at the misplaced boulder, my brow furrowed. "The Roses who are present will test your tolerance and even possible immunity to their abilities. Then, you will attempt to replicate it. We'll start with something easy. Strength is simply demonstrated."

"I don't think—"

"You will try, Blackthorne." Valor came to my side, expression stoic. I bit back the conflicting emotions around him and nodded.

The Roses that gathered all settled into a hushed state. I hated the way they stared at me, but I tuned it out.

I approached the boulder, unsure how to begin. It was Galan who joined the circle and offered me a kind grin.

Good, this is something I'm used to.

He rolled his sleeves, reached to the bottom of the boulder, then lifted it as though it were a feather. "Strength typically activates when you allow yourself to relax. Try to center yourself, then attempt to lift it," Galan instructed, setting the large rock down.

Nerves erupted in my stomach, and I took a slow breath. It slithered up my nose, the air crisp. I allowed the sensation of the sun beaming in midday to give me a swell of energy. The warmth prickled at my skin, and after a moment to center myself, I bent at the knee, careful not to strain my back.

It took me a split second to know I didn't possess increased strength. The boulder didn't budge, and when I attempted to lift it again, it pulled at the muscles in my back until they sparked with pain.

Galan offered a reassuring look, but it couldn't cloud the wave of disappointment in the people who watched.

Valor pushed the boulder to the side, his face unreadable. "Next."

Sweat glistened across my forehead as I faced another Rose, their abilities new to me. The woman, Moria, held my face in her hands, as a painful prickling coursed through my skin. A harsh breath pulled through my teeth until the prickling turned into numbness. My legs gave out quickly, and I crumpled.

A familiar Rose from Everbloom, Lyleen, caught my arm and held me up. She was told to remain close to counter Moria's ability to numb the body. Moria's powers were an anesthetic, related to the Passiflora incarnata plant family. It rippled through me, and after I already encountered the typical abilities, I dreaded what would follow hers.

When Lyleen safely lowered me to a sitting position, she pressed a hand to the back of my neck. Lyleen's powers acted as a cleanse for the body, so Valor recommended she stay close. Sensation returned to my legs and buzzed inside my arms as energy left Lyleen's palm and poured into my skin.

I glanced over my shoulder to give her a look of thanks, though my entire body still felt as though it were made of water.

"General, I think that's enough for the day." It was Casimir's voice somewhere close behind us. I heard the catch in his tone, concern bubbled beneath the surface.

"There are only three more. She'll be fine." Valor didn't share Casimir's concern, which shouldn't have surprised me. However, it solidified my reluctance to ever thank him for the coin he spared on my expenses. In fact, I intended to take advantage of it as a form of silent revenge.

The next Rose moved through me quickly. They had the ability to temporarily rob me of sight, which escalated to a level of panic that made Estelle shout, and both she and Halburn aided in a quick healing.

After each encounter, they explained their ability, how they activated it, and attempted to get me to repeat it. A low murmur of disappointment rippled through everyone when I failed to show any other unique abilities.

Then the second Rose, Elrin, approached with an emotionless expression. Though she had been kind to me on the ship, I didn't forget her snarl back in Everbloom. I worried she'd take out whatever pent-up anger she had on me.

When her hand pressed to my forehead, I tensed, ready to add another strange layer of pain to my long list. But there was no sting, no loss of sight. It was almost euphoric, and a giddy sensation rippled through me. A wave of warmth.

I heard a few people in the crowd chuckle.

"This ability takes focus," Elrin said, removing her hand. "It's like pouring…peace into another. An act of kindness—"

"That's one way to put it," someone muttered from the side, and more people erupted with laughter.

I blinked away the sensation, staring at her. "What is it?"

Elrin opened her mouth and closed it just as quickly.

It was Alba who shuffled closer, a hand over my ear. "Myristica fragrans. It acts as an aphrodisiac."

My face burned, and I shrugged Alba off. "I don't have that ability."

Elrin's brow furrowed. "But you haven't even—"

"I want to move on." I tried to ignore the embarrassment, and worse yet, the morbid curiosity about whether she had ever used such a thing with Casimir. I shook the thought from my head and looked anywhere but the two of them, lest they pick up on what crossed my mind.

Next was Orin, to my distaste. He approached, a smirk on his lips. He stopped before me. "I doubt you have this ability. However, this should be entertaining," he mused as he reached out to me.

"Orin." Casimir took a step closer, his voice a warning. "This isn't a test for your amusement. There is no reason to believe Elita would have an ability only known among Thornrose."

"Vanmore, we said *all* abilities. We won't allow it to go too far." Valor's insistence made me irate.

I cast a glance at Casimir, noting his clenched jaw, the curl of his fists. It did little to ease the tension in my limbs. My posture turned rigid when Orin closed the space, his hand resting on my forehead. I despised the contact and went to jerk back, but before I could, his eyes turned black, echoing a void that made my breath catch.

Orin grinned, the sight unsettling. Flames flickered to life behind him, sudden and rippling with unbearable heat. I gasped and tried to get away, but vines wrapped around my ankles, holding me in place. My chest rose and fell rapidly as the flames grew closer.

The smoke choked me, and in a harsh shift, I was pulled out of Mistvalle, forced back into the heat of the cottage. The embers fell, trapping me. There was no way out. Tears coated my cheeks, and I muttered a soft plea, the sound never finding my ears.

"*No, please.*" My voice was muffled, and I tried to rip myself out of the flames. Fire burned inside my palms, harsh and sharp. A shocked sob tore through me, and the flames vanished as the weight of Orin's hand left my skin.

Someone shouted my name, but I could do nothing but sputter for air, staring at my outstretched hands. Thorns covered the ground, and a few feet away, Orin glared, a cut across his cheek.

"Elita?" Casimir grabbed my shoulders, staring at me with worry as I dropped my arms.

My mouth opened and closed again in an instant. I took a shaky breath. "I—" The sensation of tears on my cheeks took me off guard, and I wiped at them, avoiding the attention of the crowd.

Casimir's expression hardened, and he gently released me, turning on Orin. "What did you make her see?" he snapped, getting in Orin's face.

Orin scoffed. "I hardly got into anything disturbing. Quite unfortunate, really. I only showed her a bit of fire is all."

Galan and Alba came to my side. Alba's hand rested on my shoulder, and the other ran up and down my arm, a small gesture of comfort.

Casimir shoved Orin, seething with rage. "What the fuck is your problem?"

Orin sneered and pushed back. "Would you prefer I have her hallucinate the prince?" he spat.

My entire body coiled, and in the next second, Casimir shoved Orin once more, causing him to lose his balance. Chaos erupted as more Roses stood as if to intervene.

"Enough!" Valor shouted, stopping Orin as he went to lunge at Casimir. "Lieutenant, you will do well to remember who Blackthorne is. You could have had her hallucinate without causing her distress."

Hallucinogenic abilities. Back in Everbloom, Alba had mentioned what Orin could do. Never would I have imagined he'd be such an abhorrent ass with its use.

Casimir glared at Orin for only a moment more before he crossed the field and stopped in front of me. He looked me over, noting the tears that slowly dried on my cheeks. "Are you okay?" he asked, reaching for my hand.

I nodded as he studied my palm. It still thrummed with energy, and on the ground beneath his feet, tiny, lethal thorns were scattered across the stone.

Estelle grabbed my other hand, placing her palm to mine. "Another act of conjuring. Much like Aeterna," she said under her breath. "You nearly killed the man." I heard the amusement in Estelle's voice, and though Orin deserved to have his teeth knocked in, I couldn't erase the sight of the flames—the reminder of the unbearable heat as my mother died in my arms.

In the Temple, under the influence of Talos's torture, I had hallucinated much the same. Flames and screaming, a return to memories too painful for me to bear.

I pulled my hands from them both and swallowed the thick emotions. "Can I be done?"

Casimir nodded, not waiting for Estelle to approve.

Far off, Valor continued to scold Orin, a finger in the smug man's face. The small scrape across his cheek wasn't payback enough for what he'd done.

The crowd either spoke in excited whispers or stopped to watch Valor shout at Orin. Casimir's hand found my shoulder blade, and he prodded me to the exit, followed by Galan, Alba, and Sol.

Casimir led me out of the training grounds. We paused outside the archway, and he pulled me further from the companions who followed us. He searched my face with a somber knowing. "Did it remind you of the cottage?" he asked, voice low so the others wouldn't hear.

"Yes." I cleared my throat in an attempt to hide how shaken up I was.

"I'm sorry. I shouldn't have let him touch you."

"It's not your fault. It's okay." I offered him a small smile. "Now, this —" I flipped my palms and studied them. "Lethal touch?" I mused. Though the moment felt inappropriate for lightheartedness, I wasn't willing to delve any further into more pain.

Sol slowly approached and paused nearby, staring at my hands. "Too bad he moves quickly. Would've been amusing to watch him be impaled."

That got a grin out of me. "Pity. I'll have to move quicker next time."

Casimir released a sigh. "He deserves it. I can't believe he'd stoop so low." He shook his head, still focused on my hands.

Seeing it as a perfect moment to chime in, Alba said, "Oh, I can. He's a prick. I hope Valor continues to emasculate him in front of everyone." She chuckled with a glance back at the training grounds.

Ever the calm presence, Galan joined us. "Perhaps a meal might do Elita well?" he suggested.

Alba gasped. "We didn't even let her eat before that whole mess. Oh! Galan, those pastries you made, tell me there's more?"

He nodded, offering a smile he reserved for her. "There is plenty left. Shall we grab some things and eat in the garden?"

I perked up. "That sounds perfect. If there's enough, I'll take three."

Casimir tilted his head, restrained amusement on his face. "You've spent a lot of energy. You could use a full meal alongside the pastries."

Alba waved her hand at him. "Let the woman indulge. Are you worried you won't get any?"

He shrugged. "I don't eat that type of food. Plus, I've been training since I was ten. For any soldier, eating enough after so much exertion is important."

"Ugh, we know you're a buff captain who trains all the time. You're telling me you *never* indulge?"

Galan watched the two. "Sir Vanmore cannot indulge foods of that kind. At least, not without great pain. I've been attempting to find a recipe that doesn't have that effect."

"Are you implying he can't have pastries? Any baked goods? How have I not noticed?" she asked, bewildered.

Casimir sighed. "Why does it matter?"

The conversation turned into a cacophony of voices—Casimir explaining that his health wasn't a conversation topic, and Alba prodding while Galan apologized. Their bickering was comfortable, and I enjoyed watching them sink into the flow that came with years of friendship.

Sol stopped at my side. "They talk a lot," she mused.

I chuckled, looking over at her. "What, you don't wish to join?"

Her gloved hands clasped at her lower back. "In conversation? No. To eat? I suppose. If only to be sure they don't subject you to more psychological harm."

"Is that a hint of concern I hear?" I prodded, leaning closer until my shoulder bumped hers. When I met her pale, almost peach-colored gaze, her eyes had gone wide.

Her attention flickered over my face for a moment, before she cleared her throat. "Won't find me carrying your slack when they've run you ragged," she huffed.

"I wouldn't dream of it." A smile pulled at my lips and she bristled, quickly glancing away.

We settled into silence and followed the three as they bickered. I chose to ignore the pit in my stomach left over from the reminder of their secrecy. I didn't want to let it weigh on me anymore.

Eighteen

en days passed since I had become the entertainment of
Mistvalle. The guard, Lady Estelle, and even Valor and Orin, all
watched me train. From sunup to sundown. The ache in my limbs would
drive me mad and exhaustion would devour me before long.

"Again, Elita," Valor ordered from across the center of the training
grounds. His cloak was discarded and he traded out his usual armor for
something lighter. Estelle wore similar clothes for training, a light layer of
leather armor. She watched us both from the sidelines.

I grunted in frustration, and tried once more, the sensation of the vines
strange as I called for them. Not the ones connected to plants beneath the
earth, but rather, my own. It didn't feel right as I shifted from trying to
feel the life in the earth, and focused on my pulse; the way the air moved
through my lungs.

The movement and thrum of the earth grew familiar to me. We worked
as one until I sensed every pulse that echoed around me. I pinpointed
them, following the heartbeat of the guards. It was a thrum I had been
unknowingly sensing since Eldravine—since hunting with my father.

When I focused, I noticed every shift, the unique weight of everyone's
footsteps. It threatened to overwhelm me, and I tried to tune them out.

Estelle had grown too eager for me to hone my abilities after, and I
tried to ignore their whispers when I mended plants. Every fiber of my
being wanted to do something for the realm. To make up for the detriment

I caused, to ease the guilt. Her excitement at how I could mend and conjure plants with ability alone made me too hopeful. Something I wasn't used to.

It was over a week of being followed, watched, and isolated. I ate my meals in Estelle's dining hall among the higher-ups in the guard. They monitored what I ate, rushed me to a healing in the morning and before bed, their attention constant. They tore me from the gardens any time I tried to return, and I missed Sol's quiet company.

I resented every second of their desperation.

It reminded me of how badly Talos wanted me to be examined and watched. Controlling every moment of my day when they had me in the Temple. I knew it wasn't the same. I had more freedom than I did in the Temple. They assured me I could come and go as I pleased. But with either of the leaders always waiting outside my tent in the morning, it was impossible to turn them down.

Valor cleared his throat to draw my attention.

I sighed, no longer wanting to train. My feet dug into the dirt anyway, and I solidified my stance. Every muscle in my arms twitched and ached.

With trembling hands and a smooth inhale, I began the process again, sensing the vines. They were within my grasp. I only needed to try a little harder. Vines. Simple, easy, and something I had done before. Yet they evaded me. I groaned and my stiff arms fell.

"You gave up too easily. Try again," Valor said, disappointed.

I glared at him, and in another bout of anger, the now familiar thorns pelted the dirt and my palms burned as the power surged through them. It was the only other ability I was able to tap into, triggered by anger.

Valor's stern expression intensified. "Control, Blackthorne. Otherwise, you will hurt someone by allowing your anger to fuel your abilities."

"I don't want to do this anymore today. I'm exhausted," I said. Sweat made a trail down my neck and into my tunic. It burned the small cuts leftover from hours spent training.

Between trying to conjure vines, their relentless questions, and having to mend plants repeatedly, I got little sleep. Nightmares and visions continued to plague me, despite the exhaustion. Soon, I'd keel over if they didn't allow me a break. But if anything, the visions made me more desperate. I couldn't protect anyone if I didn't hone my strengths.

Valor crossed his arms over his chest, expectant.

I yielded and moved back into place.

Regardless of his advice, I leaned into the anger as power sparked in my palms once more. My body ached, the tension building with every second. The energy became trapped in my veins, and a whimper of discomfort broke the silence, along with my focus.

When I saw Orin snicker on the sidelines, animosity rolled through me. My palm raised and a slew of thorns flew his way, narrowly missing him as he jumped to the side, a scowl on his face.

"Elita!" Valor snapped. His boots fell hard against the stones as he stalked over to me.

I turned to face him, defiance in my stance. "I'm done for today."

Valor pointed a finger at me, fuming. "That stubbornness won't get you anywhere. Look where it got your mother."

The words made me recoil. My brow creased, and I stared, bewildered as grief bloomed inside my chest.

Try as he might, he couldn't maintain his facade of indifference. It was the first time he looked at me as if I were his daughter, and not someone who had brought him more trouble than I was worth. The change took me off guard.

"Training is over for the day," Valor dismissed, addressing the people who stood to observe. They didn't dare grumble or disagree, even though Valor wasn't the leader of Mistvalle.

Even Lady Estelle left at Valor's dismissal. His words were loud enough to reach them all, and despite how much it didn't feel like it, he was my father, and his words didn't need to be heard by others.

I watched them depart, and the fatigue set in.

Although we were the only two that remained, I didn't face Valor yet. If I wasn't careful, I'd send a throng of thorns at him, simply because he pissed me off.

"You look like her," Valor said abruptly, thoughtful. Though I tried to resist, I eventually gave in and looked in his direction to find him at my side. "The similarities are there, I think. I see them most when you're angry. Riona shared the same expression."

I bit the inside of my cheek. His fondness of her echoed in how he spoke. To think he once knew her remained difficult for me to grasp. I imagined the woman that he knew differed greatly from the one who raised me with a cold air of indifference.

My feet shuffled, the conversation bringing me discomfort. "I grew up thinking I looked nothing like my parents," I replied. "Until I met you. Of course, outside of the Rose features. I think I inherited your nose, your eye shape and the same hue of red, too." It felt wrong to talk to him in such a casual way. A week spent under his watchful eye and his guidance while training, it chipped away at the indifference I clung to.

Memories of my mother gazing at me as she died, muttering that I looked like my father, it carried a different weight.

"It is strange, the resemblance." Valor hesitated. "Even still, you carry a lot of her mannerisms. Especially her short temper."

At that, I cracked a smile. "So she was always angry, then? It wasn't solely because of me?"

Valor appeared shocked. "I apologize. I didn't know what your relationship with her was like. It never occurred to me." He cleared his throat, uncomfortable at the turn in conversation.

I shrugged, the shroud of her indifference invisible on my shoulders. I had grown used to her treatment. It wasn't something that hurt me anymore. Her absence was worse. "She was scared, I think. Or, that's what my father always told me. Sorry—Aedric."

"Address him however you see fit. He was your father. He raised you as I chose to remain absent. I take no offense." The nonchalant way he said it made me flinch.

"*Chose* to remain absent?"

He pursed his lips, confused at my tone. I tried not to be affected by it, but it was clear in the crack of my voice that it stung.

"There was a lot of resentment. When I returned to find that Riona not only kept my child a secret from me, but also filled my place, I was bitter. Though I suspect she assumed me dead, she never went to the Forge to confirm it. I chose not to return out of my own selfish feelings. It doesn't excuse it, but I was a young man. Two years younger than you are now, actually."

I stared at him with uncertainty. Part of me sympathized, but it didn't ease the hurt that remained after years of absence. He cleared his throat and averted his gaze for a moment before meeting mine again—his anxious ticks not too different from mine.

"I did not have Captain Vanmore dreamwalk to keep track of your mother. I had him visit to keep an eye on you. To keep you safe in what ways I could, without interfering with your mother's life. If I had wanted to know what Riona was doing, I would have had him dreamwalk among her sleep."

I cackled outright. The sound was strange and nervous. He watched me, and a hint of a smile grew on his face.

"I can't imagine. If her dreams had been the ones haunted, I don't think she would have survived it," I said as my laughter settled.

"I wouldn't dare put Vanmore through that. Your mother could give quite the scolding." The fondness was always there as he spoke of her. It brought me a sense of peace.

We fell into a lull. The quiet was uncomfortable as we both struggled with knowing how to interact. He was my father, but he seemed more akin to a stranger to me than a parent, and it was the first time I had a pleasant conversation with him. The conflicting feelings warred in my mind. He had chosen to stay out of my life, yet he wanted to make sure I was safe. It made it harder to navigate my feelings.

After a long pause, Valor cleared his throat again, shifting on his feet. "I'll leave you to rest, then," he said with a slight bow of his head.

My nails bit into my palms when I tightened my fists. The words blurted out before I could stop them. "Did you ever think about coming back for us?" I asked, hating that I wanted to know.

Valor's face twisted with a sad smile. "Many times, yes," he admitted, despite seeming as if he didn't want to. Somehow, it brought me no relief. If anything, it made my grief all the worse.

I didn't want a different life. I wanted the memories I shared with the father who raised me; outside in a small garden, laughing and planting together. If Valor had returned for us, I knew it would have meant excluding my father. He was a norm, and he was someone Valor likely resented.

I went to leave, mulling over what he said, when he stopped me. "I've always wondered, what is your full name?"

The question took me by surprise. It was silly. Such a minor detail, and still, my real father didn't know. I wondered for a moment about the things Casimir never shared, as well as the things Valor chose not to know to keep his distance.

I offered him a small smile. "Elita Fullan."

"Fullan?" he paused, appearing thoughtful. "Fullan means blooming," he said.

The smile stretched into a grin at the reminder. "My father's idea."

He nodded and fell back into his usual stoic demeanor. "Get some rest. There is still more to be done with your training. But you've earned a break," he said, dismissing the conversation. I waved and took off in the opposite direction of him.

Regardless of how much I had tried to hurt him with my words, Valor didn't hold it against me. And no matter how much I didn't want to allow myself to warm up to him, the way he spoke of my mother, the way he had cared like a father would, it made it hard not to.

Nineteen

After I finished at the bathhouse and returned to my tent, I tossed and turned. Dreams of my mother dying in my arms followed me as I tried to drift to sleep. Blood trickled from her mouth, her tunic colored the same horrific shade.

As if my grief had earned me some reprieve, for once, the crimson-eyed figure didn't linger when I woke. I felt its gaze. The overbearing pressure of its presence. But it didn't show itself. I stumbled out of bed easily, without the typical restriction in my limbs, and despite my better judgment, I made my way to Casimir's tent.

The moon hid behind thick clouds as cold air blew through camp, and tiny drops of rain fell. The light sprinkle brought an icy sensation to my cheeks, and I shivered, maneuvering the woods to keep out of sight, lest I get accused of anything by Novian or Alba.

Wings fluttered behind me, the two birds never too far. They protested when the rain picked up, surging with the emotions trapped in my chest until they both drenched me.

I had visited Casimir's tent twice, and finding it was easy. The drapes were tied, and there was no sign of him awake inside, no flicker from the glow of a candle, and no sound of him stirring. I bit my lip, unsure, and second guessing if I should return to my tent. Before I turned to leave, the sight of his hands untying the drapes caught my attention.

The drapes opened, revealing a half asleep Casimir. "Can't sleep?" he asked, voice low and raspy from waking.

"I just—" The words were trapped in my throat. I stared at him, my eyes burning with unshed tears while rain cascaded down my cheeks in place of them. The sight gave him pause, a crease in his brow forming.

Memories of my mother caused me more pain than I expected them to. I had spent my entire life telling myself I was used to her callousness. But the reality that there would never be a chance to repair our relationship— that she died still too afraid to love me—was unbearable.

Tears met with the rain streaming down my cheeks and left a trail of sorrow in their wake. Casimir tensed and pulled me into his tent to get me out of the rain as it picked up, surging sideways through the forest.

My cloak was heavy over my shoulders, soaked through.

"What's wrong?" he asked, searching my face.

A sob choked out, and my hand raised, fingertips pressing to my lips to prevent another strangled cry. "I miss my mother." It was foolish after all she'd done. The way she turned her back on me when what I needed was her comfort, her time. Grief never promised to be rational.

Casimir's expression fell. His own loss and absence of his mother echoed back at me in a matter of seconds. Without a word, he pulled me to him. His arms swallowed me in their warmth, comforting and gentle. He held me close despite the rain that drenched me. My cheek rested on his chest, the sound of his heartbeat grounding me.

The rain pattered softly on the canvas fabric, quiet enough for muted cries to fill the tent. Casimir's warm palm pressed to the back of my neck, holding me closer. There was a slight tremble to his hand, as if he were unsure of the touch, before a thumb brushed over my damp hair. My eyes shut, and I allowed the comfort to ease the sting of grief. He held me in a way that displayed his understanding of such pain. It was the kind you couldn't heal from. A hole left in your chest in their absence. I used to wonder what it would be like for my parents after I died. Never did I think I would be the one left to learn how to put the shattered pieces of myself back together.

Casimir hesitated as he released me, a hand lingering on my back while he brought me further into the tent. When he gestured to the bed, I sat. He took the spot next to me, and settled onto the cushion with a comforting weight. It reminded me of his visits among my dreams.

"Don't run from that pain. Allow yourself to miss them," he said, voice gentle. "The hardest part about losing them is allowing that pain to have a place in your life. It helps to accept it, despite how impossible it feels."

I swiped at the tears. "The memory of them makes it hard to find balance." My voice broke, and I cleared my throat. "I can't control my abilities, and the grief makes it more difficult."

When Casimir glanced at his hands, I followed his gaze. They curled into fists on his thighs.

My attention flicked back to his face. "How did you do it? After your mother died?" I asked. Uncertainty crept in when I considered the pain my question might cause him.

He scoffed, his fists unfurling. "We're very different people. I doubt my methods were ideal."

I bit my lip and fought the urge to reach for his hand. "Cas?"

He sighed. "It took me years to let it go." Pausing, he straightened and met my gaze. "Those years I was absent in your dreams, I shut down. Hated everything, everyone." Casimir shook his head. "The resentment blinded me for a long time. And the ways I coped... I was drunk the first two years and made many mistakes. Training on the guard helped some. It took until I was promoted to captain for me to realize my recklessness put my squad in danger before I made a change."

Wind whistled on the canvas fabric, and rain pelted against it in a gentle thrum, the intensity of it waning. Hesitation couldn't stop me from inching closer to Casimir. His gaze followed my hand until it rested on his forearm.

We sat in silence. His expression faltered as grief clouded his eyes, creeping in like a storm. I watched him force the memories away and wished there was a way to offer him solace. It took me a while to realize there never would be any. Losing a parent was too heavy. It wasn't meant to be light.

Casimir broke the quiet. "Don't make the same mistake I did and let it fester for years. The grief will demand your attention, eventually. If you wait too long, it'll take precedence over everything else." His tone was soft, and I bristled.

Pulling back, I ran my fingers over the stitching on his quilt.

Casimir watched me fidget before he interrupted my focus. "If you want to control your abilities, you need to prevent the memories from overwhelming you," he said, as if it were simple.

"That's very helpful, Captain. Thanks." My tone was light, despite the topic of conversation.

A grin lifted the corners of his lips and my stomach flipped. He shrugged. "Let me teach you."

I considered his offer, my heart in my throat. There was mischief in his eyes and an eagerness I couldn't ignore. I took a deep breath, putting the grief aside. "Okay, teach me."

Twenty

We stood among the training grounds, the darkness as heavy as the rain that drenched my cloak, down to my tunic. When I asked Casimir to teach me, I hadn't expected him to drag me down to the field right away. I regretted agreeing.

Casimir chuckled as I glowered at him. Rain dripped off the edge of my cloak's hood. Some drops ran down my cheeks, and I shivered.

"Come on, it isn't that bad," he said, the water weighing down his hair until it fell into his line of sight.

I crossed my arms. He chuckled again, walking closer to me. "You need to focus on *not* thinking. If you allow yourself to get in your head about it, you'll get more upset," he offered, standing at my right shoulder. I fought the urge to roll my eyes.

Before I tried to summon vines, I unclasped my cloak, discarding my hood along with the heavy weight of the soaked cloth. It fell to the stones with an audible *plop*.

Ignoring the chill and dampness that made my body shudder, I inhaled and extended my arms. The thrum of the earth was second nature to me; once aware of it, it was impossible to ignore. I tried to tune in and closed my eyes to trace the earth's pulse.

My thoughts zeroed in on the movement in the ground and I blocked out everything else. The force of it surged through me, and I attempted to harness its energy within myself.

Nothing happened, and the frustration from the morning barreled through me.

I groaned and dropped my arms. "This is pointless, Cas. I've already —" I stopped short when his hands went to my shoulders, gently pressing down on them as he moved closer.

"Relax your body. Try not to tense so much," he said, his breath warm on my neck.

That didn't help.

I shivered and told myself it was because of the cold.

Relaxing my shoulders, I raised my hands and shut my eyes.

"Don't do that," Casimir chided. I looked over my shoulder at him, flustered with his proximity. "You don't need to commune with the earth. Allow your abilities to take the lead. Have you noticed any specific triggers that could help?" he asked, almost inaudible over the roar of rain.

I shrugged. "Anger, usually."

"Then you'll never be in control. You'll be at the mercy of your anger. Find another outlet." He gestured back to the empty field.

An exasperated breath escaped me, but I resumed my position.

Casimir let go of my shoulders, leaving them cold without the warmth of his hands. "Try to think of something that brings you peace." He stepped back to give me more space.

I nodded and allowed my body to relax as I inhaled through my nose and slowly exhaled from my lips. Rain cascaded down my face and left a chill on my skin. The sensation pulled me out of my thoughts and I leaned into the trickle of power that sparked inside me.

Across the field stood a wooden dummy, which appeared battered after years of service to the people of Mistvalle. It looked as if it would break with a single hit.

I shut out the thoughts that tried to spiral; the fear that I would fall short. That once more, I wouldn't be good enough. It all went quiet and turned into a soft thrum of rain, a crack of thunder, and the thud of my heart. I envisioned something that brought me peace. Or, rather, someone. I pictured my father, his face beaming with a smile that stretched from ear to ear and lit up his crinkled eyes. He would have been proud of how far I carried myself, despite everything that happened. My heart swelled with love and grief.

The sensation of power swirled through me until energy awakened in my hands, the back of my neck, the soles of my feet. It rushed through every vein in my body, pooling in my palms and chest.

Crimson and black swam in my peripheral vision, stealing my breath. The intensity made me sway, dizzy with effort.

The muscles in my arms ached, but I didn't allow them to tense. I let go, releasing the energy until it manifested as onyx vines—conjured from nothing but the power that sang in my blood.

I gasped and the vines faltered as if stalling.

"Focus," Casimir breathed, astonished. "Keep going," he encouraged, close to my shoulder again.

The power surged through tissue and marrow. The unfamiliar burning engulfed me, and though strange, it was intoxicating. There was no tether, nothing to connect them to the earth, yet I sensed every shift, the very thrum they put off. A *pulse*. The life I created.

The black and crimson threads tightened as my pulse settled. They engulfed my vision until all I could see and feel were the vines.

I flicked my wrist and the vines whipped forward and crashed into the dummy, shattering it into a thousand wooden pieces. My eyes went wide, and I stared in awe for a moment.

Casimir came closer, gaze fixed across the field. The weight of his hand brought me back, the touch tender as his palm rested on my lower back. "Gods, you're incredible, El," he said, voice full of pride.

Tears bit at the edge of my eyes. Casimir's words took root deep in my chest, burrowed beneath my rib cage. I clung to them, allowing myself to share in that pride, too.

I couldn't help but think of how proud my father would be of me. A few stray tears mixed with the rain as it trailed my cheeks, and Casimir watched, a knowing expression on his face as I beamed over at him.

"My father would be proud, I think," I said. Even as my voice cracked, the grief became less of a burden. It felt more like an echo of memories. Love with nowhere to go.

Casimir smiled sadly. "He would be beaming."

Thunder cracked overhead, lighting the clouds that shrouded the moon. I glanced up, watching it echo through the sky like crashing waves.

I turned my gaze to Casimir, half frozen from the rain, I said, "While that was incredible, I think I've lost all feeling in my toes."

Casimir's proud smile never disappeared. "The healers will demand my head after having you out in this rain."

After we rushed up the slick path to the camp, I followed Casimir to his tent and ducked inside to get out of the cold. The fabric of the tent gave little relief, and I stood in the middle of it, shivering as my teeth chattered.

Casimir tied a knot in the drapes, then went to dig through a chest near the bed. It took him a moment, and he turned, tossing a lump of cloth onto the bed. "Those should work." He gave no further explanation. I eyed the items while he went through another chest in his tent. He straightened with clothes in his arms shortly after.

I shuffled over to the bed, hesitant, and my shaky hands fumbled with the fabric, letting it unfold to reveal a dark gray tunic, the edges of it frayed from years of use, and a pair of black trousers.

Confused, I glanced at Casimir.

"What you have on is soaked through," he said, as if the intention was obvious. Only to me, it wasn't, and my eyes widened.

"Oh, I don't—" I stammered, my pulse skittering like a panicked bird.

"I'll give you some privacy." Casimir turned on his heel and went to the other side of the tent, the proximity still too close.

He stopped in the corner by the drapes and unraveled dry clothes for himself. I watched for a moment to make sure he didn't turn, then averted my gaze as he began to pull off his tunic. I reached for the clothing he gave me, and ran my thumbs over the worn texture as I pulled them closer.

I tried not to pay Casimir any mind as the wet cloak and soaked clothes peeled from my skin, falling to the floor of his tent. They met with the stone, too audible in the silence. I couldn't think of anything more mortifying than if Casimir turned around, so in a rush, I threw on the tunic, grateful for the dryness it provided against the cold. It was comfortable, well worn, and it fell past my upper thighs. I tugged on the trousers next, also too big. When I finished, I heard the distinct sound of him pulling his own dry clothes on, then silence, as though he were waiting. I took a tentative glance over at him to tell him I was done, when a flash of scarlet in his hair caught my eye.

"Is that a bloom?" I blurted.

He whipped around, then promptly covered his eyes. "Fuck. Sorry, you didn't say if you were decent," he faltered.

I pursed my lips to fight back a chuckle. "It's fine. Let me see your hair," I said, unable to hold back a smile when he let his hand fall to his side.

I tugged at the trousers as they bunched over my feet, then sat at the edge of his bed, gesturing for him to come closer, not fully meeting his gaze.

Casimir stopped before me where he tilted his head to the side to offer a clear view of the dark red petal in his hair. I ran a finger over it, the silky petal cool between my fingers. The strand of hair that held it was slightly thicker, a subtle pulse thrumming through the petal. I noted the other buds in his hair, tiny and black, well hidden.

"It's beautiful. I can't believe I didn't notice it earlier." A pang of envy took me off guard when the pad of my thumb rubbed the velvety texture. My hand dropped to my lap.

Casimir chuckled and straightened. "Hurts pretty bad." He rubbed at his neck sheepishly.

"I'm sorry," I blurted. "I wasn't even thinking."

He gave me a reassuring smile. "It's my third bloom. I'm mostly used to it by now. Makes sleeping a bit uncomfortable for a while, but nothing I can't manage."

"I have impeccable timing. I shouldn't have interrupted your sleep."

He grabbed a lump of blankets from a corner of the tent and unfurled it, letting it cover the hard stone. "Don't apologize. I'm glad you did."

A soft smile tugged at my cheeks as I pulled his quilt over me.

The petal in his hair shuddered while he set up his makeshift sleeping mat. I stared, realizing how different my life could have been if I'd known he was a Rose. There wasn't any way to change the past, but sitting in his tent, in his *bed*, it had me wishing for a life where I had known, and we could've spent those years in Everbloom, my shoulders free from the weight of loneliness.

My heart lumped in my throat, but I'd spent enough of my life not knowing why. "Cas?"

"Hmm?" He cast a glance over his shoulder, his movements paused. My heart stuttered as he stared at me beneath heavy black hair, waiting for me to say something. I thought back to all the years his scarlet gaze haunted me. Now it only brought me comfort.

I curled my legs close to my chest and wrapped my arms around them, keeping the blanket pulled high. "Why didn't you ever explain your abilities when we were younger?" The question was an abrupt shift, pulling me back through years of his presence in my sleep. It felt somewhat silly that I had once feared it.

He paused, straightening his posture. "I wasn't allowed to. Absurd, I know." He shook his head. "My mother and the general both told me it would put you in danger if you knew. Technically, I was meant to stop dreamwalking when we were children."

I bit at my bottom lip, then pulled at the sleeves of the tunic I wore. Anything to distract me from how the air seemed to buzz. "And why didn't you?" The question was quiet, nearly drowned out by the rain.

Casimir scoffed, rubbing at the back of his neck. "I thought it was amusing," he admitted. "Young and foolish. But then..." The way he looked at me, eyes clouded with something I couldn't place, made warmth creep through my icy limbs.

"Then?" I prodded in a whisper.

A small smile twitched at his lips, full of fondness. "You were alone." His voice was a soft rasp. "Every time I visited, I sensed your relief. You didn't show it, and would never admit to it, but I felt it. Then the visits got longer, and you would talk. For hours."

Insecurity swept through me, and my hands knotted into the quilt.

Before I could apologize, his eyes softened. "I like listening to you talk."

The admission forced me to look away. "Sorry. I never really asked about your life or returned a listening ear."

Casimir chuckled, drawing my attention. He sat on his makeshift bed and ran a hand through his damp hair when he got settled. "You know, I take the blame for that. I spent two years telling you I was a ghost. Younger me was quite an ass."

I pursed my lips, fighting a grin at the memory. It terrified me as a young girl, and I had foolishly believed him. It didn't help that my father believed there were souls that were turned away by Akuma—never carried into the peaceful darkness, and left to wander the realm until their soul found somewhere to rest.

Slowly, I rested on the pillow, facing Casimir with the quilt pulled to my chin. It smelled of him.

"Older you is less of an ass," I teased, watching mirth sparkle in his eyes. "Thank you, Cas."

"For what?"

"Not leaving me alone."

A pained look crossed his face. "I abandoned you for years."

The years of his disappearance still ached. But being there with him, in the quiet of his tent, I hoped I'd never have to experience his absence again.

"You were grieving. Don't be hard on yourself," I said, exhaustion beginning to pull at me.

Casimir scoffed, lying down as he tucked a bunched up cloak under his head as he did. We said nothing else as I rested my cheek against his pillow. It was silent as we both stared at each other across the space. Moments ticked by before his eyes fell first, shutting with heavy lids. I blocked out the guilt of waking him and focused on being grateful for his kindness.

Even with the threat of more nightmares, my eyes closed, and I ignored the flutter in my chest that came from being in Casimir's tent. I convinced myself exhaustion was the sole reason, nothing else.

The lie came easily.

Twenty-One

The sun coated the damp field of grass, frost melting into the earth, another harsh shift after the humid rain the night before. I leaned back on my hands, soaking in the few streaks of light while perched on a lump of stone half buried in the ground, trying to keep dry.

Calla rested on my shoulder, pecking at her feathers. Far to my right, Galan and Casimir continued their spar, using the unfamiliar terrain to present more of a challenge.

Their grunts and the sound of their armor colliding couldn't disrupt the peace I found in the private patch of land. It hid well in the trees of the camp, toward the back of it. Trees opened and allowed the light to burn on top of the rocky cliffs where Casimir and Galan sparred.

After another embarrassing morning of someone else finding me in Casimir's tent, I chose to watch the two practice. It was Galan who came looking to spar with Casimir, and when he interrupted my sleep this morning—*our sleep*—I didn't miss the way he hid a mischievous grin.

"Oh, I wasn't aware you had company," he had said, poorly hiding a chuckle.

Casimir, as always, brushed it off and thought nothing of it. His regard for me in that sense was amusing. He didn't have it in him to consider me in such a way. Galan's suspicious demeanor didn't register with Casimir, but I noticed it the moment he saw my head peer out from the blankets on

Casimir's bed. I had tried to stay hidden when Galan announced himself, but Casimir addressed me to kindly let me know he was leaving to train.

It wasn't as though we shared a bed. Casimir slept on the floor, something I needed to find a solution for if I intended to continue benefiting from the sleep free of night terrors and visions. Being so close to Casimir, I didn't have another vision of him dying. The fear was silenced when I knew he was safe.

I would continue to find my way to his tent if he was comfortable with it. Anything to keep myself from seeing him die over and over.

Alba and Galan would enjoy gossiping about us sharing a space. It shocked me when he didn't immediately leave to tell her she'd been right, and we stayed in the same tent again. Not like it was anything nefarious. But it bothered me much less than the alternative.

Though it had a similar effect, I didn't want to ask him to dreamwalk. It seemed like a simple choice to stay in his tent. It didn't feel much different from him visiting me in my room for all those years. Except for his soft breathing while he slept, and the way any time I moved a little too much, he awoke to ask if I was okay. Or his disheveled morning appearance that made him seem softer, more vulnerable.

I bit my lip and brought my attention back to the two as they paused, discussing the way Galan blocked Casimir's advances. It was always enjoyable to see Casimir step into his title as a captain and teach those he was in charge of.

Galan had been on Casimir's squad for over a year, and it showed in how the two interacted. Galan held him in high regard, and after years of knowing Casimir, it was peculiar to observe others treat him in such a manner.

Footsteps sounded behind me, and when I turned to see who the noise belonged to, my mood soured.

Orin walked our way, wearing light leather armor. Despite the chilling conditions on the mountain cliffs, he opted not to wear a cloak. His white hair swept off his shoulders in the breeze.

Not paying attention, he nearly ran into me.

"Watch where you're walking," I grumbled while I scooted out of the way. He caught sight of me and sneered. Calla squawked at him.

"Go find something else to do, girl," he said.

Casimir turned in our direction, and he gave Orin a stern look. While he was of lower rank than Orin, it seemed to be enough for Orin to leave me alone.

I rolled my eyes when Orin straightened his posture. He clearly thought himself important. I wondered why Valor chose him as his second in command. Or why Casimir spent any time with the man. Every interaction I had with him caused me a headache. There was nothing pleasant about him.

The three men returned to the conversation of blocking advances, and I deflated when I saw how Galan seemed to take it. Orin spoke to him as if he were incompetent at fighting. It made my blood boil, and I stood, which sent Calla fluttering to a nearby tree, perching next to a white raven.

Damp leaves clung to my linen trousers, and the wind blew straight through the thin fabric. I shivered and wrapped my arms around my torso as I approached them. They halted their conversation. Curiosity sparked in Casimir's eyes, whereas Orin appeared as if he wanted to draw his sword on me. It almost made me chuckle when I thought of how Casimir would react if Orin did. From what I had seen, Casimir's skill with a blade outdid Orin's. They sparred often, and when they used weapons, Casimir always bested him. Part of me wished Orin would try it, if only for something to brighten a rather slow morning.

When I reached them, I paused and tried to steady my jaw as it trembled. We were close to the edge of the cliffs and the icy wind seeped through my thin gardening clothes.

I stood close to Galan and glanced at him. Some days, it was easy to forget his age. He joined the guard just under eighteen, and he had yet to reach his twenties. It showed in his face and his uncertainty. Even so, he was one of the best teachers I had when it came to sparring.

Rocking on my heels, I tightened my grip on my tunic. "Galan, I remember Alba saying she needed your help today with something." My teeth chattered when I spoke. "Shouldn't you head that way?"

Galan's posture went rigid. "Right. I hadn't been mindful of the time. She will likely be angry with me. Captain—" He saluted Casimir. "My apologies. I have made prior arrangements that I must tend to."

Casimir smirked, not bothered in the slightest. "Of course, Hayes. Enjoy your time with Alba."

Galan's eyes widened, and he dipped his head, turning before we had a good look at the red that colored his cheeks.

We watched him go, scrambling the entire way. His desire to be near Alba always brought me joy. They were quite the pair, and I made a mental note to remind Alba she still needed to talk to him. We made a deal, and I was invested in the payoff.

When he was out of sight, I shivered and turned to Casimir and Orin. Where Casimir eyed my frigid state, Orin gave me a look of annoyance.

I released my hold on my torso and jabbed a finger at him. "What's up your ass?"

Orin sputtered. "You would speak to the general's lieutenant in such a disgraceful manner, girl?" he snapped.

Casimir scoffed and waved Orin off. "You'd speak to the general's daughter in such a disgraceful manner?" He moved closer, and I watched, confused, when he stooped and retrieved his cloak. The confusion turned into embarrassment when he wrapped his cloak around my shoulders. Orin's gaze burned through us the entire time.

After he secured it to my shoulders, he backed up. "It gets rather cold this high up. You may want to wear warmer clothes next time."

I pursed my lips and glanced down at what I wore. It was typical for gardening attire, and if I didn't leave the cliffs soon, I would be late to the last harvest of the season. Something I tried to ignore.

"Now, do you wish to spar, or continue to watch and intervene when I'm teaching?" Casimir asked.

I bit the inside of my cheek and looked at Orin. He stared at me with a mixture of annoyance and curiosity, analyzing our interaction.

Sighing, I pulled the cloak tighter. "I better go. I'm supposed to help Sol in the gardens today."

Casimir nodded and turned back to where he had been sparring with Galan. He walked away, and Orin gave me another look of abhorrence before he followed Casimir.

I went to leave, when Casimir stopped me. "El?"

"Hmm?" I glanced over my shoulder at him.

"Meet me at the training grounds to spar later?" he asked. A small grin tugged at the corner of his lips.

"Sure." My heart thudded erratically, and I darted back into the woods. If I didn't hurry, Sol would bite my head off.

When I reached the garden, no one was present.

Sol wasn't in her normal spot, and no one had retrieved baskets for picking. It was the last of the corn to need picked, and I looked forward to being done with it. The promise of moving onto something else brought me joy, and yet, Sol was gone.

I looked around the garden for any of the others. They never paid me any mind, and I never spoke to them. Sol's quiet presence was preferable in the gardens.

While the others were friendly, I basked in the silence and the ability to complete the task uninterrupted. Sol offered me a respite from all the questions which followed me everywhere I went.

Many people in Mistvalle caught wind that I was the white bloom. *Was*. Discussing the reason why my bloom never finished was a topic I avoided, and every new smiling face which inquired about it brought me dread.

No matter how much I didn't want to, I made my way over to another gardener. They tended the squash in the gardens. The cold front swooped in, nearly finishing their job for the season as well.

One man in the garden noticed my approach and straightened from where he bent among the patch of squash.

He waved, a friendly grin on his face. "Elma!"

I flinched. Of course, it was the one who never got my name right. Rather than correct him, I smiled in return.

"Morning, Matthias. Is Sol not working today?" I asked. I made it a point to remember his name, despite how he continued to get mine wrong.

Matthias tapped a dirt covered finger on a leather strap across his chest. "I don't suppose I seen her. Usually the first one in. Isla opened our gate in the 'morn."

"Would you know where she is?" Frustration pulled at me. After all the mornings she cursed me for being only a few minutes late, and she didn't even show up on the last day of garden duty.

After a moment of thinking, Matthias shrugged. "I'd do a check at the east enclave. Seen Halburn leavin' that way this 'morn. Seemed right pissed. Those two are somethin' else."

I sighed and glanced at the entrance of the garden.

"Do you know exactly where I can look?" It'd be easier to finish the task myself and be done with it. But she didn't get to put the rest of it on me. Not after how upset she got every time I was late.

"Their home. Looks a bit odd from the others. Their family comes from the Emerald Mountain. Find the house with the emerald door."

I nodded and thanked him. It would be a long walk to the east enclave. It was somewhere I hadn't explored yet, though I heard enough from Halburn when he tried to make small talk during healings.

What Matthias said about their family made sense to me. Sol always had an emerald brooch on, and Halburn had a ring which appeared crafted out of pure emeralds.

It sparked my curiosity, since I knew very little of the Emerald Mountain. The different sanctuaries didn't seem to talk about the others; I assumed to keep them better guarded.

All the years Casimir wanted me to find him, yet he never told me where to go. It made sense. They guarded their secrets close. It would have made things much easier if he could have been upfront.

There was no time to think about what any of us should have done differently, and I trudged through Mistvalle, Casimir's cloak still around my shoulders.

The warmth was welcome, though it wouldn't have been as necessary if Sol was in the gardens already. With how the sun bore down on the gardens, even on bitter days, I always left a picking with sweat staining my clothes.

It was cooler than most days, yet the markets still overflowed with bodies. The mix of norms and Roses never failed to shock me. It felt wrong to look non-Roses in the eye.

When I left the markets, I crossed the bridge. I hadn't crossed it since we first arrived in Mistvalle, and its stunning architecture stole my breath. Where the Iron Thorn was beautiful in its own way, it was dark. In contrast, everything seemed to glisten in Mistvalle.

I made it across the bridge, and an abundance of Mistvalle homes appeared before me. They wove through the rocky cliffs. The paths carved into the mountains led to the many stacking homes, all made of stone.

How they built such intricate homes made me curious. I had never seen such fascinating architecture in my life. In contrast, the path leading through the homes brought me dread. I was sick of having to climb to get anywhere.

I pushed the annoyance aside and let my legs carry me up the daunting path. The way to the Mistvalle homes proved much steeper than that of the path to the Everbloom camp. A new strain in muscles showed as much. *The people of Mistvalle must have legs of iron.*

To my delight and dismay, the emerald door stuck out among the homes made of glistening white stone. The climb would be higher than I wanted to go, but I already made it too far to turn back.

I groaned and continued on, surveying the homes carved into the mountain. They all had doors to match. It appeared to be a blank slate, except for the lone emerald door and a few others. I spotted only three other homes with different colored doors. One was a deep maroon, and two of them were a rich blue—Everbloom. It reminded me much of the color of the tents in our camp, and I wondered how many Roses were originally from different sanctuaries.

By the time I reached the emerald door, sweat trickled down the side of my face. Casimir's guard cloak proved to be too warm for such a trek. I was still grateful he offered it, and it gave me an excuse to return to his tent later.

Pausing, I caught my breath for a moment before I rapped on the door. I took a step back and waited for a reply. It occurred to me that Sol could easily choose not to answer. She didn't enjoy company.

To my surprise, she opened the door. When she saw it was me, she glared and went to close it.

"Hey!" I put my boot in the bottom of the door and a palm against it, holding it open.

Sol huffed and pushed harder. "Go away."

My teeth ground together and I stared up at her. She was almost as tall as Casimir, and had the build of a warrior, despite the fact I only ever saw her in the gardens.

We stared off for a moment too long, and she finally caved. "Your persistence is annoying," she grumbled.

I sighed with relief when the pressure released from my arms.

Sol went further inside and left the door open. She didn't invite me in, but she didn't tell me to leave.

I passed the threshold, and it was colder than I expected.

Similar to the exterior, it consisted of the same blinding white stones. The only items to break up the monotony were a woven rug made of green and brown, and an emerald colored velvet settee. It appeared vacant, not like two people lived there. While it fit their personalities, it appeared unsettling.

Sol watched me survey the room with her arms crossed. "Done judging my home?"

"I wasn't judging it."

"Then why stare as if someone died?"

I shook my head. "It's just different from what I'm used to."

Sol didn't challenge my response. Regardless of her silent demeanor, it was surprising. When she took offense, she made it clear.

Rather than scold me for judging the decor, she slumped down on the settee and pulled a quilt over her lap, then put on a pair of leather gloves. It was only then I noticed she wore sleep clothes.

No fire roared in the hearth. It lay empty, even though the temperature was frigid in the little home.

When Sol pulled her legs to her chest and burrowed deeper in the blanket, alarm bells rang in my head.

She was never vulnerable in front of people. Especially me. Yet she sat on the settee and sulked with me present in the room.

Cautiously, I walked further inside and closed the door behind me. I pushed the hesitation away and stood close to the settee. "Are you okay, Sol?"

Her head snapped up, and she glared. "Fine."

"Someone who *is* fine wouldn't answer that way."

Sol turned her head, glancing out a small window carved into the stones that made up the home.

I sighed and sat on the far end of the settee. My muscles uncoiled when I relaxed into it, although Sol seemed perturbed.

"Didn't say you could sit."

Looking at her, I said, "I walked all the way up here. I'm going to sit for a minute and catch my breath."

Sol scoffed. "Knew you were weak."

It was my turn to glare. "Unlike everyone here, I grew up without rigorous training."

She pulled the blanket closer to her chin, not replying. Her pale eyes darted around the room, appearing glossy. It made me uneasy.

The mood shifted, and I reminded myself I knew very little about Sol. More than anyone I'd met, she didn't share much regarding her personal life. When I met those in Everbloom, they freely shared much of their lives with me.

Sol wasn't that way. I hadn't even known she was from the Emerald Mountain, and I had no idea why she left.

The silence lingered for a long time before I got the courage to ask again. "Are you okay?"

She bristled and lifted her head. When she looked at me, the vulnerability made my stomach drop.

"Halburn told me to stay in."

I opened my mouth and shut it.

She was a grown woman. Why did she need his approval to leave? Although I spent much of my life not doing the things I wanted to do because of my parents and their wishes for me.

My hands fidgeted in my lap as I thought of what to say. "Before my parents died, I let them control where I could and couldn't go. It sometimes felt suffocating."

When Sol scoffed, I tried not to be offended.

She looked at me. "Did you kill your mother?"

I froze.

The room went silent, and I didn't know what to say. While I wasn't the one who burned our cottage down, nor the one who attacked them, hadn't I brought their deaths on them?

After a pause, I said, "Not directly. But she died when a man came looking for me. I wasn't there, and he killed my family instead."

Sol stared at me, no annoyance or mocking in her eyes. Her focus went to the quilt on her lap before she spoke. "When my powers activated, I almost killed Halburn…" She flattened her gloved palm and stared at it. "My mother ended up on the other side of my palms in place of him. She died painfully. I hadn't meant to."

I watched her look over her hands. Eventually, she met my stare.

"I'm grown. I know that. But I took her from Halburn. I owe him everything. He could have locked me away. He could have hated me." She swallowed and when she tucked her hair behind her ear, I had never witnessed her look so vulnerable, broken.

"Had a temper this morning. He demanded I not go out, lest I kill someone." She laughed bitterly. "As if I didn't learn long ago not to touch others."

It should have made me afraid to think she could kill with a single touch. But there was no fear when I reached across the settee and put a hand on her forearm. She stopped looking at her gloves and turned to me, eyes only a fraction wider.

"That could kill you."

"I'm aware."

Sol shook her head. "Must have a death wish. You won't find an out from your guilt at my hand."

I chuckled. "I'm counting on that." I withdrew my hand. "Sorry, I'm not well versed in comforting others."

She tucked her arms back into the quilt. "Adequate enough."

We fell into a tense silence. Sol's choice to work alone made more sense. Though part of it seemed to be a preference, some of it likely stemmed from fear.

To kill someone with a simple touch, I couldn't imagine the apprehension it would make someone live with. To feel you couldn't trust your own hands. It explained why she constantly wore gloves.

A thought occurred to me, and I stood. "Is that why I never see you training?" I asked.

Sol stared at me. She didn't confirm or deny it, which was answer enough.

"Why don't you come spar with me?"

The question took her off guard.

"But the gardens?" she countered.

I looked over my shoulder at the door. "It can wait until tomorrow. Plus, the afternoon sun burns me too badly. So, what do you say?"

From her build, it was clear she trained. She likely did it alone. And maybe I read her wrong, or perhaps I didn't understand her. But loneliness could be suffocating, and carrying guilt alone was even worse.

I wouldn't leave Sol to bear her grief on her own.

Twenty-Two

After an excessive amount of convincing, Sol agreed to spar with me. I should have told her Casimir was going to be there. Sol glared while I checked over my daggers. I ignored her while Casimir stopped at my side, his hands on the hilt of a sword as he surveyed the blade. Free of its sheath, it gleamed in the light.

To my surprise, Sol didn't pick up a weapon. She watched us prep, her arms crossed over her chest. There were times that her demeanor reminded me much of Casimir's, and the parallel was amusing. She couldn't stand him, although he was indifferent toward her.

When I finally had the nerve to meet Sol's glare, I gave her an apologetic look and tucked my daggers into the straps on my thighs. Her scowl only increased, and she walked farther to the outer circle where other guards and people from Mistvalle stood.

I pursed my lips and glanced at Casimir. He watched with his head low and his eyes peering through rogue strands of hair. A knowing look flitted in his eyes, and he straightened and sheathed the sword. Casimir put the blade back on the weapons rack and I raised a brow.

"Not interested in sparring anymore?" I asked.

"Let's do some hand to hand combat today. Brush up on how you counter attacks without a weapon."

I paled. "I hate doing that."

Casimir chuckled. "I'm well aware. But Sol doesn't seem very fond of training with weapons."

Sol surveyed the field, sizing up every person there. If only Casimir knew what she was capable of with her abilities. Hands that could poison you with a simple touch.

She didn't need a weapon.

The thought crossed my mind, and I understood what Casimir picked up on. He continued to prove his place on the guard.

Walking past him, I bumped his shoulder and grinned. "You're a good captain. You have an eye for what others need."

A pleasant, almost boyish grin tugged at his lips. He appeared flustered by the compliment.

The leather straps on my thighs released with the flick of a buckle, and I put the daggers back from where I got them. Stone scraped the sole of my boot when I turned and faced the center field.

Bodies clashed, weapons collided, and shouts of encouragement erupted in the area. I noticed a few from Everbloom in the crowd, most of which I didn't know. Among them, a long braid of light brown hair whipped around as Elrin used roots to counter another Roses burst of vines. The two smirked with every collision of their abilities, neither caving to the other.

Rather than observe them any longer, I faced Sol and trudged her way. Trees swayed behind the wall of gray stones; scarlet leaves falling in a delicate twirl. They dusted over the stones, a trail of fiery-red.

Sol watched me, her mask of indifference firm. She wore a suit of light leather armor, stained a dark green. On the field, she appeared more menacing than a lot of the guards. She stood maybe an inch or two shorter than Casimir, and I noted several guards eyeing her from the sidelines.

I stopped a few feet in front of her.

She barely gave me a grunt of acknowledgment. "Didn't tell me he would join." Her tone clipped.

"Sorry, I should've said something." My eyes averted hers as warmth prickled my cheeks. She had just begun to trust me, I didn't want to ruin that. "I could've told him I'd spar later. Although his presence has always been a bit hard to get rid of."

Sol's mask cracked for a second when confusion softened her features. "You mean to say he stalks you?"

I stifled a chuckle when Casimir stopped at my side. He glanced between the two of us, intrigued.

"What is it?" he asked.

Sol gestured to me with one hand. "You stalk her?"

I sputtered, unable to hold back an obscene chortle. Casimir was caught off guard, and he rubbed a hand on the back of his neck while he gave me a pointed look.

"A stalker? I should reprimand you," Casimir said, amused.

Blush crept up my neck. "Surely you wouldn't deny it. How many years did you interrupt my sleep with no warning or permission?"

Casimir clicked his tongue and took a step back, gesturing to the field. "Fighting words, Blackthorne. Settle it with a spar."

Sol bristled and shook her head. "Gross," is all she said.

I chuckled then walked to an empty part of the sparring field, Casimir close at my side. He didn't defend himself to Sol, and there was no need. The strange dynamic would be difficult to explain to anyone. The abilities he possessed were rare, and no one in Mistvalle had any experience with it. It belonged to his family's bloodline. He was the last one. The thought was sobering.

Dirt gritted beneath my boots when I halted in a wide enough area. Pebbles ground on the stone, and I planted my feet in a sparring position while Casimir took a spot across from me. I narrowed my gaze and surveyed how he lined himself up. His stance, the lean of his torso, the grin on his face, the dimple in his cheek…

Counterproductive.

Casimir brought his arms up in a defensive manner. "Ready?"

I sank deeper into my stance and gave a single nod. He grinned and moved quick as ever. Long strides carried him to me in a matter of seconds, but I anticipated he would make the first move. He always did when he sparred anyone.

The move was predictable, and I dodged him with a jump to the left. It would have given me more space to roll and spring back up, but that move still proved difficult for me to execute. I didn't intend to give him an easy target.

If I kept my focus on him and watched his feet, I had a slight upper hand. While I hadn't honed my fighting style yet, he seemed to have settled into his.

Casimir allowed the space between us to increase for a moment as we continued a slow rotation, eyeing each other. The noises, the scents, they rushed my senses and a sudden icy jolt shot through me. It began at my nape, sending the hairs upright.

Across from me, Casimir grinned. The light shifted, a flicker until it looked as if blood trickled from the corner of his lips. I trembled, but kept my fists in front of me. The training grounds warped around me as the chill permeated every inch of my skin. The sunlight drained from the sky as a patch of blood spread through his armor.

Sharp sickening breaths left my parted lips, and I shut my eyes hard, blocking it out. A boot scraped on stone nearby, barely audible beneath how my pulse raced.

I heard the impact of the arrow, over and over again. Tendrils of crimson unraveled in my mind until they revealed a battlefield painted in blood. It seeped into the stone and dirt. Copper stung my nose, and an arrow soared past my shoulder before it hit Casimir. Again and again and again—

"Focus, Blackthorne!" Casimir called, his tone lighthearted.

My eyes snapped open, and the training grounds were drenched in warm sunlight once more. His training armor was pristine, not even a speck of dirt I could pinpoint. He gave me a reassuring nod, as if I were nervous.

The forceful nature of the vision threatened to have me sick on the stone beneath my feet. I steadied myself, inhaled through my nostrils, and stopped the rotation, my posture more sure than before.

Snap out of it. He's okay. He's right here.

When Casimir darted for me once more, I had no choice but to tuck the fear away, ducking under his arm as it went for me. It brushed the hair that trailed me, and I heard him grunt in surprise.

As I turned, the blur of a shadow figure caused me to stumble. My knees buckled, and my head whipped around, searching for the haunting pair of eyes. The shadow remained just out of sight, at the corner of my vision.

It shouldn't be here. Why is it here? The field grew colder, and I almost missed Casimir's approach.

"Do you want to stop?" His voice was muffled, as if he spoke through a heavy door.

The echo of his heartbeat thrummed in the earth. More familiar than any other pulse. I used it to focus and shut out the presence that shifted the air around me. Casimir's deep scarlet eyes settled the fear, and replaced it with a sense of urgency and desperation. A battle loomed over our heads, and I would be damned if I was too weak, too untrained, to protect those I cared about.

Before he reached me, I held up a hand. "I want to continue. Just a bit tired."

"We can try tomorrow—"

I advanced without letting him continue. I couldn't freeze. I couldn't let fear win.

Casimir caught my fist as it flew at him. He pulled me closer, as if to trap my arms, but I went under his arm until he was forced to break his hold on me as it twisted. It was a move he had taught me when training weeks ago, and a look of approval gave me more confidence as I rounded on him again.

He countered every attack, every shift of my weight. It was clear he was cautious with me, which wouldn't help me when it came to a real fight.

I pulled in a greedy, full inhale, as we started another rotation. "Stop going easy on me. I need to know my true limit."

A smirk settled on his lips. "Would you like me to get you there?"

My eyes went a fraction wider as a spark of nerves awakened at his words. "That's what we're here for, is it not?" I chimed while settling into my stance.

Casimir's grin turned amused, and he didn't hesitate. His long stride had him on me in a matter of seconds. His boot hit mine, forcing my leg to slip outward and throw me off balance. My throat tightened, and I dropped to the ground before he could grab me and rolled to the side. I stayed low, and when he came at me again, I was the one left countering every quick attack.

He remained gentle, none of the blows enough to hurt. It was nothing more than a dance to catch his limbs, block a fist, or dodge a kick. I was exhausted within a matter of minutes, and sweat crawled down my spine.

I meant to counter attack, but he grabbed my wrist as my fist aimed for him, spinning me until my back slammed into his chest.

The arm that he held was contorted to my chest, and when I went to use the other to break free, he pulled it behind my back. He had me pinned, his body flush to mine.

"You're getting quicker," Casimir mused, his lips close to my ear.

I burned with feverish heat. "Still not faster than you."

Casimir hummed in response, a rumble against my ear. "How do you intend to get out?" he asked, tone that of a captain training a soldier. The words danced across my raised skin, quickening my heartbeat.

I tried to lock my ankle with his, but he stopped me, his knee spreading my legs. When he pulled my arm tighter between our bodies, my back and neck arched. A wisp of his breath settled along my neck. A sharp inhale caught in my throat, and his grip instantly loosened.

"Did I hurt you?" he asked, practically frantic.

To my mortification, he hadn't. The reaction was beyond my control, and I wanted to bury my head.

Spotting the people who watched, I snapped out of the moment, and wrapped my ankle around Casimir's while he was distracted. I felt the shift in his breath when I dropped my weight, despite the protest of my arms.

His leg buckled with mine, bringing us both to the ground, his body heavy on top of me while his hand and mine were pinned to my chest. I didn't have to make another move. He jumped off my back, fixing his stance.

I rolled onto my back, and grinned at him from the ground before I stood. Casimir shook off the shock, and took on a different sparring stance. Within our short back and forth, he already gathered I could read his style, and he changed it that quickly.

My arms raised to protect my front. I knew he wouldn't hit me, but sparring didn't come without accidents, and I wanted to remain in practice. If I got lazy with my form, it would offer me no protection if I needed it in an actual fight.

I took the initiative and advanced before Casimir did. If I waited for him to take the lead again, it put me at a disadvantage. I had to play my cards right. And perhaps use his hesitation to catch him off guard.

A look of approval flashed in his gaze, and I had to focus not to let it distract me, even as my pulse thrummed from the subtle show of praise.

Casimir would dodge, and I had to hope my assumption in which direction he would go was right.

To my delight, my prediction was correct.

My arm reached out when he went to jump to the right and I wrapped it around his torso, spinning myself until I was behind him, a hand on his abdomen, an ankle locked with one of his. My other hand grabbed his arm, pulling it back to me.

The field went silent, and I felt every inhale he took against my palm. A breathy chuckle left his lips.

"Much quicker than before. Well done."

I swallowed hard, my limbs still entwined with his. He was almost a foot taller—his shoulders, arms, and torso were toned from years of training. Wider than my frame, yet I had him pinned.

Another chuckle vibrated my palm. "You can let go, El. I yield."

My pulse thundered in my ears and I released him, aware of the eyes on us. Many of the others who sparred paused their own training to watch. It wasn't uncommon when Casimir was on the field.

The attention unnerved me and I moved further from him. "You let me get the upper hand," I muttered, not looking at him when he faced me. Casimir easily could've countered, and it offended me that he hadn't. But after he thought he hurt me, it was clear he wouldn't spar with me the way I needed him to.

"You're a good fighter, and we can adjust as you train more, but I won't put my full effort into an unbalanced spar."

Frustration bubbled to the surface, and for once, I wish he could treat me with indifference or at least like a member of the guard. Being coddled did nothing for me.

Footsteps crunched to my left, and I looked over to see Sol approach. Her arms remained crossed, and she stopped a few feet away, her attention going between the two of us.

She paused on Casimir. "It's insulting to go easy in a spar." Shaking her head, she pointed at me. "Spar me. I'll show you."

Something about sparring Sol was scarier than going up against Casimir. He didn't hide the fact that he took it easy on me. Something I both despised and appreciated. If I thought about how gentle he was with me for too long, I'd turn red in the face.

With a sigh, I waved Sol closer. "Well, let's see it, then."

A rare smile twitched at the corner of Sol's mouth. It was the most amused she had ever looked in my presence.

Sol uncrossed her arms, shook them, stretched them behind her head, and finished it off with a long inhale.

Casimir patted me on the back and walked to the sidelines to observe. I tried not to think about how his breath felt against my palm, then again on my ear. In a harsh shift, the vision tried to creep back in. I shook my head and copied Sol's prep to snap myself out of it. The last thing I needed was anymore distractions.

Across from me, Sol moved into a more stoic position. No leaning to one side, no open stance. She stood with her hands up to guard her face, and that was the only form she took. It was unlike Alba, Galan, or Casimir.

While I had trained since being on the ship, it was never with anyone but those three. I knew their patterns, and I also knew they would take it easier on me. Sol didn't have it in her to do the same.

Though she already saw my stance and moves, I still lowered myself into the same sparring position. It was the most comfortable to me, and the easiest to transition out of.

I hoped she didn't harbor resentment toward me after the morning disturbance. Her abilities were nothing to scoff at.

Casimir started the match with a resounding 'begin', and Sol smirked. My stomach rolled, and I chose to make the first move.

It made me uncomfortable when Sol didn't even brace. Her smirk widened. My feet carried me quickly, and it would've been better to cut in a direction she wasn't expecting, or to avoid her altogether. Sol's expression was unnerving, and I debated sprinting out of the training grounds. The embarrassment wouldn't have been as bad as the way her hand caught me, her movement faster than I expected.

Her firm hand gripped my shoulder, and she shoved me to the ground with ease. The back of my skull smacked the stone and stars swam in my eyes. I contemplated staying there and yielding, but she offered a unique challenge. It made little sense to squander a chance to spar with a new opponent who wasn't willing to take it easy.

The hold she had on me offered an opening, and I brought my legs up, wrapping them around her arm. I watched the curiosity on her face for only a second before I twisted my body. Her arm folded against my chest, and I rolled until we switched places.

Sol's face went dead serious and her arm jerked free of where I trapped it between my legs. In a blinding quick move, both of her hands pressed between us, her hands on my shoulders.

When her nails pinched at the leather armor, I lost some of my focus and it gave her the space to bring a leg up. It bent until it was at my abdomen, where she extended it, grinning again while she threw me over her head and off her body.

I groaned when my back slammed into the stones.

Sol gave me no time to recover when she pounced from the ground and dove for me. I rolled as fast as I could, trying to create more space before she got the upper hand again.

When I got to my feet, she was already too close, her leg swinging until it raised above my shoulder. She brought it down hard, and I jerked with the weight. It nearly tore my arm from the socket and I cried out, trying to move back to center myself.

Casimir went to step in, his brow creased with concern, but I held up a hand to stop him. His fists curled, but he didn't intervene.

When I faced Sol, her smirk was back.

I won't let her get away with that.

It took everything in me not to conjure vines and get the upper hand that way. Sol's abilities were touch only, and if I used my vines, it'd be an unfair advantage. I wanted to best her with combat skills alone.

A steadying breath whistled through my nose and I ran at her. My limbs pumped with adrenaline, and I leaned to the left to catch her off guard. To my surprise, she fell for it.

Her body shifted and braced for an attack to her left. I kept my face straight and continued on the same course. At the last second, she dove to catch me on the left and I ducked, spun, and kicked a leg out to her right side. The maneuver made me stumble, but it paid off.

Sol grunted when her legs buckled beneath her and she fell in a heap on the stones. I didn't let myself bask in the small win. It was pure luck I executed that move. She would get back up and I had to be ready for her next advance.

Rather than hang back, I straightened and closed the space. Before she got up, I pinned her down, my knees falling to either side of her thighs.

When her fist flew toward my face, I grabbed her wrist, shaking against her strength. Her knuckles moved closer, and sweat formed at my brow, but I held her there.

It did little to prevent her other hand from flying up. She knotted it in my hair and jerked back, grinning. *Dirty move, Sol.*

I groaned and my back arched, but I didn't release her wrist. I tried to get the skin inside her elbow between my nails to get her to ease her grip. The leather on her armor was too thick.

Neither of us yielded, and from the corner of my eye, I saw Casimir pinch the bridge of his nose. He shook his head and strode across the field until he stood over us. Due to the hold on my hair, I had no choice but to stare up at him.

Casimir tilted his head, surveying our predicament. "I'm calling it a draw."

Sol glared at him. "Neither have yielded," she snapped.

I couldn't move my head from her tight grip, causing my back to ache. Casimir eyed me, and I didn't miss the way he searched for any sign I'd been hurt. If only, like Sol, he could regard me the way a sparring partner should. It did nothing for me when others treated me as if I were incapable. After a pause, he sighed, reached forward and broke Sol's hold on my hair with pressure somewhere in her arm. She glowered at him, a silent threat. Her restraint surprised me when she didn't paralyze him for touching her.

Casimir didn't stop, and Sol ripped her arm from him as she said, "Touch me again, you'll be paralyzed for a week."

He appeared unfazed.

I shook my hair and stood, offering a hand to Sol. She took it without a fuss and straightened. With a small bow of her head toward me, she turned and left. No words from her, but it wasn't strange to me. After many similar departures in the garden, I knew it meant nothing.

Casimir, on the other hand, appeared baffled. "Did I offend her?"

I chuckled. "She's that way with everyone. Honestly, I think she respects you."

His eyes widened. "I doubt that."

"Well, she didn't poison you when you touched her." I rubbed at my sore neck. "If she hated you, you'd know. Although I wouldn't recommend touching her again."

Casimir nodded and came closer, glancing over the spot my fingers kneaded. "Are you alright?" One of his hands raised, and he moved the hair from the back of my neck to look at it.

Goosebumps spread from where his fingers grazed, causing me to shiver. "I'm fine," I stammered, stumbling back from him.

He looked amused. "I can't touch you, either?"

My face flushed. "I said I'm fine, *Captain*. Are you always so handsy with the people you train?"

Casimir smirked. "Why? Are you jealous?"

My lips pressed in a thin line, and I wished I could disappear. "Not in the slightest."

Casimir laughed, and I rolled my eyes before elbowing him in the stomach. He clutched his middle, pretending it hurt. I bit my lip and looked anywhere but him and his goofy grin.

I froze when Casimir's hand dusted across my back. I knew it was because of the dust that clung to the dark leather. Regardless, flutters erupted in my chest.

"You need a lesson or two on being handsy. First a stalker, now this," I said, shying away from him.

Casimir moved back, his hands raised. "My apologies. I'll remember not to interfere next time someone has a fistful of your hair and won't let go."

I turned to face him. "Works for me."

Casimir chuckled and shrugged. "I was only trying to help. No hands. Got it."

A horrible part of me swam with the disappointment of his hands not touching me again. I snuffed the feeling the second it occurred, and we left the training field in silence.

Twenty-Three

Exhaustion had been elusive once I started staying in Casimir's tent every night. Until the damned mending. It stole much of my time, even from training. I wished for another spar, but the leaders considered it an afterthought. They said that those skills weren't as important as my ability to mend.

It'd been over a week since my spar with Casimir and Sol, and I missed the excitement of countering attacks.

Lady Estelle was waiting for me, but I didn't hurry. I tied my boots lazily while I sat on my bed cushion on the floor—the only solution to prevent Casimir from sleeping on a makeshift bed made out of blankets. The bed frame in my tent lay empty, and I continued to spend each night on the floor of his.

Since leaving my tent, the figure didn't appear to me again. It was easy to explain it away as it became buried beneath all my other responsibilities. The symbols never appeared, and the constant reassurance that Casimir was okay ridded me of the haunting visions where blood stained his clothes and life left his eyes. With each layer of relief, I couldn't bring myself to leave Casimir's space.

A yawn pulled at the muscles in my jaw, and my rigid arms stretched with new aches.

The shaking in my fingers reminded me I needed to drink something. It was easy to forget amidst mending. It drained more from me than sparring or vines, and I rarely remembered to eat and drink before or after a session with Estelle.

Dehydration nipped at the back of my throat, and without a second thought, I reached over to a mug left near Casimir's bed, and chugged it.

An earthy liquid filled my mouth, and I clamped a hand over my lips to stop myself from caving to the urge to spew.

I glanced into the mug, noting loose herbs. They were much too strong, left overnight. I set it down and made a mental note to scold Casimir for it later. Though he'd come back with a comment asking why I drank from his mug. Exhaustion and desperation were an easy answer. It had nothing to do with how accustomed we'd become sharing a space.

My attention went back to my boots, and I finished the other one faster. I needed fresh water, and if I hid from all the leaders long enough, maybe a proper meal.

When I left Casimir's tent, the weather was oddly warm. The wither season was almost upon us, but it felt more akin to the flowering. I wanted to enjoy the change, but relief evaded me. Dramatic weather changes weren't new to me. They had happened often in Eldravine, and it made the king believe the realm was near its end.

Now it'd be true.

I shook my head, as if it would rid me of the harrowing thoughts. It helped when I caught sight of Taryn and Ulrik leaving their tent. It didn't take them long to spot me, and I grinned when Taryn waved at me.

Food and water could wait.

I hurried over to them, grinning. They met me halfway, and Ulrik was quick to duck closer to Taryn's side.

"Oh, c'mon. Elita is the last person here to be afraid of," Taryn said. Ulrik giggled, peering up at me with a soft smile. "Heading down for some grub?" Taryn asked.

I glanced toward the path down the cliffs. "I'm supposed to head to mending."

Taryn hummed beside me. She looked displeased, and I didn't have to guess why. She harbored negative feelings for the people of Mistvalle, especially their healers.

Shaking her head, Taryn said, "I wish they'd give me the room to learn here. It wasn't an easy task caring for the white bloom with little training. Would've been nice to get that here."

"I'd take you over the healers here any day. No manners, and they study me more like an object than a person."

Taryn's face twisted in disgust. "That settles it. We're taking you captive. You'll eat with Ulrik and I before they get their greedy hands on ya." She winked, and started down the path.

Estelle would be displeased.

I was too hungry to let it stop me.

We left the cliffs and chatted on and off about mundane things. I tried to explain how I mended to her, or how the healers here seemed to delight in causing their patients' pain.

She took it all in stride. Her days had been less than joyous. Taryn told me about Valor and his scolding, as if she were at fault. It brought back another rush of anger at him. Taryn was one of my closest friends, and I trusted her more than any of the healers in Mistvalle. Despite how good of a healer Halburn was.

Still, the wound in my abdomen was healed not long after we arrived in Mistvalle. The nerves still sparked beneath my skin, and the numbness bothered me some days. But I moved better than before. It had become less of a burden. Less of a reminder.

I didn't tell Taryn that, though. I didn't want her to feel worse than she already did. It was nothing she had done.

Taryn made her way into the feasting hall without me. She insisted I stay behind so none of the healers would see me. It seemed unnecessary, but I was glad I wouldn't risk an interruption.

When she returned, she and Ulrik both carried a few extras with them for me. Taryn handed me a cloth bag of dried fruit, and Ulrik timidly passed me a sugar dusted pastry.

I smiled at him. "These are my favorites. Thank you."

Ulrik grinned, remnants of the same sugar stuck to his chin. "I remembered," he said, proud of himself.

My heart swelled, and I realized just how much I had missed their company after spending most of my time on the ship with them. After we were out of sight from Orondal, there had been days that Ulrik joined Galan and I when we made bread below deck while Taryn tended to the other wounded on the ship. His joyful and quiet company was a nice change. He was always shy, but he got along incredibly well with Galan, which in turn, eventually led Ulrik to being more comfortable around me.

It was always our little group of four on the ship—Taryn, Galan, Ulrik, and myself. It still pained me to remember Casimir's silence, but I hadn't truly been alone.

Calla squawked softly close by, following us as we walked along the path and ate in silence. I was grateful for their company. Ulrik had grown taller already, it seemed, since we reached land nearly three months ago.

His red ringlets bounced as he skipped ahead of us. "Not too far, bub!" Taryn chided. He turned and grinned, all dimples and childhood mischief. His pale green eyes gave away his amusement.

Ulrik skipped faster, and I heard Taryn grumble, "Ulrik, you better stop or it's to the tents with you."

I watched as he continued to defy her and found it hard not to chuckle. She huffed in frustration and jogged after Ulrik. She scooped him into her arms, causing him to squeal with laughter.

"The tents it is, mister trouble." She nuzzled his hair with her nose and set him down, holding onto his hand. Taryn brushed her hair off her face as they walked back to me.

Water shimmered in the distance, and it drew my attention.

"We're gonna head back up to the camp. Catch you... well, whenever you aren't actually being held captive." She clapped a hand to my shoulder. "Don't let them burn you out. Skills take time. Not like anyone here would understand." She scoffed.

I smiled and patted her hand before she removed it. "I know. Thanks for walking with me."

Taryn waved while she and Ulrik left me in the clearing near the edge of Mistvalle. Calla perched on my shoulder, and settled close to my cheek, her soft head bumping my jaw.

Laughter rang in the air, not from Taryn and Ulrik's retreating forms, but from the water. It danced in the branches of the trees, rustling the leaves with joy and an endearing melody.

The odd red trees gave cover to most of the lake, like an archway made of garnet over the water, the last leaves trembling in a cool breeze. Grass crunched beneath my boots as I tried to get a better look.

I put my arms around my torso, and one of my hands still clutched to the empty dried fruit bag. A familiar white raven called from a tree overhead, never too far whenever Calla was with me.

My feet carried me closer, and I spotted many of my companions in the water as the bright blue sky cast reflections on it. Casimir, Galan, Alba, and a few others from Everbloom, waded through the lake.

I watched and wished the joy was contagious enough to ward off the negative emotion that ripped through me at the sight. Envy tugged at me as I watched them splash and cackle in the lake. No fear or hesitation in the water. No trauma to follow them.

To my dismay, Casimir caught me watching them, and he beckoned me over. I shook my head, and stubborn black coils brushed my cheeks and caught on Calla's feathers, making her bristle. I whispered a soft "sorry" to her, my attention on Casimir, who huffed in exasperation.

Before I had the chance to dart in the opposite direction, he left the water, his short undergarments clinging to his waist and thighs. I pursed my lips and tried to disregard the way he flicked his sopping hair off his forehead. Or worse, the sight of his bare chest. Scarred and toned. The skin of a captain.

My cheeks went red.

"Why don't you join us?" he asked, a smirk tugging at the corner of his mouth.

I gripped my top tighter. "Can't swim. Remember?"

"Of course…but you don't have to get all the way in. Stay where you can stand." Casimir shrugged as if it were simple.

"I can't. I have mending to get to."

Casimir deflated and came closer. Water dripped off the ends of his hair and trailed the expanse of his exposed skin. I tried not to watch it. I failed miserably.

"What's wrong?" he asked.

I winced at the question, and he observed every move I made, reading me.

"Nothing," I snapped, and instantly embarrassment forced its way to the surface. Exhaustion made it difficult to rein in my frustration. "Estelle won't be happy if I'm late again."

"Really? Because you seem a bit pissy," he mused.

My teeth clenched until my jaw hurt, and nails bit at my skin through the fabric of my tunic. I didn't know how to explain that the water terrified me. Or how I vividly remembered every second I spent in the blackness outside of Orondal, trying to find my way to the top. Or the way it seared my lungs and lit every nerve in my body aflame.

The very thought made me recoil.

Casimir watched me, his expression shifting from playful to worried. "El?"

I bristled and turned from him, careful not to jostle Calla on my shoulder. "I have to go mend."

Casimir's hand wrapped around my arm when I went to leave, and I froze. I didn't want to look back at him. He read me too easily, and there was no part of me that wanted his pity.

"I can stay close. Or teach you, if you'd like." Casimir's offer gave me no relief. I could imagine how the others would mock, and I wasn't in the mood to fend off their ridicule. Plus, the way my heart stuttered gave me more pause. I knew it would be a mistake to let Casimir get so close. I needed to clear my head.

Giving him the best smile I could muster, my arm moved out of his light grip. "Sorry. I'm tired, Cas. I want to mend, then rest."

He swiped a hand through his wet waves and nibbled at the skin on his lip. The sight made my breath hitch, and I tore my attention away from his mouth. In every shift of his body, it was obvious he wanted to prod further, but I didn't want to feel inadequate once more. It was enough to have people telling me daily I should be doing better.

Mending. Combat. Sleep. Repeat.

None of it was ever good enough, and it'd only make me feel worse to fail at something as simple as swimming. Something else everyone seemed to do with ease, and I had no inkling on how to start.

It was exhausting, and if I didn't escape the way he appeared letdown, I feared it would overwhelm me.

"I'll see you later, okay?" I didn't give him time to answer. My boot bit into the dirt as I spun on my heel, leaving him behind.

Estelle waited for me in the mending garden, sat on a stone bench, with her hands clasped in a delicate manner on her lap.

Patience exuded from her features, but I saw the pinch at the edge of her kind grin. The way her fingertips drummed together showed a glimpse of her impatience.

"Welcome, Elita. You may begin whenever you're ready." She gestured to the planters on the ground.

The mending circle was out of place. It hid in a cluster of white and silver trees, shaped like a sphere, and at the very center was a single red sapling which struggled to stand.

Inside the planter on the ground, a peony sat vibrantly, along with a cluster of mint and a rose. It was always the same three, though I never brought more than the roses and mint back, one at a time.

Estelle stepped closer and placed her hand on the peony. I never enjoyed watching it drain of life. It crinkled, wilted within a single touch.

I pursed my lips and glanced at Estelle. "Alba once told me there was a Rose that mimicked Aeterna and could drain the life of plants. Was she talking about you?" The question was silly, but the corner of Estelle's lips turned in a small grin.

"Yes, I would assume so." She pulled back and tapped her jaw thoughtfully. "I'd be shocked if it had been someone else."

"What does it feel like? To drain them, I mean."

Her lashes fluttered when she glanced back at the dead peonies. A pause. A beat of silence as the breeze twisted her thick black hair.

Estelle inhaled and stared at her palm. "Power, Elita. To take the moisture of a plant and turn it into energy of my own—to take the life of a person…" She stopped and an invisible string seemed to pull at her back and she rolled her shoulders. "Well, every ability comes at a cost. I've lost more than I have gained."

I tried not to let it bring me unease, in the same way I refused to fear Sol's abilities.

Estelle shuffled on her feet, her hands clasping behind her. "Aeterna was feared by the other deities for her ability to create life, while being able to take it just as easily. An outcast among them all, except Esen. There's a spot in Aeterna's book that mentions that. Have you reached it?" she asked, moving to sit on a stone bench, her hands now folded in her lap.

My brow creased and I shook my head. "Esen? Is he not the reason she tore through the realm?" I asked, his name one that never failed to raise the hair on my arms.

"No one can say for certain. Much of our history is lost. But the way their domains interacted, the connection they shared, he admired her. At least, that's how it's made to seem. Some would argue Esen was equally as in love with her before selfish desires led to her fall."

I hummed, looking at the flowers. "It makes little sense that Aeterna was cast out when the other deities have ravaged the realm in their own ways." I met her gaze. "Esen is meant to rule over the skies, and yet deadly storms rage in his wake. Cordelia once drowned an entire civilization, and Akuma is death itself," I said, glancing at the water not far from us. "How can they not bear the same shame or guilt?"

Estelle grinned, wide. "You're a wise woman, Elita. Now, do you think it is the deities who accept their faults that bring unbalance, or the ones who cast their shame on others?"

The answer was obvious, but it still made little sense that Aeterna would curse the earth. By the histories, she adored the land and took great pride in how it flourished. It was out of character for her to tear through her domain over bitterness and heartbreak. She was spoken of as wise, powerful, never selfish.

I sighed, my mind muddled with exhaustion. Wondering drained more energy than I had to offer. The once pink peony drew my attention. It rested in a heap of gray wrinkled petals. Wilted and weak. It was the first I went to, the only one I still hadn't figured out how to mend.

Mint was easy. A simple plant, and it smelled delightful. Spearmint rushed my senses when it got crushed. It always mended the quickest. Invigorating in more than just its aroma. Roses weren't difficult, either.

Before I knew mending was an oddity, I had mended many plants similar to it. A plucked flower here. A torn stem there.

The peonies remained elusive, and I never brought them back. They had no hint of a thrum. Estelle drained every bit of their energy. No echo. No pulse. Still, I stuck my hand into the soil by the peony. It was cold and damp; freshly watered. I didn't want to hover my hand. It needed a more intense touch. At least, I hoped it would be enough to bring it back.

I waited for the pulse that was snuffed out—stolen from the flower as it already struggled in the cold air. Dirt settled around my fingers. It lit them up, still sensing the life from the root of the rose and mint. I had to tune them out or I would never help the peony.

Close by, the waterfall roared. It drowned out most of the sounds, save for a few birds as they tried to find somewhere warmer. Damp soil stuck to my skin. Sweat prickled at the surface of my neck, though the day was mild at best. The effort of mending nipped at me, and my energy drained quicker than I ever thought possible.

When the thrum escaped me, I withdrew my hand. "I can't help the peonies."

Estelle stepped closer. "You need to try again. Mending must become more than a few snapped stems brought together. If there is no new life, there is no saved realm."

"The pressure doesn't help."

"The pressure occurs naturally. Our realm is dying. Let the desperation motivate you." She stared with expectation, with hope, and a hint of fear. She loved her people, and wouldn't rest until I did better.

Her care for the realm fueled my own, and I dug my fingers back in and allowed her smile of satisfaction to be my motivation to continue.

Twenty-Four

ches rattled every inch of me after another day of being forced to perform. Another day I wanted to refuse. But I allowed myself to be persuaded.

My desire to be needed took precedence over everything else.

Halburn would scold me, but I refused to go to the healing center. I made my way to the palace for another book to read while I rested. Dirt still covered my hands. I paid it no mind.

A handful of people meandered through the palace. It wasn't as busy as usual, something I was grateful for.

When I made my way into the library, it appeared vacant. The other side of the room held the books I was most drawn to, and I walked back to where Estelle first handed me Aeterna's story.

It was taking me longer than I expected to finish it. The differences filled me with more dread than it did answers. I often wished my father were there to help decipher it. I still wasn't comfortable enough with Valor to ask him questions regarding it. I was grateful for my time spent with Estelle. She knew more about our histories than anyone else I had met.

I brushed my hand over the spine of a book. Dust clung to my skin, a contrast to the dark soil from the planter. It smelled of old pages, and the muted room made exhaustion weigh heavier on my shoulders.

The sun continued to beat on the expansive windows. It cast a cascade of colors across the bookshelves. Exhaustion aside, I grinned at the sight, and continued my search.

None of the titles stuck out to me, and it took great effort to remind myself that I didn't have to read what was known to me. The comfort may have been nice, but it didn't help me find any answers.

Among the many spines, I spotted a book titled: *'Abilities: a Guide for Roses.'*

It sparked my interest, and I plucked it from the shelf. The other books shifted with the vacancy.

The cover swirled with vines adorned with thorns. Gold paint shimmered in the warm afternoon light, and I ran a hand over it. It appeared less used than Aeterna's story, though a lone mark folded a page in the center. I flipped to it and straightened the paper.

Sketches filled the page of vines and roots. It spoke of the different types, widths, and how to determine the difference by the thrum in the earth. It reminded me a lot of what I spent my days learning among the leaders who took it upon themselves to teach me.

Flipping through it, I watched the different titles to find something of interest. It took me a few chapters before a familiar word jumped at me: *'Dreamwalking and its History.'*

Details poured over the pages, with information about the bloodline who carried it, and what little was known in regards to the ability. It mentioned the link to lucid dreaming, a side effect often associated with the blue lotus flower. But after the few facts I already knew, thanks to Casimir, I spotted a sketch.

The woman appeared young, perhaps twenty at the time the portrait was done. Her face was drawn among many others, but the resemblance was easy to spot. Her features matched Casimir's in a way that made me smile.

'Ruelle Vanmore, Lieutenant General of Everbloom. Able to dreamwalk, describes it as awake but unable to move. Present and not.'

The next page held more sketches, more explanations. Personal experiences, and the different methods used to dreamwalk. Another page was dedicated to the act of dreamwalking while aware and able to move. The act of speaking through thoughts, by bridging a lucid dream tether. It noted the characteristics it shared with the blue lotus flower, such as anxiety relief, the ability to aid sleep.

Information filled the pages, things I had never heard, things not even Casimir had explained to me, like the tether or sleep aid. I closed the book and tucked it under my arm. I wondered how much of it Casimir knew or if anything in the pages offered more understanding of his unique abilities.

With exhaustion pulling at my eyelids, I left the palace, the book in hand. When I crossed paths with Casimir, perhaps it'd interest him. Or he'd already know everything the book said, and I'd have wasted his time. There hadn't been time to find out what knowledge Everbloom held or what his mother taught him before she died. Bringing the book to Casimir suddenly had me wrought with worry that I'd humiliate myself.

I had no idea what I would say to him. *"Here, Cas, I saw this and thought of you."* It was mortifying.

On my way back through the markets, I spotted a head of white hair in the colorful sea of bodies. Armor on and a cloak over his shoulders like always. Though it made me uncomfortable, I changed my course and went toward Orin. If anyone knew whether Casimir read it or not, it'd be him.

When I stopped beside him, he didn't spare me a glance. Crossness immediately tugged at me but I didn't let it be a deterrent.

"Orin," I said, trying to get his attention while he continued to search through a market stand filled with an assortment of weapons. He either chose to ignore me or didn't hear.

I sighed. "Orin." My tone pitched higher, and he glanced up.

Curiosity turned to abhorrence within a matter of seconds. "Who died?" Orin asked.

My brows raised. "What kind of question is that?"

Orin huffed. "What other reason would there be for the white bloom to approach me?"

I paused, insecure about my question. My hand gripped the book tighter, and I turned it to face Orin. "Has Casimir read this?" The question sounded foolish.

Orin's face contorted with confusion, and he grabbed it from me. He tucked a slick white strand of hair behind his ear and flipped through the book for a moment. He paused midway through and scanned over the page about dreamwalking.

The embarrassment increased when he snickered.

"No, I can't say he has. I haven't seen this literature before. Where did you find this?" Orin asked.

"Palace libraries."

The look Orin gave me when he handed it back held less disdain. Whatever the strange dynamic was with the two, Orin seemed to approve of the gesture.

After an uncomfortable pause, Orin waved me off. "If that is all, would you allow me to return to browsing?" His tone clipped with frustration.

"Thanks…I think." I darted out of the markets. Too exhausted to consider letting Halburn poke at me.

I trudged the path to the tents as I wiped the dirt off the book with the edge of my tunic. It came untucked, and the gray fabric wasn't dark enough to hide the stains from the soil. My nails were no better. They appeared black underneath from being deep in the planter. A bath would've been nice but I chose to wait until after I gave Casimir the book and slept.

My sleeping arrangement with Casimir continued to pay off, and I spotted the tent, close to the camp entrance. It saved me time, and I couldn't wait to collapse into the bed before he returned from swimming.

I stopped in front of the tent, undoing the many ties.

The drapes fell open, and to my surprise, Casimir sat on the floor, using my bed cushion for a seat.

Maps sprawled out around him, and he held a quill in his hand. His hair still appeared damp, and the waves curled in at the edges around his temples and ears. He wore a wool knit with the sleeves pushed up to his elbows, along with loose trousers. He looked comfortable, slight fatigue pulling at his features, and his skin slightly tanned from a day swimming in the sun.

It took him a long pause before he met my gaze.

"Back already?" he asked, setting the quill down.

"I didn't mean to interrupt. I can go to my tent—"

"No, it's fine. Tired?"

I bit the inside of my cheek and closed the drapes behind me. "I think mending might kill me," I muttered.

He quirked a brow. "Don't say that. I won't let you do it again."

Heat rippled through my limbs, and I wanted to dart back out of the tent at the sensation. "You know you couldn't stop me."

Amusement flashed across his face. "Not even if I begged?"

I turned my head to hide the embarrassment.

Casimir chuckled and brought his attention back to his maps. My fingers brushed the cover of the book while I walked further into the tent. Wordlessly, I tossed it beside him on the ground. It made a soft thump on the stone, and he glanced at it for a moment, then at me.

"What's this?" he asked.

I shrugged while he picked it up. "Just something I saw in the library. There's a whole section on dreamwalking. I thought it might interest you."

Casimir's brow knitted together, and his gaze once again darted between me and the book.

"I mean, not to imply you don't know how to dreamwalk, obviously you do. But I asked Orin, and he said you hadn't read it yet, so I thought —"

"You spoke to Orin? Willingly?" Casimir asked, stunned.

"I didn't want to bring you a book you'd already read. And, well—" My arms crossed and I knotted my hands in the fabric of my tunic. "I thought you might like it. There's a whole section in there where it mentions your mother."

Casimir stared at me for a long moment, emotions building beneath the surface until mirth shone in his eyes. He finally tore his gaze from mine and flipped through the pages. Casimir paused on the part about dreamwalking. He scanned over it, stopping when he got to the sketch of his mother.

A shaky sigh escaped his lips. "Thank you, El." I heard the catch in his voice. Looking back at me, he said, "This means more to me than you know."

Warmth pooled in my stomach, a flutter of butterflies. "Of course." I gave him a timid smile and skirted close to the bed, careful not to disturb his maps or notebooks.

My boots came off, and I set them at the end of the bed.

Casimir tore a plain piece of parchment and tucked it into the open page. He closed the book, and after a pause, he set it down next to his maps, picking up his quill.

"So, what's all this?" I asked.

Casimir looked over his shoulder at me, scarlet eyes full of warmth and familiarity. The smile made the dimple in his cheek appear.

Please look away. Don't notice the color of my face.

He shuffled in his spot, bringing a knee up toward his chest where he rested an arm, quill in his hand. "I've also been in the library a bit since we got here. They have maps I've never seen before. It's quite intriguing."

"Hmm, is it?" I teased.

Casimir rolled his eyes and threw a wadded-up piece of parchment at me. I chuckled and tossed it at the back of his head. The scarlet petal shimmered where the sun peered through gaps in the tent. I wanted to reach out and touch it.

I tucked my hands under my thighs.

He quirked a brow at me. "Why don't you sleep then and let me get back to my boring maps?"

"I like teasing you. It's entertaining. Don't take that from me."

Casimir scoffed. "You know what's more entertaining?" A beat of silence passed as he stared at me beneath black lashes. "You being perpetually red in the face. Is there something in the air of Mistvalle? Or is it a rash, maybe?"

My hands rolled into tight balls against the cushion. "It's a rash." I laid on the pillow before he could get a better look at my face.

I hadn't ever been so flustered around him. But my thoughts became consumed by his hands on my shoulders, and his breath on my ear. Sleeping in his clothes. His warm, smooth honey-like laughter. How his eyes lit up when his lips pulled into tender smile—

"I've been thinking," Casimir started to say, "would you be up for swimming lessons tonight? I'll teach you myself, of course. I've taught most of those on my squad."

I turned on the bed until I faced him, a mistake, when I noticed how close he had moved to the frame. His back was touching the wood as he brought his maps closer to where he sat, still using my cushion.

When he noticed me watching, he froze. "My back was killing me leaning over like that."

"Of course."

"So, what do you say?"

"Hmm? To what?"

Casimir chuckled. "You really do need sleep." He dipped his quill in ink and focused on his maps. "Swimming lessons. Tonight. With me."

I nibbled my inner cheek.

Something about the way he looked at me pulled at the bars around my heart. After Ronin's betrayal, it felt safer not to allow others in. Keep my distance. I feared if I let Casimir in, I would lose more of myself. Not just pieces, but everything. All of me.

Alarm bells rang in my head when I spoke. "If I can finally catch up on some sleep, you can teach me whatever you want."

Twenty-Five

The moon hid behind thick clouds, drenching us in darkness. It took Casimir a few tries before the lantern he brought flickered to life in a dance of flames. I followed him down to the black water at the end of the path I took earlier with Taryn and Ulrik. White trees and bright red leaves drooped close to the water's edge.

We set down two towels, and within a matter of seconds, I realized I should've brought extra clothing.

Casimir set the lantern on a rock near the towels. Every flick of the flame caused the forest shadows to distort and bend. The light echoed over the inky black surface of the water in a mesmerizing display. I watched in a daze, and didn't notice Casimir beside me until he tugged his wool knit over his head and tossed it on the ground. Next were his trousers, leaving him in his undergarments. Heat crawled up my neck and I meant to look away, but stopped when I noticed how far the scar stretched down his back.

It was the first time I'd seen the rest of it.

"How did you get that?" I blurted, disrupting the quiet.

Casimir glanced back at me, smirking. "Nasty run in with a drought lander," he said with a shrug. The muscles in his back flexed with every movement, and I bit my lip, tearing my gaze away.

"Sorry," I mumbled while I tried to find somewhere else to look.

Casimir chuckled, and beneath the sound, I heard the water lap when he broke the still surface. "Don't apologize. It was a bad call on my part. It had been my first scouting mission as the captain of my own team. I took on a bit more than I could handle at the time."

When he didn't elaborate any further, I couldn't help but meet his gaze. He held a hand out for me as water wrapped around his waist and soaked trousers.

"Are you sure we should be doing this?" It came out squeaky, hitched with nerves.

Casimir quirked a brow. "We're already here, and I've disposed of my clothes. You want to go back to camp?"

My eyes widened, and I was thankful for the cover of darkness when humiliation colored me pink. "I'm not sure if this is a good idea," I said. "My last encounter with swimming wasn't very pleasant."

"Exactly why you need to learn. Mistvalle is surrounded by water on almost every side. It'd be wise to know how."

My hesitation wasn't for the skill itself but for who intended to teach me. I trusted Casimir to keep me safe, but I didn't trust how my pulse quickened around him.

It took a moment to steady my heart.

Discarding my slip shoes, I set them close to Casimir's wool knit.

"Look away," I instructed, my hands going to the waistband of my trousers. Casimir cleared his throat and turned his gaze to the open water. Despite how much I didn't want to, I removed my linen trousers, leaving me in a pair of short bloomers. I wouldn't dare remove my top.

"Don't look for a moment," I said as my feet dipped into the icy water. It lit my skin with goosebumps, and I gasped. "How are you so far in?"

Casimir laughed, shrugging. "It's not so bad. Can I turn now?" he asked. Though I wasn't deep enough to hide my undergarments, I muttered a nervous, "Yes."

He turned, keeping his eyes on my face, and offered me his hand. I hoped he couldn't see how I trembled. His hand swallowed mine with rough skin but a tender touch. When he tugged on me, I followed him deeper into the water. It reached my waist, and I shivered.

"This lesson better be quick." My teeth chattered.

Casimir rolled his eyes. "It was warmer earlier, had you let me teach you then."

"And have Estelle scold me for missing a session? No thank you." My feet brushed the floor of the lake, knocking tiny pebbles out of place. Water clung to my top and undergarments, and in turn, every inch of fabric stuck to my body in a frigid embrace.

Each step I took, the water got higher until it reached my collarbones. Only then did the panic set in, and I struggled to stay on my tiptoes. The water reached Casimir's bare chest, but due to his height, he didn't struggle as much with the depth of the lake.

It made my lungs constrict, and I shifted on my arched feet. "I'm not sure I can do this," I muttered. "When I crossed the Forge—"

"I won't let you go, El." His scarlet gaze flitted over my face and his throat bobbed. He turned his attention anywhere but me. "The general would have my head if I let you drown."

"You'd make light of the white bloom drowning?" I countered, my tone roguish.

"That prophecy means nothing." He scoffed then tugged me deeper into the water. Without thinking, my hands grabbed his shoulders and I squeezed them, trying to stay afloat.

Casimir grabbed my waist to steady me. "Allow yourself to float. Let me show you how."

The quickening of my pulse would make me dizzy if it didn't quit. I nodded and released some of my grip on his warm skin. It left droplets of water behind, and I watched as they trailed down his chest.

Carefully, he released my waist. His hands hovered near my sides. "Take a deep breath, and let your body relax—I know, impossible for you," he teased. "But try anyway."

My bottom lip pulled between my teeth to hold back a smile. I watched his eyes trail over my mouth, and a muscle in his jaw twitched. Unfamiliar warmth coursed through my body in response.

The air stilled. Only the lapping water filled the silence. His thigh brushed mine as the push and pull of the lake seemed to bring us closer.

"Are you going to show me how?" I asked quietly.

A soft breath parted his lips. "Show you what?"

I had to stop myself from inching closer. "How to swim, Cas."

His eyes widened and he put more space between us, clearing his throat. "Right. It's cold. We shouldn't take too long." He never moved too far, but kept more distance from me. I tried not to take offense and attempted to do what he suggested.

"We'll start with floating on your back. It's the easiest way to at least make sure you can stay above water," Casimir said.

The thought filled me with dread but I nodded. I inhaled and let my head tilt back. It hovered a few inches over the surface, and some of my curls dipped into the water.

The icy temperature prickled at my neck, and I jolted upright.

"I can't," I stammered.

Casimir inched closer. "Do you want my help?"

"Isn't that why you're here?"

He smirked and dipped his head. "Yes, I suppose it is." He closed more of the space. "I'll just—" He paused and brought a hand around to my back. "Is this okay?" he asked, palm flattened against the curve of my spine.

I could barely nod in response.

"My apologies, I forgot you asked I not touch you after your spar with Sol," he said.

I chuckled. "I'll make an exception."

Casimir hummed in response and, with his hand on my back, some of the tension in my limbs eased.

His other hand dipped into the water. "Let your legs come up," he instructed.

I inhaled through my nose and did as he said until the weightlessness carried my legs halfway up to the surface. At first, they jolted in a panic, but Casimir's hand fell to the crease behind my knees.

A squeal of surprise disrupted the tranquility, and the urge to hide overwhelmed me. Casimir didn't mock me; his hands held on tighter and urged me to the surface. I allowed him to guide my body until I became suspended in the water, his hands still on me.

"Use slow and controlled breaths. You'll float," he said.

It sounded simple but the lightweight sensation brought me back to the vision of Akuma pulling me out of the water, and I flailed.

Casimir's grip tightened. "That's the opposite of what I said. You're awful at following directions," he mused.

"Or you're a horrible teacher," I quipped, pushing the memory back. My focus went to his chest when it softly brushed against my soaked linens. Heat crept up my neck when I had the sudden urge to run my hands over his collarbones.

"I think I'm done," I breathed.

Casimir appeared confused. "We've barely started, and you've made no progress." He searched my face for an answer, but I worried all he would see was how splotchy my cheeks were.

"It feels wrong to let go."

The admission was sobering, and once more, his eyes scanned over me. This time, they trailed from my face to the side of my neck. Insecurity weighed me down when I remembered the scar left by Talos. The skin healed long ago, but a thick, twisted white scar remained.

"You need to be able to protect yourself. It's important." The intensity of his tone took me off guard.

Casimir was right. I couldn't rely on others to always be there to save me. Even if we were far from the old dangers that used to haunt me. I nearly lost my life in the past due to my lack of important skills. Whether it was Casimir pulling me out of the cursed water so long ago or how Ronin had the upper hand on me.

If I didn't learn, I would continue needing to be saved.

I made another attempt at relaxing above the water. It shifted against my body, causing me to sway in Casimir's grip. He observed me and released some of his hold.

In the mild night, on the cusp of wither, I continued to repeat the same task over and over, even as frustration crept in. Too much time passed with me shivering and failing but I was determined to float without assistance.

Eventually, I let go enough, and my body stayed afloat on the surface without Casimir's help. I grinned with pride, even as my chin shivered.

"Good. Now, straighten and try to stay floating, but follow my movements," Casimir instructed.

When I tried to move, the lack of solid ground beneath my feet sent fear shooting through my veins.

He didn't need me to ask—Casimir swam closer, and a hand splayed across my back while the other cupped the curve of my waist. I knew he was only helping me, but the intimacy of his touch made my stomach flip. Did he handle everyone the same while training? Something told me the answer was no.

Casimir brought me closer to the shore until my feet brushed the bottom surface. To my surprise, he didn't let go. He held me there for a pause. It was subtle, but I saw how his eyes traced the curve of my parted mouth once more.

The water lapped against my freezing skin and I became too aware of our proximity along with his lack of a shirt. It made things worse when I noted the way my sleep clothes hugged my body, exposing more than I was accustomed to.

When another shiver shook my shoulders, Casimir tore his gaze from my face. "We can finish this when the sun is out. It'll be warmer." His words clipped, and he released me.

It was foolish, but I felt a pang of disappointment. I told myself it was because I had only learned to float and not swim—not related to the distance Casimir put between us.

We moved through the crisp water and back into the grass. My linen top adhered to my body like another layer of skin. The towel worked to dry off some of the water, but my top still clung to me, and the bloomers immediately soaked the trousers when I pulled them on. I wrapped my arms around myself to hide how exposed I was.

Casimir shook out his wool knit and went to pull it back on, but paused. "Do you want this? It's dry," he said, offering it to me.

"Oh, no, I couldn't do that. I'd hate to hear the stories Alba would churn if we returned to the tents with you half undressed."

Casimir walked to me—his trousers already back on—leaving behind wet prints in the dead grass. He stopped close and offered it again. "I'm not worried about what Alba thinks."

The look in his eye filled me with warmth, and wordlessly, I took the thick knit sweater from his hands. He watched me for a moment, and I swallowed the nerves.

"Do I put this over my soaked top, or...?"

Casimir tensed and turned quickly.

The wet shirt came off with a struggle, and it wasn't lost on me how it was the second time I found myself in such a state around him.

When the dry fabric caressed my body, I sighed in relief. I only wished for dry trousers to accompany it. I bent and grabbed my wet linen top and wrung it out into the dry grass.

"Are you ready to head back?" I asked, sliding on my slip shoes.

Casimir faced me, his chin quivering.

I chuckled. "I'll take that as a yes."

"Is my discomfort amusing?" He cocked his head. "Perhaps I should ask for my shirt back, then?"

"If you want it back, you'll have to take it off me yourself." I shrugged.

A flicker of something I hadn't seen before swam in his eyes, making the statement feel more scandalous than intended.

His tongue clicked as he turned toward the path. "Right. Let's head back."

Humiliation overcame me when I ran my words over in my mind several times, and I wished there was a way to take them back.

I bit the inside of my cheek and followed him to the path, neither of us saying another word.

The path was unknown to me, and I had to trail closer to Casimir than I wanted to. A thick cloud of discomfort hung over my head while mulling over what I said. I only meant it in jest, but I worried he thought I was serious. The thought was mortifying.

My hand reached out and grabbed his forearm, preventing him from going any farther. He froze and glanced down at me, shocked. I tried to apologize for making him uncomfortable, but the way he stared made me pause.

Despite the bite in the air, his forearm flushed with warmth beneath my palm. It threatened to pull me closer than two friends typically found themselves.

Casimir's body turned toward mine, but I didn't let go. My lips parted with words that wanted to scramble out. Apologies, horrible truths that took me off guard, and things I couldn't take back.

Heavy footfalls from the path interrupted the tense moment, pulling my attention up the trail to see a figure moving closer. Valor's features came into view, and my hand dropped from Casimir's arm.

Casimir glanced at me, confused. He must've been oblivious, because the sight of him shirtless and me wearing his wool knit painted a suspicious picture.

Valor froze and surveyed the two of us. "Captain Vanmore, would you care to explain why you both are out at this hour?"

"Swimming lessons, sir," Casimir said without hesitation.

Valor raised a brow. "In the dark of night, and as wither moves in?" he asked, skeptical.

I put more space between myself and Casimir. "My parents never taught me how," I blurted. "When Casimir first found me, I had nearly drowned. And with how busy my days have been with training and mending, there hasn't been room for any other skills." It came out too rushed, as if I were lying, though each word was the truth.

Valor scoffed in response, which made it worse. "Alba or Taryn would be adequate teachers, Fullan."

I pursed my lips and dared a glance at Casimir. He appeared offended and crossed his arms over his bare chest. "I've successfully taught many in our guard how to swim. Has something happened that would make you question my capabilities?" Casimir's question was genuine, and it seemed to convince Valor of the situation.

"No, Captain. However, I would insist on training in the light of day. Elita needs her rest to recoup her strength before she trains in the morning." Valor spoke as if it were a warning.

Casimir nodded. "That was our assessment as well, General. If that's all, I'd like to return Elita to her tent," Casimir said. I cast a glance at him, wondering why he chose to lie.

Valor bristled. "See that this doesn't happen again."

It was the first thing to make Casimir falter, and he met my gaze, searching for the answer to Valor's off behavior.

I nearly laughed at his obliviousness.

"Yes, of course, sir," Casimir stammered.

Valor's cheek twitched. "When you've made yourself decent, you're needed in the council hall. Lady Estelle has requested an update on battle plans."

Casimir tensed. "Yes, General."

Valor gave me another suspicious glance before he turned and parted ways up a different path, scarcely lit with small torches.

I pursed my lips, trying to stifle a chuckle.

When Casimir gave me a bewildered look, laughter burst from my chest. His lips curved in a sideways grin. "What is it that you find so amusing?" he asked.

"If it isn't obvious, I'd rather not have to say." My laughter settled, and I wrapped my arms around my torso.

He appeared even more confused. "Whatever it is, I've never seen the general look as if he wanted to kill me more."

I hummed in amusement and took a step further up the path. "We should go before you freeze to death."

Casimir nodded, and we made our way back to the tent, shivering the entire way. I didn't envy him and his lack of clothing. His wool knit offered me some respite from the cold and damp. Not enough, though, and we both stumbled into his tent. Both of our teeth chattered, disrupting the quiet. Casimir moved with purpose, digging through the chest in the far right corner. He threw me a completely dry, long-sleeved, black tunic. Continuing his search, he kept his back turned to me.

I shuffled into the left side corner, and stripped off the now damp knit, replacing it with the dry tunic. It was longer than the last one and fell to the midpoint of my thighs. I shimmied off my trousers and replaced the damp bloomers with dry ones, then went to my sleeping mat.

Sliding under my layered quilt, I shivered with delight at the relief from the wet and cold. The wool layer cradled me in a comfortable embrace, and I sighed.

Casimir chuckled in response while he gathered his things. I didn't need him to tell me—I turned over on my mat and faced the canvas fabric.

The tunic he gave me smelled like patchouli and something else. I assumed the underlying scent was just *him*. It was soft against my skin, and I burrowed deeper in the quilts.

I heard him fiddle with the buckles on his armor, then his boots. He never told me to turn, so I stayed facing the deep blue wall of the tent. It shuddered with the breeze.

Beneath the sound of wind, clattering filled the tent. It sounded like iron pots, and my curiosity got the best of me.

I faced Casimir, ready to turn in case he wasn't decent.

A cloak was already fashioned over his shoulders, nearly blending into the full black armor he wore. In his hands was a kettle, and he set it over a burning lantern, allowing the flame to lick at the bottom of it.

He moved back from it, brushed a hand through his hair, and faced me. "In case I'm not back before you're asleep. That way, you can make tea with whatever the healer gave you."

Knots twisted in my stomach. A pleasant, warm kind of nerves. I offered him a small smile. "Thanks, Cas."

He dipped his head and turned to leave without another word. I watched him go, my heart in my throat.

Twenty-Six

An hour passed and I gave up on reading through the end of Aeterna's story. If I didn't fall asleep, the next morning would be full of regret. The day would consist of more training, more mending. It continued to drain me. I considered telling them all no, and allowing Casimir to finish teaching me to swim.

The kettle whistled on the top of the small table. I walked over to it, dreading sleep without Casimir close by. I was grateful for Halburn, but the tea didn't do enough. At least the nightmares wouldn't last long. They always ended when Casimir returned.

Steaming water poured over the tea sachet. Some of the herbs escaped the cloth and floated to the top of the mug—tiny shreds of flowers, lavender buds, and other herbs. The comforting scents wafted through the space and I breathed it in. The mint and lavender were soothing, and though licorice had never been a favorite of mine, I grew to like it.

I walked back to my mat and sat with my mug in hand. The steam twisted above the lip of it, and my gentle exhales rippled across the surface, trying to cool the tea quickly.

While waiting to drink it, I glanced around the tent, and my attention fell to the maps scattered in a corner. Among them, pieces of Casimir's steel armor sat untouched. Books were stacked close to the maps, their titles all pertaining to strategy, sparring techniques, and one solely on weapons and their uses.

When the tea cooled enough, I sipped at it, eyeing the maps and the lines marked on them. A smaller parchment paper appeared hand drawn, showing guard strategies.

Casimir never spoke much about his place on the guard, but I could tell he carried his title of captain with pride.

When I drank the last sip of tea, I laid down and pushed my curls up over the pillow. It was cold on my neck, which brought me a shiver of delight.

The herbs moved through my system, attempting to drag me toward restful sleep. My body tried to resist it, no matter how much I needed the rest. My eyelids were heavy and fell shut despite the protest of my mind. Nightmares awaited me, but I couldn't bring myself to pull Casimir out of an important meeting with the leaders, no matter how much unease it caused me to be far from him since the visions started. It would be inappropriate, and cause more whispers throughout Mistvalle. There was enough to go around, thanks to Alba and the scene I caused with Novian.

I tossed and turned for what felt like another hour. The restlessness left me frustrated. Somewhere close by, a raven cried out. It grew louder as time went on, almost frantic, and I pressed a hand to my ear, trying to muffle the sound.

A soft rustle at the drapes made my body sink deeper into the mat. Relief unwound the tension in my body when I realized Casimir returned already. I must've laid there much longer than I thought. I kept my eyes shut and didn't turn to look at him. His late nights with the council were a common occurrence, and I waited for his boots to thud against the stone when he took them off.

They never did.

Soft footsteps padded closer and I sensed him staring down at me. My heart jumped into my throat, and though I didn't want to, I turned on the mat to look at him.

Terror stiffened my spine when I stared back at the figure that loomed above me.

I opened my mouth to speak, but before a single word made its way out, the person dropped and forced a hand over my mouth. On instinct, I kicked at the air and thrashed against their hold.

They smelled of smoke, and it overwhelmed me as their burly frame overpowered mine. When their hands released my mouth and moved to my throat, I barely let out a yelp before the air locked in my windpipe.

They're going to suffocate me if I don't do something. The thought didn't ease the panic. My limbs jerked aimlessly as I tried to escape the person whose face remained hidden in the shadows.

My right arm flung at them and made contact with their cheekbone, but they didn't release me. I tried to conjure vines or pelt the stranger with thorns, but my fear, like the person's hands, choked me.

The lack of air made me dizzy, even so, I brought my hands up and clawed at their arms, desperate to hurt them enough to get them to let go. The person grunted and shoved my head back on the stone. Beneath the thrum of fear, I realized how much my companions held back when we sparred. Even Sol, when she implied she wouldn't. The person put their entire weight into it, trapping my legs with their ankles while their hands dug deeper into my skin, causing pain to ripple through me.

"They should have left you to die in Orondal." The voice was husky, a male, and not one I recognized.

My head swam, and spots erupted in my vision. Black and scarlet swam at the corner of my eyes. It slowly devoured everything until it became a void as heat crept through my veins.

"You'll pay your debt to Everbloom with your life," the man spat.

The tendrils across my vision tightened, and in a last effort to get him off, I slammed my palm to his eye. It was enough to get him to release me. I rolled away and heaved for air, then scrambled to stand.

"Help!" I rasped, reaching for the drapes.

The man pulled me back, forcing me into the wooden chest in the corner. It slammed into my back and I cried out.

His hands wrapped around my throat, and I saw the first glimpse of his face. I hardly knew him, but I'd seen him every day on the ship during the long voyage. He was always quiet, tending to the ropes and supply crates. On a few occasions, he had helped me carry heavy crates. And some nights, before I started staying with Casimir, I had noticed him out later than the others. He was almost always present in the camp when I left my tent in a late night panic.

My head weighed a ton, and it lolled back, going slack in his hands as the lightheadedness increased.

I wondered briefly if he would leave my body for Casimir to find or if he would toss me over the cliff's edge—never to be found in the rushing water below.

"Hey!" A familiar accent roared through the tent, and through slitted eyes, I spotted Taryn in the opening of the drapes.

The man didn't have time to react before a wisp of long black hair appeared behind him, slamming his body into the floor.

I gasped and fell forward. My vision blurred as my chest heaved, greedily pulling in air. Taryn dropped beside me and moved me further from the man's body while Alba forced his arms behind his back. The man yowled, but she didn't release him. If anything, it looked like she pulled his arms tighter.

"Elita, look at me." Taryn's voice grabbed my attention, and I struggled for another breath. Anger and panic both swirled in her orange gaze as she surveyed me for injuries. She went rigid when she looked at my eyes. "Are you hurt anywhere else?" she asked.

I shook my head, and the pain in my neck doubled.

Taryn scanned over my neck, her face twisting with disgust. "Alba, we need to get her to Halburn," Taryn said.

Alba whipped her head our way, and it was the most dangerous I had ever seen her. An animalistic expression crossed her face. "I should break his arms," she hissed through clenched teeth.

Taryn didn't protest, but when she gently moved the hair out of my face, her worried expression deepened. "The general will know what to do with him. We need to go."

I glanced at the exit of the tent, and more dread dizzied my head when I thought about what would've happened if they hadn't been close.

I swallowed against the pain in my throat. "How did you know?" The question scratched its way out, thick with emotion.

Taryn's expression melted from anger to something somber. "Heading back from the tavern when we heard you." Taryn's voice caught, and every muscle in my body turned rigid. She squeezed my shoulder. "It's okay. We're here."

Her words did little to ease the spiral of horrific thoughts. If they had already been in their tents for the night, or if they had been a little further down the path...

I shivered and pushed the emotions away before I retched.

Cautiously, Taryn helped me stand. My legs shook with adrenaline, and I struggled to steady myself. Taryn pressed a hand to my shoulder blade and guided me toward the drapes. I watched Alba tighten her grip on the man and jerk him to his feet, and in turn, he groaned and tried to fight out of her hold—the wrong choice. His arm popped, and he yowled again.

Malice tainted every twitch of Alba's face. She never looked so terrifying, and it brought me another wave of gratitude.

Taryn didn't let me linger. She rushed me out of the tent and put more distance between us and the man who continued to spew curses.

People swarmed outside of Casimir's tent. They all appeared bewildered, and I wondered how many of them would take pity on the Everbloom man. The one who wanted me to pay for what I did. Didn't many of them want the same?

I avoided their intrusive gaze and watched my feet while Taryn walked with me. Her hand found exposed skin on my shoulder as the neck of the tunic slipped to one side, and a surge of her abilities filled my veins, and some of the discomfort in my neck eased. My lip quivered.

"Back to your tents," Taryn barked. "Bunch of nasty gossipers."

Murmurs filled the crowd as we shoved through to the path. I heard Alba and the man behind us, but I chose not to glance back, even when I heard someone running, their footfalls bringing them closer. The sound slowed a few feet away, and I heard Alba mumble something.

Galan's voice followed us. "He what?" His disbelief rang through the camp. I pursed my lips and tried to stop the way my chin trembled. "Of course. I will escort him to the general. Go with them," Galan said in a hushed voice.

I heard Alba whisper a thanks to Galan, and after a pause, she was at my other side. Her hand reached out, and she brushed curls behind my ear, then left her palm on my back.

"You're okay." Alba's reassurance seemed as if it were for herself as much as for me.

Both her and Taryn kept a hand on me, and I clung to the warmth.

We were halfway down the path before it dawned on me that I wore nothing but Casimir's tunic and short bloomers. I didn't have the energy to worry about it, and soon after, we reached the end of the path. It would have been worse to go back to camp, and the tunic was at least long enough to almost reach my knees.

The subtle thrum of Taryn's abilities helped to bring my heart rate back to a steadier rhythm, but if I thought too long about how grateful I was, I worried tears would fall and never stop.

I held the emotions back. My hands trembled at my sides and clenched into tight fists until my nails dug into the clammy skin. I tried not to pay attention to Galan behind us when he broke off and made way for the palace where they were having the council meeting.

Taryn and Alba brought me into the healing center, and in the late hour, many of the healers stood frantically when they noticed us enter. There were no other patients, as far as I could see. Few lanterns flickered, casting orange light over the white floors.

Familiar blonde hair caught my attention as Halburn scurried across the room.

"By the goddess, what caused this?" he asked, ushering us over to a far off cot. Halburn stood before me when I sat and immediately looked me over, pausing when he noted my eyes, then flinching at the sight of my neck. He glanced at Taryn and Alba with wide eyes.

"Someone from Everbloom attacked her while she slept," Taryn explained.

Halburn's expression soured. "Did she lose consciousness?" He directed his question to Taryn, and she shook her head. Halburn faced me. "May I scan you?" he asked. I gave a timid nod, and he placed a hand to my neck. It made me flinch, and he muttered an apology.

The room went silent as he focused, his eyes darting back and forth as he began his healing work. I was grateful he was present despite the late hour. His presence no longer made me uneasy, and I couldn't bear the way the other healers stared. Pity consumed their expressions, and they whispered among each other, making my face warmer.

Alba whipped her head around to glare at them, which cut off their whispers. My gratefulness burned at the edge of my eyes.

When the doors to the healing center swung open with ferocity, my entire body coiled.

Heavy footfalls echoed through the building, and I looked past Alba and Taryn to see Casimir storming toward us. His nostrils flared and fury burned in his gaze. In his full black armor, the cloak billowing behind him, he appeared more shadow than man.

The tension left my shoulders at the sight of him.

Halburn moved back when he finished his healing and went to shuffle through an herbal cart.

Casimir stopped in front of me, not bothering to address anyone in the room as he assessed the aftermath of the attack. He appeared haunted when he took note of my neck. Without a word, Casimir reached forward, hesitant. Both of his hands cautiously ran over the sore spots left by the man who attacked me.

I gulped against his fingertips as he eyed the damage.

Casimir's fury was palpable, and it distorted his expression. "Gods, Elita... What happened?" The tremble in his hands matched his voice. "Who did this?"

Taryn moved closer. "A man from Everbloom attacked her. Alba and I heard her scream when we were walking through the camp."

Casimir tore his gaze off my throat, and his eyes met mine. My fingers anxiously ran over the edge of the tunic he gave me.

"He came in as I fell asleep. I thought it was you," I whispered.

Horror crossed his face, and his shoulders shook with a heavy exhale. "Who was it?" he asked.

Alba looked from me to Casimir. "Did Galan not say?"

Casimir dropped his hands from me. He turned to Alba and Taryn. "*Who was he?*" he snapped.

Alba's brow pulled together. "It was Karion."

Whoever it was, Casimir seethed with anger and disbelief at the name. He faced me and searched the rest of my body for any other injuries, freezing when his gaze locked with mine. Sadness etched his brow, and gently, he turned my face, looking at the corner of my eye.

Taryn tucked her hands into the loops at the edge of her trousers as she said, "Karion's son died in Everbloom when the guards first came down. He'd just joined the Everbloom guard."

Casimir's fist clenched at his side. "Galan was right not to bring him into the council. He would already be dead."

My eyes widened. "Grief makes people do foolish things."

"You would defend him when he tried to kill you?"

"If I didn't bargain for Ronin—"

"No," Casimir cut in. "Had he been innocent, it was the right choice. You didn't know." Some of the anger dissipated in his features, and his tone softened. "We will deal with him as the general sees fit."

I bit at the skin inside my cheek.

Taryn came closer and put a hand on mine as it fiddled with the frays of my borrowed tunic. I halted the movement, and she gave me a knowing look. Without a word, she leaned in, embracing me with the careful touch one would handle an infant.

My walls crumbled.

Tears streaked my cheeks, and a sob tore from my chest. Casimir tensed, then pulled the privacy drape to my cot closed in a rush.

Taryn's arms squeezed tighter, and Alba put a hand on mine. Their presence was warm, a much needed comfort. I caved to the swell of emotions despite how long I tried not to break in front of others.

Taryn whispered her reassurance, and through the tears, I looked at Casimir. I saw the swarm of fear in his eyes, outweighing the rage. For the first time in months, he stared at me the way he had after Ronin—that same tangible fear I felt from him when he carried me onto the ship.

When my sobs settled, Taryn pulled back and wiped the tears from my cheeks. Alba moved her hand from mine after a gentle squeeze. Halburn stood off to the side, giving us space. I was grateful for his ability to read the situation.

A few quiet moments passed before more footsteps reverberated in the healing center. Three people, if I counted right. Their pace was urgent, and without warning, the curtain pulled back, making me jump.

Valor eyed the people around the cot, wild fury making him appear dangerous.

Estelle paused just inside the drape, a hand resting on her chest. It dropped slack at her side when she took note of my appearance. Galan followed them, and his attention fell to my neck the moment he spotted me. All of their stares burned against my skin, and I recoiled.

Casimir noticed and came closer to shield me from view as he faced his back to those who walked in. I tugged on the tunic until it was further down my thighs. I didn't have to ask anyone—Taryn already moved to pull the thin blanket over my lap.

"Halburn, how is she?" Estelle broke the quiet.

Halburn took a step closer and bowed his head in her direction. "Blackthorne will be fine. There's a lot of redness, a few blood vessels burst in her right eye, and she'll be sore for a while. All in all, we're lucky it's not worse."

Estelle nodded and faced Valor. "Well, General, it was one of your own. How do you wish to proceed?"

I peered around Casimir to see Valor. He stared at my neck, and I wished for the ability to disappear. The fury of a father burned down the hardened exterior he built, showing the remnants of fear in his gaze.

The nerve beneath Valor's eye twitched, and I watched him contemplate. It didn't take long for his features to darken. "Someone willing to take the life of another based on grief driven madness has no place here." His words dripped with malice. "A man willing to kill an innocent woman out of spite forfeits his right to exist."

Casimir appeared relieved at the response. I should've been indifferent or even grateful. But to watch a grieving father continue to pay for my poor decisions… My guilt continued to take precedence over actual sense.

Estelle stared at Valor, calculating her response, before she said, "For the time being, I will have him held in Mistvalle's prison. Decisions can be made once we are all level-headed."

Valor's fists curled. "You misunderstand me, my lady. The man has lost the right to live and shall be dealt with accordingly."

An unbalanced weight settled on my shoulders—gratitude for Valor's care for me, and dismay for the consequence dealt to another father blinded by grief.

Casimir's relief changed to a look of forlorn when he noticed my torn emotions on display, packaged in a shameful tear.

Halburn came over to the cot and pressed a warm cloth filled with what felt like grains of rice to my tense shoulder. I gave him a nod of thanks and held it over the front of my neck.

Halburn turned and cleared his throat. "Might I suggest you all take this elsewhere? Blackthorne needs rest. She's had enough stress."

Valor halted his conversation with Estelle, and uncomfortable silence wrapped around the small group of people. They all stared at me with pitiful expressions.

I held the warm rice cloth tighter when Valor took a few steps closer, standing at Casimir's side. The facial changes of a father were hard to miss. I had grown up seeing such fretful gazes many times.

It was more than I could bear, and I looked down at my lap, watching tears blot the fabric.

Valor sighed. "The council will meet and discuss what action to take. Until then, Karion must be guarded indefinitely."

I watched Casimir's feet shift. Clearly he didn't approve of what Valor said, but it brought me a shred of relief to know, for the time being, another person's blood wasn't on my hands.

Despite the tears that trailed my skin, I glanced up at Valor, and hoped he could see my gratitude. The sight of my face continued to cause him, and the others, to go rigid.

"We will have him taken to a cell and guarded at all times," Estelle confirmed, then took a timid step toward me. "It should go without saying, but you may rest. Do not worry yourself with mending or training. I'm relieved to see you mostly unharmed, dear girl." She offered a small smile and turned to pull Halburn to the side.

The two disappeared to the other side of the drape, and soon after, Alba gave my hand a gentle squeeze. "I'm so happy you're okay." Tears filled her eyes. "Try to rest."

With that, Alba stood and grabbed Galan's arm. They both left, along with Halburn and Estelle, leaving me with Taryn, Casimir, and Valor.

Casimir never looked at Valor. He watched my every move, glancing at the redness left by Karion's hands.

Taryn sighed as she stood. "Listen, we're all worried, but let's give the girl some privacy, alright?"

Casimir didn't move.

Valor took a step toward the drape before he paused. "Don't leave her side, Captain." Though it sounded like an order, something told me Casimir wouldn't have left even if Valor tried to make him. I was grateful when Valor departed, and the area cleared until it was only us three.

Some of the tension fell from my shoulders, and the way the herbs remained in my system made me yearn for sleep. When I tried to yawn, the muscles in my neck sparked with pain. I flinched, closing my mouth as soon as it opened.

Taryn noticed, frowned, then reached across me to the cart filled with herbs and tinctures. After trying to search through them with her arm outstretched past me, she huffed in frustration and got up.

While she dug through the cart, Casimir finally moved. He took timid steps closer and lifted a hand to my right temple. The pad of his thumb rested close to my eye as his hand trembled.

Taryn returned and froze when she noticed Casimir standing in front of me. She pursed her lips and stopped beside him. When she tapped his arm with a glass bottle, he barely glanced at it.

"Three drops. That's it. It'll do good for the aches and whatnot. Best to stay here for the night if she takes it."

Casimir nodded and took the bottle from her. She gave him a two-finger salute and darted behind the curtain, closing it more when she disappeared.

I heard murmuring on the other side; Estelle and Halburn. From what I made out, it sounded like Taryn dismissed the two.

When the noises settled, Casimir dropped his fingers from my face and undid the lid to the bottle. It came out with a glass dropper, and I tried not to grimace. The memories blurred, but I never forgot the days spent in the cell with Talos's torturous herbs.

But it wasn't Talos. It was Casimir, and his hand shook when he brought the dropper to my lips. He waited for me, and I couldn't bear to look at him when I opened my mouth. My focus went to the vaulted ceilings and when the tincture dripped on my tongue, I waited for a sensation I knew wouldn't come. There was no fire or ice shooting through my veins. It was mint and lemon, with an herb I couldn't place.

I swallowed and tried to relax my jaw as it quivered.

Casimir set the bottle on the herb cart. "You need to rest."

Lanterns flickered outside the curtain, and one shuddered close to my cot. "It's a bit bright." I didn't mean for the words to come out cracked, but I hardly sounded like myself. Inflammation tightened my throat until it hurt to speak.

Casimir's jaw clenched. He leaned over to the lantern near my cot and blew it out. It made little difference with so many still lit outside, but it would be enough.

I turned on the cot and brought my legs up. The sheets shifted and started to fall, but Casimir grabbed them before they reached the floor. He rested the sheet over my legs, feather-light as it caressed my skin. The pillow on the cot wasn't as comfortable as the one in the tent, but it would do.

Casimir fidgeted with pieces of his armor. He paced around. Eyed the herb shelves. Every move he made showed his unease, and after what felt like nearly an hour, I thought perhaps Casimir needed whatever Taryn had him give me.

My limbs melted into the cot and I released a blissful sigh.

The aches in my neck eased, and I sank deeper into the pillow. "How will you sleep?" I asked.

Casimir scoffed and faced me, putting his back to the shelf of herbs. "Don't worry about that."

"Cas—"

He grabbed a nearby chair and brought it beside the bed. He gestured to it and sat down. The stool had no back to it, and I saw how his eyelids drooped with exhaustion.

I patted the cot. "At least rest against something."

Casimir's gaze flicked from my hand to my face. A pause. A breath. Finally, he moved the stool closer and rested his back on the frame of the cot.

I grinned. The action felt odd and misplaced, but the herbs washed away the pain. I wasn't just numb. Something in the tincture made my thoughts swirl in a giddy way and colors distorted around the outline of the shelves and carts.

Casimir gave me a quizzical look before he picked up the bottle he'd used and eyed it. After a moment, he scoffed. "Taryn…" He swirled the contents of the tincture and set it down. "I hope you're prepared for strange dreams."

Chuckles cut through the tension. I covered my mouth. "Why?"

His hand rose and brushed the rogue curls from my face. Warmth pooled my cheeks.

Casimir paused, his fingers tucked by my ear. His focus lingered on my neck. "Psilocybin. It'll be fine. Try to sleep."

I hummed and curled on my side, facing him. His hand fell, taking with it his warmth.

It didn't take long for the pull of sleep to claw at me. When I closed my eyes and inhaled, Casimir's familiar scent filled my nose. His head rested on the cot near me, the weight a comfort.

Twenty-Seven

The sun blinded me and pulled me out of a deep sleep. It poured in through the massive, arcing windows overhead. My arm flew over my face to block it out. When my arms ached and my neck didn't want to move, memories of the night before made me jolt. My nails dug into the cot, and I took a shallow, shaky breath. It made the discomfort worse.

Petaled hair swam in my vision. I turned with stiff muscles to see Casimir sit, his movement sluggish, and an indent on his cheek from the side of the cot. He blinked hard a few times, trying to wake himself up. Scarlet eyes searched mine while I attempted to slow my breathing. Casimir took note of the panic, his brow furrowed.

He straightened on the chair, leaned to the side, and brought back a mug. "Are you okay?" he asked while I took it from him.

I nodded and drank the water. He appeared unconvinced, but didn't prod any further. Beneath my eye twitched when I swallowed, and I shook my head, neck stiff, and handed the mug back to Casimir.

He frowned but set it aside. "Halburn stopped by while you slept. He's wanting to check on you before you leave. Do you want me to grab him?" he asked.

The urge to refuse was irrational, but it came on quickly. The last thing I wanted was someone putting their hands on my neck, but I steadied my nerves and offered a small nod. The tightness in my throat made me uneasy, and I struggled with wanting to speak. I didn't want to irritate it further, and Casimir quickly caught on. He stood and wrapped his cloak around his shoulders. He didn't go beyond the edge of the privacy curtain, and I saw him gesture for Halburn. It took him a matter of seconds to appear, and I assumed he'd stayed close throughout the night.

If Halburn was shocked by my appearance, he didn't show it. His expression was stoic as he approached the cot. "I'll do a quick healing before you go. It should help with some of the swelling. Is that okay?" he asked. It wasn't common for him to be patient, but I was grateful he gave me a moment before I gave a stiff nod.

His hands were cold as they settled on the sore places on my throat. The sensation sparked in the swollen tissue, and I winced. It brought back every agonizing second I spent with Karion's hands pressing into my neck.

Casimir stayed close, his face a shroud of concern.

When Halburn finished, he stepped back. "Well, it's a bit worse than last night. As is the nature of this type of injury. I'll send you out with some herbs to soothe your throat and the inflammation." He looked between Casimir and me before walking to the curtain. "Do you need anything else?"

A single word rasped out of my throat. "Trousers." It was hoarse and painful. Both men winced before Halburn left out of the drapes.

I moved to the edge of the cot, every inch of my body aching. Casimir stepped closer, ready to help if I needed it. When our gaze locked, the sadness that spilled over in his eyes made my heart sink. He lingered on my neck, and I assumed the bruises were worse.

Halburn reappeared quickly with the herbs, tinctures, and trousers. Casimir gathered the items in a small cloth bag and turned to give me privacy. My entire back sparked with pain as I pulled on the trousers. I didn't utter a word, and when I finished dressing, I tapped Casimir's shoulder.

He turned, and not a second after looking at me, he unclasped his cloak and placed it over my shoulders. I gave him a small smile of gratitude as he carefully secured it. He adjusted the neck of it, hiding some of the aftermath on my skin.

"Do you want to go back to the tent? Or I could take you to your old tent, if you'd prefer." Until Casimir said it, I hadn't even thought about how it'd feel to go back there already. My shoulders tensed, and I contemplated for a moment.

The walk to my tent would take longer, and it was closer to the center of the camp, which made it more likely to stumble across people. I wasn't ready to interact with anyone, even the few I was comfortable around. Then there was the fact that the majority of my things were in Casimir's tent. It'd be inconvenient to switch to mine, and all I wanted to do was bury myself under a blanket and try to sleep.

It gave me a sliver of peace to know I wouldn't return to it alone.

Finally, I looked at him. "Your tent?" I fought the urge to clear my throat, knowing it wouldn't help.

He nodded and led me out of the healing center. The markets were crowded, and I nearly bolted back inside to the quiet safety. Casimir noticed the shift, and his palm rested on my back and he became a shield between me and the crowd.

The path to camp was thankfully empty. Almost no one lingered in the upper cliffs during the day, and we arrived at the tent in a hurry. No one stopped us, and to my relief, there was no one close to the guard tents.

Casimir paused in front of the drapes. His shoulders pulled tight with tension before he opened them. A knot formed in my chest, and I didn't enter at first. Items had fallen in the wake of my struggle. My bed cushion was folded over, the blankets and pillow sprawled haphazardly. Tears bit at my eyes, and I looked away, struggling to step inside.

"We can go to your old tent." Casimir's voice displayed his distress over the sight. He looked over at me, but I shook my head.

"I just… It's worse than I thought." The words were scratchy and strained, but it wasn't as difficult to speak after Halburn eased some of the inflammation.

I walked further into the tent, and Casimir began righting the thrown items. "Take the bed. You should rest."

The suggestion loosened my shoulders and I scurried over to the bed. I removed Casimir's cloak and went to bury myself in the blankets, hopeful for more sleep.

When I curled on my side, pain sparked through my back and air hissed through my teeth.

Casimir stood upright, searching my face. "What is it?"

The night came back in flashes, and I sat back up, reaching for my sore spine. "I fell into the chest last night. With everything else, I didn't think about it until now."

"Does it hurt?" he asked, coming closer to the bed, his brow creased with concern.

My lips pressed together and my hands rested in my lap. Casimir gave me a knowing look and sat on the edge of the bed.

"Do you need me to look?" The question came out unsure.

If not for how uncomfortable it was, I would have said no. But with every turn of my torso, the injury demanded attention. I nodded and faced my back to him. His hands went to the bottom of the tunic, and he slowly moved it upwards, exposing my back.

A sharp inhale startled me, and I glanced over my shoulder at him. "What?"

"Gods…it's bruised dark." The touch of fingertips took me off guard. They were cold, and he was careful, hesitant, as he mapped the bruise. The pressure wasn't enough to sting, but the soft brush of his fingers made my shoulders relax some. "You should have Taryn or Halburn look at it when you're ready." He lowered the tunic and I turned to face him.

The way he watched me, the sadness when he glanced at my neck… The weight of the events crushed me. While I never knew his name, Karion spent much of his time helping me on the ship with mundane tasks. A quiet man who carried grief he never spoke out loud.

And he tried to kill me.

My lip quivered as tears clung to my lashes. Casimir tensed and reached for me. I let him pull me close as quiet weeping filled the tent. I didn't linger on how I nearly sat in his lap, my knees bent over his thighs while one of his hands caressed my back, avoiding the sore places. I buried my face in his chest and clutched the crease in his light armor. The soft wisp of his breath through my hair was calming as he held me, giving me somewhere safe to fall apart.

Casimir's other hand rested over my shins, keeping me close. I heard the shudder every time he exhaled, the slight show of his lingering fear. He whispered into my hair that I was okay, a reassurance he repeated again and again. For himself as much as it was for me.

It wasn't the last time he held me in the quiet while I wept.

Taryn came by before sunset. She brought more supplies from Halburn, warm soup, and she worked on healing the bruises on my back. By the end of the day, she left. Every well-meaning visitor did.

In their absence, the panic that threatened to keep me up at night brought Casimir back to the bed. His arms enveloped me, his fingers wiped the tears, and when I was calm enough to lie down, he made tea, kept the lantern lit, and took the floor cushion.

It wasn't nightmares that kept me awake. The return of wicked memories led to quiet conversations in the night. They grew longer the more my throat healed. Casimir followed my lead each time, either distracting me with stories of his time on the guard, or listening as I spoke the fears out loud. I ruminated over what I could have done differently, but Casimir was quick to remind me none of the fault was mine to bear. There was a promise of more self-defense training when I eventually healed.

For three days, I didn't leave the tent.

For three days, Casimir was my quiet comfort.

Twenty-Eight

The library became a sanctuary for me when Casimir resumed his captain duties. It stayed vacant most of the time as talk of looming battles weighed on everyone.

I kept my focus off such a heavy topic and spent much of my time reading, seeing Halburn, and allowing Taryn to handle the bruises on my back.

Estelle hadn't asked me to resume mending, and I didn't feel ready to begin training again. It'd been six days of doing the bare minimum, at the urging of everyone to take it easy and allow my body to recover. It was the first time since the cottage that I had the time to heal before anything was asked of me.

I continued to take advantage of the downtime.

My fingers brushed over the spines of several books while I kept an eye out for something to read.

Karion's attack left me unable to return to Aeterna's story. It had been the last book I read before his hands were around my throat, and though I wanted to move on from the event, my body had other plans. The distaste for the story became visceral, and even my bed cushion turned into another thing I sought to avoid. Casimir and I swapped places, and he slept on the bed cushion close to the bed frame that I now occupied.

While browsing, a title caught my attention, and I pulled the book from the shelf. It looked newer than the others, and I wondered how Mistvalle acquired such an assortment of books, let alone one that still had crisp pages.

I ran my hand over the cover and found too much joy in its silver flourishes and how they shimmered in the lantern light.

'*Tethered by Vines.*' It lacked any strategies or information on abilities. There was no true history. It was simply a book to distract me from the things that weighed on me.

Sol sighed beside me, impatient. Of all my companions who offered their company, she was the one who despised staying up late. But she waited, anyway, her back against a bookshelf while I browsed.

I flipped through a few pages before sticking with it and whipped around to face Sol. I offered an apologetic smile. "Sorry. I've grown bored with all the practical literature," I explained.

Sol raised a brow and put out her hand. I placed the book in her palm, and she turned it over, flipped through the pages, then grunted—a sound of understanding rather than mocking.

"Light reading. Got it." She handed it back and retrieved her lantern from the floor. "Council starts soon."

She didn't have to remind me. I stalled on purpose. It only ever brought me more unease to hear their plans regarding potential war. Their updates from those close to the borders who had been watching the king left me with the most fear.

But the meetings happened late most nights, and I'd yet to willingly stay in a tent alone. Though nearly a week had passed since Karion's attack, it remained fresh in my mind.

No one had forced me to have constant companions, though I knew they wouldn't have protested the idea of keeping me guarded. The company came at my request. It had been far too difficult for me to muster the ability to ask, and when I did, they all eagerly agreed to work out times to stay with me.

It was more than I could've asked for, and I tried not to feel guilty for disrupting their schedules. They never complained. The closest it got to a grievance was Sol's subtle shift in mood when she grew tired.

We left the library and entered the silent grand hall. Many of the leaders would already be in Estelle's council room, I could only hope they wouldn't stare at me as much as they had the last few times.

The bruises on my neck hadn't finished fading, and neither had the burst of blood in my eye. Halburn had brought it upon himself to show me how it looked in a small mirror. While I understood the sight was jarring, I hoped that the council members would keep their attention elsewhere.

Sol led the way through the halls, her silent demeanor a comfort.

Her lantern cast warm shadows on the slick alabaster walls. I tried not to focus on the time of night and the fact that we would walk in late. It drew more eyes, and it never failed to be my fault. The book would be a decent distraction.

Whenever they planned a council meeting, someone kept me company until Casimir was done. The timing didn't work out most nights, and I joined him in the council room until he was finished.

I should've been embarrassed— always needing company to feel safe. But Casimir insisted, and Estelle was quick to make arrangements for me to attend comfortably.

When the doors opened to the meeting, I waved goodbye to Sol, muttered a thank you, and darted for the soft burgundy chaise in the corner of the room. I didn't want to intrude by sitting at the table. It'd be a distraction, and it was more comfortable in my own space with a book.

When I sat, my cloak wrapped around me, shutting out the icy bite in the marble palace.

After I got adjusted, I glanced at the table, finding Casimir in his usual seat, already watching me.

It'd nearly been a week since the attack, but his demeanor remained changed. He was perpetually tense. He had muttered a few more apologies, carrying a guilt that didn't belong to him. I assured him I didn't blame him in the slightest.

I broke eye contact and cracked the book open. There wasn't a chance to start reading.

"Have we settled on a decision concerning Karion's sentence?" Estelle asked, diving into a topic that had brought me dread since that night.

Casimir's unnerving stare made sense.

I closed the book and set it beside my thigh. The chaise didn't seem as comfortable, and the room became eerily silent. More eyes burned against my skin. Never looking at me, but rather at the aftermath that told the story of what transpired.

Valor ducked his head. "You already know my thoughts."

Casimir tore his gaze from me. "And mine as well."

I tensed at the implication.

It shouldn't have brought me negative feelings. Over the past few days, it became obvious I—like Casimir—carried a guilt that wasn't mine to bear. And while things could've been different in Everbloom when they captured Ronin, I did what I could with the information I had. The man needed someone to blame, and you couldn't blame the dead. Rather than Ronin being the responsible party, it fell on my shoulders.

A few tense moments passed before Estelle looked at me. "Elita, I know it may be difficult, but I would like to hear your thoughts. Your voice matters here. You're the one who suffered at his hand."

Tears abruptly blurred all the faces that waited for my answer.

All the times I'd been harmed at the hands of a man, I was never given the chance to hold them accountable before. For the first time in my life, my choice would determine a guilty man's fate.

My mouth opened and closed. A tear broke free and I wiped at it with the back of my sleeve. The weight of such a decision wasn't lost on me, and I stared into the faces of those who cared for me. Valor, Casimir, and Estelle. They gave me the space to think it over. I hoped they wouldn't resent my choice.

I brushed off another stray tear, took a steadying breath, and sat straighter. "I don't—" The emotions cut me off as I stifled the urge to cry. Casimir's fist curled on the table. Valor didn't remove his gaze from me, and he offered me a nod of encouragement. "I don't think I can agree to a death sentence." I paused when the abrupt reminder of Ronin's attempt on my life increased my fear of Karion. Hadn't Ronin tried to do the same? As revenge for the death of his daughter?

When I didn't elaborate further, it left the meeting in a lull, a few people turned their heads and muttered. In turn, Valor glared at those who lost their patience.

One of the men rolled his eyes, a childish action in such a place. He waved a flippant hand in Valor's direction. "That's enough of an answer. We have more pressing matters," the man said.

I regretted not begging Sol to stay in the library a few hours longer. The man's dismissal was humiliating.

Estelle slammed a hand on the table, and the room went silent. Whoever the man was that spoke, he held his tongue and recoiled into his chair.

"You will not dismiss the pain of this woman. You may leave if you insist on airing your stupidity," Estelle snapped. She let the threat linger before she faced me, her expression softer. "Now, Elita, if you need more time, we can give that to you. Karion is under constant watch, and we're taking every step to ensure your safety."

My shoulders drooped and I stared at my hands as they quivered in my lap. Her words should've been enough to reassure me. But it wasn't, and I didn't want to spend more of my time worrying that he could find his way to me.

I met Estelle's patient gaze and spoke with shaky resolve. "I want him gone. Not dead, just gone." I hesitated and looked to Valor. "Is there a way to do that?"

Valor appeared thoughtful for a moment before he nodded. "We can send him to be held in a different sanctuary." He turned to Estelle. "Lady Estelle, I would request some of your guards to escort him. Unfortunately, the risk of Everbloom sympathizers remains."

Estelle bowed her head. "Of course, General. I will have it arranged."

The sentence was over within a matter of minutes. It felt like an eternity to me, and when they turned the conversation toward the method of Karion's transfer, I held back tears and opened my book.

The war plans became a distant murmur while I read until they dismissed the meeting, and Casimir left his place at the table to retrieve me. He stopped by the chaise and waited while I got my things together and stood, leaving my warm spot behind.

The room emptied quickly, except for a few who spoke near the exit. I was grateful for the hasty departure, which left me with one of the few people I felt safe with.

Casimir wore the same expression he once had after Ronin sheared my bloom. It was clear that he avoided staring at my neck. He knew it bothered me.

"Are you okay?" he asked.

I shrugged. "Not really. But I will be." I had survived enough, and the words rang true. Though the damage was done, and memories would remain, it wouldn't always be so heavy.

Casimir pursed his lips and tipped his head toward the exit. "Want to head back to the tent?"

Not *his* tent. Just the tent. The one we found ourselves sharing. It never failed to make my pulse flutter.

Before answering, I noticed Valor near the door. When I glanced his way, he turned his head, and his worried, fatherly behavior almost made me chuckle. Despite the hardened exterior he tried to uphold, the cracks in the walls continued to widen the more we interacted.

It was a relief.

"Actually," I said, looking at Casimir, "I'll catch up. I need to speak with Valor about something."

Casimir's brow furrowed. "Will you be fine walking back on your own?" he asked. The question poorly hid his concern.

"I'll make Valor escort me back." I gave a halfhearted smile to Casimir and hoped it'd be enough.

I wasn't ready to walk alone at night, even as I tried to work past the trepidation. There were many things in life you could bury, but the attack wasn't one of those things, and the leftover fear sank its teeth in deep. I hoped Mistvalle would feel safe once more when Karion was far away, and the attempt on my life became a distant memory.

Casimir appeared on the verge of protesting, but to my relief, he let it go. "Try not to make too much sound when you come to bed—when you come to sleep—when you get to the tent." He cleared his throat and looked away. "There's training for the guard early."

I held back a grin. "Of course, Captain. Quiet as a mouse." I waved and went in Valor's direction.

In the hushed council room, my leather flats made an obnoxious sound, slapping on the marble floor. It drew Valor's attention, and he dismissed a conversation that didn't seem to hold his interest.

The council member caught sight of me, understanding crossed his face, and he bowed out of the room. Casimir left behind me, and only Valor and I remained.

Stiff silence settled among the marble walls when everyone departed. It proved difficult to start a conversation with him, but after a moment, I rocked on my heels, clutched the book tighter, and opened my mouth to speak.

"Have your guards left?" Valor asked.

I pressed my lips in a line and glanced over my shoulder as if I hadn't seen Casimir leave. "Yes. I was hoping you could walk me to camp?" The question wasn't genuine, and Valor raised a brow.

"Is that so?"

"I mean, yes, but I also wanted to talk." I struggled to admit it, no matter how silly it seemed. He was my father, even if he had been absent my entire life. He was there now, and questions continued to bother me.

Valor gave a single nod. He gestured to the door, and I left the threshold first, trying to muster the topics that pestered me the most.

We walked through the halls while I contemplated. Valor gave me the time to think it over, though I suspected he didn't know how to talk to me either. He missed twenty-one years of my life. He didn't know me.

I looked at him when we reached the top of the stairs to the palace. "Before I found Everbloom—well, actually, when I was at the Temple, the prince said something about my father that has continued to bother me."

We started a slow descent of the stairs.

"I'll do my best to answer. However, I did not speak with your mother or father for many years. Not since before you."

I froze on the steps. "Did you know my father?" I asked, taken off guard.

Valor grew tense. "I wouldn't say I knew him. We had crossed paths a few times. He was a good friend of your mother when she and I—" He stopped short.

A weight lifted that I hadn't noticed before. "So, they weren't together when you and my mother were involved. He knew I wasn't his?"

Valor didn't hide his shock. "I hope you haven't thought so low of me since Everbloom." He shook his head, a rare small smile tugging at the corner of his mouth. "They weren't together until after I left. He would have known you weren't his. Did he treat you as if you weren't kin?"

Grief stung my eyes. "No. Never. He was a wonderful father."

Valor's soft smile turned somber. "Good. That's good to hear."

We both moved in sync, descending the rest of the stairs.

The night sky was clear, and stars shimmered among the black canvas. A waning crescent moon loomed over the top of the trees, creating a soft glow.

No one lingered in the markets or the courtyard of the palace, and with wither beginning, there was no chirp from bugs. Only a rustle from leaves that couldn't hold onto branches any longer. They dusted the cobblestone path.

At the beginning of the incline to camp, I paused. Valor followed suit and continued to wait for me to speak. I couldn't bring myself to meet his stare when the words stuck in my throat.

I inhaled, and the crisp air filled my lungs. "The prince implied he knew about Roses in hiding. He assumed I had been one of them." I swallowed the lump in my throat. "He had my father's notebook and claimed my father knew things he shouldn't have. But it's difficult to accept that he guessed at the sanctuary's existence. I can't understand why he wouldn't take me somewhere I would be safe."

I faced Valor and tried not to drown under the pressure of his guilt. It distorted his face, and, like my mother when she looked at me the same way, I noticed how young he still looked.

"Especially since he suspected my bloom was the one prophesized." I scrambled for the right words. "When you suspected the same, why didn't you come back for me?"

Valor released a heavy exhale and gestured to a stone bench near the start of the path. I shuffled to it and we both sat.

It was clear the question made him uncomfortable, and his foot softly tapped the cobblestone.

"When Vanmore first appeared in your dreams, he was only meant to confirm my assumption that you were my daughter." His foot stopped tapping and he met my gaze. "He found much more than that. When he dreamwalked, he told us it wasn't right, and the very act of bridging the connection drained him. Something about your mind made it difficult for him. We had his mother, Ruelle, dreamwalk."

The mention of Casimir's mother pulled my shoulders with tension.

"It's difficult for us to understand what a dreamwalker encounters in someone's mind, but she witnessed fragments that implied you were the white bloom. When we had that information, it drove many people to unthinkable actions." Valor tore his gaze away and tipped his face to the sky. "Rather than want to protect you, there were many who wanted to remove you from hiding. They wanted to inform the king that the goddess had gifted them their final sacrifice."

I copied him, looking at the stars to ground myself. The thought that Roses and norms alike would trade me for their gain made my stomach churn.

Valor continued, "They were too tempted by the prospect of freedom from sacrifices. They didn't take into account what it would expose you to. Rather than living in peace until it was time to fulfill the prophecy, they would have given you up, allowed you to live in the Temple and be submitted to their evil practices."

I knotted my hands in my lap and cast my eyes downward as tears pricked in them.

"For that reason, many Roses were banished to prisons in far-off sanctuaries. We never sought to retrieve you because we hoped you'd be safer that way. The prophecy was buried, and we spoke of it to no one. I never thought that by keeping you there, I put you in more danger."

Tears trailed my cheeks and dripped off my chin. I watched the drops soak into the fabric of my sleeves, unable to look up.

The emotions boiled over, and a soft sob slipped out.

The burden of the white bloom crushed me, and I wept in the courtyard. There wasn't even a chance to feel humiliated. I carried too much, and I couldn't hold the weight of that, too.

Valor put a hand on my shoulder, timid and unsure. It was enough to bring more tears skipping down my cheeks, fast and warm. I met his broken expression, and the sight of a grieving father was more than I could take. It brought back the memory of the father who raised me. Carrying grief for things they couldn't control or change.

I brought my focus back to my hands, unable to hold Valor's shattered gaze anymore.

The sobs turned into soft sniffling, before the tears settled, and the cold air froze my damp skin. A shift in the mood happened as swiftly as the show of emotion, and Valor gently patted my back before he removed his hand. He cleared his throat and I caught him glance at the markets. The uncertainty was endearing. His fleeting gesture to offer me comfort meant more to me than I could bring myself to articulate.

I straightened and wiped my face. "I'm ready to head back, I think."

Valor gave a curt nod and stood. I followed suit, offering him a small smile of gratitude. When his cheek twitched as he returned the gesture, the scar across his face pulled. He put his hand out, ushering me to go first up the path.

I held back the questions about his past and walked a few steps ahead of him. The silence was lighter. There wasn't a cold indifference. It didn't compare to the silence in the presence of my mother. In all his years of absence, he still managed to offer more warmth and comfort than my mother had in my nearly twenty-two years of life.

At the top of the path, I hesitated. More so when Valor went past the entrance—past the guard tents.

He turned, noting my absence. "Did you forget something?" he asked, taking a few steps back to me.

I shook my head, looked over my shoulder at Casimir's tent, then tugged at my cloak, bringing it tighter around my body. "I, um…I've not stayed in my own tent since the attack."

Valor hesitated, then nodded in understanding. "Of course. Get some rest, Fullan." I watched Valor turn and leave, and—not wanting to be alone in the middle of the camp—I darted to Casimir's tent.

Careful and silent, I untied the drapes, not wanting to wake him. I jumped when his fingers brushed mine, undoing the last tie as I reached for it. It fell open and he stood on the other side, looking as if he hadn't slept at all.

He held the drape open, and I ducked under his arm, thankful for the warmth of the tent.

I noted the lantern still burning on the table near the bed. There were books strewn across the blanket, which hadn't been disturbed. A lone spot in the chaos remained clear, more proof that he had stayed up.

The sound of him securing the drapes made me face him. Red petals stuck out in his hair, and I watched when they shuddered any time he moved. Until, finally, he met my stare and ran a hand through the mess of waves and petals.

"Did you wait up for me?" I asked—immediately regretting it. "Sorry. Never mind."

Casimir's eyes flickered to my neck, then back to my face. He took a tentative step toward me, slow, cautious. Something about the way he moved made my pulse flutter.

He stopped inches away. The proximity made me dizzy and I peered up at him. His hand lifted, timid, tender. His knuckle gently tipped my chin, locking our gaze. Then his fingers moved across my cheek, brushing the hair off my temple. My breath hitched. I saw the way he observed me, his focus on my eye that continued to heal.

The pad of his thumb rested at the dip in my temple. "You apologize as though people don't worry about you," he said, voice soft. "The red is nearly gone."

The energy in the tent shifted, spinning with the change in Casimir's demeanor. He appeared too soft, too vulnerable. Close and unguarded.

Casimir met my wide gaze, then pulled back, breaking the spell.

"I—" I paused, searching for what I wanted to say. The words poured out, my chin trembling with nerves. "You told me to find you, even though you knew Everbloom wasn't safe."

He froze, waiting, still close enough I could see the small scar at the edge of his jaw. Part of me wanted to trace the line of it; to listen to the story of how he got it.

"Why?" I whispered, afraid if I spoke too loud, his walls might go up.

Casimir swallowed thickly, and sadness swept across his face. "I thought I could keep you safe until your wilt." There was no hesitation, no attempt to hide the truth. Pain echoed in Casimir's voice when he spoke. "I suppose the notion I could protect you from harm was naive. Though, I don't think I'll ever stop trying."

"Cas—"

His jaw tightened, the vulnerability sealing away. "Sorry. The decision about Karion put me on edge. I had encouraged his son to join the guard. If he wanted someone to blame, it should've been me." He averted his gaze and went to the bed, beginning to clear the books.

I hesitated and tried to let what he said sink in. I realized that, once more, he carried guilt that didn't belong to him.

Wordlessly, I discarded my slippers and cloak, then shuffled over to the bed, helping him clear it. The book titles consisted of battle strategies, along with one that appeared to be a guide for managing a squad.

His guilt bled into his work, and the mess started to look more like desperation. A plea for control. For a way to keep those in his care safe. It wasn't meticulous instructions or strategies that he jotted down on paper. It was words scrawled in haste, ramblings about Galan's counterattacks being slow. The name Sabian was written down along with the need for better armor. More names I didn't recognize accompanied items or skills Casimir thought needed improving. Even Orin, who Casimir listed as poorly skilled with a blade.

I stared at the paper too long, my fingers pinching the edge of the page, and I felt Casimir watching me.

When we locked eyes, my brow furrowed. He surveyed every change in my face, waiting for me to speak.

I straightened with books in my arms and tucked the paper into the stack. "You're a wonderful captain, Casimir," I started, hesitant, "but you can't save everyone. Don't try to carry that burden."

Casimir scoffed and turned, catching me off guard.

He set the things he gathered onto the table, and I followed, setting them down to free my hands so I could gently grab his arm.

The wind whistled outside, slapping the fabric of the tent. The strong breeze filtered in through the seams, icy and dry. It drowned out the silence, the force of it a mirror to the emotions that swam in Casimir's eyes.

"You could train them until their fists bled, their swords grew dull, and their abilities reached their peak, and you would *still* lose people, Casimir. People will make their own choices. Karion's son did when he *chose* to join the guard. And so did I, when I crossed the Forge, when I followed Ronin. None of that falls on you."

The sight of tears glistening at the edge of his eyes made me rigid, and I squeezed his forearm, moving closer.

"You'll bleed yourself dry trying to keep everyone safe. Please, don't hold yourself accountable for other people's choices."

He smiled sadly. "I'll try, only if you stop blaming yourself first."

I opened my mouth to explain that it was different, that my choices had caused other people harm. But I shut it quickly, realizing his point.

Casimir gently removed my hand and reached for the cushion on the floor, dragging it beside the bed frame. "I have to train tomorrow." He straightened and blew out the lantern.

"Cas—"

"I know my limits, Elita." The darkness couldn't hide the emotion that choked him. "Taryn will be here early to check in and stay with you."

"But—"

He crouched at the mat, and pulled a blanket over it.. The finality of his silence brought me to the bed frame, and I curled on my side, facing the wall of the tent. I pulled the quilt over my body and wished there was a way to prevent him from carrying the impossible.

But it was a mirror to how desperate I was to keep Casimir and all those I cared for safe. I couldn't fault him, and yet it pained me to see the same fear in his eyes whenever he looked at me.

I sighed and brought the quilt to my chin. *We're safe right now. That's enough.*

Twenty-Nine

aryn sat behind me in Casimir's tent, her hands flat to my spine. My tunic was rolled up, giving her a good view of my back. It was much too early in the morning, and the early wither air was unforgiving. Goosebumps rippled across my exposed skin. I was grateful Taryn's palms were at least warm.

Casimir sat on the mat, pulled further from the bed, with the book about abilities resting in his hand. Petals continued to pop up throughout his hair, with a new one threaded to a slightly thicker strand that hung close to his eye. It looked bothersome, and he pushed it away from his face once more. Until his wilt happened, he couldn't trim his hair.

It'd been a quiet morning after he woke me shortly before Taryn arrived. My sleep was peaceful, and the figure didn't visit again. I clung to the tender memory of him holding me, though I wouldn't ever admit to it. Part of me expected to forget the fleeting moment before I fell asleep, but it stayed with me.

When Taryn's hands pressed to the center of my back, I winced, a sharp hiss of discomfort pulling through my teeth. Casimir's head snapped up, and he looked at me with a crease of concern above his eyes; the look that became almost constant after the attack.

"I'm okay," I assured him, pressing my arms closer to my chest to keep the tunic secured to my front.

"Sorry. The center had it the worst," Taryn muttered as the sensation of her abilities increased. "Say, when you're done with that book, any chance I can swipe it from ya?" Taryn directed her question at Casimir.

It drew his attention away and I relaxed some, my shoulders falling. Taryn's hand moved slowly, brushing over the sore knots leftover on my spine. Her abilities flitted beneath my skin and brought more relief. I sighed, my head dipping down. Taryn chuckled.

Casimir flipped the book in his hands and looked at the cover. "Will the healers still not train you?" he asked, stunned.

Taryn scoffed. "They won't even let me get a word in. Stubborn pricks."

"I'll be sure to loan it to you after I finish. Their chapters on healing are the most extensive," he mused as he turned the book back over to continue reading.

Taryn hummed low as her hands settled on a single spot. The tension was worse there. It ached through tissue and bone.

I tore my focus from the sensation and ran my fingers over the quilt in front of me. My legs were crossed, knees resting half beneath the warm covers. The stitching distracted me, and I drew patterns over it.

After a while, Casimir stood, setting the book on the table. "I need to head out. The general has been requesting battle plans, should we need them." He grunted, slipping on his boots. He looked at me, then at Taryn. "If the healers won't come to their senses, I'll have a word with the general and Lady Estelle. There's no reason to deny you training. You've proved your worth and more." There was a look in his eye, one I couldn't entirely understand. I owed my life to both of them and their shared effort bringing me back. It was no small thing. Casimir had watched Taryn do more than her fair share on the ship, as well. She tended my wound at the expense of her own sleep anytime it wasn't doing well. When Casimir had fixed my sutures, the lack of supplies left me with an infection. It was thanks to Taryn's constant efforts that it cleared up at all.

Taryn's fingers twitched against my skin. "I'd say you owe me after all the messes I had to get you out of, boy," she teased.

Casimir scoffed and grabbed a stack of parchment paper. "I'll be busy until the last meal. Will you or Alba be able to stay with Elita?" he asked, glancing at Taryn.

"Don't you worry, we'll figure it out. Ulrik is with his gran, spending time with the other little ones here. I'll be available for a couple hours."

Casimir nodded, undoing the drapes. "Thank you, Taryn," he said. "I'll talk to the general."

He left, tying the drapes behind him. It was silent for a while, Taryn's hands just easing the pain.

I heard the camp bustling outside of the tent. It was always loud when the first meal loomed close. Everyone made their way down the cliffs, ready to integrate with Mistvalle. Their absence became a relief after Karion's attack. I didn't feel comfortable when the camp was full.

It hurt to be an outcast among both Everbloom and Mistvalle. But I was grateful for the small circle of people I trusted. They accepted me despite my faults. They never treated me like a burden.

When Taryn's healing continued longer than normal, I glanced over my shoulder at her. "Is something wrong?" I asked.

A sideways grin tugged at her cheek. "Nope. When I stop, I feel the way your shoulders tense. Is it still hurting that much?"

My heart swelled. "Yes. But you don't have to—"

"Oh, come off it. You deserve some relief, white bloom. The lingering pain can make the memories harder. No need to suffer more than necessary."

The emotions lumped in my throat, and I pressed my cold fingers to my lips. Tears stung my eyes, and Taryn's abilities echoed with more intensity.

"Now, no sense in stuffing your emotions. You'll trap them in your body. It's okay to cry." Her tone was soft, almost motherly.

It was enough to get the few tears to fall. Relief, rather than more pain. It felt good to let them go. The soft sniffling filled the tent, a release of the emotions I had ignored since the attack.

Taryn removed her hands, then wrapped her arms around my shoulders, squeezing gently not to irritate my back. "There it is." Her voice was choked up.

I put a hand on her arm, holding on to the comfort. Her head rested on the back of mine. "He's gone, Elita. He won't hurt you again. You're safe."

The words brought more tears streaming down my cheeks until they fell on Taryn's sleeves. She held me tighter, one of her hands moving to run down my arm.

We sat like that for a minute. When my crying ceased, Taryn let go, and moved to sit beside me.

I smiled softly at her, wiping my face. "I needed that."

"Yeah, I could tell. Healing isn't just patching up wounds, you know. Our bodies carry those things. It stays with you. Don't let those memories take anything else from you. Healer's orders." She winked, then patted my hand.

I adjusted my tunic, tucking the end of it into my leather trousers, then I plucked the vest I had embroidered off the quilt beside me, sliding my arms back into it.

Taryn clambered off the bed, then walked over to the table. She flipped through the book Casimir left, waiting for me to redo the ties on the bodice. I didn't tighten them as much as I normally would.

My stomach dropped when I noticed Taryn swap the book about abilities with Aeterna's story. She ran a hand over the cover before she opened it to the page I had last been on. I watched her remove the parchment I used as a bookmark near the end where the differences were more evident.

Taryn hummed a short tune while she flipped through before she stopped. "That's odd," she mused. I could sense what she was trying to do, but I took the bait.

"What is it?" I asked while I got up. Taryn watched, surveying my face for any changes. But her abilities helped numb a lot of the soreness that remained, and I moved with ease.

I stopped at her side and looked at the page she paused on. It was maybe ten pages ahead of where I stopped. Immediately, I was pulled in by the symbols on the paper. I ran a finger over one of them, recognizing it from my dreams. The figure had shown them to me again the night before. Regret set in that I hadn't continued.

"Have you seen these before?" Taryn asked, watching me from the corner of her eye. She knew I hadn't picked it up in a while after I had complained to her about my mental blocks that followed the attack. I saw her concern, and I tried to give her a reassuring look.

"Actually, yes. I've seen these in dreams." The moment I admitted it, a visceral tug in my chest made me feel as if I shouldn't have. I ignored the sensation. "I suppose I should've kept reading. I've never seen these anywhere but in my dreams."

Taryn's head tilted. "Definitely odd. Perhaps you should show Valor or Estelle. See what they think. There isn't any explanation for them. It seems like it says someone came across them, but not where or what they were for."

I bit at my lip and looked away, ashamed that I hadn't kept reading.

Taryn picked up on the change, and she set the book back onto the table and grabbed her cloak. "Say, you wanna show me what all the fuss is about with mending?" she asked, no pressure in her tone.

I hadn't practiced mending again since Karion's attack. Part of me missed the sensation. The act of healing a plant on my own. Though I didn't show any promise in normal healer abilities, it was similar.

The black wither cloak I had grown to love rested on the back of a chair. I grabbed it, and wrapped it around my shoulders.

"Just don't tell Casimir. He's been on me about taking it easy," I said, untucking my hair from the cloak.

Taryn pursed her lips, trying to hide the mischief on her face. It didn't work. "Hmm, he's been on you? Not exactly taking it easy—"

"Taryn," I grumbled, my grin falling.

She laughed, raising her hands. "Okay, okay. Sorry. I couldn't help myself."

I rolled my eyes, and after we both put our boots on, Taryn followed me out of the drapes, still chuckling to herself.

The mending garden was vacant. It wasn't somewhere that other people spent time, since Estelle had prepared it especially for me. The planters were set to the side, covered by faded yellow straw.

Taryn scolded me when I went to pick one up, and grabbed it herself. She set it down where I pointed, though I felt guilty that she had to lift the heavy planter. She reminded me that I still needed to rest. Mending would be enough excitement.

The planter sat in the dry, frozen dirt. I lowered myself in front of it, my knees settling in a familiar spot.

It was strange to be back. But when the straw was brushed away, showing flowers that should've been wilted already, my heart soared. Mending was something only I could do. An ability given to me by Aeterna.

I tore some of the plants, feeling their thrum weaken in my hands when they were severed. Taryn watched, her brow knitted together.

When my hand hovered over them, it trembled. Part of me worried I wouldn't be able to mend them. It had been awhile since I last tried. But to my delight, the fibers mended, slow and intricate, stitching back together. The thrum increased, a pounding heartbeat in my palm. Until the torn rose was mended, standing tall again.

Taryn scrambled closer to the planter. She whistled, a face-splitting grin on her face. "Well, I'll be damned." She brushed her fingers over the petals, staring in awe. "How does it feel to heal something so broken?" Taryn asked, glancing at me.

Pride swelled in my chest, and I tore the mint, mending it just as quickly. "It feels powerful," I said, my voice low, almost lost in the breeze.

Tary nodded, her grin soft. "Wanna know something even more powerful?" She paused, eyes somewhat glossy. "Every time you refuse to yield, refuse to let all that darkness win, you're mending yourself. Taking what others meant to cause you harm, and refusing to stay down—*that's* powerful."

The trees rustled, dusting vibrant orange curls across her face. Her smile couldn't hide the shadow in her eyes. The remnants of something too painful to speak.

I knew that look well.

"Thank you, Taryn," I said, the smile not as genuine as my gratitude.

I stared at her, watching as she changed the conversation to hide the hurt in her eyes. She began to talk about the similarities in mending and being a healer, and I listened without interrupting.

She avoided my gaze, but I didn't look away. My face fell, and I watched her carry on about many mundane things, wondering what she had to endure to have so much wisdom to offer.

Taryn found my gaze, her smile forced. I realized I hadn't been listening, and I saw just how much she didn't want me to prod.

I stopped myself from asking, and hoped when she was ready, she'd share with me one day.

But I wouldn't force it.

Some memories were too agonizing to speak of.

Thirty

After informing Estelle I felt ready to mend again, the day unfolded in chaos. Valor had concerns on whether I had recovered enough, but Taryn told him I would be able to do it. They observed me, performed healings with Halburn and Estelle to be sure, and for the first time that day, I found myself back in the tent, the book in my hands after I couldn't escape the thought of the symbols.

Despite how late it was, I hadn't changed out of the burgundy linen dress I wore. An embroidered vest—which I had spent far too much time stitching during my days of rest—was tied over the dress. It wasn't the most comfortable attire, but I had missed wearing dresses, and, considering I didn't intend to sleep when Casimir got back, I kept it on.

I sat on the edge of the bed, my nails digging into the cover of Aeterna's story. It was quiet after Sol left me at the drapes, and I awaited Casimir's return. The overlap never took long, and on time, the drapes fell open, revealing Casimir, his hair damp after the bathhouse. He wore a pair of loose green trousers and a soft gray knit, already dressed for sleep.

The lantern on the table trembled when a breeze came in from the entrance, illuminating his features as he found me across the tent, my hands drained of color around the book.

"Is everything alright?" he asked. His brow furrowed while he tied a quick knot in the drapes before he came to stand in front of me.

"Taryn found something in the book this morning. I've been thinking about it all day, but going through it by myself—" I pursed my lips, feeling ridiculous. Casimir put a hand out for the book.

I passed it to him, the parchment marking the page with the symbols on it. He flipped through it in the quiet. The crease in his brow deepened as he stared at the page of symbols.

"I've not seen these before. What made you linger on them?" he asked, running a hand through his damp waves.

The tug of resistance in my chest returned, but I ignored it. "I've seen them in dreams before. When you stopped dreamwalking after we first got to Mistvalle. I'm not sure what they mean."

He glanced up from the book, then closed it. "Did Taryn say anything? Has she come across them before?"

"No. And I didn't feel like discussing it with Valor." The answer was partially true. I had considered telling Valor and Estelle, but whatever the block was, it kept my lips sealed shut each time I almost brought it up.

"I've not seen these in any literature I've come across." He leaned over and set the book beside my thigh. The familiar scent of patchouli followed him, and in such close proximity, his warmth reached me. It was comforting, and my shoulders loosened some.

Casimir straightened, but he didn't move to go to the floor mat.

I fiddled with the edge of my sleeve before I spoke. "I thought about going to the library to look for books on symbols. But then I got back to mending, and Estelle had me—"

"You started mending again?" he asked, tone apprehensive, but laced with enthusiasm.

I offered him a soft smile. "Yes. It felt like it was time."

He grinned in return, the tug of his lips showing the dimple in his cheek. "Sorry, I didn't mean to interrupt. Are you planning to go look in the morning?"

"Actually, I was going to ask if you'd take me there tonight. If you're not too tired, of course." It shouldn't have made me nervous to ask, but my hands continued to fidget in my lap.

Casimir's attention went from my face to my hands. His grin turned into a smirk. "The library is typically shut at this time."

"Yes…" I paused, halting my nervous movement. "I was hoping a *captain* might be able to help me get in?"

"Hmm, I see. Using my title to get you places?" His tone was playful, and the change nearly made my heart leap from my chest.

"If you don't mind?" The nerves crept into my voice, and he moved back a few steps to grab a cloak from a chair near the desk.

"Not at all. I've been waiting for your rebellious side to come out. Never thought it'd be breaking into a library for books. But who am I to judge?" He tossed the cloak to me and I caught it, rolling my eyes.

"No mocking," I chided as I stood from the bed to wrap the cloak around my shoulders.

Casimir chuckled while he passed me a pair of leather slip shoes. I slid them on, and for a moment, he simply watched.

The dress swished at my calves as I walked toward him. He eyed it, a glint in his gaze.

When he noticed how I observed him, he adjusted his posture. "Is that the vest you've been working on?" he asked while he opened the drapes.

I brushed a hand over the small flowers, admiring the stitching as if I hadn't spent much of my time on it. I looked back up at him. "It is. I couldn't bring myself to part with it just yet."

"I can see why. It looks nice," he replied, causing my cheeks to go a shade pinker.

I tore my gaze from him and left the tent. Casimir didn't follow at first. He went back to the bed, grabbing the book.

"It might be useful," he said as he tucked it under his arm so he could close the drapes.

With that, we left the camp, moving as if we were committing a crime. I had to hold back my laughter as Casimir caught up to me, a mischievous look on his face.

There was a time when his visits once made me feel a similar way. A secret shared between us two. Visits in my room when no one was meant to know of my existence. It didn't matter it had been in my head, to me, it was the most excitement I got in the cottage. It was fitting that Casimir was the one to help me sneak around in the palace.

Before we left the cliff path, Casimir grabbed my arm and brought me to a stop. My eyes widened when he leaned close, inches from my face. "I know where the guards take post at night. Just stay close, okay?"

I nodded, unable to speak. Casimir led the way, and I stayed at his right side. Our arms brushed as we shuffled along the path, further from the cliffs.

We moved quickly, and thanks to Casimir, we were able to avoid the guards who were on patrol for the night. He ducked us behind a couple of trees, away from watchful eyes. With his title, I was sure he could talk himself out of a scolding from any guards. But I didn't discourage the behavior. Not when it was so endearing.

The thought startled me, and I tried to avoid Casimir's gaze when he glanced back at me. We arrived at the side of the palace, but he didn't try to bring me to the front steps.

"What are we—" A strangled yelp caught in my throat when he pulled me along, going for a door I hadn't seen before. It was well hidden on a small path of ashen white stones, behind a wall of withering trees.

Casimir fiddled with the door for a second before it opened, revealing a hall that was almost pitch black, if not for the two lanterns at the very end. I looked over at him to find his eyes already on me. He smirked, seemingly proud of himself.

"I figured we could avoid having to speak to any guards this way." He gestured for me to go in first, and I obliged.

When the door shut behind us, we paused, listening for anyone nearby. There was no shuffle of feet or hushed voices, and we took that as our cue to start down the hall.

Casimir took the lead as we neared the lanterns. He kept an eye out for anyone patrolling the halls, but with no one in the area, we moved quickly. At first, I didn't recognize where we were, despite the nights I spent going from the library to council meetings. It wasn't until we went down a well-lit hall that I got my bearings.

We made our way into the library without being noticed, and I was grateful for how sure Casimir moved throughout the palace after his many days and nights spent there.

The library was darker than the rest of the palace, and when we first entered beneath the arch, Casimir told me not to move, and I listened to him retreat back out of the library. The lack of visibility only lasted a moment before Casimir returned, a stolen lantern in his hand and his lips fixed in a sideways grin.

I rolled my eyes as he closed the space. The closer he got, the further I backed into the library shelves until they somewhat hid us and the light he carried.

"A lantern? Are you sure that's a good idea?" I whispered.

He shrugged, then started down the line of books. "If we get caught, I'll just tell them Lady Estelle gave us her blessing."

My brow quirked. "And if it's Estelle we come across?" I deadpanned.

Casimir paused and turned, almost causing me to run directly into his chest. He looked down at me, amusement on his face. "I'll claim you threatened me. I had no choice but to let you in."

I lightly shoved at his chest. "I'm sure she would believe you." The moment felt lighter than any had since the attack, and I found myself staring at his face for too long, my hand on his chest.

Mortified, I dropped my arm and cleared my throat. Beneath the sound of my pulse racing, I heard him chuckle. I ignored it and scanned over the books on the two shelves on either side of us. They reached to the ceiling, and I worried we wouldn't be able to find anything of use with how it overflowed with books.

After I quietly walked back and forth, eyeing both shelves, I met Casimir's gaze—the one I tried to pretend I didn't notice following me the entire time. "I think we'd have better luck on the shelf where I found Aeterna's story. There are a lot of histories and symbolism mentioned in the titles. I don't see anything here."

"Lead the way," he said, voice low and soft.

Being alone with Casimir shouldn't have made my stomach flutter with nerves. We shared a tent each night. But it was in the way he spoke. The tone that laced with things I couldn't place. Things I must've been imagining.

He followed me to the back of the library where the wall of books stood. The lantern cast warm light on them, and shimmered in the gold paint on the book spines, illuminating their titles.

Somewhere outside of the library, I heard the shuffle of boots. They never came too close, and I kept my focus on the titles of each book. Whatever the tug was inside my chest, it seemed to lead me to the right. I continued down the line of books, my focus staying four shelves above my head. And though many strange things followed me throughout the realm, I kept the tug to myself. I didn't speak a word of it to Casimir, even when I found a book that felt magnetic. A pull so strong, I knew it had to be what I was searching for. It was too high for me to reach, and I looked to Casimir.

Although I hadn't said a word, by the way he watched me, a question in his stare, it was clear he picked up that something was out of the ordinary. I felt guilty for keeping things from him, and reminded myself that some things were too strange to explain. Including the figure that had followed me some nights. The one with terrifying eyes.

I hoped the book, the symbols, might help me understand it.

"Can you reach that one?" I asked him, pointing to the shelf. While there was a ladder at the other end of the long wall of books, it was rickety, and I didn't want to give away our presence.

Casimir quirked a brow at me as he set Aeterna's story on a shelf close by. "I'm aware I have a height advantage on you, but…" He raised an arm, going for the shelf, but fell short by a good margin.

I sighed and gave the ladder another look. "I really didn't think this through—Cas!" Hands gripped my waist and hoisted me up as my squeal echoed through the library. I grabbed onto Casimir's forearms as he steadied me, his entire body shaking with muted laughter.

"Sorry. I should've given you a warning. Grab the book," he said between his chuckles.

I shook my head and released my grip on his arm as I went for the velvet book cover. When I pulled it out, I realized I hadn't read the title. It was too high for me to see, but the moment I could, goosebumps erupted over every inch of my skin.

'*Esen's Reign.*'

My rigid body was slowly lowered against Casimir's chest until my feet found the floor. The panic thrummed in my veins, the sensation not belonging to me. I almost didn't notice that Casimir hadn't released my waist until he gave me a gentle squeeze, pulling my gaze off the title.

I looked over my shoulder, my mouth open as if to speak. No sounds came out when I realized how intimately he still held me. My back was against his chest as his hands slowly slid off my waist.

The looser his grip became, the more I turned to face him. The shelf was at my back, and I pulled the book to my chest as he took a small step back.

"The title...I don't know why I grabbed it." My voice caught around the words. Between the panic and the sudden uptick in my heartbeat, I struggled to speak.

Casimir shuffled closer to the bookshelf until his back leaned on it, and he put his hand out for the book. I handed it to him, resting against the wood like he did, our arms nearly touching.

He flipped through it, letting the pages flutter quickly. After how loud I had squealed his name, we'd be discovered soon if we didn't hurry. But with him so close, coupled with the tug to the book in his hands, I couldn't be bothered with the sense of urgency.

It took him a couple flip-throughs of the book before he stopped at a page, the symbols bold and sharp on the paper. He inched closer to give me a better look at them. Unlike in Aeterna's story, these had more definition, and there were descriptions for each of their purposes.

Only four of them stuck out to me. They were the same symbols that followed me in my dreams. The ones that bled flames.

Energy. Life. Balance. Death.

I brushed my fingers over the page, following the swirls along the rune for energy. A horrible longing filled my chest, one I couldn't understand. The rune almost felt alive.

"Is that the symbol you've seen?" Casimir asked.

"Yes. And these…" I ran my finger to the rune for balance, then life. Before I reached the symbol for death, I paused. I couldn't bring myself to touch the last rune, and withdrew my hand.

"'Energy, balance, and life?'" Casimir mused. "That sounds a lot like how your abilities manifest." He closed the book and offered it to me. I stared at it, unable to take it from him. It wasn't like Casimir to miss a shift in my emotions, something that was inconvenient at times. He pushed off of the bookshelf and searched my face, trying to find the answer to my hesitation. "What is it, El?"

"It's nothing." The answer was shaky, and he tilted his head, standing directly in front of me.

"You lie poorly, and you look like you've seen a ghost. What is it?" His voice was softer as he noted the way my hands shook.

"It didn't give me the answer I was hoping for. If anything, I feel as though I have *more* questions now. It gets exhausting." My voice trailed off into a whisper as I leaned my head back and let it rest on the books behind me.

Casimir hummed low in his throat and offered the book to me once more. "There's more in this book. Perhaps you'll find something in there that makes sense."

I glanced at the book, then back at him. He was only a few inches away, his scarlet eyes fiery in the lantern light. Slowly, I took it from his hands, our gaze locked the entire time.

For a foolish, fleeting moment, I thought he might kiss me. It took me off guard, but I didn't shy away. We froze, both of our hands still on the book. I was brought back to the night in the water when his eyes traced my lips. *Had I imagined it?* A flutter of nerves built in my stomach. As soon as they appeared, they scattered at the sound of boots thumping hard through the library.

Casimir released the book and moved as though to shield me. Both of his arms caged me in as my back leaned deeper into the bookshelf. His face landed inches away, a few strands of his hair brushing my forehead. My eyes went wide, and I held my breath, sure that he'd close the distance —

"The palace is off limits at this hour. State your business!"

The voice made my stomach drop, and I ducked my face toward my shoulder, hiding from the intensity in Casimir's eyes. *Gods, this looks incriminating.*

"Vanmore?" Orin's voice was unmistakable, and I wished I could vanish.

I remained between Casimir's arms, my heart in my throat. When I peered back up at him, he stared at me in a way no one ever had before. The moment felt more scandalous when I caught a fleeting look of disappointment in Casimir's eyes. *That isn't helping.*

"Don't tell me you're sneaking around with Elrin again after all this time—"

"No," Casimir cut in, moving back to reveal my beet red face.

Orin appeared dumbfounded. His mouth gaped, and he looked at Casimir, then me again. I offered a sheepish wave, which only made the embarrassment worse.

Orin shook his head and fixed his expression. "The general will kill you himself," he said, giving Casimir a stern look.

"It isn't like that, either, Orin. Elita needed my help finding something."

Orin's face showed his skepticism. "Yes, I see. I apologize for interrupting," he gestured to the bookshelves Casimir had me pinned against a moment ago, "whatever that was. I'm afraid I have to cut this little meeting short. Lady Estelle and the general will be displeased to know you've been sneaking into the palace."

Casimir let out an exasperated sigh. I couldn't bring myself to do anything but grip the book tight in my hand.

"We got what we came for, now if you'll excuse us, we'll be leaving," Casimir said, glancing back at me. I gave a small nod of agreement and clutched the copy of 'Esen's Reign' closer to my chest, proof that we weren't leaving empty handed.

Orin watched us go, his arms crossed over his chest. As we went under the arch, he called after us, "Next time you wish to sneak around, perhaps don't shout someone's name in the dead of night."

The back of my neck burned, and I kept my head down while I picked up my pace. Casimir laughed beside me, not holding back his amusement.

I glared at him and shoved his shoulder. "Very funny. You know, I'm interested to hear what this business is with Elrin. Maybe I can ask her—"

"Okay, okay. My apologies." Casimir raised his hands in mock surrender.

We made our way back to camp without another word. Where Casimir seemed to still fend off more cackling, I couldn't tear my thoughts from the runes and what they meant. Their order was deliberate in my dreams, they always appeared the same way. Energy, then life, balance…and death.

The lighter feeling dissipated, and I was left wondering if the cycle of runes held any weight on my fate. For the white bloom to bring balance, perhaps my life was always the price I had to pay. I longed for it to be mending, but it felt foolish to think that could be my purpose.

At the entrance to camp, Casimir slowed his pace, not going for the tent just yet. I watched him, and let his behavior pull me out of the daunting thoughts. Rather than turn in for the night, he walked closer to a fire that still crackled in the center of camp, the seats vacant.

I followed him without thinking, and matched his pace, walking beside him. When he paused behind the circle of logs that people used as seats, he glanced over at me, his lips pressed in a line as he hesitated.

"Cas?" I spoke his name quietly, and in response, I watched his features melt and his eyes soften.

His body turned to face mine. "Elrin and I were on the guard together." The words surprised me, but I just listened. "The sneaking around…that wasn't anything nefarious. She asked me to train her in private. Something about not liking how a few of the guards spoke about her abilities."

It was my turn to hesitate, unsure what he was trying to say.

"I'm not sure why I agreed to become something more with her." He shook his head and looked at the fire. "I didn't have romantic feelings for her. It wasn't my intention to ever hurt her, but I know intention means very little when I chose to give it a chance. I thought maybe time would change how I felt. It was naive."

When he didn't continue, I summoned the courage to speak. "Why are you telling me this?" I asked, holding the book close.

Casimir met my gaze, and I saw a hint of shame in his eyes. "What Orin said in the library, and how Elrin first treated you… I thought it'd be best to explain things."

I offered him a soft smile, and placed a timid hand on his arm. "It's okay, Casimir. I know who you are. You don't have to explain yourself."

"With this, I do," he said, searching my face.

I pulled my hand back, and adjusted the cloak over my shoulders. "If it gives you any peace, Elrin and I got along well enough on the ship. She helped Taryn with some of my care."

Casimir hummed, looking away again. "That does, actually." He cleared his throat. "We should go back to the tent. Give you a chance to read some of the book before it gets too late."

I glanced back at the cover of 'Esen's Reign,' more apprehensive than I had when we first went to look for it. "I suppose you're right. I won't get any answers from a closed book."

In a routine that had become all too familiar, we made our way to the tent where Casimir held the drape for me, and I scurried to the bed. My slip shoes were left on the floor near the frame, and the cloak rested back on the chair.

While I changed into sleep clothes in a corner of the tent, Casimir got his space ready, giving me privacy. Dressed in my own linens, I burrowed into the quilts and opened Esen's story, hoping what I found wouldn't leave me with more questions, and even less answers.

Thirty-One

Three weeks passed in a blur. Each night I left the mess hall and my last healing of the day to find my way to Casimir's tent. In that time, the bruises on my neck disappeared. My back was no longer sore, and the proof of the attack faded.

If only the memories would fade, too.

I continued to tell myself that staying with Casimir was only to keep the nightmares at bay, and for protection. Nothing more. Our days blended with my training, his duty to the guard, and after Karion's attack, I still hadn't been on my own.

Valor and Casimir agreed Karion's actions might give others the courage to finish what he started. It seemed unlikely to me, but the two insisted it would be safer if I kept company whenever possible.

Although I was never alone, outside of trips to the bathhouse, I still managed not to open Esen's Reign unless I was with Casimir. I read it on the days it was too frigid or wet out to train or mend, while Casimir continued to plan strategies for battle. While his quill softly scratched at the parchment, I buried myself in Esen's story.

Many pieces of it appeared to be lies. A bias carried out by those who told his story. It spoke of a god who was selfless and kind. An anomaly among the other deities. He was said to rule with fairness, and love for the human race.

Most of the pages were filled with praise for him. Admiration for his strength, the rain he conjured to water the land, the wind he controlled as it moved through the trees. Paintings depicted a figure of light, with white wings to carry him above the clouds. His irises a golden ring among a pool of black.

There was no shortage of stories to tell of his strength and wisdom. But to my dismay, there was never an explanation for the symbols. His story mentioned Aeterna many times, but it didn't ever relate to how he aided in suppressing her presence. It bled through the pages with words that proved the god had been obsessed with her, rather than the innocence he feigned.

Casimir always made a point to remind me to read between the falsehoods. To look at what frames the runes inside the book. And each day, I tried. Only to be disappointed once more.

The weeks passed without any answers. But I continued to get quicker with mending, and more efficient with a blade.

That day, I stood in the training grounds with Galan. He stayed ready across from me, a sword held in his hands as he waited for me to make the first move.

The sword I picked felt heavy, but I was becoming used to its weight and the swing, despite the times it seemed as if it would pull me down with each arc of the blade.

I was getting braver in training. The sound of the sword moving through the air was addicting, and with a quick and sure stride, I charged forward and swung, the steel of my blade locking with Galan's, ringing throughout the field. I grinned, even as my arms trembled with Galan's strength pushing against mine.

Our swords remained locked for a moment longer before I twisted, our blades both scraping against the stonework.

He jumped back, holding tight to his sword.

Despite the cold in the air, neither of us wore gloves, our hands bare to the hilts. Calluses covered my palms, something I hadn't experienced before. Blisters changed over to thicker skin, growing accustomed to the leather in my hands.

"Your swing has drastically improved," Galan said, panting. It created clouds of hot breath in front of his face. Despite the season, some days, it still got warmer than what was typical. The shifts in the weather were off-putting.

It hadn't rained since the morning after Karion's attack, but I ignored the dread it brought, and focused back on Galan, grateful for his encouragement.

"It doesn't feel as heavy anymore," I said as I fixed my stance.

He pursed his lips, appearing exhausted. "Are you wanting to continue?" He sounded hopeful I'd say no.

I chuckled, relaxed my posture, and lowered my sword. "I suppose we could be done for the day. Wielding a sword is something that never crossed my mind back when it was just myself and my parents. It feels good to do something like this," I said.

"You seem to be doing well. Emotionally, I mean," Galan said, although he seemed to stumble over his words as he spoke them. "Not to say there was anything wrong before. It is good to see you at peace."

I smiled, and nodded in agreement. As I placed my sword back into its sheath, I relished the sound it made as it slid into the leather.

"Would Captain Vanmore have anything to do with that?" Galan asked. My head snapped in his direction, unable to conceal the overwhelming embarrassment.

He chuckled. "My apologies, I don't mean to intrude. It is hard to ignore how the camp talks. It would seem your tent has become permanently vacant, and his has an additional resident."

I turned to hide the pink across my cheeks. "He's my oldest friend, and his abilities help with my nightmares. Plus, I still don't feel comfortable being alone," I said, scrambling for an explanation.

Galan watched as I fumbled with my sword, trying to ignore the way his question made me flounder. "Of course. I didn't mean to imply anything," he said, trying to hide a smile.

"And what of you and Alba?" I asked.

His smile fell and his face turned red.

Good. At least we're even now.

Galan put his sword back in its sheath. "That is private."

I grinned as I adjusted the blade over my back, pulling the leather straps in front of my chest to tighten it. "Hmm, is it though?" I teased. "You two have been absent an awful lot lately. Sol keeps complaining that she can never find you two when she's finished sitting with me." I raised a brow. "Not to mention you two darting out of the feasting hall at the same time, absent from your stall duties…" I trailed off as his blush grew, eyes wide. Chuckling, I said, "It's okay, Galan. You two deserve to enjoy your time together."

He dipped his head, smiling. "She's quite incredible, isn't she?" Galan mused, his eyes practically sparkling.

"She is pretty great," I said. Their growing absence made more sense, and I reminded myself not to get too upset with Alba for not telling me she finally talked to him. I couldn't imagine it had been Galan who admitted to it first.

After we both returned our weapons, we went to leave the training grounds. Any lighthearted conversation died when Casimir and Valor walked onto the field, wearing their full armor, cloaks draped over one shoulder, and weapons on their bodies.

I froze and watched their approach. The grim look on their faces brought me little comfort. That morning, I'd barely seen Casimir dart out of the tent, much earlier than normal as Sol replaced him.

For the first time in weeks, visions bled into reality, and the sight of Casimir in armor made me rigid. The field around me flickered from the training grounds to the battlefield, an arrow spearing through Casimir's chest.

Galan paused beside me, pulling me out of the hallucination. He stood straighter, saluting them when they stopped a few feet away. "General, Captain," Galan addressed them, the light tone gone.

Casimir's gaze found mine, intense, unwavering. The worry was visible in every shift of his body. My stomach dropped at the sight, and my fists curled.

"What is it?" I asked.

Valor noted the silent exchange, eyeing the two of us. "Vanmore has received word that the king's army marches in Tyvolia. They are moving to attack Mistvalle." Valor's voice never hitched, it didn't falter. He showed none of the fear that stole my words.

It took less than a second for my heart to hammer painfully. Nerves tingled throughout my face, my chin and temples going numb. I tried to breathe, to ease the panic that continued to escalate.

The visions…

Everyone looked at me as my breathing hitched. "What do we do? Can we go to another sanctuary?" I asked, trying to hide the fear.

Valor's jaw clenched, and his hand tightened on the hilt of his sword. "If we flee now, we risk the safety of the other sanctuaries. You may still be the answer to saving this realm. And if they take down Mistvalle, or take you captive, there won't be any way to confirm those suspicions." Valor's words made my head swim.

All I could think about were the visions, the ones I tried to convince myself were just nightmares. But I used to be haunted by visions of my own death, unclear and horrifying. The prospect of going to war with the Iron Thorn threatened to make me ill. Casimir couldn't fight. I couldn't let him.

Casimir took a step closer, eyes fixed on me. "We have plans to journey through the mountain pass before their army arrives. There isn't much time. There's no telling how long they've been marching. We may only have a week," Casimir said, his words doing little to soothe the dread.

"A week?" I whispered, afraid if I spoke any louder, I would lose my composure. *This can't be happening.*

"It could be more," Valor cut in. "There is no way to know for certain. We have scouts going out tonight to ride to the cliffs. They will report back on what they find."

I noted Casimir's full armor and alarm rippled through me. "You're going to scout?" I asked, sounding more upset than I meant to.

Valor appeared shocked. "He is the only captain the Everbloom guard has, Fullan. He'll ride through the mountain pass with his guard," Valor said, voice stern. "Hayes, you will join Captain Vanmore on this scouting mission. Myra and Sabian will be joining as well. Lady Estelle has asked me to remind you of the raiders from the Drought that reside among the mountain pass," he said, turning his attention to Galan.

Galan gave a curt nod. "Yes, General. I will prepare now." Galan dismissed himself in a hurry. He didn't give me another glance when he strode off, leaving me with Valor and Casimir.

They both watched for a moment before Valor spoke. "Lady Estelle has asked us to keep you nearby in the palace, under the Mistvalle guard's watch. For your safety."

The thought of being held in the palace gave me no relief. Being held captive, even if for my safety, made me want to bolt.

Casimir stepped in before I had the chance to get upset. "However, we won't be doing that," Casimir said. I didn't know what to make of it when Valor appeared shocked. "Sol and Alba have already offered to keep her company in shifts." Casimir paused, and met my apprehension with a look of understanding. "With all due respect, sir, Elita is capable of more than many of those on our guard."

The panic spread through my chest the longer I looked at him. It became a suffocating, desperate need to protect him. "Exactly," I said after a pause. "So let me scout. I want to go."

They both stared at me in shock, the dismissal already clear on both of their faces. "Absolutely not." Both of them spoke in unison, the refusal final.

"But I've been training for months. The guard has—"

Valor raised a hand to cut me off. His expression changed from shock to frustration. "Your ability to mend is needed here. We can't afford to put you at risk. Vanmore's team has already been briefed, and your presence would disrupt them. You may not join the scouts," he said, crushing my hope in an instant. "Now, if you'll excuse me, I need to return to make a plan of action." Valor gave a small bow of his head before he left the field.

I watched him go, frustrated that he hadn't given it a moment of consideration. And even more upset that Casimir agreed with Valor's choice, despite having taken up for me a moment before.

The visions of him dying had become less and less, but the threat of a battle left me more afraid. Each death I witnessed, he wore full armor, too far for me to reach. The nights in his tent, close to him, there was relief from the horrifying sight. But the talk of war brought it to the forefront of my mind. I couldn't let him go.

Some time passed with Casimir waiting for me to react. I mulled over the rejection, observing the way he shifted on his feet. He ran a hand through his hair, ruffling some of the red petals woven throughout his black waves. I sensed his apprehension.

"I'm probably one of the best riders you have from Everbloom. Many of them had never seen a horse before coming here. Why can't I come?" Rather than sound confident, the fear crept into my voice.

He sighed, his hand raising to tuck a red petal into the confines of his hair. "You've only been training for a few months," he said, as if it were obvious.

"You just told Valor I was better than many of those on the guard. Where'd that belief go?"

"What squad training have you had? You've done plant manipulation and some combat. Have you ever worked in an organized team? Has anyone taught you proper protocols?" He listed his reasons off, but they were of little interest to me.

"I'm a good rider, and I have the skills to help. You're the one who has been teaching me. Alba and Galan, too. Why has anyone been training me if I can't serve on the guard?"

"The general already said no. I'm the captain of the team, and I also say no." His refusal made me recoil.

"It's a scouting mission, and you act as if I can't follow instructions," I retorted.

"The last time you were given instructions meant to keep you safe, the Iron Guard attacked Everbloom." Laced in his words was the bitterness he refused to speak. It slipped out, and I saw the regret flare in his eyes. But it was too late to take it back.

I faltered, taken off guard. The guilt was never far, and it nearly suffocated me then.

My fists clenched, and I took a step away. "I'm going to see Halburn and head to the feasting hall. Don't bother escorting me. I'll go on my own," I said, leaving before he got another word in.

The healers scrambled like roaches. They bustled through the healing center, making preparations in anticipation of the king's possible arrival in a week. They had to be ready in case people got caught in the chaos when the fight came to Mistvalle's gates. It made me nervous to see. They usually worked seamlessly, never frantic. Everyone had a duty, and they performed them with ease. Seeing them in disarray didn't help my anxious thoughts.

Halburn sat in front of me, holding my hands while his eyes darted from side to side. From his expression when he finished, he didn't seem pleased.

"Well?" I prodded.

He scratched at his chin. "The mending seems to be very draining for you, on a cellular level." He leaned to the side, jotting something down. "The bruises have healed, at least. Have you noticed any problems when you mend? Lapse in memory? Trouble with sleep?"

My spine stiffened, but I shook my head, refusing to mention the hallucinations. "Outside of being exhausted, I've had no issues." When I stood, I brought my discarded cloak over my shoulders.

Halburn got out of my way. "I'll speak with Lady Estelle myself, but I've gotta warn you, mending is taking a lot out of you—energetically. If you aren't careful, it could be deadly."

Unsure what to do with the information, I chose to shrug it off. "I'll keep that in mind. Thanks, Halburn," I said, waving as I left.

I didn't need him to tell me the mending was causing me too much strain. The exhaustion clung to me like a shadow, a constant companion despite my nights of peaceful sleep.

Desperate for a moment to turn off my mind, I headed through the bustling markets—watching for the sign to their tavern, even if I didn't intend to partake in drinking ale. I thought better of doing so by myself after my first experience.

To my delight, the tavern didn't have a large crowd. The last meal of the day was underway, and only a few people sat at tables, their chatter soft in the dimly lit building.

A fire roared in a hearth across the room, and close by, a woman played a melancholy melody on a fiddle. The sound carried, and I realized it was the first time I'd heard music since leaving Eldravine.

While looking for somewhere to sit, Taryn's red hair caught my eye. She slumped at a table alone, staring into a mug of ale. The sight made my heart plummet, and I walked over to where she sat.

The sound of my boots thudding on the wood floors wasn't enough to draw her attention, nor the scraping of the chair—not even when I sat across from her.

Taryn continued to stare into the mug, which swirled with froth. I waited a moment before I caved and reached across the table, putting a hand on top of hers. When she looked up, it hit me that I hadn't seen her in two weeks. Not after her last time healing the bruises on my back. The realization filled me with guilt.

Her orange eyes watched me, waiting for me to speak first. I saw the flush in her cheeks, and worse, I saw the subtle tint of pink at the tip of her nose. She'd been crying.

"Are you okay?" I asked, despite my better judgment. I knew Taryn, and as expected, she withdrew her hand from the table and looked away. Her shoes tapped the floor, and she fidgeted in her seat.

Sighing, I settled into my chair. "You know I won't leave you alone unless you tell me what's wrong."

Taryn turned, glaring at me. "Just leave me be. Can't a woman sulk in peace?"

I shook my head. "No, Taryn. Not when people care about her."

She scoffed, but didn't ask me to leave. Rather than pry, I waited. Taryn seemed to struggle with getting the words out. I watched her war with herself until she caved, sighing.

"Valor told me about the king. Angry man, that one," she scoffed. "He blames everyone but himself for why that happened. And now the people of Mistvalle await the king—" She stopped and tapped her foot faster on the flooring. "The prince, too. Their army is marching here." I watched as she scraped at the mug with her thumbnail. "And even with looming war, and Casimir's recommendation, the healers here won't train me." She laughed, the sound hollow. "I'm useless, even when I offered to be extra hands in case the fight shows up here. They still refused."

"I'm sorry, Taryn. I didn't know."

She shook her head and offered me a sad smile. "It's nothing. Just needed to clear my head for a bit, and this was the best place. I'll make it. I've survived worse." Taryn sank into her seat, running a finger over the lip of her mug.

I watched Taryn chug the rest of her ale, barely going up for air. She set the mug down with a heavy slam. "Well, better head back to the camp. Need to sleep some of this off before I get Ulrik from his gran."

"Are you sure you're okay?" I asked, my tone soft.

I could see the tears well in her eyes but she smiled anyway. "Don't worry about me, white bloom. I'll be just fine as long as that king and his son never show their faces here." She shook her head, then tucked her disdain away. "See ya around. Try not to drink as much as I did." With a two-finger salute, she ducked out, not giving me a chance to say another word.

Guilt became a familiar friend. It knotted in my chest until it became a little harder to breathe. Everyone continued to pay for my actions regarding Ronin. It didn't matter anymore that I had only tried to save him. It didn't matter that I thought he was innocent. They lost Everbloom on account of me—maps left behind in haste to give away another sanctuary. Now Taryn suffered as a result of my choices, and I worried Casimir would pay the ultimate price because of where my choices brought us all.

I sat with the guilt, despite how much I didn't want to carry it. Determined to repay for my foolishness, I resolved to prove my value and earn my place in Mistvalle.

The people I cared for wouldn't suffer for me any longer. I'd mend until my abilities ran dry if it meant buying them even a few more seconds. I refused to let my power go to waste. If I had the chance to protect them, I wouldn't stop until they were safe.

Until they were free.

Thirty-Two

ol found me in the tavern with an untouched mug of ale in front of me. I couldn't bring myself to drink the bitter liquid, even as I longed to numb my mind. She didn't sit. For the first time in a while, I took note of her anger. She had become less agitated with me over time, but once more, I felt her burning glare on me.

I sighed and met her pale gaze. "I've had enough people scold me today."

Sol's nostrils flared. "You weren't at your tent."

My brow furrowed, and after giving it thought, I remembered that she had offered to stay with me in the library again during Casimir's normal council hours.

"Oh…Sorry, I didn't realize the time—"

"The time?" She scoffed and jerked her chin, not looking at me. "Alba didn't know where you were. Off with Galan." She shook her head, blonde hair brushing her shoulders. "People worry about you. Don't put them through more than necessary."

The crease at my brow softened and I ducked my head, embarrassed. "I didn't mean to worry you, Sol. Thanks for coming to find me. I'm sorry you had to. There isn't any council tonight, and I forgot." I stood from the table, and left the untouched mug behind.

Sol watched, her anger dissipating. "Don't apologize when people care about you."

"Does that imply you care?" Despite my best efforts to keep it in, a small smile tugged at the corner of my lips.

Sol bristled, whirling around. "Don't ruin it."

The smile turned somber, and I followed her through the tavern. It didn't matter how many people told me to stop apologizing. Carrying the weight of their concern, their care, it made me feel like I was a burden on them. Though, I would have done the same for any one of them.

When we left the tavern, Sol slowed until we walked side by side. Her silent presence comforted me. Out of everyone, she offered me space to speak when I needed to but never forced it out of me. I found myself glad that Estelle brought me to the gardens and crossed our paths.

We walked through the markets that had cleared and settled for the day. Few people remained, most of them shopkeepers who were closing and locking their doors.

The lanterns lit the paths. They flickered and made shadows on the stones. I tried to ignore the dread about the looming war, and kept my eyes on the warm orange glow.

As though the gods thought I needed more unrest, I spotted Casimir and Galan near the stables on our walk to the path that led up to the camp. The two appeared deep in conversation, both of them in full armor, their cloaks resting on their shoulders.

Casimir had his sword of choice at his hip, and two daggers strapped to the side of his trousers. Arms crossed over his chest, he assumed the authoritative stance of a captain.

Galan donned the short sword he always used, and despite his attire, he seemed uncertain in the way his feet shuffled and his hands fidgeted with the strap that held his sword to his side.

Alba approached from where the stables were, carrying something for Galan. I slowed, trying to watch their exchange, the two of them endearing.

With Galan busy, Casimir spotted me and Sol. He didn't beckon for me to speak to him. There was no sudden change of heart to have me go along on the scouting mission. He simply stared. It made knots of unease twist inside my chest. It terrified me to have him out of my sight.

I bit the inside of my cheek and kept walking.

Casimir's refusal left me feeling hopeless. If they would let me try, if they trusted my abilities, I could keep him safe. He knew my abilities more than the others. He knew what I could do. My muscles were used to combat, sparring, and running—the swing of a sword, the feeling of vines. I was proficient with a dagger, and quick on my feet. And as if a perfect fit for the scouts, I was skilled on horseback. But they were leaving me behind because of my abilities. I thought it would make them see me as strong. It just gave them another reason to guard me close.

Sol shook her head after we passed them. "They don't know that pass. Your father has no sense."

I hummed in response, then looked over at her. "Don't call him that," I said, still unsure about his place in my life.

At that, a smirk pulled at her lips. "Returning the favor. I don't appreciate how often you mention Halburn."

"It's not my fault I got stuck with him as a healer," I retorted, unable to hold back a smile.

"Better him than the others, I suppose," she mused.

"Plus, I like having something to tease you about. You offer very little in that department." I bumped her shoulder with mine, and she cleared her throat, eyeing the path up to the Everbloom camp.

Sol crossed her arms, ducking into her emerald cloak. "Then I'll continue to mention your father."

I chuckled, amused. "Fair enough."

We carried on, the only sound came from the rustle of bare branches in the breeze. When we reached the top of the cliff, Sol stopped. She never did stay long in the camp. It made her uncomfortable to be around people she didn't know.

"Will you be fine until Alba arrives?" she asked.

I nodded. "Yes, thank you, Sol."

She dipped her head and turned, retreating down the path. I watched her leave, the solitude sinking in the further she went. But I had already disrupted her evening, I didn't want to inconvenience her more by asking her to stay until Alba got back.

When I walked further into the camp, my attention was drawn by a large group of people outside a lone tent. It was peculiar, and I paused. Five guards gathered at the open drapes, whispering along with a healer from Mistvalle.

My interest piqued, and I moved closer, as many others started to. I kept my distance, at the edge of the crowd, and listened to what they were saying.

"She is too ill to leave with the scouts, Lieutenant," the healer said, and I noticed him addressing Orin.

Orin's expression remained unchanged as he contemplated the situation, seeming unconcerned about the woman's state.

"She'll need to rest for a few weeks before she can resume with the guard," the healer explained.

Orin looked displeased. "We may not have a few weeks. The king could be halfway up the mountain pass in Tyvolia for all we know. We needed her for the scouting mission," Orin snapped.

"There is nothing to be done, sir."

I watched as the two scrambled. They went in circles with the same conversation looping over and over. It took a fraction of a second for a ludicrous idea to fill my head as they argued over the woman's health. My feet carried me backward as I watched the crowd. They had a short time to find a replacement, and I knew where Casimir and Galan were, already preparing to leave.

A list ran through my mind: Leather armor and a guardsmen cloak from an unattended guard tent. Daggers. A shawl.

I left the crowd and went to the tents that belonged to the guard. It wasn't unusual, not with the many nights I had spent in Casimir's tent.

Casimir's cloaks all carried the insignia of a captain. I couldn't use his, and I made a quick change and went for Galan's tent, ducking inside, knowing that it was unoccupied. I'd have to apologize later for rummaging through his things.

The clothing chest in his tent was similar to Casimir's. It sat in a corner and I went straight for it, tugging out a guardsmen cloak. I hoped it wouldn't fit too poorly.

I grabbed some other things from his tent, like a tunic and leathers. While he was taller than me, his frame wasn't too bulky. I'd fit well enough in the leather armor he had if I tightened it just right. With a shawl to wrap my hair and half of my face, and a hooded cloak, I hoped I could get away with it.

As I walked down the path, a mix of determination and anxiety filled me. The shawl was already over my face, with all of my hair tucked into it as well. I only hoped no one had time to update Casimir on the woman's condition, and I'd need to avoid eye contact if I intended to pull off my ridiculous plan.

My breath made the fabric over my mouth warm and moist. I tried not to let it bother me, knowing I'd have to wear it at least until we were too far to turn back.

I stopped at the training grounds, and located my preferred daggers. The smooth, cool metal felt solid as I secured them in the leather straps at my waist. My pulse raced, but I didn't have time to second guess my decision. It was reckless and foolish, and I didn't care. The stars aligned for me and I would take my chance.

Fiery determination fueled my every step. The only thing capable of stopping me would be if Casimir noticed something was amiss.

Casimir and Galan stood in the same spot I left them, but Alba was absent and another guardsman had joined them, wearing similar armor to mine and Galan's. I didn't know him well, but he was familiar. His hands held onto his horse's reins, and he had a bow and a quiver of arrows slung over his chest and back.

When I approached, Casimir barely glanced toward me. "Myra," he greeted. "We were meant to be heading out already." He sounded agitated. I ducked my head apologetically and said nothing. My eyes darted to the ground to avoid meeting his. He seemed to accept it, and without a word, I went toward the stables.

I heard the crunch of his boots behind me as he followed to retrieve his horse. It made me nervous to be close to him in the stables, but he didn't say a word to me.

He grabbed his already prepped gelding and left the stables, Galan swapping places with him. I tried not to look at Galan either, keeping my eyes on the slick black mare I had visited a few times. She reminded me of Mora, and I hoped it wouldn't give me away. I didn't know what horse Myra would have picked, but I continued with putting the saddle on my mare.

It didn't take me long to prepare her. I was thankful for the years I spent around horses, and the time in Mistvalle I got reacquainted.

I walked the mare out of the stables and hopped into the saddle with ease. I hoped none of them would notice, but they all appeared preoccupied as they struggled to get into their own saddles. It took a lot of self control not to laugh when Casimir fumbled for a moment, before he swung himself over, settling in with a huff.

Once all four of us mounted, Casimir led his gelding to the front, turning it to the side to look at all of us. I busied myself with the reins, my eyes pointed down.

"It will be a long ride up the mountain pass before we reach the lookout where the king's army would most likely be visible from. There are no guarantees." He paused, and I worried he was looking at me, but when I dared a peek at him, he paid me no mind. "There are raiders in the mountain passes, and we will need to be vigilant. I don't want to have to remind you twice. Eyes up." It sounded like a command. I glanced at him, hoping the night and the shawl would provide me enough cover for him not to recognize me. It seemed to do enough.

He hardly looked my way. "Let's head out." He turned his horse and led the way.

Galan followed directly behind him, and the other guard and I took up the rear. I didn't mind the distance. If he noticed it was me before we got to the lookout, he'd send me back, likely to be guarded at all times in Estelle's palace, like Valor intended.

We all moved at a steady trot through Mistvalle and only picked up speed once we were out of the forest gates. I hadn't ever seen them before. They were tall, reaching three times my height, and made of glistening silver. Two Mistvalle guards held them open for our departure, and once we were through, Casimir set a quicker pace.

I sped up with ease, enjoying the speed of the mare as she galloped. Wind howled in my ears, threatening to rip the hood from my head. It was exhilarating, and I hadn't realized how badly I missed riding fast. The path we rode on was well-tended, surrounded by towering trees as we made our way through the forest.

Grateful for the shawl, I pulled it tighter around my face to shield myself from the cold and its bite. Any skin exposed stung where the icy air hit. It would've been unfortunate had I forgotten my riding gloves.

Trees and rocks passed us in a blur. Despite how novice they were to riding, Casimir looked as if he'd been riding for years. He led us well through the twisting trees, and the horses all followed him after being trained to do so.

My only concern for myself was not being used to a long ride. I knew my muscles and legs would ache before long, but I ignored the worry. The ride was thrilling.

It occurred to me that Casimir would discover it was me. We just needed to get too far to turn back.

We rode on for hours. My arms and thighs hurt worse than I had anticipated. They were sore, but I persisted. We were too far to turn back, and I would not expose myself by complaining. Casimir's inability to send me back filled me with a swell of confidence.

Casimir brought us all to a sudden stop, pulling me out of my thoughts. He turned his horse and faced the group.

"Everyone keep in mind the prep with the last scouts. The rough terrain is just up ahead. We need to be cautious," he said, looking at each of us. I averted my gaze when he glanced my way.

"Will the horses make it through fine?" the other guardsmen asked, sounding nervous.

"They know these mountains, and they know this pass. I wouldn't worry too much, Sabian," Casimir replied.

My focus went to the unfamiliar face, seeing some of his features in the darkness. Sabian had long red hair and appeared to be Galan's age. He also wore a look of uncertainty.

I shifted on my saddle, allowing my muscles to stretch and get out of the position they'd been stuck in for the hours of riding. Since we stopped, I wanted nothing more than to take off my shawl and breathe for a moment. I didn't want to be scolded by Casimir unless I had to, so I refrained from taking it off.

After a momentary pause, Casimir turned his horse to the pass. "Stay close and follow my lead. You as well, Myra."

I nearly forgot that it was supposed to be me. I gave a single nod.

We began our slow pace through the more dangerous path. I didn't notice at first, but Sabian came closer to my side, his horse next to mine. "Are you okay, Myra? You're more quiet than usual," he whispered so only I heard.

My body tensed and I gave him a nod to get him to leave me alone. It didn't work.

He continued to watch me. "Was it Novian again?"

My curiosity got the best of me, and my head snapped up.

I regretted it in an instant.

After meeting many Roses, I understood our eyes were not identical. The red was different for everyone, and Sabian looked surprised by mine.

His brow furrowed in confusion. "What—"

I clicked my heels against my mare and she picked up speed, trotting for a short distance until I put a good amount of distance between us and Sabian. I stayed a few paces behind Galan, and tried to keep my head down. There was no room to worry about what Sabian would do. The sight of the terrain took precedence. Jutting rocks, fallen limbs, and a rough incline covered the path.

My stomach sank as I stared at it. It was a path carved for more experienced riders, and even after I grew up with horses, it made me uneasy.

We remained silent, and I followed behind Casimir and Galan in a straight line. There wasn't room to ride side by side anymore, not unless we wanted to risk causing another to go off the path and into the rocks.

The visibility of early dawn didn't help us navigate the treacherous trail, and my heart hammered painfully against my ribs. It worsened as I watched Galan and his uncertainty, along with his inexperience. He fidgeted in the saddle, his nerves affecting the way he rode. I kept a close eye on him. I knew him well, and it made me even more anxious. His posture wasn't right. The way he guided the horse was unsteady and unsure. He wouldn't be able to do it.

I observed him, paying attention to how his mare responded to every slight movement of the reins. Every second made it worse, and I panicked as I watched it unfold in front of me. I saw it coming. It didn't stop my stomach from churning when it happened.

Galan tried to tug his mare to the right to dodge a rock, but it was a mistake. I saw what he couldn't and tried to shout for him to stop, but it was too late. I couldn't do anything except watch as his mare stepped on a loose rock, slipping. It happened within a matter of seconds. The mare reared up in a panic as the ground moved beneath its hooves. Galan yelped, falling back with a horrible thud. He let out a roar of pain as he rolled on the ground.

Swiftly, I brought my mare to a halt and dismounted before Casimir could maneuver his horse around on the narrow, uneven path.

I ran to Galan, evading his agitated mare, which stomped and huffed in a panic. I crouched at his side as he writhed in pain, gripping his arm.

I tore the shawl from my mouth while my hands grabbed onto his shoulders to steady him. "Galan," I said sternly, trying to get him to calm down. He continued to groan, his eyes shut. "Galan, breathe." I tried again, my hands squeezing his shoulders.

He peeked through slitted lids, the discomfort plain on his face. Still, surprise won out. "Elita?"

I inspected his head for a moment, then brought my attention back to his arm after confirming there was no visible head trauma. "Can you move your arm?" I asked, ignoring his bewildered stare.

Casimir dismounted with a grunt, reaching us in a few quick strides. "What happened?" he asked.

No matter how much I didn't want to, I gave in and glanced over my shoulder at him.

Casimir's eyes met mine, and his nostrils flared. "You didn't." He stared at me in disbelief.

"He hurt his arm," I said, not trying to engage in an argument while Galan lay there injured. I turned my focus back to him—his face still contorted with pain. With a careful touch, I assessed his arm. "Can you move it?" I asked again.

"Not without great pain," he groaned.

Casimir bent at the other side of Galan. His anger permeated the air, searing with an almost palpable intensity. His stare burned into me, but I refused to look up. My focus stayed on Galan.

I unclipped his cloak, and cautiously moved it out of the way to give me a better view of his arm. It twisted in an unnatural manner, with his sleeve torn and his skin scraped. I gulped down and finally met Casimir's gaze. Worry and frustration both crossed his features.

Casimir stood as Sabian approached, after he tied up the horses. Sabian shared the same bewildered look when he saw I was not Myra.

I tuned them out as they discussed the situation and tried to help Galan. Each horse had a saddlebag with healing supplies in case something happened. In a few seconds, I unclipped the leather bag from my horse. My knees met the dirt as I kneeled next to Galan and pulled out the supplies that might be of use.

A salve and some bandages were the best I could do. "Sorry," I muttered. He didn't have time to react to my apology before I wiped the salve over the torn skin. He shut his eyes again and pursed his lips. I fought the urge to keep apologizing.

The wrap was worse than the salve while I tried to cover his wound and bring the wrap around his arm like a sling. Galan grimaced when I helped him sit. He winced as I secured the bandage over and around his arm. With a gentle tie, I finished my patch-up job and stood.

Casimir and Sabian's conversation came to an end, and my focus shifted toward them. Casimir fumed as he stalked over to me, looking every bit a captain, and I braced for the scolding.

Casimir stopped a few inches in front of me. "You directly disobeyed the general and captain of this squad. I should have the general refuse you from training and have guards attached to your hip," he snapped, eyes flaming.

My brow furrowed, and I took a step back. "Casimir—"

"Captain. On this mission, I am your captain. Do you have any idea what you've done? Did you even think about the people you left behind to find your tent empty, or were you okay with leaving them to fear what became of you?"

My face paled, and I swallowed the guilt. Alba was meant to stay with me, and I couldn't imagine what she must have thought when she found both mine and Casimir's tents empty.

I didn't shrink away from Casimir's intensity. He was right. It'd been selfish of me. "That wasn't my intention, I just—" The explanation caught in my throat. How could I explain that I was terrified of losing him? That I selfishly left behind my friends, my father, to protect him?

When Galan groaned and tried to sit more, he brought our attention back to him. I swooped down, and offered Galan an arm to help him stand. He gave me a grateful look, but couldn't do much more than that. Sweat glistened on his brow and he appeared ill. The adrenaline would wear off, and the pain would be unbearable.

I turned to look at Casimir. "He needs the healers in Mistvalle. We can't do anything for him here."

Every word I said seemed to make him more irate.

Sabian walked to us, standing on the other side of Galan, cautious of his hurt arm as he tried to help take on some of his weight.

"Captain?" Sabian sounded unsure.

Casimir let out an exasperated breath and turned, running his hands through his hair while he took a moment to think.

The red of his petals were more visible as the sun rose. A stark difference when the light hit the red just right. They took some of the edge off his appearance as he fumed.

Galan continued to grumble and moan in pain, shuffling from one foot to the other. I didn't know how he would make it back down the mountain if he couldn't ride.

After a moment, Casimir turned, observing the three of us. He looked displeased. Whatever choice he made, he clearly didn't like it.

"Sabian, you will ride back to Mistvalle with Galan. I need someone with him who can manage his weight on a single horse if need be. It will be a slow descent." He turned his attention to Galan. "Do you think you can ride on your own? Sabian will ride close as a safeguard."

Galan gave a weak nod, and I watched it unfold, biting my tongue when I nearly argued that I could find a way to manage Galan's weight. I would get to stay, and despite how angry he was with me, it kept him close.

Both men brought Galan over to his mare, struggling to get him up. They looked at the horse, at Galan, and tried a few different ways. It took me a few shaky inhales before I had the confidence to step in.

With trembling hands, I conjured black vines, and allowed them to twist outward. They were thick and sturdy as they wrapped around Galan, hoisting him up into the saddle with ease. Sabian and Casimir did nothing but watch, bewildered.

Galan's nervousness was palpable, but as soon as he got on his horse, the vines uncoiled from him in slow motion. I had to make sure he was steady before letting go. The energy it took made my exhaustion worse, but I tried not to let it show.

Galan gave me a nod of reassurance, and I released the vines. They fell to the ground, becoming one with the earth, and I exhaled.

My pulse thrummed with the remnants of the energy that surged through me, and I couldn't stop the small smile that tugged the corner of my lip up.

Sabian let out a low whistle. "That was impressive," he said. Casimir glared in his direction.

If it weren't for the horrible situation, I would've grinned.

Thirty-Three

asimir and I rode on in silence. He never told me to turn around and follow Sabian and Galan. He had waited while I mounted my horse, and without a word, he led the way up the path. The sun was high overhead, shining down on us as we returned to a smoother forest trail. We slowed as we left the dangerous path. My mare bristled, her head dipping as the need to stay alert died down. The arduous trek left both horses exhausted, and though we needed to finish the scouting mission, I let her move at an unhurried pace, even if the reprieve was only brief.

When we were out of the worst of it, I had expected Casimir to pause and scold me again. He never did.

Unfamiliar sights made it easy for me to ignore Casimir's cold shoulder and focus on the surrounding beauty. Even as the tree's leaves were almost entirely gone, a few red and white ones clung to the branches, reluctant to let go. The possibility it could be the final wither to grace the realm haunted me. A truth I tried to ignore.

Despite the rigorous training, and the many days spent in Estelle's presence with all her hope, the thoughts plagued me in the silence of our journey. Thoughts of ruin, cursed air, and the wishes of a dead man consuming the realm entire.

The withering trees and glow of the sun weren't enough to distract me. It all blended, and soon the sights no longer interested me, which made the thoughts more consuming.

I gazed at the back of Casimir's head, observing his bloom.

From what the prophecy said, with the white bloom severed, another bloom could not take its place. With the untimely end of my bloom, it had doomed the realm. It was Ronin's words that haunted me then, and it appeared my horse sensed the tension in my body as she whinnied and snorted.

My time in Mistvalle had pushed Ronin further from my thoughts, but he was never gone. A reminder to guard my heart. I couldn't allow myself to think about him for too long. It hadn't occurred to me before, but following the visions of Casimir dying, I realized I had already put him in danger once. He was trained, stronger, and he was able to take down Ronin. But what if he hadn't been? The unease threatened to throw me into a spiral, and without thinking, I clicked my heels and my mare picked up speed, outdoing Casimir's pace.

We never reached a full gallop. The mare worked at a steady trot while my hands worked the reins, trying to rid my body of the horrible sensations that arose. I wished things could've been different. That I would have never left the Temple. My bloom would've already saved the realm, and no one would have ever had to die because of me.

When I envisioned a different outcome, thoughts of Casimir teaching me how to swim, or the look of pride on his face when I conjured my vines, made me question if I would've chosen another path. And without realizing it, my horse picked up a gallop through the woods.

I wanted to outrun the fear and the way my heart fluttered when I was with Casimir. It was a feeling I wanted to forget and leave behind.

Behind me, Casimir shouted something. I tried to listen, but my head swam in a sea of panic.

I had closed myself off when Ronin brought the dagger to my hair, yet I found myself trusting my companions from Everbloom. I wasn't wary of Halburn and his strange demeanor, and Sol became a friend. Valor was less of a stranger, and someone I no longer resented. And Casimir...

Gloved hands grabbed my horse's reins, pulling me to a stop with a protest from my mare.

My head whipped in Casimir's direction, my eyes wide.

"What are you doing? There are raiders in these mountains, and you're practically giving them an easy target," he snapped. I took the reins from him while my horse stomped in place. "Do you purposefully try to be difficult?" he asked, expression full of frustration.

"I can ride just fine, and the path is clear," I retorted, unwilling to admit how careless I'd been.

Casimir huffed in disbelief. "Have you lost your mind? This is exactly why the general and I had agreed you shouldn't come. You have no idea how to take orders."

"And you have no idea how to give them," I bit back. "You hardly said a word to the entire scouting party, and when Galan got hurt, your first instinct was to get upset with me when you weren't even paying attention."

His cheek twitched, the only display of his slow rising anger. "Every inch of ground we cover, the paths we take, I plan them out ahead of time. With the team *I'm* assigned. We all play a part, and I didn't account for someone who rode out on arrogance alone. Your impulsivity continues to put people in danger, and somehow, you still haven't learned." The words were heated, laced with frustration that had been buried.

My stomach dropped, and I tore my gaze from his. I didn't know how to tell him that I only meant to keep him safe. That my rash choices were not made simply to prove myself.

But no words would leave my lips. A pang ached in my chest. The sense of safety torn from me. I tried to ignore the sinking sensation, the one I once felt in the presence of my mother. A burden. A risk no one truly wanted to take on.

I tried to quell the emotions, but the damage was quick and harsh.

A short lapse of time passed before Casimir clicked his heels. "We need to move. We'll lose the light if we don't hurry."

Without a word, I followed him, my head hung low.

The parallel to how right I thought I was when I fought for Ronin's release followed me then. Decisions I made in haste without thinking what might come of them. Had I asked for time in Everbloom to find a solution, had I only returned to my tent… But I didn't know Ronin's true intentions, and had he been innocent, they would have killed him, and I would have been complacent. The thoughts plagued me, and my hands grew sore from rubbing the reins viciously the entire ride.

Much of my life was spent in secrecy, without experience in the realm, or working with others. But those excuses were just that: excuses. If I didn't learn to sit with uncertainty, discomfort, and rejection, I would continue to make choices that brought more ill outcomes. I didn't want my companions to be burdened by me.

In the same breath, going back to a life of quiet obedience went against every instinct in my body. I didn't want to be a burden, but I refused to be a prisoner. After a life of hiding, I wanted so much more.

Our days were numbered as the realm's end and the king's army both hung over our heads. I wanted to be of use, and when we returned to

Mistvalle, I would earn my right to be on the guard. To be someone who they could rely on.

It took us the rest of the day to get to the lookout at the top of the mountain pass. Orange painted the sky, making the clouds turn into a lovely display of fiery waves. With any luck, we would have enough visibility to make the trip worth it. Either that, or we would be there until the next morning.

Our horses came to a stop at the top of the lookout. The altitude resulted in the frigid air biting my skin. In spite of the cold, the sight stole my attention, blocking out some of the trepidation at being so high up.

Tyvolia lay below, a stretch of desolation and ruins.

The sight was unsettling.

Casimir dismounted first. His boots landed hard on the withered leaves, making a loud crunch in the muted woods. Not even birds sang their song. A sense of eeriness filled the air.

The ground was strange beneath my feet when I got off my horse. After such a long ride, the solid, unmoving earth made me waver. My legs ached in new places, it ran from my inner thighs to my knees. It was by far the longest ride I'd been on. I didn't understand how Casimir stood so steady. He showed no signs of being bothered as he dug through his saddlebags, his gloves discarded on top of the saddle.

After a few gentle strokes across my mare's neck and a whisper of my gratitude, I went through my own leather bags, and hoped to find some food to fill my grumbling stomach. It twisted with a hunger I ignored for far too long. The full meals had spoiled me in Mistvalle.

After searching, I came across dried meat and a waterskin. There was no bread tucked away, and my anticipation sank a little. Galan was part of the kitchen preparations in Mistvalle, and he always made a delectable loaf. But it was only the dried meat and a cloth full of an assortment of different nuts.

A disappointed sound escaped me and I went to sit against the bottom of a tree, my hands full.

Casimir didn't search for food. He held a long bronze spyglass and scanned over it, flipping it around in his hands before he extended it. Then he grabbed out what appeared to be a map and left his horse tied to a low-hanging branch. He approached the edge of the lookout, sure of himself, even as my nerves spiked when he neared the drop-off.

I fixed my attention back to the items in my lap, and started with a bite of the dried meat, which had no flavor. It went down with a struggle, and I opened the cap of the waterskin, and drank a few sips to wash it down.

With deft fingers, I sorted through the cloth until I found the walnuts, crunching down on them in hopes they would be better than the meat. They weren't. I groaned and put the food away, taking another swig from the waterskin.

When I glanced in Casimir's direction, I froze.

His posture was rigid as he looked out at Tyvolia, the spyglass pressed to his eye. He didn't move. It looked as though he had stopped breathing. A shiver rippled up my spine.

I set everything on the ground and stood.

The leaves crunched beneath my quick strides until I made it to his side, my gaze searching the barren lands for what he saw.

Without a word, he passed me the spyglass. The metal was warm in my palm after he had held it for so long, and my fingers shook when I raised it to my eye.

I searched and saw nothing, until Casimir's hand moved to my elbow, pointing me toward what he had seen.

My knees buckled.

In the distance was a sea of what appeared to be tents, misplaced and vibrant. Familiar red and silver flags stood in the camp, with the insignia of the Iron Thorn stitched into them. The same one that matched the scar on my neck.

Absentmindedly, one of my hands pressed to the sacrificial marking. The sight of the flags couldn't compare to the horror I felt upon noticing the masses which moved in a wave, too distorted from far away. From what I could tell, it was at least a thousand soldiers.

My vision blurred at the edges as I stared in a mixture of disbelief and dread. They were too close. There were too many.

Casimir took the spyglass from my hands, and I stumbled back. As if distance from the lookout could erase the glaring reality below.

When we had sailed to Mistvalle, part of me hoped to never see the symbol of the Iron Thorn again. But it had arrived at our doorstep, with a thousand soldiers ready to do whatever they could to capture the Roses. And kill those who didn't comply.

A sick sensation overwhelmed me, and I wished I hadn't drunk so much water a few moments before. It swirled in my stomach, threatening to come back up.

The vision of Casimir falling repeated over and over. Dead by a spear. An arrow. A sword. Always through his chest.

Casimir watched me. "Elita?"

"I've doomed us all." The words fell from my lips. "The prophecy must've been mistaken. I've only cursed this realm and everything I touch."

I saw the flash of guilt in Casimir's eyes while he watched me fumble with my words. "None of this is your fault—"

"No." I cut him off. "You were right. I shouldn't have come."

I turned on my heel, my movement stiff and filled with apprehension, desperate to turn from the sight below. We had to get back. A week would have been a gift. Now we'd be lucky to make it four days before their army reached the mountain.

The sound of Casimir's footsteps followed me as I made my way back to my horse. We had to warn everyone. They needed more time. I reached for my horse's reins and missed as I grew lightheaded.

Casimir's hand wrapped around my wrist, stopping me when I went to grab the reins. I looked his way, wide eyed. It pained me to stare at him, the visions twisted my head, and the hysteria would drive me to a breaking point.

"What are you doing?" he asked, sounding more confused than angry as he slowly released my wrist.

"We have to get back and warn them. We need to be ready," I said, voice shaky.

"And we will. We have time."

"Time?!" I cried, the sound echoing in the woods. "They are practically breathing down our necks!"

Casimir stared at me with pity in his gaze. I despised it.

"We'll leave once I've marked their location on the map. You'll be safe in Mistvalle. Lady Estelle will see to it."

I recoiled from him. "I'm not worried about myself. I'm worried about the thousands of people in Mistvalle that are about to be at the mercy of an evil king. A king who still believes their bloom can save this realm." I froze, staring at the red in his hair.

Casimir noticed my gaze and sighed. "Don't worry about my bloom." Though he acted unconcerned, it didn't ease the pit in my gut.

He walked away, going to his horse. I watched as he marked the map with the tip of a dagger. Soon it would be dark out, and we'd have to make the trip down the pass with no light to guide our way. The realm was against us.

When he finished, it was as he said. Casimir got up into his saddle, and I wasn't far behind.

Urgency propelled us both, and we rode faster than we should have down such a steep path. The horses handled it with ease, likely used to the trek, since other scouts had been that way many times.

We rode side by side. Casimir didn't insist on taking the lead. He finally seemed certain of my ability to ride.

The trees whipped past us in a blur as the darkness fell like an ominous blanket. Something inside me said to ride faster, to get out of the mountain pass. My pulse thundered along with the hoofbeats. It threatened to make me dizzy.

We were nearly at the area where Galan fell off his horse when a horrible feeling consumed me. Something was off.

Calla swooped close, screeching in my ear. She got too close to the mare, fluttering fast at her side, almost as if to get us to turn.

The mare bristled beneath me, sensing it at the same time as I did.

"Duck!" I yelled out as the sound of a bowstring releasing came from our left.

Casimir didn't hesitate. His head ducked down toward the horse's mane and he veered hard right. I copied his movement.

We moved as if we'd spent years practicing and perfecting our rhythm. Casimir led the way, and I wasn't far behind, copying every turn or jump he and his horse made.

As we galloped into the trees for cover, the path quickly vanished, swallowed by the dense foliage. Even as we pressed on, I could hear them not far behind us.

Casimir made another sharp cut through the thick foliage and I followed, a scream catching in my throat when he came to a sudden stop, his hand wrapped around my reins.

He jumped off his horse and took my hand, tugging me off the saddle before I could protest. Without pause, he brought me close to a tree. An arrow hissed past us, sending his horse into a frenzy. I watched in horror as it ran off into the woods. The presence of an archer made my blood run cold and I stared at Casimir, nearly crumbling.

"Cas—"

He put his palm over my mouth and shook his head. "It'll be fine. Stay hidden. Don't come out until I say."

I pushed his hand off. "Are you mad? We need to go," I said, my tone urgent, afraid.

"They're too close. I can handle a few raiders."

"No, you can't go—"

"Stay here, El, please." The desperation in his voice took me off guard. I stared at him, searching his face. I saw something similar to what had been haunting me since the visions started. He'd seen me die before. Brought me back with his own hands.

After a reluctant pause, I nodded. He appeared relieved and moved back, drawing his sword. It sang out of the sheath, making my stomach churn.

The sound of footsteps grew louder as the raiders approached. From the sensations in the earth, it was too many for him to handle on his own, but I knew my fear wouldn't help him. He was a captain. He trained often and kept his skills honed. And even then, all I felt was dread as he walked out from behind the tree.

The night was horribly quiet in his absence.

I tried to do what little I could and tied my horse to a tree. We didn't need to be down two mounts. After securing my mare, I remained behind the trees, waiting. It didn't take long, and I realized how right Casimir had been. They were too close.

Through the night, the clash of swords reverberated in the air, shattering the silence. Raiders howled, and voices carried through the trees. It had to have been ten or more. It was too much.

Weapons continued to clang, the sounds getting closer. I heard Casimir grunt as he fought them off. I wished then that he possessed the same strength as some of the other Roses. He may have been skilled with a blade, but I feared it wouldn't be enough.

Daring a glance, I peered from behind the tree, catching the shadows and blades as they moved in the night. Casimir swung his sword while using a leg to kick another charging raider to the ground. His blade locked with a curved sword, and he shoved them away.

I watched with my heart in my throat.

Another arrow sang through the trees somewhere, still missing its target. I was both grateful and frustrated with the night. They couldn't aim well, especially as Casimir dodged, kicked and rolled. He held his own until something shifted.

Someone else charged from the woods, sounding as if they wore metal armor. When they collided with Casimir, a startled gasp caught in my throat, the sound echoing.

Casimir stumbled up from the ground, taken off guard. His hesitation cost him the upper hand.

With a sickening sound, the person slammed him into a tree, using the edge of a sword to smack against his temple.

I didn't have to think. I sprinted out of the trees, screaming his name as heat and energy surged through my body. Powerful and familiar, and I reached for it, letting it consume me.

Thorns splintered from my hands, and sent the raiders jumping with screams of panic. Roots tore through the woods, wrapping up bodies in a quick sweep.

The intensity was almost too much as I ran and released my abilities on the raiders. I ducked under a swinging dagger, and threw a hand out to wrap another raider in roots without faltering.

Roots and vines tangled as they sought their targets. They wrapped up the struggling raiders along with the ones Casimir had already knocked out. The roots pulled them into the woods, and their screams of terror reverberated.

With their relentless grip, the roots completed their task, leaving me to confront the raider who had taken Casimir by surprise—the most imposing figure in their group. They smirked, their face dirty and half covered. They wore scraps of mismatched iron proudly.

Without wasting another moment, I charged toward the raider, my hand gripping the dagger. They jumped out of the way with a cackle, and brought down their short sword.

I moved to dodge, my legs unsteady still from the ride. The raider's blade curved as they spun to catch me.

Fabric tore, and heat spread from my collarbone to my shoulder, burning beneath the adrenaline in my veins. I clenched my jaw, and corrected my stance just as they brought the short sword down again for another hit.

I blocked with trembling arms; the dagger suspended between us while vines wrapped around my arm, giving me more strength. I pushed against their blade, using the vines to engulf our locked weapons.

They stared in horror as the vines crawled up their hands. The raider yelped and dropped their sword, trying to free themselves from the vines. Only they couldn't, and my roots already took hold of their ankles.

The raider stumbled backward. They fell to the dirt with a thud, and my roots tightened, crumpling the metal. When they screamed, I let go with a whip of my hand, sending them across the forest grounds until their calls for help were but a whisper in the trees.

I gasped, my lungs heaving with the exertion.

The absence of the raiders left an eerie silence among the trees. They rustled, withered leaves brushing over the ground.

I ran over to where Casimir slumped near the tree and tugged his heavy frame into my arms.

"Casimir?" I tried to wake him, scanning over his body for injuries. Blood shimmered at his temple, coming from somewhere in his hair in a waterfall of red. "Casimir," I said sternly, shaking his shoulder. His chest continued to rise and fall with shallow breaths, but his eyes remained closed. I looked around the woods frantically, unsure what to do.

There was no one there. I was alone as Casimir lay unconscious and bleeding. The guards and healers of Mistvalle were too far away. Galan and Sabian were long gone.

I made a horrible mistake.

Thirty-Four

The soft breeze carried the peaceful chatter of bugs, creating a stark contrast to the grim situation. My head pounded until it made nausea roll through me. Using my abilities drained me, but it was the only way to get Casimir's heavy frame onto the saddle.

His body slumped when my vines let go and I gasped, shoving him back up as he fell. My muscles burned in protest at his weight, but I got him settled on the mare's neck with the help of my vines.

Careful not to hurt the horse, I entwined vines around Casimir's body, looping them until they held him tight to the saddle. Sweat dripped down my temple even as the night grew colder.

There was no other option than to leave the area. We had to get somewhere safe before the raiders returned. Gods forbid they brought more with them. I had only tied them up, and if my experience with Ronin was any indication, it wouldn't take them long to find a way out. Some of them likely still had their weapons on them. I didn't have time to worry about it.

Taking extra care, I squeezed onto the saddle, mindful of Casimir's limp body. His broad frame made it difficult to fit. One of us would end up falling off. For good measure, I conjured vines to knot around us both and the mare, despite her protests. When I assured her in a gentle tone, she settled, allowing me to secure us.

The horse responded to the gentle kick of my heels and picked up a slow trot. Our combined weight would make the journey much harder on her. I needed to remember to reward her with extra apples when we returned to Mistvalle.

We picked up speed, and I did my best to wrap my arms around Casimir's broad body while holding the reins. I gave it my all to ensure he stayed steady and remained on the saddle alongside me. It proved more difficult than I expected.

I ignored how Casimir's back scraped against my torso, causing the wound across my chest to burn. I didn't have time to assess my injuries. My biggest concern was Casimir's head, and the fact he still hadn't opened his eyes.

Trees and brush passed by in the blackness, keeping the path to Mistvalle elusive. Beads of cold sweat formed on my face as shock from my wound overwhelmed me.

Blurs of black and white darted in my peripheral vision as Calla and the other raven followed us, their cries loud in the night.

The horse continued to pant as she galloped through the woods, dodging the twigs and thicket. Our two bodies were heavy on the mare's back, though there wasn't much to be done to ease her burden. My arms struggled to hold on to Casimir as he slumped on her mane.

I let out a string of curses as his body shifted to the left, causing my muscles to ache and beg for relief from the tension. I had to get him out of the forest.

Summoning every ounce of strength, I hoisted him higher on the horse, securing my arm around his waist as my other hand clenched the reins. The strain caused my fingers to cramp around the leather.

My heels kicked into the horse's side, imploring her to ride faster. She snorted in protest but picked up speed despite her exhaustion. I hoped she sensed my gratitude, as well as the urgency.

I glanced down at Casimir. His head bounced with every gallop of the horse and it caused more worry to fester. He already had a head injury, and the jarring motion could worsen it. There wasn't much to do, and I pulled him closer to me in an attempt to help, when abruptly, the mare reared up.

Casimir's weight was too much, and we slid from the saddle, the vines snapping. I cried out when his body collided with mine, a dead weight on top of me. My head swam with the impact.

A few feet in front of the mare, a wide stream ran through the woods, slippery rocks breaking up the area as the water roared. The horse trotted anxiously along the edge of the stream.

I rolled Casimir's body off mine and took in a greedy gulp of air. My back and neck ached from the fall, but from what I could tell, I was unscathed. It didn't matter, though, not as the energy drained from me, leaving my abilities depleted. We were stuck.

I surveyed our surroundings and spotted a grove of trees that would—if we were lucky—provide enough cover. My hands looped under Casimir's leather vest and I pulled him backward, dragging him through the dirt and brush to get us both out of eyesight, despite how it pained my shoulder and chest. We weren't far enough, but I couldn't think of any solutions that didn't involve trying to force the mare to cross the water. My wound and overuse of my abilities made it impossible to conjure anything.

When I clicked my tongue, the mare turned. Her training overpowered her fear and she trotted over at the sound.

I grunted and struggled with Casimir's weight until, finally, I laid him over an exposed tree root, his head resting on it. Sweat prickled at my brow and I huffed, slumping next to him. I lifted his head from the root and moved it to my lap, glancing over the gash on the edge of his scalp where the raider struck him. Blood clotted over it, making it jagged and black.

I gulped and fumbled along the pack at my side until I found the waterskin. I pulled it out and set it on his chest before I took the edge of my cloak in my hands. My dagger hissed out of the sheath, and I cut through the fabric.

The cap to the waterskin came open with ease and I poured a small amount onto the piece of cloth. My hand trembled when I brought it to Casimir's temple, where I applied gentle pressure to his wound. He didn't flinch or move, though I had hoped his eyes would snap open with the wet contact. Horrible thoughts awakened, and I hoped he would wake up— that the hit to his head hadn't been too much.

His chest continued to rise and fall. His pulse felt strong against my fingertips. Hope was unfamiliar and more cognate to a curse, yet I indulged in it, anyway.

To my surprise, the horse idled close by, though I didn't take the time to tie her reins to the tree. I had to trust that her training would be enough, and she would stay by my side until the sun rose again, and we found our way back to Mistvalle.

Far from the danger, my adrenaline faded. My back melted into the sturdy tree, my eyes heavy after using more of my abilities than I ever had before. I shut the forest out, telling myself I'd only rest for a minute.

Movement in my lap made me jolt awake, heart pounding till the noise drowned out anything else. Sleeping in the uncomfortable position caused soreness to settle in my neck. It was of little concern to me when I noticed Casimir stir awake. A groan parted his lips. Some of the tension left my shoulders, and I pressed a hand to the side of his face.

I brushed his hair back from his temple. "Casimir?" I spoke softly, trying to get him to wake up.

His face displayed his discomfort, and when drops of rain pattered on his skin, his eyes snapped open. The sight filled me with relief, even as a storm rolled in.

Casimir appeared dazed, his gaze finding mine through the heavy blink of his lashes. A flash of panic filled his expression. "Elita," he rasped.

My hand trembled on his cheek, and I slowly pulled it away. "Are you okay?" I asked, moving his hair back from the gash on his scalp. He winced and tried to sit.

"The raiders," he said, half raised on his elbows. "Where are they?" He searched our surroundings, confused.

"We're safe. For now, at least." I tried to help him sit, but he didn't seem to need it. He brought a hand to his head, grimacing when he touched the wound.

"How…" His gaze came back to mine, and he searched my face, before his eyes trailed over the rest of me. They froze on the cut through my tunic. "You're bleeding." He scrambled up too quickly, and swayed where he knelt.

I stopped his hand when it reached out to check my wound. "Rest. Please," I said, gently lowering his outstretched arm. "You've been out for gods only know how long. They hit you pretty hard."

He stared at me, his jaw twitching while he mulled over my words. When he swayed again, he seemed to agree, and sat back down with a huff, appearing dizzy.

I passed him the waterskin. "Drink." It wasn't a suggestion, and he took it from my hands.

While he chugged the water, I stood, my head swimming when I did. I hadn't dared a glance at my wound. There hadn't been time. It throbbed, the blood on the light gray tunic still dark red where it touched. The sight of it brought back horrible memories.

I pushed past the unsteadiness and forced my legs to carry me to the mare while the rain picked up, sweeping in sideways while thunder rumbled overhead.

The mare seemed anxious about the storms and I tied her reins to a tree, thinking it would be wise to make sure she couldn't run off. We'd need her as soon as the rain settled and Casimir wasn't unsteady.

I took the saddle, blankets and bags off her to use for some shelter against the harsh rain.

Casimir watched as I made my way back, even as the rain obscured visibility. I ducked near the tree and dropped what was in my hands. "I'm going to need your cloak."

Rain whipped through the trees, soaking our shelter. To shield us from some of the cold and wet, we placed leaves and saddle blankets on top of the cloaks that we propped overhead. It did little to combat the downpour, and water dripped through the fabric.

Casimir continued his search through the saddlebags, finding what we had on hand to tend to our wounds. He pulled out sutures, oils, and herbs. The bandages were no use. They were drenched the second he pulled them out of the protective leather.

I saw the worry on Casimir's face as his teeth worked at his lower lip. Carrying the minimal supplies he gathered, he moved closer. "I need to assess your wound," he said, gesturing to the blood on my tunic.

"But your head—"

"Enough about my head," he interrupted, scooting closer in the cramped space. "Will you let me help?"

My lips pressed into a line, and I glanced at the tear through the tunic, from my left collarbone to my shoulder. After I nodded, he moved closer, and his hands ducked into the fabric, tearing it wider to expose the cut.

His face twisted with concern, his gaze finding mine. "And you rode with me on that horse for how long?" He sounded bewildered. "You should have left me to the raiders," he muttered, his attention fixed back on the wound.

"Yeah, like you would have left me if it were reversed," I said, knowing such a thought wouldn't ever cross his mind.

Casimir sighed and shook his head. Once more, he inched closer, the heat from his body tangible in the cramped shelter. He eyed the space beneath my collarbone, assessing the damage.

When his fingertips ran over my bare skin, the wound twinged with burning pain. The nerves screamed at the contact, and I had to quell the urge to recoil.

He took his time looking it over before he glanced at me under his dark lashes. "I'll need to close it." His voice strained. I winced, wanting to move away, but his warmth was comforting, and there was nowhere to go.

His heavy, wet hair fell into his eyes, and without thinking, I brushed it back. Casimir stared at me, his expression unreadable.

"Can I begin?" His voice caught.

Even though I didn't want to, I nodded and pushed the torn flap of my tunic back to tuck it behind my shoulder. I tugged on the front of it with that same hand, exposing the length of it.

"Remind me to have you fitted for proper armor when we get back. Your torso will be made of scar tissue before long," Casimir said, his face twisting. I quirked a brow at him. "Yeah, I didn't think that through before speaking."

Casimir threaded the sutures with steady hands, covering the hook with salve. He took a moment to rub it over his hands as well. His throat bobbed when his gaze fixed back on my wound.

Apprehensive, he said, "I'm going to begin."

It did nothing for my nerves.

"Are you sure you can do this?" I asked.

"Of course. I captain a team of soldiers. I've sutured many wounds. It's just, on the ship—" He didn't finish. His jaw clenched, and he sighed, releasing his tense shoulders. "Try not to move too much, okay?"

I bit the inside of my cheek when he leaned toward me, the suture hook between his fingers. My free hand shot up, grabbing onto his shoulder with a shaky grip. He peered at me, wide-eyed.

"Sorry," I breathed.

Casimir shook his head and let my hand stay. He inched closer, straining to see with the limited light we had. The soft glow flickered from the lantern that we retrieved from the saddlebag.

It would have to be enough.

The anticipation built while I waited for him to begin, and I pursed my lips when the cold steel touched my skin. Casimir released a nervous exhale, and the hook broke through the edge of the wound.

Tears stung my eyes, and I whimpered, almost pushing him away.

"Elita," he said softly, a reminder not to move.

My fingers dug into his shoulder as the suture thread pulled through my flesh, and fire shot through my nerves. No matter how hard I tried, I couldn't prevent a few tears from slipping out.

He muttered apologies over and over, but continued. I held on to him, trying to focus on anything but the way the wound pulsated.

Casimir paused to look at me and his expression turned remorseful. Tears streaked my cheeks, but I didn't hold it against him.

"It's okay," I said, even as my chin quivered.

His attention went back to the wound. I averted my gaze to the top of our makeshift shelter, unable to watch. From where he laced the sutures at the edge of my shoulder, it seemed he was close to being done.

Breaking the tense silence, Casimir said, "I apologize for how I reacted earlier." He paused, and I glanced down at him. "I was mad at myself, and having you here…it scared the fuck out of me."

My fist knotted in his tunic as I stared at his petal covered hair while he worked, unsure what to say. His words had hurt me more than I could articulate.

Casimir continued, "You saved me, and not only that, but even managed to get me somewhere safe while wounded. I wouldn't have made it without you here."

Air hissed through my teeth, interrupting the moment. He pulled the last bit of the sutures, tying them off. He let go of a heavy exhale and sat back on his heels.

Casimir grabbed a dagger from the ground and cut through the threads, leaving behind uniform stitches. The threads lined with precision, an impressive work given the lack of visibility.

Before I could attempt to cover my chest, he grabbed my hand, stopping me. Casimir opened the salve and applied a thick amount to his fingers before grazing it over the stitches. My teeth clenched, but it was over in an instant.

"Finished." His voice strained, and he didn't meet my gaze. Casimir fumbled with the salve, closing it back, my blood on his hands. He began to desperately scrub it off, wiping them on whatever he could to rid his hands of the rust color.

It was my turn to reach out and stop his hands. His ember eyes appeared haunted. It wasn't hard to guess why, and memories rushed back to me of the day in the clearing, his hands painted with my blood after he brought me back.

"Casimir?"

A shade of red colored the tip of his ears, visible with our proximity. He didn't shake off my hand.

"Are you okay?" I asked.

The question made him pull away, his mask of indifference shadowing his features. "Fine."

In the silence, Casimir gathered the supplies and stuffed it back into the saddlebag. The twitch of his cheek and the tension in his jaw betrayed his attempt to hide the emotions.

After the long silence on the ship, we never spoke about when he brought me back. He never spoke of Ronin or what taking a life did to him. The memory of words whispered in a tent in Everbloom followed me —his desire to honor his mother's belief. While his actions were justified, it didn't seem to erase the guilt he carried.

It was my turn to inch closer.

My advance caught Casimir's attention. "What—"

"I'm going to check your wound, and you're going to let me," I said while I retrieved the waterskin. There wasn't much left, but it would be sufficient.

Casimir watched, his jaw remaining clenched. He flinched when I brought a piece of wet cloth to his wound, wiping at the cut across his temple. It wasn't as deep as I'd thought; a relief. It wouldn't need to be sutured.

His warm breath threatened to break my focus. He was close enough to scatter hairs from my face with a sigh. It made my hands tremble, but I didn't retreat.

I met his gaze. "You don't talk about what happened. Or, not with me, at least," I said, blotting the cut.

Casimir tensed. "There's nothing to talk about."

"Please, Casimir. Don't keep carrying it alone."

He searched my face, hesitant. Tension rolled through our shelter, palpable while I waited. Casimir fidgeted, a hand running through his hair, then tapping on his thigh.

I lowered the cloth from his wound, but I didn't move back. Our legs brushed when I shifted.

Silence filled the next few minutes before his shoulders hunched, hair falling over his forehead. "It's absurd," he said with a bitter chuckle. "What kind of captain can't accept that they had to take a life?"

Scarlet eyes met mine. Emotions swam in them, threatening to spill over. The sight made me rigid.

"Not for a moment do I regret it. If I could go back, I wouldn't change my decision to take his life. Not after he—" Casimir looked away. "It doesn't change how it felt to kill someone."

No amount of uncertainty could stop me from reaching out and resting my hand on his as it shook on his thigh. It settled with the weight from mine. I heard the shudder of his breath, heavy with the memory. It pained me when I watched him war with his own mind.

Outside, the rain continued to surge. It turned our shelter into nothing more than a heap of sodden fabric. A mirror to the rush of emotions flashing over Casimir's demeanor. They drenched him until tears settled at the edge of his eyes. He glanced at the top of our shelter. I watched him work through it, my hand never leaving his.

Eventually, he lowered his gaze. "You died, El." His voice caught, and the tears he continued to fight glistened at the rim of his eyes. "When I got to you, there was no pulse, no breath. I've never—fuck." Casimir turned his head, clenching his fists.

He could barely look at me. "I have dreams where your ribs crack under my hands. And your blood on my skin…those memories are the hardest. I wouldn't change what I did to Ronin, but if I could, I'd go back and try harder to get you to stay in Everbloom."

Nerves flitted through my veins when I squeezed his hand. The pressure was light, just enough to get him to look at me. When he did, the air caught in my lungs.

I forced myself to speak. "None of what happened falls on you. Please, don't keep blaming yourself. It was my choice to leave."

Casimir shuffled, his hand slipping out from under mine. "That doesn't change the fact I didn't try hard enough to change your mind."

His ability to hold on to the guilt made me deflate. Nothing could've stopped me from leaving Everbloom. Not with how everything transpired. The discovery about Valor, and the way they regarded Ronin's life, clouded my judgment.

It felt wrong to continue to allow the past to haunt us, yet Casimir couldn't bring himself to look me in the eye, even in such a small space. As quick as he opened up, he closed himself off.

With no warning, Casimir snuffed out the lantern, drenching us in darkness. "We'll ride when the rain stops," he said. "There isn't much time to warn Mistvalle. Sleep while you can."

"But—"

"It's too cold, and we've soaked our means of warmth." He hesitated, and without the light, I struggled to understand why. I heard him sigh, and jumped when he grabbed my wrist, tugging on it.

"What—"

"Body heat," he said, though it sounded like he didn't want to.

I was thankful for the cover of night, because my face was surely as red as his petals.

Unable to respond, I let him pull me closer. The sound of my pulse drowned out the thrum of the rain. It wasn't the cold that made me shiver, but his touch.

He laid back, his body stretching out on the damp ground. With a tender touch that made my stomach flutter, he led me to his side, allowing me to nestle into the crook of his arm.

Casimir's palm cupped my waist and held me to him. My hands moved to tuck beneath my chin, pressed to his chest. He turned until his body faced mine, our thighs brushing while he draped his other arm over me. No one had ever held me in such an intimate way and it threatened to make my heart leap from my rib cage. Inside my head, a storm of conflicting thoughts brewed, threatening to overflow.

The slope was too slippery. The heart was a foolish thing. Casimir was nothing more than my friend; my ghost. Yet when he pulled me even closer, his hand gripping my waist, the reality of my feelings flooded me.

I had fallen for him.

It was the worst mistake I made.

Thirty-Five

When I opened my eyes, a serene sunrise greeted me, casting a warm glow on the horizon as the rain subsided, leaving thick pockets of illuminated fog. The sight of the forest was jarring after I fell asleep in the makeshift shelter. Casimir's absence brought another wave of unease.

I shivered on the cold ground, noticing the lack of cloaks and saddle blankets. The few items that were gone brought me enough alarm, but the mare was nowhere in sight, either.

An awful thought crossed my mind; that the raiders had shown up and taken our things, and Casimir had attempted to fight them off with his head injury.

Just as the distressing thoughts started to take shape, footsteps to my left interrupted them. With the mare's reins in his grasp, Casimir emerged from the trees in the grove and made his way toward me, leading the horse.

He stopped a few feet away. "I didn't want to wake you until I had everything ready to depart. You seemed to be sleeping well," he said, interrupting the silence of the early hours.

Our cloaks hung out of the saddlebags—returned to the mare—and he had washed the remnants of blood from his hands. It appeared he'd been awake for some time.

When I stood, my back and arms ached from the overuse of my abilities, and the sutures stung as my arms raised over my head to stretch. I winced as my arms fell back down.

Casimir observed me. "How's your wound?" he asked, coming closer with the horse in tow.

"The skin feels tight, but it'll be fine."

"I know it goes without saying, but we have to leave. If we don't return to Mistvalle before night falls, the soldiers won't have any time to prepare."

I nodded in agreement before eyeing the horse with apprehension. It would be much easier to ride with Casimir awake and able to hold himself up, but fitting two people on the horse was no easy feat.

He noticed my hesitation and took a step closer. "I'll mount first. It'll be easier if you sit in front." He didn't wait for me to reply. In one fluid motion, he swung a leg over the saddle and pulled himself up. He stared down at me. "Let me help you." His hand reached out toward me.

My palm slid into his, and he pulled me quickly. If not for the stirrup, I would've fallen flat onto my back. I sat half in Casimir's lap to avoid sliding up and over the pommel.

Even with the dread for the impending fight, my stomach somehow found it appropriate to flip when he enveloped an arm around my waist. It brought me back to our limbs tangled in the dark of night, keeping each other warm.

"Ready?" he asked, his mouth close to my ear.

The only response I could give was a nod.

My heart won out the war with my head, and I resented it.

Casimir wrapped his free hand in the reins, holding them tight in his fist. With a kick of his heels and a jerk of the reins, the mare took off.

Descending the mountain pass was a swift ride that contrasted with the arduous trek up. With fewer people, and no mishaps, we made it back to Mistvalle with the sun high in the sky.

We rushed through the open gates, and the sound of thunderous hooves echoed through the entrance, making the guards scatter. The horse charged ahead on the stone paths of Mistvalle, and the familiarity filled me with a brief sense of peace, despite its impermanence.

King Lendorr and his soldiers marched on, and before long, a battle would ensue. Finding a way around it would be impossible. The Rose people wouldn't go without a fight, least of all, when Lady Estelle believed the answer to helping the realm was in my abilities.

Amidst the bustle of the crowd, we hurried toward the stables, the weight of dread following us. Casimir pulled us to an abrupt stop and my hand fell to his knee, bracing myself while the horse protested the sudden change in pace after she ran for so long.

When Casimir dismounted, I let out a sharp gasp, lost my balance and tumbled to the side. His hand wrapped around my bicep, and I grabbed onto the saddle. When my feet settled onto the stone, my legs wobbled, reminiscent of when we left the ships. Casimir released me once I got my footing.

A crowd of guards flooded the area. Among the crowd, Galan and Sabian appeared to be geared up to leave, accompanied by Valor. Their eyes went wide when they caught sight of us.

Disregarding their conversation, they all moved toward us, Valor leading the group as they clambered. I became more aware of my torn tunic and rested a hand over the fabric that had fallen off my shoulder. It wasn't a moment later that Valor stood before me, his hands grabbing my shoulders.

Pain sparked in the wound, but I just stared, bewildered.

"Damn it, Fullan. What were you thinking?" he stammered. It took him only a second to note the blood on my tunic, and he released me, his expression horrified. "What happened?" His gaze flicked to Casimir. "Were there raiders?"

Casimir took a step toward Valor, offering a small dip of his head. "A surprise attack when we left the lookout." He hesitated, before saying, "General, the king's army moves in Tyvolia. At most, we have four days to prepare.".

Valor's face flashed with anger. "Four days?"

Casimir gave a grim nod.

After a moment of contemplation, Valor shook his head and brought his attention back to me. "And what could have possessed you to leave the safety of Mistvalle to go on a mission you were refused? You could have been killed, Fullan."

I flinched at the change in how he addressed me. It wasn't with indifference, no, it mirrored the care of a father. I had been scolded in a similar manner much of my life when I got too reckless in the village. Now, the same fear of a father stared back at me.

It was Casimir who took another step, somewhat blocking me. "Sir, I would be dead if it weren't for Elita."

Valor's jaw clenched and his fists fixed into tight balls at his sides. The anger in his expression still burned at me, and underneath the surface, I saw the surprise and fear.

It made my head spin, and I faced Casimir, adjusting the torn piece of my tunic as it threatened to fall again.

The constant conflicting emotions toward Casimir, or toward my blood relation to Valor, were too much. The need to isolate myself threatened to suffocate me. A festering desire to hide my heart. I didn't need Valor to play the role of a father. I didn't want Casimir and his warm hands and his steady heartbeat against my ear as I fell asleep.

The thoughts sent a jolt through me, swirling in confusion and distress, and I was grateful when Galan stepped forward, his arm wrapped in a sling. His hair was disheveled, and he hadn't bothered to change his armor since they returned. They must have jumped right into explaining what happened, and I wondered how long it took them to return. Galan had been too injured to go down the mountain with haste.

Despite his exhausted demeanor, Galan spoke up. "General, our scouting team owes a great deal to Ms. Blackthorne."

My cheeks burned when both of them defended me. The months spent training paid off, and while I knew I was capable, their support gave me another swell of confidence. Enough that when every head turned in my direction, I didn't want to hide. I had proven myself.

Valor appeared split. He was unapologetically stubborn, and I wondered if it was him I got the trait from rather than my mother. The thought was another pull toward trusting Valor.

The crowd waited in anticipation for Valor to say something. He was deprived of the chance when Lady Estelle emerged from the stables, donned in a beautiful display of shimmering armor.

Silver swirls twisted through rose gold armor plates. She glimmered from head to toe, and her hair was once more twisted into elaborate braids that kept it away from her face.

No one had to be told to move out of the way. The crowd parted as she came closer, taking in our appearances. I prepared myself for another scolding, or perhaps a demand for me to spend the next few weeks locked in the palace under constant guard.

It took me by surprise when a pleasant smirk graced her face. "Our white bloom shows her strength once more. Even so, her general means to discredit her." She sauntered closer and placed a hand on Valor's shoulder. "Perhaps you should view her as a soldier, and not your blood." Her hand dropped when she spoke to him.

Valor straightened, his mask of indifference falling into place.

Estelle approached, taking my hands in hers. Her eyes danced as she began a quick assessment of my wounds. Everyone gave us space. Some backed away or left altogether.

When Estelle pulled back, her face fell. "We will get you to Halburn at once. Both of you," she said. Her attention fell to Casimir beside me. "Once you both have been mended, we require a meeting with the council to make plans. Vanmore, we will take your map in the meantime to begin preparations."

Everything moved in a blur. Casimir handed her the map he had marked on the cliffs. It seemed pointless. The king's army wouldn't have remained idle. They would already be closer than what he marked. The thought made the hair on my arms stand.

Galan was the one who ushered me from the dispersing crowd. Most of the guardsmen followed Valor and Estelle toward the palace to round up the council members.

I stared at the bandages on Galan's arm when we exited the busy area, noting the bloodstains that leaked through the white of the bandages. The sight of it made my stomach churn with nausea. As the battle on the horizon drew closer, my nervousness grew.

Another pair of footsteps trailed behind us, and I didn't have to look to know they belonged to Casimir. I felt the familiarity in the thrum of the earth. It brought me relief when Estelle sent him for a healing. He needed the attention of their healers.

I passed Galan and hurried into the healer's center, not needing anyone to help me find it. It had become like a second home. Especially after they discovered my mending abilities. Every healer wanted to study me. All but Halburn, and I was thankful for his disinterest.

The indifference disintegrated when he caught sight of me and the top of my tunic, torn and bloodied. I could practically hear his thoughts chastising me, a frustrated melody of his wasted endeavors.

Halburn met us halfway. "Now what've you gotten yourself into?" His voice echoed in the vacant building. Most of the healers appeared to be elsewhere, likely in preparation for the battle.

A bitter taste filled my mouth when I remembered how Taryn told me they turned down her offer to help. She was of no use in Mistvalle, and yet I wished she was the one scolding me rather than Halburn.

Not in the mood to answer his question, I moved over to my usual cot and sat with a huff. Exhaustion and anxiety plagued me. An exam, along with a healing, were the last things I wanted. If we didn't have the king breathing down our necks, I would've trudged up the hill and tucked myself away in my old tent—far from Casimir, with the drapes double knotted—and attempted sleep.

The reality remained that King Lendorr was mere days away, and I needed to be in the best shape possible if there was any hope to convince Valor and Estelle to allow me to fight with the people of Mistvalle and Everbloom.

Halburn sat in front of me and I tugged on the torn piece of my tunic, no longer bashful around him. He'd seen my torso more times than I could count, and it didn't faze me.

However, Casimir's burning stare did.

Warmth spilled across my face, and I avoided his gaze by looking at the sutured skin. It appeared as if a seamstress stitched it in a well lit room, rather than a battered captain who had one lone lantern to light his work.

Halburn released a heavy sigh. "This will heal much better than your old one. But you'll probably have nerve damage. Please, try to avoid any more wounds like this."

I wanted to roll my eyes, but thought better of it.

I shrugged and said, "Captain Vanmore implied I'm to be fitted for proper armor. Then maybe I can stay out of your hair." From the corner of my eye, Casimir tensed. I tried to ignore it.

The likelihood of him having armor found or made for me was slim to none. I saw it in his worried gaze as it roved over my scarred skin. The hope of fighting alongside the guard dwindled with each second I spent in Casimir's watchful presence. He had told me he wouldn't stop trying to protect me, and the weight of his fear began to drag me down. I reminded myself how desperate mine made me, and tried to sympathize.

My jaw clenched when Halburn placed a hand on my skin to begin the healing process. Casimir continued to watch, his arms crossed over his chest.

"Are you going to stand there and gawk, or are you going to get your head checked?" I didn't mean for it to come out with so much bite, and Casimir appeared confused.

Galan was close by, but he showed no sign of offense. He offered me a single nod and left, even though his presence wasn't the one that made me irrational.

More healers ushered into the room and Galan strode over to them. I hoped they could heal his arm before he was required to fight. They needed every member of the guard they had.

Casimir remained near even though I snapped at him. Every flick of his gaze made me want to hide, lest my heart run off with my head once more.

When a healer approached him with a kind smile and a gentle prodding to a different cot, I sighed in relief. The healing process continued with Halburn, and my shoulders drooped. Energy surged beneath my skin, no longer strange to me.

The wound wouldn't be gone, but I only needed it manageable. I didn't intend to remain in Mistvalle when they marched.

Halburn finished with my wound, and I barely had my tunic sorted over the sutures before I darted out of the healing center. I needed space and a clear head.

Casimir and Galan were both preoccupied with their own healings and I sprinted down the pearly white steps, going straight through the markets, which were eerily empty.

Estelle wanted me back at the palace, but I couldn't bring myself to go. Not yet. Every inch of my body was over-exerted and exhausted, but I made it up the familiar path.

The emptiness of the camp was unsettling. All the tents remained, but no one was there. It occurred to me they must have moved families to a safer area.

Navy blue fabric shuddered in the breeze when I approached my tent. It stood undisturbed, bringing an odd sense of comfort as I walked back inside the protective drapes. My bed frame lacked a cushion. It sat among Casimir's things—which seemed more scandalous to me then, and I hated how it came across to other people. Their assumptions would be incorrect, but it didn't stop the mortification when I considered the gossip that spread throughout the Everbloom camp.

I disregarded the thoughts and made quick work of swapping my bloodied clothes for new ones. I adorned myself with a pair of tight black trousers, a more fitted gray tunic, and a leather armor vest. It was stained black, but the ties were a contrast of scarlet.

Once my boots were on, I draped a wither cloak over my shoulders and fastened the silver clasp. If I were going to ask to be on the guard, I needed to fit the part. Valor would oppose me, and there were likely others who'd agree with a refusal from him. With any luck, Casimir would be a voice of encouragement.

I doubted it.

Thirty-Six

The council room was more intimidating than I anticipated. Faces scowled when I entered—their bodies were donned in armor, with weapons close by. They appeared less like the usual timid council, and more akin to warriors ready to ride into battle. An eerie silence fell over them. Whatever they'd been saying died in their throats, and I tried not to let it deter me.

I squared my shoulders and walked into the room. With any luck, they wouldn't notice the way my hands trembled at my sides. Valor's scowl, along with Casimir's gaze of dismay, made some of my resolve wane.

They would oppose me without a second thought.

Halburn and Sol drew my attention. They sat in full armor among the rest of the council, close to Casimir. Where Halburn watched me enter, disappointed, Sol gave a rare look of approval that gave me a spark of courage.

Lady Estelle sat at the head of the table, and amid hardened soldiers, she offered me a welcome smile.

"Elita, what a pleasure it is to have you here. Captain Vanmore was discussing the run-in with the raiders. Thank Aeterna you were there to assist him."

It caught me off guard, but I smiled and dipped my head. Casimir shifted in his seat, appearing flustered. From the expression on Sol's face, it amused her.

"Thank you, my lady," I said in return. The nerves simmered beneath the surface, and I choked them down. On shaky legs, I made my way closer to the council table, using Sol and Estelle's approval to give me confidence.

I didn't fit. I didn't belong. But I refused to turn around.

Estelle gestured toward a spot at the table, and my heart raced. "Please, have a seat."

Before I had the chance to reply or sit, a chair scraped hard across the floor, and a man with striking blonde hair stood, his face twisted in what looked like disgust. It would take more than that to make me recoil.

"My lady, she has no place at this table. She isn't a member of our council, nor the guard," the man spat, his glare fixed on Estelle.

Her pointed smile sent a shiver down my spine. She didn't appear to take kindly to being questioned. "Bolin, I can assure you, she is welcome at my table. If you take issue with that, you may be dismissed."

Bolin sputtered, but he didn't dare challenge her again. When he sat with a deflated huff, I stood taller. I wasn't ready to sit, not yet. While her word implied I was welcome, it wasn't enough. I wanted to become a formal member of the guard.

I swallowed the nerves and met her gaze. "Actually, my lady, that's what I'm here to discuss—" The words barely made it out before Valor stood. Another opposing voice, and I worried he would drown out anything I said.

"I will not accept you on my guard. There is no room for someone with less than six months of training under her belt. Captain Vanmore may have spoken of your heroic efforts, but that doesn't change the fact that you directly disobeyed a general and captain without a second thought." Valor was quick and harsh. I expected nothing less.

Inhaling through my nose, I replied, "I ask you to reconsider, General. This isn't a scouting mission. I have seen the army that marches, and I want to fight."

Valor scoffed, his expression hardening.

Estelle raised a hand to silence him as he went to speak. Even though I was willing to fight for what I wanted, her being on my side upped my odds.

"Let her speak." Estelle's voice chimed throughout the council room. Halburn's attention turned to her, his distress clear.

I tuned him out and gave Estelle a nod of thanks. "My abilities are unique and could be of use on the battlefield. Especially when you take into consideration that existing roots in Tyvolia are weak from rot." Images of Lendorr and Talos flickered in my mind. "And I have met the king and his son. My knowledge may be of use."

It was a mistake to look at Casimir. He appeared haunted, and his plea for me to breathe, to stay, became overbearing. *I can't sit in safety while others pay for my choices. Not anymore.*

"What do you know of the men who march?" Estelle asked, bringing me back to the present.

I hated to remember my encounter with them, but hoped it would help me. "The people in the Iron Thorn are unaware of their true nature. They march for a king who has sentenced many to death for simply protecting their children." Horrible memories surfaced. Ronin's daughter, his wife, their blood on the king's hands. And so many more. "My lady, if not for the cruelty of the king, we may not be in this position. It was the death of Ronin's daughter and his wife that led him to his actions. And he isn't the only one. Many more have endured the same at the hand of the king."

Despite holding Estelle's attention, another stood, and I had to fight the urge to roll my eyes at Orin when he spoke. "How convenient for you to blame the king. Were you not the one who bargained for the norm's release in Everbloom?" Orin's smooth deposition couldn't hide the pleasure he got from watching me wince.

The room fell silent, all eyes on me. Another version of myself would have crumbled at the accusation. While it stung, I knew there was truth to it.

"Yes, Orin. I bargained for his freedom. His intentions were unknown to me. There isn't a realm where I wouldn't have done the same." Shock rippled through the room, and a few people snarled. "I've seen enough in Mistvalle to know norms and Roses can coexist in peace, yet you were quick to sentence a man to death—a man who appeared innocent." The memory of defending Ronin in the fortress made my skin crawl, but I continued, "How can we claim to be any better than the king if we're quick to kill those different from us?" No matter how much I believed the words, they tumbled out.

Orin sneered at me. "Do the lives lost in Everbloom mean nothing to you?" he spat.

My brow furrowed, and I took a step closer to the table, standing across from him. "I feel the weight of every life in this realm on my shoulders," I hissed and placed a hand on the table, not cowering when he glared in my face. "The Roses and every innocent person in this realm. Not norms, but *people*. Ronin was a man twisted by grief, and the king was the cause for that."

Orin scoffed. "Playing ignorant doesn't suit you. You denied your destiny, and the gods have punished you for it."

Sol shook her head. "Nonsense of a heretic," she said, further infuriating Orin.

"The prophecy called for her sacrifice. If we could change the events, I would've escorted her to the Temple myself—"

It was Valor who stood, a finger jabbed at Orin. "Know your place. Elita is not on trial for her misgivings. Remind yourself of that."

The room shifted, swimming in the emotions that warred at the table. Conflict made the flicker of the lanterns taunting; they cast shadows off the bodies which stood, unrest fueling the flames.

"Enough!" Estelle's voice rang throughout the room, silencing anyone else tempted to speak. Her red gaze flickered to Orin, glowering until he yielded and sat in his seat. There was no wiping the smirk from his face.

My palms burned with the familiar sensation of power surging below the surface. I had to control myself if I wanted a place on the guard. Giving in to my emotions was not an option.

The disapproval of my father among the others almost made me give in. To turn away like the frightened girl I was taught to be. No more training or risks. Just peace until the realm ended.

But I didn't want that. Not anymore.

There was a time where I would have given anything for freedom and peace. But I had too much to lose. There were too many people I cared for who were ready to fight a battle my choices brought to their doorstep.

Despite being terrified, I faced Estelle and removed my hand from the table. "Lady Estelle, I came to this council to be granted permission to fight with the other Roses. I'm prepared to serve on the guard." I ignored the sound of another chair scraping the marble floor.

In my peripheral vision, Valor tensed. "Estelle, you cannot truly consider allowing her—"

"You will accept whatever member I deem part of your team, General. And should you refuse, you are free to stay behind in Mistvalle."

My eyes went wide, and I stopped myself from spewing words of gratitude to Estelle.

Valor's jaw clenched, and his gloved hands balled into tight fists. Sol smirked and appeared seconds from laughing at him.

I found Casimir's gaze, my heart plummeting. The fear in his eyes was plain for all to see—desperate, pleading. Our thoughts didn't need to mingle for me to know how horrified he was.

"General, Captain, welcome your new member to your guard," Estelle offered me a kind smile and sat down. "Be sure to find her proper armor before we ride in two days. She'll need it."

My stomach flipped with both fear and excitement. Responsibility fell like a familiar blanket over my shoulders. I grew up with the weight of the kingdom on my back. Taking on the duty of the guard, by choice, gave me a new sense of purpose. One I hadn't felt in a long time.

Taryn was the first to congratulate me when she found me in the armory with Sol. I stood on a platform, surrounded by seamstresses who surveyed me. The stone room was dimly lit and empty except for a few chairs and displays of unused armor.

In normal Taryn fashion, she didn't make a fuss because of the prophecy. She didn't bring up her doubts. Her amusement was a nice respite, and I was grateful for Taryn and Sol's easy company.

"I'm surprised Valor didn't make a bigger deal. You should've seen the mess he was in when you didn't wake up for a few days in Orondal."

Taryn shook her head while she ran a hand through Ulrik's curls while he rested on her lap.

Sol leaned on a pillar close to the platform, her arms and ankles both crossed. When I left the council room, she followed along, and in her own way, seemed giddy. She took joy in watching Casimir sulk.

I met Taryn's gaze, an eyebrow quirked. "He could use some work on his communication skills. When I first woke up, he implied that, if not for Casimir, he would've left me behind."

At that, Sol chuckled, trying to hide it behind a cough. I rolled my eyes at her.

Taryn shrugged. "Some people are just no good at speaking their feelings. I could name one in this room." She gave me a look, and my cheeks grew warm.

It made it worse that I knew exactly what she meant.

When I turned to let them continue their measurements on my legs, I looked at Sol, changing the subject. "Perhaps I should have let them know I've never trained in full armor before," I said, ignoring the way the Mistvalle armorer looked alarmed.

Sol's emerald armor shimmered in the lantern light when she shifted. "A captain who didn't train you in armor?" She shook her head. "A fool. Typical for a male."

I stifled a laugh and surveyed Taryn and Ulrik, already in their sleep clothes. "What will you two do while we're gone?" I asked.

Ulrik sat straighter, sadness in his pale green eyes. "You're leaving?" His voice was small, a whisper in the large room.

Taryn looked down at him, a soft smile on her lips. When she met my stare, I saw the somber shift in her expression. "They've just got to handle something, bub. But, Elita will be back soon. Plus, she's got that smelly captain to keep her in check."

I chuckled when Ulrik's face lit up, knowing who she meant.

"He's a nice captain," Ulrik said. "They'll both come back?"

Ulrik was looking at Taryn, and I was grateful for it. My smile fell, replaced by fears I was too stubborn to confront until then.

There was no guarantee that any of us would make it back. The goal was to stop Lendorr and Talos from taking Mistvalle—from hurting the people there. We'd be lucky if even half of us made it back in one piece. It was a sobering thought, and made it easier to understand why Valor was so adamant about not letting me go.

Taryn patted Ulrik's back, whispering to him. She wouldn't lie, but I could tell she avoided the truth.

They both grew distracted when the squawking exchange of birds echoed in the archway, the doors held open by stones. Calla jumped along the steps, the white raven accompanying her, seemingly to pester her.

Ulrik giggled and slid off Taryn's lap to creep closer to the birds. He stayed quiet, never getting too close. He stopped a few feet away and crouched, wrapping his arms around his legs.

Taryn sighed as she got up from her spot. Her arms crossed over her chest, and she stopped to stand close to me. "You better come back, white bloom." It was spoken softly, more emotion than Taryn typically displayed.

I looked at her, a halfhearted smile on my lips. "Really encouraging, Taryn. Thanks."

In spite of herself, she grinned. "There's very few people here I actually like. Don't leave me to care for the bird. I've got enough on my hands with that one." She tipped her chin lovingly at Ulrik.

"I wouldn't dream of it. I'll do my best."

The women measuring me finished and left us. They grinned when they passed by Ulrik, his frame small and drowning in the long cloak he wore.

Taryn took another step closer, a goofy look on her face. "Plus, I've got an ongoing bet with Alba. Can't win if you or Vanmore dies."

Sol sputtered behind me, covering her mouth.

"Not amusing. Don't you two have anything better to do?" I grumbled, stepping off the platform.

Taryn waved her hand dismissively, and went over to where Ulrik continued to watch the two birds—just blurs of black and white as they lifted into the night.

I watched Calla go, remembering when she first ever came to me. Before the fire. Before everything changed.

A pang of guilt washed over me when I realized how long it'd been since I thought of my parents. Perhaps that was part of healing. Not the absence of grief, but rather than drowning under the weight of it, I continued on, wading through the changes.

I was surrounded by people I cared about, and people who cared for me. They continued to lift me when I didn't have the strength to do it myself. They carried me through the worst of it.

It was easier to recognize it then—the reason I wanted to ride with the guard and fight. I had something worth fighting for.

Sol pushed off of the pillar, and the dim orange light reflected on her armor, like a flame consuming a forest of emerald trees. Her entire demeanor changed without the linen gardening clothes or the light leathers used for sparring. I only hoped I'd exude the air of a warrior the way she did.

She paused close by and stared at the retreating birds, indifferent. It was an improvement to how much she originally disliked them.

Taryn lifted Ulrik from the ground, his lanky limbs seemingly longer each day. I watched, smiling when Ulrik wrapped his arms around her shoulders.

I glanced between Taryn and Sol. "So, would either of you be interested in helping me figure something out before we leave?" I asked.

Taryn chuckled. "Of course."

In contrast, Sol shrugged. "Depends."

Not bothered by her indifference, I smiled. "I just need help figuring out how to keep my hair out of the way. It's a pain." The curls were finally beneath my collarbones, but still shorter than I was accustomed to.

Sol observed my hair before she ran a hand over her own, which was cropped shorter than mine, a sharp cut at her jawline. It seemed she didn't share the sentiment.

Taryn came up beside me, eyeing my hair. "Eh, shouldn't be too difficult. We'll fix you up with something."

"Well, Sol, you're welcome to join, even just to watch and keep us company." I threw on my wither cloak. It didn't give me immediate relief from the cold, but I didn't mind.

Sol's boots shuffled on the icy stone floor. After a moment of contemplation, she nodded.

Taryn made way for the exit, Ulrik content to rest in her arms. "Not to be morbid, but I really did mean it. You better come back."

I bristled, feeling the weight of her request.

"I'll do my best. Promise," I said.

A glance at Sol gave me pause. In her expression was a warning: there were no guarantees. Even so, I would try my hardest to keep my word. If not for them, I made the promise for myself, too.

After all this time, I should've been used to the notion, but I wasn't ready to die.

Thirty-Seven

Sol sat across from me on the floor of my tent while Taryn knelt behind me, trying to get my hair braided. Ulrik's head rested on her lap, asleep despite the glow of the lanterns.

When I flinched, Sol raised a brow. Time passed in a blur of black curls falling into my eyes. An hour wasted on efforts that seemed fruitless.

Grumbling, Taryn released my hair again, causing a mess of onyx to trail over my forehead. I blew upward and sent them sprawling.

"That's all I've got in me. I can't get the shorter curls to stay in the braid." Taryn shifted, pulling Ulrik higher into her arms.

I rubbed at my neck, sore after the many silly maneuvers she had me perform to make sure it would stay in place. Although that didn't compare to how my scalp ached from her constant pulling and adjusting.

Sol sighed and got up. "Let me," she said.

Taryn scoffed. "Like you'll be any better at it."

"Adequate enough. I've braided my own."

I couldn't imagine Sol with braided hair. She always wore it the same, but if she got mine to stay, it'd be preferable to Taryn's rough attempts.

"Give it your best, Sol," I said.

Taryn acted as if she wanted to protest. But she caved and moved out of the way to let Sol replace her.

Sol settled in the spot behind me, her hands gentle when they brushed through my hair. A shiver shook my shoulders, and Sol paused before continuing to softly gather my hair. I chuckled.

"What's amusing?" Sol asked.

"Nothing, I just didn't take you for the gentle type. Or the type to braid hair. You're soft, admit it."

Sol stopped and cleared her throat. "Say a word to anyone, you'll be bedridden for months."

A bout of laughter nearly sputtered past my lips, but I stifled it. Taryn seemed to find it amusing, but she turned her head, not willing to anger Sol more. Her hand ran over Ulrik's hair while she watched us.

It didn't take Sol long to wrap a halo braid around my head. Secure, and more uniform than anything Taryn conjured. I didn't hold it against her, considering how long her hair was.

After Sol perfected the braid, all three of them left my tent. Sol assured me that she would find me before we rode out to manage my hair. There was no way I would keep the tight halo braid in my hair for the next two days.

I stood in the middle of my tent, alone at night for the first time since my encounter with Karion. My gaze flickered to the empty bed frame, noting the absence of my cushion. There was no part of me that wanted to return to Casimir's tent. Not only would he scold me, but I would have to be close to him.

An uncomfortable heat crept up my cheeks when I thought of falling asleep on the ground with him. It was foolish, and I resented my heart and even Casimir.

Part of me knew he wouldn't hurt me. But it didn't erase the things he had already done to cause me pain and apprehension. From hiding the truth of who my father was, to the silence after I'd lost everything. He hid the fact that Ronin was in Everbloom, knowing Valor and Orin planned to kill him.

The more I thought it over, the stronger my conviction became. I couldn't go back to his tent. I needed to focus on preparing for the fight that was fast approaching. If I found the time, maybe I could even spar with Alba, Sol, or Galan. Either way, I needed to avoid Casimir.

A rush of panic hit me when I thought of the visions. The battle had arrived, and I almost darted out of the tent to beg Casimir not to go. To stay where it was safe. But I knew he wouldn't even consider it.

Sighing, I shook out the rest of my braid, allowing the tension to release some from my scalp. Despite my absent cushion, I resolved to sleep in my tent. And so late in the day, I wasn't willing to risk retrieving it.

It would be a horrible night of rest.

Using what remained in my tent, I laid out a few of the extra wither blankets on the ground and fashioned a cloak into a makeshift pillow. It wasn't much, but it'd have to do. At least until I snuck into Casimir's tent to get my things back.

The harsh icy winds blew through the tent as if the fabric weren't even there. Quickly, I threw on a nightgown, missing the warmth of my tunic and cloak the second they were off. I shivered and nestled into my blanket. My ankles rubbed together, trying to create some friction to warm my body. It offered little relief.

I laid there for what seemed like an hour before I gave up, sitting straight. It'd been a month since I used them, but I needed something to help, or I wouldn't get any sleep before the battle. So, despite the bitter cold, I stumbled out of my tent, carrying a tea kettle and the herbs that Halburn gave me.

Very few people bustled through the camp. Most of them appeared to be getting ready to depart to wherever the safe stronghold was. Estelle only mentioned it in passing, but she assured it would be enough to keep those who did not wish to fight a safe place to wait it out.

I tuned out the unusual chaos and walked over to the fire ring that had seen better days. The lack of use left it neglected and covered in fallen leaves. I hoped the dead brush would help the fire start quicker.

To my delight, it sparked easily, and I went to work filling the kettle from a nearby well. Within a few minutes, everything was ready, and the iron kettle rested on a hook above the fire.

The flames licked up the edges of it, closer than necessary, but I wanted to return to my tent before my fingers froze.

Soon, the pressure in the kettle intensified until it emitted a gentle whistle. I pulled it off before it got any louder, and made my way back into the tent, shaking from the cold.

I popped the sachet of herbs into the kettle and left it alone, shuffling back into my blankets with a mug and the herbs close by. The scent filled the tent. Swirling in clouds of licorice and mint steam. It soothed me.

Comfort burned into longing when I thought of the times Casimir made me tea to aid in his absence.

Time passed in a blur of exhaustion as I poured the tea, sipping on it the second it cooled enough not to scald my tongue. The flavor wasn't as familiar anymore, and the licorice aftertaste bothered me long after I finished the drink.

I set the empty mug down and curled deeper into the blankets.

While the herbs worked their way through my system, an abrupt swell of regret came over me—regret for lying next to Casimir; regret because I wanted to again.

The thoughts mixed with the herbs. They moved fast, firing off in flashbacks of kind ember eyes, and flickering back to years long past—an unsure lanky teenager popping into my dreams, his hair cropped short, and his responsibilities too big for his shoulders.

Numbness took over my limbs, and my eyes fell shut. The sensation was unnatural, not a peaceful lull into darkness.

Anything was better than the memories of Casimir before his years of disappearance. They were lonely years, and I wondered if they felt that way for him, too.

The pain melted and the herbs pulled me deeper.

Wisteria trees blossomed, their flowers swaying in a fresh breeze, white catching in the rays of light. Misplaced flowering bushes sprang from the ground, creating a circle around a white rosebush.

None of it should have been possible, yet they appeared placed by Aeterna herself.

The breeze rustled again, taking with it a few stray white petals. They swirled in the light, glimmering to reflect the sun. My heart stuttered as I watched them fall in an elegant dance.

When they touched the grass below, more flowers sprang up in their wake. I watched in awe. A strange sensation thrummed through my body, and the pull to reach out and put my hand to the earth became magnetic. My limbs moved of their own accord and my palm found the damp grass. It rustled against my skin, warm and soft. Then, the greenery vanished, like smoke beneath my fingers. It revealed a stone platform, a misplaced sphere in the earth. When I flattened my hand, energy coursed through my veins, symbols came to life, and thudded in tune with my heartbeat as they appeared. The same runes I had seen before. Energy, life, balance, and death.

A breath fell from my lips as they came to life, carved into the stone. They echoed with a soft ruby glow.

"He searches for you."

The voice drenched me in comfort, unable to startle me. It wrapped around me, and a deeper knowing settled in my soul.

Akuma stood across the field, never moving closer. The hood of his cloak rested on his shoulders, revealing white hair that fell like a waterfall, cascading down his back.

He watched me, black and icy blue eyes pulling me in. My fingers twitched on the stone, the energy dissipating until it left a hollow sensation in my chest.

"If she awakens, he will find you." Akuma's words carried in a delicate breeze and I shut my eyes, letting the melodic tone fill my head.

The warning had the opposite effect. An odd smile tugged at my lips— not my own.

When I opened my eyes, Akuma stood before me, towering and transcendental. Stars echoed in his onyx skin. A night sky using his body as a canvas. Petals scattered in the breeze, the white catching on his cloak. More flowers bloomed behind him, a sea of roses that buried the stone platform.

Every inch of space that the god of death closed caused the white roses to turn black with rot, and sadness evaporated the smile on his lips. Knowing echoed in his eyes.

"He cannot find you. He will not have you."

The scene distorted behind Akuma, darkness consuming the field. Before I could speak or move, his palm flattened to my chest, searing my skin.

"Stop!" I cried, stumbling back.

Black and crimson flickered at the edge of my vision, weak. A voice whispered in the corners of my mind, too quiet to make out the words, but visceral enough to feel the sting of betrayal.

I gasped and sat in a panic. The wither air did nothing to stop my nightgown from being drenched in sweat. I placed a hand to my burning chest, my heart hammering until it made me dizzy.

Movement in the drapes of my tent made me jump, and I turned to see Casimir there. In his black armor, he resembled a shadow.

"Fuck, Casimir, do you have any sense of boundaries?" I rasped. My hands gripped onto my blankets, causing my fingers to cramp. There was no time to come down from the nightmare.

"Now you know how I've felt," he said, walking into the tent.

My brow creased. "Absolutely not. I've never walked into your tent without you opening the drapes for me. Have you come to chain me to my bed so I can't join the guard?"

Casimir stammered, his eyes wide. "No, I—" he paused, scanning over my makeshift bed on the ground. His hands clasped behind his back. "You never came to my tent. For your bed mat, of course." He stumbled over his words. "I wanted to make sure you were okay."

I was grateful for the cover of night as my cheeks burned a furious red. "I'm fine. I figured it was time I went back to my tent."

Casimir surveyed the space, going from my makeshift bed to the kettle and mug still sitting beside me. "I apologize for waking you."

The words pulled me back to the dream and my knuckles rubbed at my sore chest. The feeling it evoked was unmistakably familiar.

In stark contrast to normal nightmares, this dream was tangible. It felt real. The sensation of the grass, the sting from Akuma's hand. Worry crept in when I noticed the absence of the earth's thrum.

My knuckles quit kneading, but the fragments of betrayal rattled in my chest incessantly. Whatever he had done, the pain ran bone deep. Unwilling to be excused as just a dream.

"El?" It wasn't new for him to shorten my name, but it quickened my pulse.

I glanced up at him and dropped my hand. "I'm fine," I said again, wrapping my hands into the blanket. "You can go rest now. You'll need it before we return to the mountain pass."

The images from the dream burned across my vision, but I didn't want to tell him. It wasn't uncommon for me to have odd dreams after taking the herbs, and I let that explain it, despite how my soul ached.

Casimir pressed his lips in a tight line and gave a reluctant nod. "Again, I apologize for disturbing your sleep." He turned to leave, but paused in the drapes, he looked back at me, his gaze intense. "I know you won't change your mind, but I wish you'd reconsider joining the guard."

The words made my stomach drop. "Casimir—"

"Lady Estelle's insistence is suspicious, and the general agrees. Your presence on the battlefield isn't wise."

I bit the inside of my cheek and looked away.

The doubt took root in my mind lightning quick. I resented him for disturbing my sleep to leave me with paranoia.

I didn't reply. I'd have more luck arguing with a rock than Casimir.

With no more cryptic warnings, he left and tied the drapes closed.

I laid back onto my makeshift pillow, which was damp from sweat. My pride wouldn't let me follow him back to his tent, even if I only planned to grab my bed cushion and leave.

His suspicions made me nervous, but they wouldn't deter me. I'd make it my goal to avoid him until the guard began their march. My plan only worked if he didn't storm into my tent again.

I feared if he did, maybe I'd listen—and perhaps I'd ask him to stay with me. The thought made me more anxious than riding into battle.

Following Casimir's interruption to my sleep, rest evaded me. I tossed and turned the remainder of the night, unable to get his warning out of my mind. I didn't want to believe Estelle had any ill wishes for me, and yet, the seed of doubt took root, already growing out of proportion.

I needed to sort through the thoughts on my own. After clambering out of the makeshift bed on the ground, I had walked to the stables in the early hours.

Apart from the gentle rustle of straw and the distant chatter of stable workers, it was quiet and empty enough that it gave me the space to be alone with my thoughts.

My mare shuffled in the stall while I brushed her silky coat. The bristles ran over her dark hair, leaving behind brush lines. With my opposite hand, I pet her mane. "I never did thank you for getting us out of those woods. Hopefully, I'll get to ride out with you. You're resilient."

"Nix is a fine choice."

The interruption made me jump, and I turned to see Valor approach me.

I faced the mare—Nix—again, and with a smile, I gently patted her mane. "I've visited these stables often and never knew her name."

Valor stopped outside the stall, eyeing the mare. "She's one of the best, according to Lady Estelle. A well-trained horse for long journeys."

I set the brush down and looked at Valor, crossing my arms under my cloak. "She got us out of those woods with little protest. I'm impressed with how well she handled two riders."

Valor met my gaze; his red eyes akin to looking in a mirror. "I take it you have not changed your mind regarding tomorrow?" he asked.

I sighed. "First Casimir, now you."

"Don't confuse people wanting to protect you with people doubting you, Fullan. I don't believe a single Rose here would doubt how capable you are, especially after you saved Captain Vanmore on your own." He paused, his stare unnerving. "But the prophecy remains. Whether we understand it or not, you are the white bloom, and there may be hope for the realm."

I averted my gaze. "I wish people would stop saying that," I grumbled. My fingers found the fraying edges on my cloak and I fiddled with them.

Valor hesitated, then said, "No one asks to be chosen by the gods. Regardless, they saw fit to choose you."

Knots twisted in my stomach when I recalled a similar conversation with my other father long ago. The wound lingered under the surface, awaiting the right words to trigger the pain.

No, I didn't choose it. But no Rose ever had.

Out of habit, I ran my hand through my hair, waiting to feel buds brush up against my skin. Silky and strange in my curls. But there were none, and I grieved for the ones I lost.

I dropped the strand of hair. "Prophecy or not, I'm going to help fight."

"Then I hope you are prepared to do what you must. On the battlefield, it is your life or theirs. I pray you'll be able to bring down your sword on the enemy when faced with that choice."

I swallowed hard. The thought hardly crossed my mind.

When I fought the raiders, I only wrapped them in vines and sent them away. None of my efforts were lethal. I had never taken a life, and the thought made me ill.

My silence was enough for Valor, and he put a hand on my shoulder. It took me by surprise, and I stared at his grim expression.

"If you can't take a life, you have no business being on that field."

In an ideal realm, I would do what needed to be done. But the haunting images of Casimir stalking toward Ronin, sword in hand, made me unsure. The death of my parents, the woman in Woolfolk, and even Ronin—they all haunted me, but I wasn't the one who ended their lives. The only blood on my hands was figurative.

After a pause, my gaze found the scars on Valor's face. "Have you ever taken a life?" I blurted the question.

Something flashed in his eyes, and his jaw clenched. He dropped his hand from my shoulder. "Many, yes."

The answer made me flinch. "Do their deaths stay with you?" The question was foolish. By his expression, it was one that haunted him.

He inhaled, his posture rigid. "Every one of them."

Although I anticipated his answer, I despised it all the same. I wanted to fight. But the idea of being haunted by more ghosts made me hesitate.

There couldn't be hesitation when my sword or daggers came across an enemy. If they were prepared to cut me down, I had to be willing to do the same.

Fear sparked when I realized I didn't know if I would be capable of such a thing—to watch the light leave someone's eyes at the end of my blade, their blood painting my hands. The thought horrified me, but not as much as the thought of allowing others to die because of my foolish choices.

Valor, Estelle, Sol, Casimir, and many more, were going to ride to meet the king where he marched. They were going to risk their lives for their people. For every Rose who lost their life at the decree of a king.

We had a chance to buy our people more time. A victory may win us the opportunity to save the realm. If nothing else, my presence could act as a shield. A wall of roots or vines to tie up enemies. I wasn't sure if I could end a life to save my own. But I knew I would do anything to save those I cared about.

I met Valor's gaze, my resolve sure. "I can do what must be done, General."

Shock and dread crossed his face, but he didn't try to sway my decision, nor question my resolve. "Then we welcome you to the Everbloom guard. I trust you know your limits better than anyone else here." He paused, searching my face. "Even so, I implore you to only take calculated risks. Your abilities may be the realm's last hope."

Thirty-Eight

Dread followed me to the armory the next day. Every soldier rose before the sun. Frost covered the ground in a thin layer that crunched beneath my boots as the soft glow of dawn shimmered in golden waves through the dead grass. The wither whispered in the breeze, and I longed for snow.

The last people in Mistvalle were all members of the guard, or volunteers to fight or heal. The families, and those who did not want to fight, found safety in the mountains. Estelle explained they had a stronghold for such times.

I managed to avoid Casimir the previous day, and although we were bound to cross paths, I hoped it wouldn't be until the army was already riding. If he wouldn't stay behind, neither would I. Though it was foolish, I wouldn't leave his side on the battlefield if I could help it.

The visions would not come to fruition.

Inside the armory, it overflowed with soldiers. Galan was present; his arm mostly healed after Halburn helped him. He stood across the massive room, his armor already on. It was more akin to what the guards of Mistvalle wore, with heavy iron pieces.

Before I had a chance to go speak to Galan, I saw Estelle approach, already in her armor. She wore a grin that split her face with excitement. And though she looked kind and pleasant, Casimir's words continued to make me wary. I hated that he not only disturbed my sleep, but also my internal peace. To live in a constant state of paranoia was exhausting.

Estelle reached me, and her grin softened to something more somber when she took note of how my hands fidgeted with my tunic. "We have your armor ready, Elita."

"I would love to see it," I said, the words true despite how nervous I was.

She clasped her hands together, her red eyes gleaming. With a graceful wave of her arm, she gestured toward the arches at the other end of the room.

Armor clanged throughout the massive hall as the soldiers prepared themselves. Low chatter filled my ears, and I tried to ignore the way some of it silenced when we passed other guard members. Many of them were quick to glower at me as we passed, as if I'd done something terrible by joining the guard.

From Everbloom to Mistvalle, it seemed there was no escape from the way eyes followed me. To go from no one ever sparing me a glance in Eldravine, to being perceived by so many people—to feel their disdain—it was overwhelming.

Estelle either didn't notice or chose not to pay it any mind. We crossed the room to an archway that led into a separate room. It was darker than the open space we left and full of armor displayed on long dark tables, and some held up on armor racks. I surveyed the small square room, eager and in search of the armor that may have been mine.

Estelle moved with ease, accustomed to her heavy armor. She plucked up a few pieces off a table with one hand and beckoned me with the other. I stopped close to her shoulder, and watched her unravel all the pieces of cloth. She laid them next to the more sturdy pieces of armor. My eyes drank in the rich burgundy swirls throughout the black iron, and with a timid hand, I took a vambrace out of her hand.

It had a good weight to it, and intricate swirls carved into the metal. There was a breastplate to match, along with a few other pieces. While it wasn't a full set, it would provide me with more protection than the usual leather armor vests.

The under clothes were black, and the combination brought me a swell of joy. "Can I put them on?" I asked, with barely a glance in Estelle's direction.

"Of course. I will leave you to it, dear girl." Estelle appeared pleased with my reaction and stepped out of the archway, disappearing around the corner.

Greedily, I picked up the pieces of my armor. I threw off my other clothing and pulled on the black leather trousers and the tight black tunic. I tucked the fabric into the waistband of my bottoms and pulled on a black vest that went halfway up my neck.

It proved more difficult than I expected to get myself in the armor. The ties on the vest were the hardest part as they laced up behind me, but I managed to pull them tight.

Once that was on, I grabbed the breastplate and stared at it for a moment. The Mistvalle insignia was carved into the center of it; a circle of thorns intertwining. I ran a thumb over the design and couldn't wait another second. I got it on and clasped the sides of it together with the black leather straps. It felt foreign on my body, and somewhat heavy. It wasn't overbearing, though, and I hoped during the ride it would become more comfortable on my shoulders.

Next, I tugged on my vambraces and buckled them on my forearms. Then the shoulder pieces, which connected with the breastplate. I struggled with them, but once the first was done, the second went on easier. The new pair of black boots slid on and I fastened them tight to my calves. They were comfortable and light on my feet, but offered enough protection from the cold.

Leather thigh straps waited for me, and I put them on, knowing I would need them to hold my daggers. To my delight, a thick black wither cloak laid on the table. I brought it across one shoulder, securing it with the clasp at a strap near my collarbone. With everything on, I felt more like a warrior, and less like the lonely girl who used to live in fear.

I adorned my hands with a pair of black leather gloves, tucking them into my vambraces. Once Sol showed up to braid my hair, that would be the final piece outside of the weapons.

A grin stretched across my face, and I left the room, my head held high. I both looked and felt like part of the guard.

When I turned the corner, Estelle stood close by, speaking with Valor. Their attention turned to me, and their reactions were complete opposites. Where Estelle beamed at me, Valor's upset was clear.

He strode over to me, inspecting the armor. "Is red a safe color, my lady?" he asked. Despite the bite in his tone, Estelle remained unaffected.

"You look every bit a soldier, Elita," Estelle said. "How does it fit? Is it to your liking?"

I gave an eager nod. "It fits perfectly. Thank you."

Valor surveyed my armor, walking around me in a full circle. He seemed uncertain, though he didn't voice his apprehension. If not for Estelle's insistence, there would've been minimal effort in finding me any armor. Her belief in me gave me more confidence.

Estelle stepped forward with my two daggers in hand, and offered them to me. Before my gloved fingers even brushed the hilt, footsteps reverberated in the stone room.

Casimir stormed through the archway, his livid gaze fixed on me, burning with disbelief. The sole of his boots thundered on the marble floors, his nostrils flared. I thought I'd seen anger the night he came into the healing center after Karion. This was different. Horrified fury singed the air.

He wore full black armor. An onyx cloak rested over one of his shoulders, a curtain of night billowing behind him.

The armor from my visions.

Alarmed, Estelle lowered the daggers and waited for him to approach. It didn't take long for him to reach us with his determined stride. My entire body tensed, preparing for what he was going to say.

Casimir didn't pause. He didn't formally address either leader. "Are you two insane?" Casimir snapped, his face twisted with a rage I'd only ever seen twice before. He eyed my armor as if disgusted.

Estelle was the first to take offense. "Watch your tone, Captain. Decided by my council, and my own word, Elita is part of our guard and is capable of fighting, if she so desires." Estelle wore her own armor as if it were a crown. Her presence demanded respect and silence, yet Casimir spoke in defiance.

"She has no business being on a battlefield. She has only been training for the past four months. *Four.* There's no sense in having her fight when she isn't needed. And to make matters worse, you've painted her as a red target for the enemy."

I grimaced. The giddiness died out, replaced with a horrible sinking sensation. "Anyone capable of fighting is needed. I won't sit in the safety of Mistvalle while others fight a battle that followed me here," I said, voice steady.

Casimir's expression flashed with frustration, his shoulders squared at me. I wouldn't falter under his gaze. I didn't want his blatant disapproval to affect me, but it weighed on me nonetheless.

Before Casimir got another word in, Valor stood beside me. His presence, along with his willingness to take my side, gave me the reassurance I needed.

"Captain Vanmore, that will be enough. Ready yourself in the stables so we may return to preparing Elita." Valor's attempt at a dismissal did nothing, and disbelief mixed with my frustration.

"She'll only be a distraction for those who still have hope for her bloom. The desire to protect her will get soldiers killed," Casimir retorted.

Valor's eyes narrowed. "Our guard is well trained. We put all lives above our own. If you have a personal issue, you may deal with that on your own before we ride out."

Casimir's jaw clenched, and his hand tightened around the hilt of his sword. I watched him fume, the energy palpable.

Unable to bear it any longer, I closed the distance until we were nearly chest to chest. Shock softened his expression and his eyes bounced over my head to the two people behind me before he met my glare.

Outside the archway, the sounds of metal clanging and chatter continued, oblivious to our standoff. Not even the chill that swept through the armory could quench the flames in his gaze.

Seething, I grabbed Casimir's arm and led him out of the side hall. He started to protest, but gave in, trailing behind me with my grip still on the cold black vambrace around his forearm.

Bewildered expressions passed us as some of the conversation settled. We moved through the bustling crowd, ridden with the scent of sweat and iron. The watchful soldiers didn't deter me, and I brought Casimir into a vacant side room. All the sounds and murmurs faded into the background when we came to a stop.

I became too aware of my grip on his arm, and I dropped it, facing him. "What is your problem?" I hissed.

Scarlet eyes searched my face, an inferno of a thousand emotions all swirling at once. His sudden silence made me irate.

Tension pulled at my shoulders and I rolled them, standing straighter. "Is this about what happened on the scouting mission?"

His anger dissipated some, and his apologetic demeanor made me want to shrink away. "No. The fault was on my shoulders. I should've never put that on you." His voice was much softer, the guilt seeping through.

I ignored the warmth at the back of my neck and I steeled my resolve. "Then why are you trying to humiliate me? Even Valor has more confidence in me than you're willing to give."

"That's different."

My eyes widened. "That's *different?* Valor was just as reluctant at first, and yet he took up for me while you gave them reason to doubt me. Why?" I wanted to grab Casimir by the front of his armor, to shake him and plead with him to allow me to protect him. I wasn't weak, and if there was any way for me to keep those I cared for safe, I couldn't sit in the safety of Mistvalle.

Casimir bristled, his focus anywhere but on me.

Something snapped in me, and my hands clenched until they ached. "What is this? What are you trying to do to me? You train me and tell everyone about how capable I am, now this. What changed?"

His ability to avoid my gaze was staggering, and the pit of frustration turned into a raging fire. I stepped closer, my boots loud on the marble. We stood chest to chest once more.

With nowhere else to look, Casimir's gaze flicked down to mine, and he swallowed. "Please, El. Stay here." It was just a whisper.

The words made me take a step back.

Years of his constant pleas for me to find him flooded back. Since we were merely children, he begged for me to leave the safety of my family to go to where he was, and now he was asking me to stay. To hide. When I was finally strong enough to do something, he wanted me to turn my back on the people I doomed.

I forced myself to speak past the frustration. "I don't need your blessing to fight. I'm going."

Casimir didn't retreat, and his hot breath fanned my face when his head dipped toward me. "As your captain, I forbid you."

"You *forbid* me? Ha!" I turned from him, creating distance before I cursed him to Akuma and back. "All my life you disturbed my peace, and begged me to leave my family to find you—to find Everbloom. Even when it wasn't safe. You didn't care about what would befall me then. Why does it matter now? You aren't my ghost anymore. I don't need you to protect me."

Frustration ravaged me, but I still faced him.

The rest of the words I wanted to yell died in my throat.

Casimir's face distorted with desperation that made me freeze. His eyes dimmed to a smolder rather than an inferno. His confidence was gone, stripped away to show a man who was terrified.

Every drop of fury drained from my body and I waited, watching him wrestle his inner battle.

When he closed the distance between us, his steps timid, my heart jumped into my throat. He stood inches from me, eyes searching mine behind thick black lashes.

His breath hitched when he inhaled, the only sign of his hesitation. One of his hands raised, unsure, hesitant, before it cupped the curve of my neck. "I may have been your ghost, but you have haunted me every moment of my life since I met you. And I—" He stopped, a shaky sigh parting his lips when his thumb brushed my jaw. "I can't lose you, Elita. Not again." It was a whisper, a confession, a plea.

The air evaporated from my lungs, and the floor caved beneath my feet. The only anchor in every unsteady flutter inside my chest was *him*. The vulnerability split him open, and I nearly crumbled at the sight.

I needed to say something. I wanted to say so many things. But my throat closed. Panic replaced the euphoria that had bloomed.

Hide your heart.

My fingers twitched at my sides. I wanted to reach out to him. There were so many things I wanted, and yet—

"Casimir…" Nothing else came out, and I watched as a wave of sadness swept across his face. Every crack in his well-built wall sealed shut, and he took a step away, his hand falling to his side.

No, no, no. My skin prickled with a cold sweat.

"Casimir, I'm sorry—"

He winced, taking it wrong. He had never looked so vulnerable or wounded in front of me. And no matter how much I wanted to tell him that my heart had fallen into the same trap, the words wouldn't leave my lips.

Heavy footfalls interrupted the stiff quiet, and my head snapped up to see Valor approaching.

424

Nausea swept through me, and I had to force myself to glance back to Casimir. "I'm sorry, but I haven't changed my mind. I'm going to fight." The words fumbled out. They weren't what I wanted to say, but there was no time, and the fear was inescapable.

My eyes pleaded with Casimir to understand, but he already tucked his hurt away and turned to face Valor, his back to me.

Horrible and sudden tears welled up, blurring my vision. I forced the emotions somewhere deep down. There was no time for them.

We were going to fight a useless battle. The realm was already dying. My bloom was gone, and my abilities barely had time to take root. Still, the hope remained. A future where the Rose people could be free, and the fate of the realm didn't rest on our shoulders.

None of that would ever come to fruition if the king captured the Roses. We would wilt and die in his dungeons.

We had to win.

Thirty-Nine

I couldn't focus. The ringing in my ears drowned out every word Valor said while crowded bodies moved through the stables. *Why did he say that? Why now?* My stomach turned once more. I had to bury the nerves before they overflowed and clouded my judgment. The truth did nothing but cause me more agony.

Sol noticed something was off while she braided my hair into a tight halo around my head, but I couldn't bring myself to say anything to her. To speak it out loud once more would make it too real. She likely would've laughed outright, entertained by the accidental rejection.

Casimir's insistence that I stay out of the fight made more sense as my mind swam through all the wrong thoughts and worries. To know he would be on the battlefield, his words following me like a different type of ghost; it made me afraid.

In the white noise, my heart thrummed too hard. If I didn't get a handle on it, I would be vulnerable in the fight.

Every movement in the stables blurred. Someone shoved Nix's reins into my hand and told me to gather outside for further instructions. My hands trembled around the leather and I cursed my foolish heart for causing me grief when I needed to focus on what awaited us after we passed through the mountains.

Our journey would take us along the same pass Casimir and I had returned from a few days before, and I wondered how they intended to navigate the rocky cliffs where Galan got hurt.

Two hundred soldiers were prepared to head to battle, and we had narrowly made it through the cliffs with three guards on horseback.

While many of the soldiers were riding out, some would follow on foot with shields. We didn't carry flags or other useless items, not like the king's army who awaited us in Tyvolia.

I kept my worry over the trail to myself. Casimir was a skilled captain, and he would've explained everything to Valor to make a plan. I trusted them both to guide our people through.

When I left the stables with Nix, the sun blinded me. It shone down on my armor, casting a red glow on the stone beneath me. I tried not to think about how it resembled a pool of blood.

Bodies and horses alike crowded the courtyard. People stacked carts full of supplies—materials to prop up tents, spare weapons, rations, and items for the healers that would accompany us.

I was grateful to see Halburn among the crowd of healers, even with his strange tendencies and poor bedside manner. He was the best healer they had, and it gave me a sense of peace to know he would be there to take care of the wounded.

Halburn noted me watching the healers prepare, and he paused in his work. Confusion twisted his expression as he strode over to me. I braced myself for another scolding.

When he stopped in front of me, the bafflement was clear on his face. "You didn't change your mind? I thought for sure you'd back out," Halburn said.

My hand knotted tighter around the reins. "Not you too."

He puffed his chest and stood taller. "Well, are you riding out of defiance or necessity?" he inquired.

I hated the implication.

Shuffling on my feet, I said, "Anyone able and willing to fight should. I'm no exception."

"Except you are. The white bloom has to—"

"I've heard enough of the prophecy, Halburn. My old wounds have healed, have they not?"

He fidgeted with his armor, the only outward sign of his upset. "Well, yes. But those new ones haven't, and you've skipped healings."

"Please, don't be another voice of doubt. It won't help me when we reach the king's army."

Halburn's cheek twitched, and he released a reluctant sigh. "At least try not to get yourself into a mess. Can you do that?" He knew as well as I did I couldn't promise that.

I nodded anyway, before adding, "And if not, you'll be there to fix me up." The quip was lighthearted, but the fear slipped into my tone.

Halburn shook his head. "Well then, don't act surprised when I never stray too far from you. It'll be annoying, I can promise that."

The words should have brought me some relief, but panic rose instead. Even as he donned armor and had weapons strapped to his back—the thought of him worrying about me in the midst of a fight made my skin crawl.

In Mistvalle, I was far from my ghosts, but the lives that were lost on my account were never too far from my thoughts. I didn't want him to be another lifeless face to haunt me.

I pushed away the fear and nodded at Halburn.

Nix shifted next to me, sensing the change in my mood. I tugged her to the side—out of the way—and mounted the saddle.

The courtyard swarmed with clanging armor and the echo of weapons singing into sheaths. It made the overwhelm worse as the ringing erupted in my ears. I swallowed the lump in my throat and brought my mare from the ever-growing crowd.

Out of habit, my eyes scanned the masses for those I knew. In the swarm of bodies, it was hard to make out where anyone stood. I spotted Sol speaking with Halburn to the far side of the courtyard. They appeared to be in deep conversation while Sol spun a dagger in her fingers.

I found Sabian, Orin, Estelle—

Casimir was hard to miss, his hair dotted with red petals. He reached his twenty-seventh bloom. I wondered what it would be like to witness them wilt. I tried to ignore the pull to him in the throng of people.

Even though his expression remained filled with angst, his attention fell to one of the other guards. His face pulled with concentration as he helped the young norm attach a quiver of arrows to his back. I had to turn my gaze from him before I either made my way over there or he caught me staring.

If we both made it out alive, I didn't know where to go from there. He already shared his feelings, and there was no way to undo it. If I was braver, maybe I would've confessed the same. How he made my pulse race, he always had. It never occurred to me before why that was. Why every visit in my dreams made my skin prickle beneath the dismay. A friend, a ghost, a curse, a delusion; it never occurred to me I saw him in any other way. Not until Mistvalle. Not until I let myself trust him.

It hurt worse to think of losing him as a friend in the process, too. If my cowardice caused him to pull away, I wouldn't be able to bear it.

I was grateful when Estelle rode forward on her gray gelding. Her armor glistened in the light. She held no fear of the Iron Thorn's army, that much was clear.

All the chaos and chatter died when her horse trotted to a higher level in the courtyard. She looked out over the soldiers, norm and Rose alike. Valor joined her, wearing black and red armor.

Estelle spoke for them both. "We have a two-day journey through and out of the mountain pass. We cannot allow Lendorr passage through the mountains."

I grimaced at the name, my hands damp with sweat in my gloves.

Estelle continued, "The Rose people have not abandoned hope for this realm, and we will fight for the freedom to save it on our own terms, not by being held captive and sheared senselessly. We will find the answers here when we have won our peace."

The bodies in the crowd shuffled. Clanking armor and hoofbeats filled the silence when she surveyed the mass of soldiers.

"You ride not solely for Mistvalle, but for the freedom of our people. I thank you for your bravery."

Mutters erupted in the crowd, and the sound of hundreds of people scrambling into saddles filled the space. Horses scraped at the stone with their hooves and snorted with anticipation. The energy rang through my body, a tangible echo. It reverberated in my veins and I shivered at the sensation. Adrenaline surged through me as I waited with the other spectators.

In the swell of disarray, I hadn't noticed Casimir take up my side. I nearly jumped out of my skin when his horse stopped next to mine. His gloved hands held tight to his reins, and it brought me back to how he held me on our way down the mountain pass—after a night spent laying at his side. My heart skipped when I recalled every shift of his arm as he brought me closer, trying to keep us both warm.

While my thoughts swam with memories that did little to prepare me for the battle, Casimir held firm to his captain demeanor. It brought me relief to know he wouldn't abandon the comforts of our friendship. The desire to reach out and take his hand made me flush with warmth.

He glanced over at me. "Are you ready?" he asked. His tone sounded more like a captain.

I swallowed, my hands trembling on the reins. "Will you stay close?" The question fell from my lips in a whisper. I watched the way he shifted and his gaze flickered around us. Every move he made read differently to me than before.

"Always, Elita."

My heart hammered, and I hoped the cold explained the sudden flush of my skin. "Then I'm ready." The words didn't ring true.

Casimir noticed the change in my tone, and his expression shifted into something softer. A look I realized he reserved only for me. I never saw him look that way at anyone else, and he had looked at me that way since we first met.

"Unless I'm injured or dead, I won't ever be too far. You have my word." His lips lifted with a sideways grin, but his words only caused my heart to plummet.

"Cas—"

"I'll be fine."

It did little to reassure me.

I didn't have the chance to say anything before Valor ordered everyone to begin the march through the Mistvalle gates.

Casimir fell back into his captain persona and prodded his gelding to move forward. He didn't have to tell his guards to follow suit. They all copied him and made five uniform lines behind him.

I felt out of place riding at his side, but I didn't back off. No matter how much I didn't want to admit it, I trusted him. I'd stay by his side in battle, and when we returned, perhaps then the confession wouldn't be as difficult. We'd come back, and he could have my heart.

Everything hung on the uncertain hope of winning the fight and on my ability to rise above the betrayal that continued to haunt me.

Trotting through the gates another time offered less enchantment and more alarm. Several guards stayed at the entrance, while others were scattered throughout Mistvalle to ensure the safety of the families who remained.

Hooves trampled over the dirt in a thunderous cacophony. It rattled my bones and my pulse quickened along with it.

I kept my composure and remained close to Casimir. When Valor took up my other side, it brought me another unfamiliar layer of comfort. It surprised me, and I ignored the urge to flee from it.

Between them, I was safe.

Forty

The journey through the mountain pass was deadly quiet. No one spoke the further we trudged on. We went a different way to accommodate the extra bodies, and didn't return to the treacherous path.

My body leaned back in the saddle as we made our way down another steep hill. At some point, Casimir had gone forward to catch up with Valor to speak with him, and I lingered at the back of the line. It was the last bit of peace I expected to have before the fight that I was ill-prepared for.

I wouldn't dare speak that truth to anyone. They already knew. Valor implied as much when he spoke to me in the stables, but I still allowed my need for redemption to pull me into a fight, when I didn't know if I could take a life. The very thought made me wince. I wasn't uncomfortable with my combat abilities, but I feared what would become of me if I destroyed that part of who I was. Some of the last innocence I clung to.

When I noticed the swarm of soldiers slow their pace ahead, my face prickled, going numb with panic. I clicked my heels to Nix's sides to pick up a trot.

It didn't take long to spot Sol and Halburn, both making their way back toward me. I didn't realize how much distance grew between me and the rest of the party.

As the day wore on, the trees and unfamiliar terrain blended. Every step closer to Tyvolia showed more signs of the desolate Drought Lands. The trees appeared sickly as black rot made its way up their bark. It ate away at the once beautiful white trunks of the trees, and it brought a chill up my spine.

The sight of it was unsettling. It'd been months since I'd seen such death as it consumed every living plant in the vicinity. It caused a strange ache in my body, as if I sensed their necrosis. A shred of pain thrummed in my veins, and I ripped my gaze off the grim sight.

Halburn and Sol made a turn behind me and guided their horses along my side. It helped take my mind off the sensations that singed my blood.

The steep hill leveled out, and the trees thinned until we could see through them and into the scorched land of Tyvolia.

Air caught in my lungs, and Nix protested at the sight, snorting with displeasure. A fetid breeze howled through the vastness, and it burned inside my nose.

The soldiers dispersed left and right, creating a line of riders with shields in the front, and healers and supplies toward the back.

Every inch of my body trembled with resistance, but I pressed through the group of healers and supply carts. Estelle's armor was easy to spot in the massive crowd as it blinded against the setting sun. Next to her was Valor, Orin, and some of her better soldiers, who were never too far from her side.

That morning, I had wanted nothing more than for my companions to give me space. In stark contrast, a swell of relief hit me when Galan joined our line. Never too far, Casimir brought his horse in front of the four of us. I spotted more familiar faces from Everbloom joining us. Sabian, Myra, Abner, Elrin, and a few others.

Every hoofbeat brought us closer to the king's army, and the panic wrapped its way around my throat. My pulse thundered in time with every move we made. It turned my stomach in a nauseating way.

It eased some of the panic when I brought my horse right beside Casimir's. He was the captain of the Everbloom squad, and I knew I should have stayed back. But his closeness brought me a sense of safety no one else could.

Casimir's gaze met mine, a silent exchange that left the air heavy with unspoken words. His promise to stay close remained, and I made it my goal to be near the ones I cared for most.

Each step forward, the sight became more unsettling. Death consumed every inch of the land. Fear coiled in my body at the realization that soon the entire realm would be consumed by the same desolation if we didn't win.

Worse yet, if the prophecy had been mistaken.

If we won the fight against the king's army, we faced another obstacle. From what was known, my sheared petals would prevent me from blooming again.

The mystery around the white bloom and the prophecy remained, and in it, a flicker of hope. If my abilities could accomplish what my bloom did not, there may be hope yet.

We only had to make it out alive.

Darkness settled over us like a suffocating blanket, and everyone scrambled in disarray to set up camp. In her strategic planning, Estelle had accounted for a designated area where the injured could seek refuge if they made it off the battlefield.

Being in such close proximity to the king's army, the panic in my body couldn't settle, it steadily rose. I hadn't anticipated the fear that came when Valor rode out to look for signs of the king's forces. Sure enough, King Lendorr moved closer with every passing moment, his soldiers following with flags that billowed in the foul wind, and torches that lit the night sky.

The fight loomed over our heads as fires crackled to life in the dark camp. The shadows it cast resembled monsters crawling across the ground, and I looked away from their menacing glow.

I tied Nix's reins to a freshly placed wooden post and left her among the other horses to rest and eat. The morning would bring one last charge for the enemy, and Nix needed the reprieve.

The exhaustion pulled at my eyelids until they ached, a reminder I needed rest. I tried my hardest to ignore reality and went toward a small tent that Sol stood outside of.

Myra and another woman I didn't know shuffled into the misshapen tent, and I did my best to hide the annoyance from my expression. I didn't want to share a tent with so many others, but there were no other options. On the list of things to worry about, my sleeping arrangements weren't one of them.

Sol seemed more hesitant to duck into the tent, and didn't hide her distaste for our predicament.

I walked past her and bumped her shoulder with mine. "Don't pout, Sol. Halburn will take your gardening privileges away again," I joked. Irritation flashed in her pale eyes, and I stifled a laugh.

"Don't be surprised if you only have half use of your face tomorrow," she retorted.

"As long as I can still ride." I shrugged, ducking under her arm when she held the drape open.

Sol took the mat next to me—Myra and the other woman took the two across from us. The tent was cramped, but the fatigue settled deep in my body, and I didn't stay awake long enough to be bothered.

White willow trees swayed in a crystal, shimmering breeze. The air that danced through my hair smelled faintly of lavender and cloves. It should have brought me peace, but I recoiled when it reached my nose.

Colors distorted around me. Darkness slithered toward the light, only to be consumed by the fog that glimmered as if a thousand diamonds had burst.

"You shouldn't be here." The voice threatened to split my head in two. It echoed in a husky whisper that dripped with a hundred voices threaded into one. My pulse quickened in response and I turned, only to see nothing there with me.

The voice chuckled, becoming a familiar echo that caused heat to bloom in my veins. "Your choice to fight will doom them all."

Warmth crept through the field, a false sense of comfort. It brought with it memories that didn't make sense to me. Flashes of a winged man clinging to a veiled figure.

Sorrow choked me.

"I have waited centuries for you."

Goosebumps erupted over every inch of my skin and I tried to run, but tendrils of light wrapped around my ankles, stopping me. The darkness flickered with golden irises—eyes shadowed by the thick fog. I watched them change to green for a split second, then pools of black wrapped around gold irises once more.

"It's only a dream," I whispered, even as shards of light crept through tissue and bone, leaving behind a trail of warmth my soul seemed to remember. A gasp tumbled past my parted lips when it crawled through the veins on my arms, reaching my collarbones.

The ground trembled beneath me with the sensation of thunderous footsteps. Cloves filled my nose once more, wafting closer with every step.

"Let me go," I rasped.

The voice distorted with a chilling laugh before all the color drained from the once enchanted forest. Every tree became devoured by rot, and the shimmering fog turned into smothering smoke.

"Your defiance will cost you everything."

Fire licked up my legs, and I opened my mouth to scream.

The figure stared down at me. Inches away, its breath was icy, but real. Crimson and black gazed at me, watching every change in my facial expression. I tried to move, to alert Sol or even the other women in the tent. But my limbs felt melded to the ground, and I could do nothing but gaze back.

A soft hush came from the figure, like a mother trying to calm a frightened child—then its claw-like hands snaked up the sides of my face until they cradled either side of my skull.

My breathing came faster, threatening to make me sick. A strained whimper barely made its way up my throat before the figure pressed into me, igniting an inferno throughout my entire skull.

Every inch of me trembled, my muscles desperately trying to thrash out of the figure's grasp. It gave another soft hush before the fire turned into ice racing down the back of my neck.

The thrum in the earth pulsed through me until the panic became overwhelming. Too much energy surged into my veins, and in an instant, I felt every heartbeat around me. It was too much, and I tried to cry out again, my lips parting with a strangled sob.

"Elita?" Sol moved beside me, and I tried to look over at her—to beg her for help.

Tears trailed my temples, falling into my hair as the energy around me pressed into my chest, suffocating me beneath the pulse of every person in the camp.

"Elita? Hey, can you hear me?" Sol's voice grew frantic, and when she sat up, I shut my eyes hard, hoping the figure would vanish. Firm, warm hands grasped my shoulders, giving me a gentle shake. "Elita." Panic seeped into Sol's voice just as the feeling returned to my limbs.

The thrum of energy wove into my very being.

I gasped, my eyes opening to see the figure replaced by soft pink irises. Sol searched my face, her hands still on my shoulders. "Can you hear me?" she repeated, her thumbs pressing into my shoulders with comforting weight.

My throat ached with discomfort, dry and scratchy as I inhaled. I tried to still the way my heart raced. As the intensity wore off, I allowed my ankles to roll and my legs to carefully stretch out. My flesh held onto remnants of the vision, now nothing more than a subtle sting beneath the energy left behind by the figure.

She didn't see the figure. No one else can see it.

Ice crept up my spine, but I mustered a nod to answer Sol. She sighed and released me, sitting back on her heels in the cramped space. The other women stirred by my feet, and grumbled for us to be quiet.

Flames cast shadows on the outside of the tent, and a sliver of orange bled through the slack drapes, illuminating Sol's worried expression. "Bad dream?" she asked, putting a hand behind my shoulder as I sat up.

Voice strained and shaky, I replied, "I'm fine." The lie was obvious on my tongue. The new figure, the one with golden irises, lingered in the back of my mind, its voice a taunting echo. A horrible dread settled in my bones; a knowing.

Whoever Akuma had meant, his presence still lingered in the tissue of my skin, burns left behind from the strands of light.

He found me.

"Sleep. I just need a minute. I'm okay, really," I whispered.

Sol's brow furrowed, her palm still against my back. "The tears and shaking say otherwise."

I didn't reply for a moment, and when I looked down at my trembling hands, curls fell across my cheek, catching on the trail of salty tears that clung to my skin.

In the silence, Sol reached out, timid as though I would spook, before she brushed the hair behind my ear. I looked at her, not shying away from her worry. She knew I was lying, and there was no point hiding my fear.

"It was a nightmare. But I'm okay. I just need to go for a walk."

"Elita…"

At our feet, someone moved again. "Can you two be quiet?" one of the women muttered. I couldn't tell who it was, but their annoyance was clear.

"It's alright, Sol," I whispered, offering her a look of reassurance. "I've had nightmares all my life. Try to get some rest. I'll be back."

Sol pursed her lips and looked as though she'd protest me leaving. Eventually, she sighed, and shuffled back to her spot beside me. "You need rest, too," she grumbled.

I didn't know how I'd sleep again after the figure reappeared, but I nodded, anyway. "I'll be sure to get more sleep."

When I left the drapes, the foul wind did nothing to relieve the cold sweat that coated my skin. I tried to hide my unease when I noticed how the camp continued to bustle with soldiers, and torches illuminated the night—offering me minimal coverage.

Casimir was nowhere to be seen among the people who stayed awake to keep watch, and though I was grateful he would get rest before the fight, I needed him. I needed to see that he was okay.

My eyes scanned the area, hoping to find him or any sign of his whereabouts. When I spotted a familiar sword perched outside of a tent, I stumbled that way as sweat dripped down the side of my neck, despite the icy breeze.

Beneath the fear of the figure, the vivid dream flashed in my mind, and I grew desperate to speak with Casimir. I needed someone who knew me, and who knew my nightmares.

The fragments of light in the dream—the golden eyes, they had never appeared before, but my soul knew them. The hair on the back of my neck raised as I reached for the tent, fueled by desperation.

Before I opened the drapes, someone cleared their throat behind me. I whipped around to see Valor with his arms crossed over his chest a few paces away.

"You may regret going in there. Five full-grown men have to share that space," he said.

I bit at the inside of my lip and moved back.

"Is there a reason you wish to disturb your captain's rest before battle?" Valor asked. He appeared withdrawn, but I heard in his tone the way he fell into the role of a father.

My hands balled into fists at my sides while I fought back the humiliation. "It isn't your concern. I'll return to my tent now."

Valor put up a hand to stop me. "Of all the years Vanmore dreamwalked, do you truly believe he never mentioned your sleep disturbances?"

I was tempted to wrap vines around Casimir's ankles to drag him out of his tent. "It didn't cross my mind, no," I snapped. "That's private, and not something I wanted him to share."

"Do try not to hold it against him. It was his duty. There were many things he would not share, but your repetitive visions of death caused him alarm," Valor elaborated.

On cue, my legs burned again. "Oh" was all I said, unsure how to escape the panic that crept up my throat.

I didn't want to tell Valor about the new dreams that disturbed my sleep. Even as I grappled with the fact that the visions of my death came to fruition once before, they weren't ever clear. They had pieces missing or warped together. The eyes that haunted me in those dreams were Casimir's that gazed back at me, and the hands that ripped at my hair were Ronin's. And many years before I knew my bloom was white, the petals that fell were red. I didn't trust the visions.

But the voice, the golden gaze...

Esen.

The realization tore through me, and my soul withered in response. Terror became a tangible stone in my chest, and I had to glance away before Valor saw how afraid I was.

He didn't ask questions, and regardless of his interruption, I was grateful for the patience he gave me. Since I couldn't wake Casimir, I took a few steps back from his tent, and to an empty corner of the camp. Valor followed, and the way his demeanor softened reminded me more of the father who raised me.

Away from the flickering lights and Casimir's crowded tent, I tried to release some of the tension from my shoulders. My efforts did little to relax my body, which was wound tight.

Valor's arms uncrossed, and he stood half turned toward the camp, keeping watch.

I struggled to find the words I wanted to say.

If I explained the dream, he would have someone escort me back to Mistvalle with haste on the basis of a bad omen. Perhaps that wouldn't have been such a bad thing. Esen's threat echoed through my thoughts and sent a wave of unease coursing through me.

My fingers pulled at the edges of my cloak. "Do you think the deities speak to us?" I asked.

Surprise flashed beneath his stoic mask, but he stifled it as quickly as it appeared. "That's not something I have experience with, I'm afraid." He paused, appearing thoughtful. "There are many things we do not understand about the deities, or even this realm, for that matter. I wouldn't dwell on things you may never have answers to."

I didn't meet his gaze, and settled for glancing at the night sky. The stars flickered above. Too serene for how tormented I was.

"I think they show me visions." The confession sounded foolish, but Valor said nothing, even as I sensed him observing me. "Since I was a little girl, I dreamed of a man shearing my hair and ending my life. That very moment replayed in my nightmares many times before, and eventually came to be." My voice caught at the brief mention of Ronin. "I think it may be happening again," I said, the fear obvious. It'd been months of witnessing Casimir die, and now the threat of a deity seeking to punish me entwined with that fear.

A threat. A warning. And I feared what would become of those I cared for if I didn't take Esen's word seriously.

Valor's jaw clenched, and he glanced over his shoulder at the quiet camp. His gaze met mine, and worry etched his brow. "What did they show you, Fullan?"

"I don't know what to make of it," I whispered. "There were white trees that turned black with rot—and something grabbed me…I don't know how to explain it. It was like strands of light, but wicked. I felt it burning under my skin." A shiver rippled through my shoulders as I recalled the nightmare. The voice continued to echo in my skull.

Valor's efforts to appear indifferent vanished, and his face appeared ashen. "Have you had this dream before?" he asked.

I shook my head. "No, this one was new."

Some of the alarm drained from his features. "The misgiving before a battle can bring about strange dreams. Don't dwell on distractions," Valor said.

Even as the sensations from the vision lingered, I nodded in reply. There was no sense in delving further into detail. Not when I struggled to understand the visions myself.

Valor appeared content with my response, though I never uttered a word. I was thankful when the conversation ended, rather than him pressing for more information.

Casimir wouldn't have caved as readily as Valor did, and perhaps not waking him was a gift. He would have tied me to a tree until the fight ended. The vision that did come to fruition haunted him, and unlike Valor, he wouldn't have taken a new one lightly.

In the lingering silence, I walked back into the camp, and closer to the flames that lit the darkness. Valor followed without a word. I found myself grateful for the space he gave me to sort through my thoughts.

Hesitation swirled in my mind as Esen's warning replayed. It committed to my memory and preyed on my weak resolve.

"Your defiance will cost you everything."

I nearly prayed to the other deities for answers or favor, but the cognizance rushed in with truths I had long ago ignored.

The deities wouldn't rescue me from a prophecy they wrote.

Forty-One

Sol sat next to me near the fire in the center of the camp. Despite the thick gray clouds, the sun had risen, casting a soft, diffused light. The morning brought a biting cold as a harsh breeze swept through, chilling me to the bone. I was grateful for the fire and my warm wither cloak that provided enough respite.

In a bout of nerves, I already devoured my bread, and my stomach churned with the full sensation. Sol picked at her piece of wheaten bread, her legs stretched out until her black boots almost touched the stone ring around the fire. We were some of the only soldiers held up with eating, and despite my best efforts, it was impossible to ignore the way everyone paced around the camp while they prepared to ride out.

Near a stack of shields, Estelle stood with her head held high, and her armor caught the meager light the sun offered. She appeared ready to fight, and I envied her confidence. Estelle had traded off with Valor late in the night after she rested, and it gave me a sense of peace to know that he got some sleep. Valor became another person to care for, and another one to fret over. I didn't have time to know him well, but the thought of losing another parent was crippling.

One of the last people to rise was Casimir, to my bafflement.

He stumbled out of his tent—the last of the five. It perplexed me until I noticed two new blooms in his hair. One more petal, and he would achieve a matured bloom. The appearance of the new blooms did nothing for my nerves. I knew the pain it brought.

I stood without uttering a word and left Sol to her meal.

When I strode over to Casimir, his eyes widened—still wearing the remnants of sleep as if it were his armor. "Morning," he greeted, his voice a low rasp.

"You have new blooms," I said, scanning over his hair to be sure I counted right. Twenty-nine blooms, and they overwhelmed his hair. It wasn't subtle, and the king would spot it with ease.

Casimir released a heavy sigh and ran a hand through his hair. He grimaced when his fingers caught on a petal, still sore. "That's unfortunate timing," he grumbled.

"Will you be able to fight?" I asked. The panic leached into my voice, but there was no way to hide it.

"Of course." He sounded offended.

The crowd of soldiers continued to scurry as they readied for battle. It made it difficult to talk to Casimir as the noise built into an overwhelming clang of metal and armor.

I kept my focus on Casimir while people passed by in a hurry. His eyes never left mine, even as Valor's voice carried over the chatter and disorder. He was a captain on the guard—his duty was to the general—yet he didn't look away. The timing was inappropriate, but my pulse quickened with every passing second of our gaze locked.

Galan jogged our way, shattering the tension.

I gulped down the emotions and faced Galan as he slowed near us. "Lady Estelle is preparing to address the soldiers before we ride out. She is requesting Captain Vanmore's presence in the line of leaders," Galan said.

"He needs to eat and see Halburn." The words slipped out.

Casimir raised a brow. "If Lady Estelle requests my presence, I will head that way at once. Don't worry about me." His tone edged in warning, and I flushed with embarrassment.

Galan's amusement only made it worse.

I bit the inside of my lip and gave a brief nod to Casimir. I had worried it would be him who would be distracted, and even Valor shared that concern. But it was my feelings that were a hindrance.

Unspoken words threatened to spew out of my mouth. It wasn't the time nor place and it was more akin to a desperate need to leave nothing unsaid before we left the camp. I didn't let myself linger on those thoughts, and walked back over to where the other guards were.

Sol was up and finished with her food, and she already had her horse ready at her side. She tipped her chin up in greeting when I stopped beside her. My time spent speaking with Casimir cut into my preparations, and Nix was one of the few horses that remained unready. I groaned in frustration and parted from Sol once more. I heard her chuckle and thought better of glaring in her direction.

Between the vision and Casimir, I became distracted by the wrong things. My head had barely warmed the mat before I woke from the haunting vision, and I resented myself for not taking more care to be rested.

With no one else lingering back, it was easy to get Nix saddled. Every tie and fastening of a buckle was like second nature to me, and when she was ready, I tugged on the leather reins to lead her toward the mass of bodies who all awaited Estelle's call to battle.

I dwelled at the back of the legion, and watched with a pit in my stomach while Casimir joined the line of leaders. Fatigue clung to his features, and his red petals lacked subtlety. They adorned his black hair like a red crown atop his head; a stark contrast to his black armor.

I turned my attention to Valor. He scanned the throng of soldiers, sizing them up. Every leader appeared primed for the fight ahead. I tried to allow it to give me some courage, even as I trembled.

Estelle mounted her gelding first. "Our fight today is centuries in the making." Her voice rang through the camp, silencing every murmur among the company. "Lendorr marches intending to capture and shear every Rose he can, for a kingdom that was long ago damned. We will no longer hide in the shadows, fearing a fate that was thrust upon our people." Estelle paused, her eyes surveying the gathered soldiers.

"Lendorr believes our blooms can still salvage the damage done to this realm, but the blood of our people will not pay for his ignorance," Estelle thundered. "We will no longer suffer at the hands of cruel gods and kings. Lendorr will fall, and in his defeat, Mistvalle—and the Rose people—may have peace. Until this life ends or we find hope anew through the prophecy." Her words thrummed through every soldier.

The energy coursed in my veins. It called to my vines, and the power that always lay in waiting. It was the push I needed, and as Roses and norms shouted in agreement, I swung up into Nix's saddle.

There was no other choice—no path I could foresee. The only way to unravel the prophecy or my abilities was by emerging victorious. It steeled my resolve, and my voice joined the shouts of two hundred soldiers.

Hoofbeats pounded the barren land of Tyvolia. It thrummed in my veins, energy coursing beneath the surface. It was more noticeable than it had ever been after my encounter with the figure, and knowing what we were going to face, I forced the thoughts of it to the back of my mind.

In the distance, ruins rose and fell, crumbled until they became one with the dust of the earth. Once formidable, the kingdom of Tyvolia lay in waste. The stone castle, with half of it fallen, remained a haunting reminder of its former glory.

I had never been in Tyvolia before, yet I'd seen that very land many times in my visions. It filled me with unbearable fear, and I tried to stamp it out before it could hinder me.

Twisted empty pine trees lined the ruins, menacing like teeth in a snarling jaw. The abandoned cobblestone streets cracked, nearly one with the dust. Among the ruins, the king's army stood idle, their horses scuffing at the stones. The sound reverberated through the still land.

A thousand of the king's army stood in opposition—a sea of garnet and ivory. Our two hundred soldiers couldn't fight an army of a thousand.

It seemed doomed before the battle began, but we rode on. Turning back was no longer an option. If we retreated before the fight started, the king would close in on Mistvalle, and the people we left behind would perish.

During the morning preparations, Estelle had briefed everyone on their strategy for the battle—the same one Casimir had been in charge of alongside Orin the past few months. We were to stop the advance first, and see if they continued theirs. She recognized the slim chances of King Lendorr changing his mind, yet she clung to the belief that speaking with him might spare any bloodshed.

I knew better than to hold on to hope. There would be no bargaining with the king, and he would strike first, and hard.

The grim reality brought more disquiet, and shaky breaths came out in rapid puffs of air from my tight chest. The cold air threatened to freeze my lungs, but I couldn't settle the petrified gasps.

The sight of Tyvolia was jarring the farther we rode from the cliffs that protected Mistvalle. It surpassed Orondal in its wretchedness, and the stench seared my nose and throat.

Clouds moved and hid the sun. Among the swell of gray in the sky, birds circled. It appeared haunting, yet when a familiar flick of black flew close to my shoulder, I was grateful. Calla perched on my armor, and I tried to allow her presence to ease my worry.

My gaze fixed back on the ruins. Soon, the desolate lands would be painted with the blood of both norm and Rose.

I shuddered, and Nix protested beneath me. I needed to get a grasp on my emotions and bury them until the battle ended. Otherwise, I would put myself and my companions in greater danger.

None of the obstacles in my path stopped me, and I needed to come to terms with my choice to ride alongside the other soldiers. My friends urging me to stay out of the battle didn't hinder me, but I couldn't shake the feeling that ignoring the voice in my dreams would have dire consequences.

Nix shifted once more, this time rearing up as if frightened. I held on and my thighs tightened against the saddle. The vision swirled in my thoughts, and Nix seemed to be another protesting presence. Calla squawked and her wings brushed my cheek. Both companions sensed the unease. My stomach dropped.

Sol rode up beside me and grabbed part of Nix's reins. It was fortunate we were in the back of the legion as our horses came to a complete stop.

"Settle, Nix." Sol's thick accent carried in the stillness where we came to a halt.

One of Sol's gloved hands reached over and ran across the expanse of the mare's neck, trying to soothe her. It took a moment, but eventually, Nix calmed down. I glanced up to see Sol's expression pulled together with apprehension, and farther ahead, Casimir and Halburn left the line of soldiers to retrieve us.

"Steady your mind," Sol said. The implication was there without her having to say it. If I didn't, the cost would be ruinous.

Before Casimir and Halburn made it to us, I urged Nix to follow the soldiers that still marched. We met them halfway, and I noted their worry, but I didn't entertain it. The visions had to be dismissed from my mind, otherwise I would die in the Drought Lands.

I refused to bow to the fear. I didn't survive a shear to die at the hands of Lendorr. He had spilled enough Rose blood.

When Casimir noticed Sol and I approaching, he pulled his horse back around and led the way back to the company. Their armor glistened in the rising sun and the line of shielded riders in the front slowed their trot. The abrupt halt made my skin prickle.

Lady Estelle would size the enemy, and I only hoped our archers were quicker than theirs.

Wind howled through the arid land. It shook dead branches in the distance, and whipped loose coils of hair in my line of vision. I wished then for a moment to pull Sol to the side to have her fix my unruly hair as the braid slowly unraveled.

In light of what we faced, it was but a slight inconvenience.

A hundred yards off, King Lendorr's army came to a halt. Their horses anxiously scuffed the cobblestones, and the shaking of their soldiers' armor reached my ears. In the front of their line, soldiers stretched across with shields drawn up.

From where we paused, I noted the king in the middle, behind the tallest shields in the line. Subtlety wasn't in his nature, and he wore white and red. The stark contrast against the barren earth was abhorrent.

Estelle didn't stay behind her line of shields as the king did. Valor accompanied her, trotting through the rotted trees and crumbling stone pillars. Dust kicked up beneath their mounts.

The sight of Valor forsaking the security of the shields as he moved closer to the king had my hands cramped painfully on the reins.

Vivid memories I fought against emerged, and I was reminded of the way the king mocked my grief over my parents. He hadn't killed them, but he would have. It was sobering, and I wanted to bring Valor back to safety. But I wouldn't make such a scene in front of an entire army, and I settled for bringing Nix closer to the front line, even as she protested—much like my companions who were never too far.

If Valor wouldn't stay in the safety of the shields, I would summon one for him if need be. It was second-nature to call to my abilities. The power surged in my veins and I remained just behind the line of protection, ready in case they needed me.

Never too far, Casimir, Galan, and Halburn joined me.

"Is there something wrong, Elita?" Galan asked. I tried not to let his question affect my focus as I stared at Valor and Estelle. I needed to be ready. Calla shuddered on my shoulder. She seemed to brace, and it did nothing to ease my worries.

Halburn moved closer. One of his hands remained at the long sword strapped to his hip. "Do not over-extend yourself, Blackthorne. Avoid using your abilities," Halburn spoke in a whisper.

"I will do what I have to if the king attacks. It's my duty as well as yours to do what we can," I replied. There was no room for them to argue as the king began his own trot toward Estelle and Valor. The army did not follow, but a display of white and silver did.

Talos.

My stomach churned, and Nix took a few steps back, tuned to my every emotion.

The prince donned silver and ivory armor, which blinded me worse than what the king wore. His blonde hair was slicked back, and he carried the confidence of a well-trained soldier, his expression emotionless.

Breathe.

The air caught somewhere in my chest, and the constriction ached. Sweat dampened my nape, and memories rattled my mind, threatening to make me lose my meal. They came in horrid flashes, not quite right; fragments of agony I tried to block out—liquid burning down my throat and through my veins. A knife torn through the skin at my neck.

Visions that were new to me became tangled with the scene before me. Memories that weren't mine, yet they unraveled in my mind as if I had seen it all before. Mighty wings blocked the light from the sun, and a sense of betrayal was thick in the air, suffocating me.

The hallucination burst in an instant, and I nearly retched.

"Elita?" Concern dripped off Casimir's tongue. I hardly heard him over the rush of blood in my ears.

A harsh inhale whistled through my teeth, and I tore my eyes off Talos to look at Casimir, my voice strained. "The Prince. Talos."

Casimir tensed, and fury flashed in his gaze. He fixed his attention back on the two men. I didn't miss the way Casimir's hand tightened around the hilt of his sword or how he moved his horse a few spaces ahead of mine.

"Hayes, find Sol," Casimir ordered. "We need someone at Elita's side at all times."

I gaped at him. "No. Don't let my presence here be a hindrance. I can hold my own." It wasn't being alone I was afraid of. "I have my abilities. I'll be okay."

"Did your abilities keep you safe from Ronin?" Casimir's question made me flinch.

"That was different, Casimir—Look at me." I steadied my voice, trying to get him to turn his gaze.

Reluctantly, he faced away from the scene in front of us.

"Please, have faith in me. I can't bear to carry your doubt," I whispered.

His jaw clenched but he gave me a curt nod.

Galan returned with Sol in tow. Once more, the four companions surrounded me. I didn't let it distract me or make me feel weak. Instead, it empowered me.

I straightened in the saddle and watched the scene unfold before us as Lendorr and Talos met Estelle and Valor halfway. Silence fell over every soldier. No one dared to move or speak as the king pulled his gelding to a stop.

Ten members of the Iron Guard accompanied them, flanked by five on each side of the prince and king. Their armor was blood red and detailed with glistening silver. On their chest they held the Iron Thorn insignia— the same marking that scarred over on my neck.

I urged Nix to step closer to the line of shields until I was right behind them. My companions moved with me, but I stayed in the front between the four. I was aware of the inevitable result, but I still wanted to listen to what the king said.

Estelle took the lead. "You're far from your kingdom, Lendorr." The king bristled at her tone and how she addressed him.

I flinched when Talos sneered.

"How dare you disrespect your king?" Talos snapped. His voice threatened to send me back.

"He is not my king, boy." Estelle's voice was sweet and smooth like honey, and it irritated the two men all the more. "You march on my border and threaten the peace of my people. I cannot allow that." More bite made its way into her tone.

King Lendorr scoffed. "You own nothing unless I or the gods deem it so. Your kind has caused mine enough anguish as is, and I will not allow my kingdom to suffer any longer. We have come to reclaim the sacrifices that the gods have given us."

Valor shifted in his saddle, and it caused the first slip in my mask of indifference. I watched how the Iron Guard surveyed him, and how the prince rested a hand on his own sword. My hands found my daggers, and I bit the inside of my cheek to stop myself from yelling at them to retreat.

"You have no claim here. Have you not spilled enough of our people's blood?" Valor's voice thundered through the desolate land.

The king glared. "I know your face, Rose," Lendorr said, his focus fixed on Valor. My blood ran cold. "There won't be an escape for you here, I assure you of that."

Surprised murmurs erupted in the crowd of soldiers.

"Enough," Estelle hissed. "My people will not be accompanying you back to your kingdom of bloodshed. The white bloom is no more, and any bloom you take will only continue to curse this realm."

King Lendorr paused, his eyes narrowed. I watched him mull over her words, knowing there was no realm where he would turn around empty-handed.

The quiet was heavy as we awaited his reply.

My hands clenched tighter to my daggers, and on instinct, vines began to take shape, forming in the air around me. They coiled across the earth, stopping at the foot line of the shielded soldiers.

Casimir moved closer. "Not yet. Wait for the command."

The vines didn't dissipate nor move any farther. I allowed them to remain ready, should Valor and Estelle need cover for their retreat.

Every shift in the earth reverberated in my body with the movement of each horse and soldier on the barren field. I sensed the tremble of the people around me and in the king's company. It threatened to overwhelm me.

Finally, the king's face twisted into a snarl. "We won't hear your lies. You will return to the kingdom willingly or your people will die here. I can already see which of your Roses are ready for a sacrifice."

Ice crept down my spine, and I looked to Casimir. His gaze never wavered from Estelle and Valor, but my heart was in my throat as I watched the red petals in his hair shudder in the breeze.

Calla cried at my shoulder and lifted. Hovering above, she circled over our heads, meeting a blur of white wings. Casimir's owl.

I tore my eyes away to see Valor and Estelle already had their hands resting on their weapons.

"Try to take my people, and yours will pay with twice the bloodshed," Estelle crowed.

The king jerked his head back as if she slapped him. His nostrils flared, and the shift in the earth turned from a subtle hum to a thunder of energy.

Soldiers in the king's army moved.

Collectively, their heartbeats quickened. Their stances shifted.

My breathing picked up with the intensity, and without meaning to, my vines shot forward.

Everything moved in a chaotic blur as they slithered over the earth, increasing with every inch of land they covered. I didn't have to tell them where to go or what was coming.

The vines shot up and stretched in front of Valor and Estelle in a wall of black tendrils. They coiled tight together, and I felt it in my body when arrows dug into the fiber of the vines.

I gasped, and Nix protested beneath me at the intensity. Casimir shouted something in my ear, but every noise became another buzz of energy in my veins.

Valor and Estelle roared in the distance as they pulled their swords behind the wall of vines.

My body shook with adrenaline and I jumped off Nix's saddle and brought my hands to the earth. I needed to ground myself. I had to feel where the archers were.

As I found the thrum of their pulse, I waited for the change as they released their arrows. My eyes shut, and I forced the power swirling through me to focus on them. A web of vines rippled through the earth, and I didn't listen for the screams. The contact sang in my blood.

Chaos broke around me, but I kept my focus on the earth even as the horses pounded against the ground, threatening to disrupt my focus.

Shields clanged when the soldiers broke into a sprint. Our own archers let their arrows fly, and I sensed each body that fell when they found their mark. It horrified me and broke my focus.

I fell backward, gasping.

Casimir yanked me up in a rush searching my body with livid eyes. "Are you hit?!" he yelled over the roaring in my ears.

I shook my head and searched the ground for my daggers. I hadn't noticed when they left my hands, but I grabbed them up quickly.

"Valor?" I asked as I mounted back onto Nix's saddle. Our soldiers ran past us, rushing the enemy as the fight broke out.

"The vines were quick enough," Casimir assured. "Now focus," he ordered.

Every inch of me quivered with adrenaline, and I didn't spare him a reply. I kicked my heels to Nix's side, and we broke into a gallop.

Through the thrum of disarray, the words from the vision rang in my mind; *"Your defiance will cost you everything."*

Forty-Two

I stayed on Nix's back as long as possible, maneuvering the gray stone ruins. The walls of the fallen kingdom created an obstacle, making it harder to stay mounted. Enemies charged from all sides, but Nix was quicker, skilled, and agile. We dodged around another half-deteriorated wall, her hooves skidding along crumbled debris.

Vines rippled through the air in my wake, snapping at soldiers' ankles and taking them off guard to give our ground troops the upper hand. Black tendrils left a trail everywhere I went, withered on dusty cobblestones beneath me—giving the appearance of rot consuming the forgotten kingdom.

In my peripheral, I caught sight of Valor as he charged through the masses, throwing bodies as though they were small stones. They tumbled across the cracked gray cobblestones, some slamming into the trees that clawed at the sky at the edge of the paths. The trees shuddered beneath the force of the bodies before they fell into a pile of dust.

It was a poor choice for a battle, and the castle and its walls made it more difficult to keep an eye on the enemy. In all directions, signs of life stretched far and wide. Cottages turned into piles of rotten wood. Streets that stretched deep into the blackened woods. Streams were dried up, another obstacle for the riders. Bridges collapsed into the gaps, creating a dam of stone.

I conjured more vines when the flood of enemies increased. They lashed out and whipped around another few bodies, slamming them into each other in a mess of armor and disgruntled screams. I tucked my daggers away to focus on using my abilities. Halburn warned me against relying on them too heavily, but I hadn't taken a life while using them.

Not yet.

Each encounter with another snarling face, I feared I would have to use the daggers. Even the use of my thorns gave me pause. Valor's warning echoed in my head, a reminder that any hesitation could kill me. It was their life or mine, and I had to make that decision with each enemy I encountered.

My companions became lost in the disarray and at the collapsed steps to the fallen castle, I caught sight of King Lendorr cutting through our soldiers as if they were nothing.

I didn't have time to focus on him. Another enemy charged for us, and I wrapped a vine around their ankle, pulling them off their horse.

Nix and I fought the growing crowd of bodies, but it was too much to stay mounted when another soldier yanked at my arm, trying to throw me off. I grunted, and a slew of thorns splintered from my hands near their feet. They fell to the ground, reaching for their boots.

If I didn't dismount, I risked Nix's safety and my own. My head begged me not to, but I hopped off the saddle and sent her in the opposite direction with a command. Her absence brought me a wave of sadness, but I trusted that Estelle was sure of their training and that she'd find her way safely to camp.

I didn't have time to watch her go. A sword swung over my head and I barely ducked in time for it to miss loose strands of my hair.

Pouncing up, I called on my vines and they tore through the air, ripping the sword from their grasp. They were quick to recover, and I noted the color of their armor. Iron Guard.

My anger flared, molten heat traveling from the back of my skull and down my spine. Without meaning to, thorns erupted from my palms and pelted their armor; denting the metal as some thorns scraped at the skin on their face. Blood trickled down their cheek, slow and gleaming scarlet. My body ran cold. Rather than fall, they lunged at me.

I rolled under their fist and kicked out a foot to knock them down. My abilities struggled with the split in my focus, but I sharpened my intention and wrapped vines around their body, pulling out a dagger with one hand. They thrashed against the vines, and my hand holding the blade shook at the sight.

Before I unfroze, a sword plunged through the man's armor, and blood sputtered from his mouth, spatters landing on my face.

A horrible sensation twisted my gut.

I glanced up to see Sol. She tore her sword from the man's chest and gave me a pointed look before turning when another enemy lunged for us. I gripped the dagger tighter in my hand and slid over the dusty earth, cutting at the ankles of another Iron Guard. Their screams threatened to split my skull.

I jumped to my feet and surveyed the crowd. Bodies swarmed, their swords locked in combat. I tried to ignore the blood that cascaded through the air as Sol cut down another enemy. It sprayed on the crumbled ruins, drenching the stone like spilled wine.

It put me in harm's way to get distracted, but my gaze searched for more of our soldiers. In the throng of bodies, I caught sight of Galan. I nearly retched when he grabbed an enemy by the head and twisted.

There was no time to focus on him.

Another body charged at me, and I threw my arms over my face on instinct. My back slammed into a tall stone pillar as roots wrapped around my forearms, blocking the fall of their sword. It tore through a layer of them and I pushed back. The hit rang in my bones.

Before they swung again, I kicked a leg out and brought my boot to their cheek. It sent them sprawling into a wall of stone with a sickening crack as their jaw clenched. Dust spiraled down, and clung to the soldier's hair.

There was no reprieve.

Another body dove for mine and I twisted, swinging a dagger through the air in an arc. It came down hard and cut through their thigh. I jerked it out of flesh, and blood speckled my armor in return.

I used another round of vines to tie the yowling enemy up. I couldn't bring myself to end their misery. Their eyes locked with mine, catching me off guard.

For most of my life, I never could meet a stranger's gaze. Now, I watched as horror flickered across the soldier's face while I held their life in my hands. It chilled me to the bone.

Sol slashed through another enemy without a thought, and I envied the callousness she harbored. The body fell with a sickening thud, coated in blood and dirt.

In the mass of enemies locked in battle, I noted a bright display of armor. Estelle moved through the swarm with ease. Bodies fell in her wake. Shock slithered down my spine when the enemies gasped and sputtered before they shriveled into nothing more than a husk trapped in metal armor.

Something slammed into my back, and I tumbled across the ground.

I caught myself on a pile of rotten wood and rolled without pause. A lance plunged toward me and I barely blocked it with the vambrace on my forearm. They had me cornered.

Fear poured into my palms, needles beneath my skin, and thorns exploded from my hands, tearing through the woman's armor. She shrieked for only a second before she went limp. Holes dotted her armor, and blood pooled beneath her body.

No. I hadn't meant to kill her.

I scrambled back from her body. Her life force drained into the barren earth, and I felt every agonizing second of it in the energy that thrummed in the air.

I lost Sol in the crowd of bodies, and I yearned for my companions, as though their presence could save me from such a feeling. There was no escaping it. I killed her, and the look of terror was frozen on her face.

Blood drenched the desolate land, and screams echoed in the ruins. I watched as an Iron Guard plunged a sword through one of the Mistvalle soldiers, and in turn, the guard lost his head at the end of Sabian's sword. It painted the dirt red as it rolled far from its shoulders.

An arrow sang through the air, almost clipping my shoulder, when a body moved in front of mine. They raised a forearm shield, blocking me from the projectile.

White hair flew free from its braid; strands streaked with blood. Orin whipped around and glared. "Focus," he snapped.

I stammered and took a step back. "I killed her." My voice didn't sound like my own. I didn't understand why I told him.

Orin's nostrils flared with annoyance. "Good. Prove it wasn't a mistake you were allowed in this fight and push back." His words steadied me, and I mustered a nod.

Orin left me there as he lunged for an oncoming enemy. He drove a spear through the person's body and left them suspended.

I sprinted the opposite way of him and through a thinner part of the masses. I ducked under a swinging blade and dodged arrows that soared close by. Before I ended up at the end of another blade, I ducked behind a rotted pine tree farther from the crumbled walls, trying to catch my breath.

Sunlight poured in sideways through the trees, casting streaks of light through rotted bark and branches. Dust shimmered, suspended in the air after the land had rested for centuries, nearly untouched.

Hills rose and fell in the distance, dotted with blackened trees. It looked as though it had been burned, their life stolen by flames rather than a curse. The thought crossed my mind that soon the entire realm would resemble Tyvolia.

The armor plate weighed too heavy on my chest. I gasped and pressed a hand to it. My fingers twitched, longing to remove it. I needed to breathe. The armor wouldn't let me *breathe*.

Overhead, a raven called.

Calla moved through the trees, darting in front of me. I flinched when I noticed blood on her beak.

Someone's eye rested in one of her talons.

She swooped, and landed on a branch above me. The eye rolled across the dirt, far from me. She left the tree, and perched near my feet. Her head tilted to the side, and as though she knew I needed it, she hopped onto my leg, resting.

Calla's presence allowed me to gather my composure and tear my attention off the desolate land of Tyvolia.

I tore my gaze from her and continued to inhale slowly through my nose. Icy air filled my lungs, and while I searched the crowd, I spotted a familiar head of petal-covered hair.

My heart jumped into my throat.

Casimir was far across the battlefield in an old crumbled courtyard. He used two swords, one of which I didn't recognize. With both hands on the hilts, he stalked toward an enemy.

I froze, watching as he cut the guard down with ease. No hesitation. After he shared how Ronin's death haunted him, I worried he would freeze. A sigh of relief parted my lips, but the feeling didn't have time to take root.

Calla lifted, squawking just as the sound of a whip cracked close by. It warped the air around me, appearing from behind the tree. It encircled my leg, and the impact of it made me scramble across the ground on my hands and knees.

It struck the air again and I rolled until a rock slammed into my chest plate and I sputtered. The skin on my thigh burned, and I glanced down to see a cut through my leather trousers, along with a horrible gash that bubbled with blood.

I gritted my teeth and turned to see an Iron Guard swing a whip over their head, poised for another strike at me.

They never brought it down.

Halburn cut through the guard with his sword, and his shoulders moved with rapid inhales. The blood that painted his face in speckles of scarlet disrupted his kind demeanor.

He stalked over to me and helped me stand. "Stay on guard." I barely heard him over the roar of battle. "Now, don't move for a moment," he said, and his hand covered the gash on my leg.

I hissed through my teeth as the sensation of him healing the tissue made me flinch. Before an arrow could catch us off guard, I dipped into the energy buzzing in my veins and summoned a pillar of vines around us.

"We don't have time for this." The tremble in my words gave away how much it stung. But if we stopped fighting, more people would die, and pausing allowed me to remember the woman's face as I ended her life.

Halburn pulled back and shook his head. "You've overused your abilities. If you continue like this, next hit, you might not get up." He spoke gravely, lines hardening his face. "If you can't use combat, then you need to get to camp."

I used the moment to settle myself. Every fiber of my being ached, and I sensed exactly what he meant. The thrum was practically gone, numb at the back of my skull while the wall of vines faltered. Heat wouldn't prickle in my palms, and the pulse within the earth became a whisper.

It wasn't difficult to agree with him. He sensed more with his abilities than I could, and I nodded, my neck stiff. "Why else have I trained if not for this? I can fight, Halburn." The confidence settled on my shoulders, comfortable despite the weight of responsibility.

Halburn didn't appear convinced, but he accepted it. "Well, that oughta hold for now. Try not to use your abilities unless there's no other choice."

I glanced down to see that he stopped the bleeding, though the wound remained. It would be enough. "Thank you." My gratitude brought a scoff from Halburn as he stood straight. My efforts to hold the vines waned, and without meaning to, they dropped. The battle overwhelmed my senses. My face blanched when I saw another Mistvalle soldier take an arrow to the chest.

"Focus on your enemies. Not anyone else's." Halburn's words echoed in the desolate ring of trees as he sprinted away. I watched as he caught another Rose who nearly fell to the dirt.

I scanned the fight as it unraveled around me. My chest ached with adrenaline and guilt. There was no room to grieve an enemy who tried to kill me. It was her life or mine. Yet the agony still tugged at the corners of my mind as I sprinted through the herd of people who continued to take each other's lives without another thought.

Bloodshed raged around me.

The way my pulse thudded in my ears drowned out the echoes of agony—like a thousand hoofbeats hammering inside my rib cage.

A sudden shift stiffened my spine, and the vibration in the earth caused my skin to prickle.

The sickening familiarity made me whip around, and I searched the chaotic mass of bodies locked in fierce conflict. My heart plummeted as a jolt of fear paralyzed me.

A pair of pale green eyes stared at me beneath disheveled blonde hair, the sight pulled straight from my nightmares.

Talos.

Forty-Three

Panic tore through me in a rush of agonizing breaths. I stumbled back, and almost fell to the ground as he began his advance. I searched the crowd in desperation for familiar faces but saw none. An icy sensation crawled over my skin, memories resurfacing that I thought I had buried. I couldn't fight him. Not with the way my arms quivered.

Air became trapped in my lungs.

Breathe.

His footfalls echoed in my head, and I sensed it in my entire being. I recoiled as visions of the cell in the Temple blinded me. It changed from the ruins of Tyvolia to the clearing from my dream, and golden light crept across the earth, slithering at my feet.

"Please," I whispered.

Sweat beaded at my upper lip and tasted of salt. I gasped for air, but it proved futile.

Please, breathe.

"You're leaving? But I've only just found you." His voice clawed through my skull, bringing me back to every moment in the Temple.

The ruins swam in a dizzying display—a sea of gray and black spun behind him while I walked backward, trying not to fall.

More broken memories split my mind, the sensation agonizing. Every step Talos took shifted the scene around me. Light shimmered in a sudden swell of fog, thick and suffocating. The taunt of the figure repeated in a whisper that wrapped itself around me. It changed again and again, too rapid for me to understand.

Grief shot through me, and I gripped the daggers until the tension forced me back to myself.

The fog evaporated, and Talos watched me, his gaze swimming with keenness. Something inside me snapped, a fear not my own. It threatened to send me into the ruins, the mountains, anywhere but in the presence of the prince.

I tried to quell the fear before it got me killed and quickly decided against using my daggers. They'd be no use against the long sword he carried with him, the blade dragging across cobblestones.

Halburn's warning was fresh, but I had to do something. I reached for the energy in my veins to conjure vines, thorns, anything to give me the advantage. The pull at my energy left my gut hollow and I stumbled as my knees buckled.

Talos smirked and his eyes flashed with amusement as he took in my struggle. He closed the distance with every failed attempt to conjure. The next reach for vines made my vision blur. They were no use.

When I finally caved and willed my legs to turn and run, I didn't get far before his hand grabbed my arm and pulled me into his chest. His scent filled my nose, and I thrashed in an attempt to escape the aroma of clove and copper.

Hot breath coated my neck, and rather than fight, my body froze, every limb filled with ice.

"I told you that you would help me find them."

"No!" I struggled in his grip, the battlefield a blur around us.

He turned me around until I faced him, smirking. One of his hands worked its way up my spine until he held the back of my neck. "How simple this could have been had you stayed in the Temple. So much blood spilled for the deities to bring you right back to me…"

Talos's fingers knotted in my sweat-coated curls while the other hand ran over the curve of my throat. He pressed a thumb to the side of my neck where he left the sacrificial mark.

The battlefield flickered behind him, the sky shattering in a burst of light. The warmth never hit my face, even as it blinded me. Streaks of light wove through the air before they evaporated entirely, swallowing us in thick, dark clouds.

Talos's gaze fell to mine, the soft emerald darkened by the gloomy sky. "Don't fret. I do not intend for you to die by my hand here." A smirk tugged at his lips.

Harsh breaths poured from my lungs, and desperation burned in my chest. The sensation made me dizzy, but nothing could quench the flames as they trickled through my veins. Black and crimson twisted at the edge of my vision.

For a split second, Talos staggered, his hand loosening on my curls while his gaze shone with reverence. He searched my face, a golden glint in his eye. "It is as Esen said."

I took advantage of his vulnerability and threw my head back, taking him off guard. An agonizing scream left my lungs empty when I jerked forward, his grip on my hair causing tears to bite at my eyes. It was nothing compared to the force of my forehead cracking his nose.

Talos's grip loosened on me and I dropped from his arms, scrambling back from him. Rubble scrapped at my palms while warmth coated my lips.

Blood dripped from my nose into my mouth and I spat, trying to stand on weak legs. My knees buckled halfway up and I ducked my head, swaying with a hand on my thigh. The wound bubbled with bright red blood as Halburn's patchwork job came undone.

My eyes shut, a horrible choice, but I couldn't keep them open as my head drifted, the sun caressing my skin when my chin tipped skyward. I heard Talos recover and knew it wouldn't take him long to come after me. The royals weren't incompetent. He'd likely been training since he was old enough to pick up a sword. I couldn't beat him with skill alone.

An exhale parted my lips, and copper stung my tongue. I looked to Talos, his hungry gaze nowhere but me as he stalked my way.

His arrogance cost him the upper hand when Sol slammed into his back, her gaze lethal as she drove him to the ground. Her hands went for his face, but he was too quick.

Talos threw her off then rolled across the rubble until he got to his feet, his own chin painted scarlet while his nose bled. Satisfaction rose inside me, a sliver of pride for repaying the prince by spilling his blood.

Sol's attack gave me enough time to stand straight, and my hands went for my daggers. Talos charged at Sol, his sword drawn. She moved in a blink, ducking under his blade to bring up her sword, narrowly missing his arm.

"Vines!" Sol shouted, the demand more than my body could give. It twisted at me and I pushed against the fatigue, zeroing in on Talos as I attempted to conjure vines. If I could get his arms pinned, Sol would be able to kill him with a single touch.

Refusal sparked in my veins, the energy evading me. The block suffocated the thrum, and every push to summon them tore beneath my skin.

Sol grunted in frustration, dodging another attack from Talos.

He kept his back to me, and without my vines to aid us, I took the opportunity to run for him, my gait unsteady. Wetness coated my thigh, the movement jarring the wound. I continued, my teeth clenched as I closed in, daggers raised. In the second it took me to fix my stance, he tossed Sol to the side.

Air dispelled from my lungs when an Iron Guard intervened, slamming a fist into my chest, throwing me through ruins. My torso folded around the curve of a crumbling wall, and robbed me of air. I curled into a ball, grasping my middle.

Before Sol and I had the chance to recover, Talos towered over my hunched frame, his hand outstretched toward me. I groaned, unable to take a full breath. I stared up at him, the rays of the sun blinding behind him once more. It lit his head, a misplaced halo in his hair.

His gloved hand wrapped around my upper arm and he pulled me close —the sun made his irises appear golden.

"I have come to take back what is mine." His voice dipped low while his hand found the back of my neck. He held me there, fingers snaked through my hair. "You will not escape this time."

My chin quivered as he let go of my bicep, his other hand still wrapped loosely in my hair as he turned to leave.

Within an instant, he froze.

Casimir stood a few feet away, swords in hand, and murder in his eyes. "Release her," he growled.

Talos barked a laugh, thunderous in my ear. His hand went to the back of my neck as he forced my knees to the cobblestones. The wound on my thigh glistened against the sudden stretch of skin.

Casimir's presence should've brought me comfort, but all I could see were the visions of him dying among ruins as a battle raged behind him.

The fear ruled my body, and I reached both hands back, wrapping them around Talos's forearm.

Power seared through my palms. The effort blackened my vision, and a muted scream rattled from my chest. Thorns tore through steel and caught in Talos's arm until he released his grip.

He roared in anger, and I rolled, putting distance between us while my hands already searched for my daggers, still crouched low. I pulled both out and held them in front of me, even as tears obscured my spotty vision.

Scarlet dripped from punctures in Talos's vambrace, but he recovered swiftly, already swinging at Casimir with his blade.

Casimir's sword locked with his, and the sound rang through the battlefield. He kept them crossed and pushed against the prince's blade.

"Get out of here, Elita," Casimir ground out between clenched teeth.

My eyes widened, and I stared at the back of his head. "Casimir—"

The next sword to swing was Sol's. She charged at Talos's blind side, moving far too quickly for him to dodge. Before it could land a blow, an Iron Guard blocked her swing and sent her blade soaring through the air, glinting in the light.

Chaos ensued as guards came to Talos's aid. Casimir shoved against Talos, and sent him stumbling back just before he blocked an attacker that approached behind me. There was no reprieve, and Talos took his chance, closing in on me as Casimir cut down another guard that went for me.

My legs were nonexistent beneath me. They felt detached, even as I stood, my ribs screaming at the movement. I sputtered, and blood painted the dusty road beneath me, sinking into the cobblestones that held the memory of bloodshed from centuries ago.

Talos reached for me just as I raised a dagger. He scoffed and blocked it with his blade, holding me there as my arm trembled.

"Don't fight it," he said, voice low and carrying an intensity I didn't understand. He never tore his gaze from mine, even as war waged around us.

Quickly, I brought my other dagger up, but he smacked it out of my hand, then missed as he tried to grab my wrist. The battlefield tilted, and the ground vanished beneath my feet. The force of his blade sent me back to my knees, the second dagger clattering to the ground beside me.

I called to my abilities, clawing at the corners of my mind to activate them. My eyelids drooped with the effort, too heavy to hold open as he reached for me.

A flash of black armor appeared, wrapping a gloved hand around the prince's blade without flinching. Talos had no chance to respond before Casimir used his free hand to drive one of my fallen daggers into the shoulder of the blinding white armor.

It was the first time I'd seen the prince show fear.

Casimir twisted, earning a howl of agony from Talos. He released his sword, letting it fall. Of all the guards, Casimir excelled at hand-to-hand combat. It showed as he dodged Talos's fist. Then again in the way he forced the prince's chin into his knee, slamming his jaw shut. More blood poured from his nose. Hit after hit, Casimir was relentless, the softness in his gaze replaced by malice while he spilled the prince's blood.

It wasn't a straightforward attempt to end Talos's life. The dagger held firm in the shoulder of his armor at Casimir's disposal, he could've ended it in an instant. No, Casimir dragged it out. He didn't give Talos a moment to recoup before he hit him again, purple bruises blooming on his pristine skin.

My head lolled as my hands sought out my other dagger. If I could throw one just right, aim for Talos's throat, maybe then Casimir wouldn't destroy the very person he was; tearing away at the prince, desperate for retribution.

A guard stopped my hand, and I repaid his interruption with a dagger to the foot, and a fist to his knee. He fell as quickly as he tried to attack me, and the effort left me more drained.

Talos sucked in a loud breath, dodging the next attack before he attempted to grab Casimir's arm, sluggish as his face bloomed with bruises.

Casimir was quicker, and with a hand holding the dagger wedged in the ivory armor, he drove Talos to the ground, disrupting the rubble. His boot fell hard on the polished white glove until bones snapped. Unbridled hatred flashed across Casimir's face, and he pressed harder, pulling Talos's other arm backwards.

Talos yowled, the sound catching more attention.

An Iron Guard charged for them, stopped by Sol who burned his face, the scent horrid as blisters formed beneath her palms. Shrieks of agony tore through the guard until he fell in a heap. She didn't hesitate, her sight was on Talos.

Another guard charged in, ramming into Sol's side. It was the last thing the guard did as his head severed from his shoulders at the end of Halburn's blade.

"Leave, Blackthorne!" Halburn thundered, his sword plunging through another enemy.

I sputtered again, coughing blood while I hunched over. The pain in my ribs doubled, made worse by every forceful exhale in my lungs. When hands grabbed me, pulling my limp body close, I didn't have to wonder. I didn't recoil.

Behind Casimir's shadowed form, Sol swung at Talos, taking his place. The weight of his hands on my shoulders made me crumble, the sky spinning as I tilted to the side. His arms lifted me from the ground, and the sounds of war became a muted ringing in my ears.

Halburn and Sol fought the onslaught of the Iron Guard who came to Talos's aid. In the flood of bodies, more Mistvalle guards filtered our way. I spotted familiar faces as Moria and Elrin came to help them. Bodies fell in Moria's wake as they lost their ability to move, and Elrin finished it with a sword to their chests, brutal and quick.

Gray ruins pulled me out of the fight, the sounds growing distant while we left the others behind. Casimir muttered something while he sat me down among cramped ruins, the floor above us low over our heads. The wall of crumbling stone shielded us from Talos and the Iron Guard.

I swayed when his hands left me, and my eyes slipped shut while the thrum of my abilities fought to recoup.

"Elita." It was loud, forced. Casimir's voice slipped between his responsibility as a captain and his concern. "You need to return to camp. You—" More blood sputtered from my lips, speckling his face. "Fuck. I can't—" Casimir watched me writhe, my face pinched by discomfort while I clutched my fractured side. He looked over his shoulder, back to where we came from.

The fighting continued with the sound of clashing blades. He brought his focus back to me. "Let me try something." He tore off his glove, and his hand shook as he ducked it into the neck guard of my armor, forcing the leather back. His skin was damp with sweat when it touched mine, resting from my collarbone to the curve of my neck.

He crawled closer to me in the cramped space, one of his knees resting between both of mine. My head lolled, eyes heavy with the pull to cave to the agony. Casimir's hand tucked deeper into my armor, his skin warm against mine.

Using his other hand, his knuckle gently lifted my chin, locking our gaze. "Eyes on me, Elita." His voice was a low rasp, the words a gentle command.

I rested my head back on the ruins, never breaking eye contact as his free hand went to my waist to keep my body from slumping. A warm sensation pricked beneath my skin, not like the touch of a healer, but it eased some of the pain. I had felt it before, and I thought back to the ship. My lips parted, sighing when some of the agony died down. He stayed there, eyes vigilant as he scanned the ruins.

When my jaw unclenched, the discomfort a distant hum, I placed a palm to his arm that was wrapped around my side. "What are you doing?"

Casimir's brow furrowed, as though the question was inappropriate in such a circumstance. "The book you gave me." It was the only answer he offered.

I nodded, closing my eyes for a moment. The pages filled my mind— passages where it poured over the shared effects of the blue lotus flower and their correlation with dreamwalking. He managed to relieve my pain. I took a moment to be grateful I gave him the book and the time he had to hone his ability.

Something slammed into the other side of the wall, and dust rained down on us, settling on Casimir's petals, dusting the shoulders of his armor. His cloak was gone, lost somewhere in the battle. I noted the cuts across his face, the hollow look in his eyes. The fight had already taken so much from him, and I wished I could return the relief his abilities gave me. If not for the blood that choked out of my throat, I would've thought I was healed.

"That feels nice," I muttered, tasting blood when I swallowed.

Casimir's nostrils flared, unable to pull himself out of the fight. But I couldn't linger there. I needed the mental reprieve as much as I needed a healer. It allowed my pulse to settle, the thrum of the earth slowly returning to me.

His hand went to leave my armor, but I stopped it, pressing a bloody palm to his. "Please, just a moment more."

"I can't, Elita...I can't focus. You being here—" His jaw clenched, the ability in his hand faltering until pain hissed through my teeth. "I'm begging you, let me finish this fight. I can't keep searching for you in the chaos. And seeing you like this..." His other hand left my waist and came up, his glove wiping the blood on my chin.

I winced, my face sore. The memory was faint, unfitting in the despair that ensued on the other side of the ruins. Even so, I stared at him, grabbing his wrist as he went to wipe my face again. "Please tell me I have all my teeth," I said, my eyes filling with tears that made me feel weak. Sadness drew lines in his face, his brow pulled together. I shifted and sat straighter against the wall. "I can fight, Captain." My voice was quiet but steady, his title bringing us back to the moment. The wounds that covered me ached, but there wasn't a soldier unscathed.

Casimir's grip tightened on the skin beneath my armor, his abilities flickering like a candle, the effectiveness waning. "You're so damn stubborn, Blackthorne," he whispered, his tone a pitch lighter as softness returned to his eyes. He leaned closer, his forehead nearly touching mine. "Don't resent me for this."

Before I could reply, he tore his hand out of my armor, the relief going with it. I didn't have a moment to stop him, grab his arm, or ask him to stay.

He peered around the ruins, and a second later, Halburn appeared, kneeling at my side. "Goddess sake…" He shook his head, and pressed a hand to the wound on my thigh.

Casimir stood, collecting his sword from the rubble. "Take her to camp, healer. That's an order."

"Casimir—Hey!"

Halburn loosened my chest plate, the release taking me off guard. He worked quickly, his concern evident when he bypassed every question or warning and put his hand into the bottom of my tunic, resting on the side of my rib cage that brought me the most pain.

"Couple of cracked ribs." He shook his head, and glanced at Casimir. "I've got this one. Go help my daughter."

My heart sank like a stone in my chest when I thought of Sol fighting Talos. I hoped the other Mistvalle soldiers had been enough help to keep her safe. The vision of her dead on the battlefield nearly had me up and out of the ruins, desperate to make sure she was okay.

Casimir's eyes searched mine, the brief look reminiscent of a silent goodbye. Dread outweighed the relief brought by Halburn's hands.

"Don't let her come back here." Casimir's command was final, meant for Halburn. Then he was gone, his scarlet petals catching the light just as he ducked out of the ruins, his sword drawn and ready.

My entire soul withered in his absence, and for a horrible flicker in time, I worried it would be the last time I saw my ghost.

Forty-Four

The silence that followed Casimir's departure was deafening. It rang in my ears until even the fight was lost to me. Halburn's abilities worked at my ribs, then my thigh. He worked quickly, eventually using both hands to focus more energy on the two wounds. The smaller scrapes and bruises would have to wait until the battle was over.

I stared at the ruins above my head, the stones centuries old, and still standing. They trembled with every hoofbeat or slam of a body. Footsteps approached many times, someone sprinting on the other side. I kept waiting for Casimir to reappear with the news that Talos was dead.

But we remained undisturbed, hidden among the aftermath of Cordelia's fury. The battle of Tyvolia ended when the floods wiped the entire civilization away, drowning them in the depths of the sea. She was never regarded in history as a murderer, not the way Aeterna was.

I sat in the presence of her destruction, the water dried centuries ago, but the stain of bloodshed couldn't be washed away. Her story wasn't unlike Esen's. Jealousy drove her there. The deities were never short on arrogance.

Sweat glistened at Halburn's brow, and I stared at him. Exhaustion was evident in his features. His hands trembled on my wounds, his abilities waning the more he used them.

Rubble scraped beneath my foot when I shuffled, moving back from him. It broke his focus and his head snapped up.

"I'm okay, Halburn. Don't spend the last of your energy on me."

He shook his head, reluctantly removing his hands. "Coulda used more healers here."

I bit back a reply, knowing that Taryn was better off in the safety of Mistvalle with Ulrik. But he wasn't wrong. There hadn't been many that accompanied the party, and most of them stayed back at the camp to heal the injured farther from the battle.

Another body slammed into the wall behind me, shaking my torso. I sat up slowly, testing how my rib cage felt. It still sparked with discomfort, but it was bearable. The blood on my thigh was dried, the wound no longer gaping.

It'd be good enough.

I went to stand, every bone in my body shaking. Halburn scrambled to grab my forearm.

"And where are you going?" he asked, exasperated.

"I'm going to fight."

"Not so long as I have breath in me. We're returning to camp." He moved quicker than I thought possible for the timid healer, scooping me into his burly arms. I grunted in protest.

The ruins fell away when he stepped out of the shadowed corner Casimir brought me to. Sights and sounds all rushed back to me, jarring compared to the muted effect of the stones.

Arrows swished through the air, catching in armor. Swords continued to collide, cracking like thunder. Screams echoed in the forgotten kingdom. I searched for familiar faces, only to find none.

The guards that fought were of Mistvalle. They continued to hold off the Iron Guard, as well as the enemy soldiers who didn't carry the same scarlet armor. Casimir, Sol, and Talos were all missing. Lost to the chaos.

My pulse quickened just as Halburn's pace did, sprinting through the crowd of enemies and companions.

The wounded were scattered across the cobblestones, their hands reaching for Halburn. He never paused to help them. I watched in horror as their eyes trailed our retreating figures, tears streaking through blood and dust that coated their cheeks.

"We have to go back!" I shouted over the disarray. My legs squirmed, trying to get him to release me.

"The captain ordered me to—"

Halburn tripped, sending me across the rubble. His boot caught on a dead body, and their lifeless eyes found me a few feet away. I scrambled up, not allowing myself to stay down.

An enemy soldier closed in, going for Halburn. I went straight for the guard, my daggers swinging at them. I caught the edge of their arm with my blade. They jerked back, and I tugged at the hum of my abilities as they simmered beneath the surface, gradually recovering. I wrapped a thick vine around their ankle, and slammed them to the ground.

More Iron Guards and enemy soldiers continued to close in around us, the area thick with desperation to help Talos. Their presence confirmed that he wasn't far.

Vines flicked and whipped through the air. They slapped bodies back from Halburn as he stood and grabbed a sword from the cobblestones. I flung the enemies into the ruins, and dust erupted around their fallen bodies. Halburn gave me a warning glance, the meaning clear: if I overused my abilities, I'd be right back where I was.

I released the pull on my abilities and sucked in a steadying breath, my side pinching with agitation.

Footsteps quickened against the earth, singing to my abilities. Without having to think, I whipped around and charged at the enemy. Their armor differed from the Iron Guard. It appeared dull and without the intricacies the king's guards wore. My vines easily overpowered them. They crumpled like parchment against the thick vines as I tore through the crowd. I ran at another enemy and released a blast of thorns, just as they swung for a Mistvalle soldier. They howled and tumbled to the ground. Even as their energy drained, I tried to block it out. I released another whip of vines and knocked the oncoming bodies to the ground.

Exhaustion caused my abilities to falter. Sparks erupted behind my eyes and I clenched my jaw, taking a moment to center myself. Halburn covered my brief pause, plucking up a discarded spear. He sent it soaring through an enemy's gut.

Between the parting crowd, I spotted black hair speckled with scarlet. Casimir continued to fight Talos, carrying two swords once more.

While the two fought, Casimir's focus on Talos, I spotted an enemy soldier as they closed in on Casimir's blind side. I moved without a thought, darting in their direction. I pulled out my daggers, trying to preserve my abilities. I jumped up with my blades raised above my head. They came down hard, and the person sputtered as my blades locked us close. *No.* My hands twitched as I pulled the daggers out of the young man's neck. He appeared no older than sixteen.

Bile clawed its way up my throat, and I turned my face to the side as the contents of my stomach poured out onto the ground. My ribs screamed at the force of it.

When the retching settled, I dropped next to the young man. His eyes gazed at the sky, void of life.

"No, please," I whispered. My hands wouldn't stop shaking as I looked over his armor. It wasn't thick enough to block any attacks. The thin steel barely fit the young man's frame.

A sob of disgust tore through me. Tears painted his armor beneath me as blood pooled around his neck and head. My screams drowned the sounds of war. I scanned the bodies around me, noting the armor that matched the young man's. They scattered the land of Tyvolia, their faces void of life, yet still clinging to their last moments of terror. These men and women were not Iron Guard. Many of them appeared to be younger than me. The realization threatened to make me sick again.

A hand pulled me off the ground, and I tried to fight it. "Are you hurt?!" Elrin's voice caught me off guard.

My mouth opened to speak, but another sob made its way out. Elrin looked over my armor, then at the boy I killed.

One of my shaking hands grabbed her elbow. "They aren't soldiers. They're just children. The king brought people from the villages."

Alarm flashed in her expression, and I watched as she took in our surroundings. The bodies that lay dead on the ground were mostly young men and women, too inexperienced to fight. They had no chance.

Called on by a cruel king who sent them to die. We couldn't win.

Not with the blood of the kingdom's youth on our hands. We would lose trying to be everything the king was not.

Forty-Five

When I was younger, I used to read books from my father's library that told stories of fierce battles, long since passed. They spoke of warriors who defended the kingdom to keep its people safe. Full of paintings of kind kings who sacrificed themselves to defend the weak.

My father would remind me that people often falsely recounted history. Those who wanted to appear self-sacrificing never were quite as pure as they wanted others to believe.

I used to roll my eyes at him and continue reading. A decent king wouldn't put his people in harm's way. It made sense in a perfect realm. How could someone be so cruel as to sacrifice their people?

Even the Rose sacrifices were painted to make sense. A necessary evil, demanded by the gods.

But the barren land covered in the dead bodies of the kingdom's youngest soldiers proved my father to be right. The king they served would sacrifice them to get what he wanted.

I wrestled with the urge to be sick as I fended off another enemy who closed in on Casimir and Talos. If we didn't get out soon, another young soldier would lose their life at the end of my blade. My energy was already spent, and the aching was back tenfold in my side.

Elrin tore through the crowd of Iron Guard, and similar to me, she tried to only disarm the younger soldiers.

My heart plummeted when I pulled another body to the ground with too much force. Controlling the vines as my emotions raged was impossible, and it made it too difficult to avoid killing the innocent soldiers who were forced to fight the king's battle.

When a roar of pain broke through the chaos, I jerked my head around to see Casimir grasping his shoulder while blood coated his hand. The Iron Guard responsible lost his hand not a moment after.

No, no, no. Please.

A splitting grin twisted Talos's face while he backed away, retreating. I didn't hesitate. I summoned vines across the earth, meaning to wrap them around his ankles. To my chagrin, he cut through them with his sword. Talos's eyes flickered in my direction.

Casimir steadied his stance, and I moved to go to his side, but something knocked into my back.

The ground scraped across my face until I skidded to a stop, a few feet from a jagged wall of ruins. It burned from where small rocks tore through my cheek and I gritted my teeth against the pain.

I turned quickly to see an Iron Guard swinging a mace toward me. My body rolled to the right, but part of it grazed my arm, and a scream erupted from me as it jerked out of my skin. Without meaning to, I released another round of thorns. They rippled through the earth, taking down several enemies in their wake.

I gasped when their energy died in the dirt. For a pause, I didn't move. Agony tore through me. The gash in my arm couldn't compare to the sensation of the soldiers dying at my hands.

A familiar face swam in my line of sight, and I blinked back tears.

Halburn's expression distorted with panic as he scanned over my body. "By Aeterna's earth, your arm..." he said, his voice low.

The noises buzzed in my head, and I couldn't tell if he was whispering to himself or if he was talking to me. Nothing else he said registered.

Death ensued around us, and I needed to move. If I didn't, Halburn would die simply for being too close to me and trying to help. Despite how my arm burned, I sat straight and watched as the two armies continued to slaughter each other.

Halburn's touch on my arm made me grimace, but I allowed him to heal what he could.

Between the mass of people in combat, I spotted Casimir and Talos with their blades locked. With his other hand, Casimir's second sword swung through one of the enemy soldiers who wore no insignia.

My stomach churned, and I grabbed Halburn's arm, fixing my gaze on him. "The king brought innocent people here," I rasped. "Many of these soldiers are barely out of childhood."

Halburn gave me a heavy look just as an arrow sang through the air near the side of his head. He didn't even flinch.

"Get her up!" someone's voice roared over the sounds of war.

I glanced at my side to see Sabian holding up a shield with one arm while he used the other to swing a short sword at an attacking enemy.

"You can't heal her here!" Sabian shouted, taking his eyes off the battle that raged around us.

It was the last thing he did.

An arrow speared through his chest, and he sputtered, eyes wide with shock.

"No!" I tried to jump up, but Halburn pushed me to the ground, grabbing Sabian's shield to cover my body. Disbelief rattled me, and Sabian's lifeless face stared back at mine, inches away.

My eyes shut hard enough to sting, and I tried to rid myself of the horrible sight. Guilt wracked every bone in my body, and I fought back the sobs that threatened to swallow me.

More arrows whipped around us and fear grabbed hold of me when I realized Halburn's hand was gone from my arm. Without thinking, I threw the shield off and searched for his blonde hair among the bodies that littered the ground.

To my relief, he stood beside me, fighting off more enemies as they stormed the area. The relief didn't last long when I realized how overwhelmed we became as soldiers came to Talos's aid.

Casimir continued to hold his own, even as blood shimmered on his armor. We needed to get out before my vision came to fruition.

I got to my feet, and with my uninjured arm, I reached out, focusing my dwindling energy on building a wall of vines at our backs. Halburn didn't break his focus, and I was thankful for it.

Sabian remained at my feet, his eyes never closing. Though I would have done the same for a fellow Rose, I couldn't push away the shame. If I'd only been more careful. If my presence hadn't distracted Casimir and Halburn.

The vision from the night before came to the forefront of my mind, and dizziness overwhelmed me. Halburn's armor swirled in a display of shimmering emerald in front of me, and the earth seemed to tilt.

"Steady, Blackthorne!" he ordered.

The vines faltered behind us, and before they finished falling, he grabbed my wrist and pulled me closer to his side. He continued to swing while the voice echoed in my head: *"Your choice to fight will doom them all."*

Halburn struggled with my weight as I leaned on him, swaying on my feet. The vision became overbearing, the weight suffocating, and my sight blackened.

"I can't see," I rasped.

Halburn tensed beside me and advanced through the ongoing battle. I listened as he swung his sword with abandon and continued to dodge attacks to the best of his ability. We moved through on his experience alone. I was nothing more than a dead weight as he pulled me along, my vision gradually returning.

I tried to tune out the voice, but it repeated the warning again and again until my head threatened to burst.

The calamity began to dissipate around us the farther Halburn ran. It took all my effort to block out the shrill voice and focus on where we were. We stumbled through a broken wall in the former castle. Rubble scattered and echoed as our boots kicked them away. Sparks of white burst behind my eyes, and I pressed a hand to my temple.

Crumbled ruins shielded us from the fight we left behind. It looked out of place in the desolation of Tyvolia, but I knew what glory used to stand in the empty stone walls.

Halburn came to a halt and released my weight from his arm. I slumped against a stack of old stones that threatened to slip out from under me. The uproar faded, and with no stragglers among the ruins, my body finally had a moment to settle—a moment to note Casimir's absence.

He stayed behind.

I gasped and pressed a hand to my throat. The panic ravaged my mind, and Halburn watched with his brows knitted together.

"You've got to gather your feelings. We can't stay here," he said. The frustration in his voice was clear.

While my body fought the panic, Halburn took the time to heal my arm more. I tried to ignore the prickling as he mended it.

The only respite it offered was to halt the bleeding. Even Halburn's abilities couldn't repair tissue in a single healing. It would take time for it to return to normal. It made me weak, and it would affect my swing with vines or blades.

Halburn removed his hand after a minute, and he took me by the shoulders, surprising me. "Don't go back out there, Blackthorne. Wait here and I will have someone return you to the camp."

My stomach dropped, and I immediately shook my head. "I can fight, Halburn. I *have* been fighting. I'm going back for Casimir."

Halburn was taken aback before a knowing look swept across his face. "I knew it the moment you showed up to ride out. Lady Estelle shouldn't have allowed you to step foot out of Mistvalle. If you go back for that captain, you'll only get yourself and him hurt."

"I'm the only one who can conjure! And we can't keep harming those young soldiers—"

"And *that* is why. They are your enemies, and they killed Sabian, and have killed many others." He shook his head. "You've overused your abilities, and if you don't stop, you'll be just as dead." The words were harsh, and he sighed. "Don't leave the ruins. Sol will take you back."

I opened my mouth to protest, but he sprinted away, his sword drawn. His heavy footfalls echoed in the hauntingly silent castle. Rubble shifted, knocking until they fell to dust.

When he disappeared, the horrible thought I might never see him again made my stomach twist with grief. It was foolish, and it did me no good to grieve over those who still walked among us. Not when Sabian's body lay forgotten back where he tried to protect us.

The sight of his eyes followed me—as did the horror in the young man's face who I had driven my daggers into. They haunted me, and I hated how Halburn's demand for me to return to the camp tempted me.

For all the training and belief I had in myself, I failed miserably. Perhaps the vision was right, and I displeased the gods.

Pain sparked in my side, the ache not nearly as bad as when Casimir brought me back, but enough to make it hard to twist my torso. I placed a hand to the sore ribs, my palm moving with my shallow breaths.

None of the uncertainty I had held any relevance when I focused back on the fight that continued outside the broken side of the castle.

The different armor from the Iron Guard to the soldiers of Mistvalle and Everbloom all clashed in a sea of glistening colors. Their weapons sang in the distance, and it reverberated through me. It became a powerful thrum in the earth and it pulled me closer. My feet met with the crumbled stones beneath them, and my eyes scanned the fight.

The king's army was winning, and I watched with realization as the Roses tried to avoid lethal force on the enemies that didn't don the horrible red and silver. We couldn't bring ourselves to be as cruel as the king was, and it was costing the blood of our people.

Anger bit at the corner of my eyes, and surveyed the fight for Sol or any of my other companions to appear—petal-filled hair or Galan's much too unsure demeanor. Anyone to help me make my choice. Anyone to help me fight.

Sol was nowhere in sight. I tried to force back the worry and reminded myself that Halburn likely needed to search for her. But I wouldn't wait for Sol to come and retrieve me.

Terror latched onto me when I spotted Valor in the hoard of soldiers. He tore through the crowd of enemies, tossing them away without another glance. His strength was his best weapon. Bodies flung across the land in sickening blows, shattering the ruins they collided with. He held the upper hand with ease, and soldiers cowered in his presence. Valor trained his gaze on King Lendorr, and in foolish arrogance, one of the gray-armored soldiers came up behind him. The soldier brought down a dagger, but Valor was too quick for him.

I watched Valor freeze before he could even raise his blade.

The blood drained from my face when the king charged for Valor as he stared at the young soldier in disbelief.

Numbness crept across my skin, and before I gave myself a chance to rethink it, my legs carried me through the battle that continued in a sea of blood. The loose stones shifted under my boots, and I caught myself before falling to the ground. Dust covered my armor, changing my cloak from black to a curtain of gray. It whipped behind me, a nuisance. I released it, leaving it to fall to the ground.

Valor fought off the enemy without lethal force, and it somehow made the panic worse. I couldn't lose another parent, and his hesitation, no matter how brief, would get him killed.

Every muscle in my legs stung with the exertion, but I sprinted as fast as possible, my sights set on the king as he prowled at Valor's blind side.

Lendorr didn't see me coming, and with the waning energy left in me, I conjured vines. I tried to wrap him in them, but he was quicker than I anticipated as he turned his head in my direction. His sword sliced through my vines.

I grunted and dodged an oncoming enemy, using my vines on them to clear my path. The vines faltered, weak and strained. Part of it turned to a wisp of dust. There wasn't any time to let it deter me.

King Lendorr snarled and turned from Valor.

Good.

I threw out another throng of vines toward the king, trying to at least distract him to give me the upper hand. They lashed out and shuddered.

Lendorr didn't fall prey to the bait, and for a split second, I doubted whether I could take the king alone. There was no time to let the uncertainty stop me. His gaze was already locked on me, and he closed the space with his sword drawn.

I ducked under his blade, rolled, and pulled out one of my daggers, aiming for his leg. My entire body trembled, the pain humming beneath the adrenaline.

Instead of making contact with his shin, he brought his knee up, and clipped me in the chin, which sent me sprawling back. My teeth clenched painfully and I tasted blood. Spots flickered in my eyes, and the exhaustion nearly made me succumb to the blow.

My chest tightened, but I couldn't cry. Never again would I allow him to catch a glimpse of my tears. Not after he mocked the death of my parents. The memory released a burst of fury, and I got back up as he swung for me.

I jumped out of the way and with one hand in the crease of his armor chest piece; I pulled him forward, and slammed his face into my knee. I tried to bring my dagger to a weak spot in his armor, but he twisted his body. It caused my arm to contort horribly, and I cried out as my hand released his armor.

The king spat blood into the dirt and glared at me. "You don't belong here, foolish girl."

His words made me flinch. Another reminder of the vision that haunted me every moment of the battle. I didn't allow myself to linger on the visions.

Returning his gesture, I spit blood at his feet. When he looked at me in disgust, a grin split my face. His expression twisted with anger, and he charged for me.

My first instinct was to run, but I held my ground. With my arms in front of my face, I conjured a wall of roots. Thicker and more capable of stopping his blade.

The king grunted when they caught his blade. It stuck in the thick roots, and he tugged at it. The sensation rattled through my veins, every tug of his blade sang through me. I winced but kept steady. It was my chance to turn the fight to my advantage.

A sharp hiss pulled between my teeth when I released my focus. I moved to the other side of the roots and brought my dagger down until it found the weak spot in his armor.

Lendorr bellowed and tore his arm away just as he pulled his sword from the roots. He swung, and I moved back once more. A dance of back and forth, waiting for the other to falter.

I wasn't quick enough, and the tip of his sword ran across the top of my armor, where I didn't have any protection.

The sting of it sent me to my knees, and I pressed against the cut. It wasn't deep, but it was enough to make moisture bite at my eyes when it tore across the flesh that had yet to heal beneath my collarbone.

My energy dwindled fast, and if I didn't gain the upper hand, I was going to die. I couldn't carry on without reprieve or a chance to regain my energy. It wasn't like the days spent on the training grounds. The battle was adrenaline and constant movement. If I froze for a second too long, it'd be the death of me.

The pain in my muscles radiated bone deep, and I glanced up to see the king closing in on me once more. I didn't want to stand. I didn't want to fight anymore.

That wasn't an option, and I rose.

The king scoffed even as he bled from beneath his armor. It painted the white pieces with scarlet.

I took a fighting stance across from him and waited for him to make the first move. If I didn't reserve all the energy left in my veins, I would fall over from exhaustion. I struggled to size him up. His combat style was unknown to me, and while I sparred with my companions in Mistvalle, it was never with the intent of harming each other.

I tried to pay attention to how he moved. He was slower than before, taking on a more cautious approach. If I couldn't overpower him with hand-to-hand combat, my chances were gone. Lendorr wouldn't let me catch him off guard again.

Every inch of space he closed made my muscles taut with tension. I tried to remain ready.

Silently, I called to my thorns, but the energy died in my veins, and it made the unease worse. If I stayed there any longer waiting for him to make the first move, I wouldn't make it out of Tyvolia. Not as a throng of Iron Guards started to move through the area. They stormed across the field, coming to their king's aid.

I broke into a sprint.

Coils of sweat-covered curls scattered across my line of sight. I grunted and ignored the minor inconvenience. It was my last chance to finish it.

If the king fell, they'd have no choice but to retreat or they risked losing both the king and his heir. Silently, I hoped Talos was lying dead somewhere in the sea of bodies. Then it ended with Lendorr.

The thought gave me the last push I needed, and I roared above the sound of clanging armor and locking swords. Every pulse thrummed in my veins, and I lunged for the king with my dagger above my head.

He went for his sword, but I anticipated he would.

A single vine sprang up from behind him and knotted around his hand as I jumped into the air, taking hold of his armor while my body twisted. I wrapped myself around his back, raised my dagger against the blinding sun, and plunged it toward the king's neck.

Something rough yanked me back by my hair, and I scrambled as the dagger soared through the air. It clattered far from my grasp, and in desperation, I tried to conjure thorns again. They never came.

An Iron Guard held onto my hair, and I thrashed in his tight grip. It burned as he pulled my head back, exposing my neck.

The king straightened, flicking his hair off his face. He plucked up his sword and stalked over to where the Iron Guard held me, despite the way I lashed in their grip.

Ruins distorted behind him. The land of Tyvolia spun until a sick sensation rolled through me. My vision darkened at the edges, waves of crimson and black burning through the air in horrible threads. Air pulled for my lungs, and the energy dissipated. No thrum. No vines.

"You should have given your sacrifice as you were meant to, girl," the king taunted.

He closed the space, and a horrid grin twisted his face as he raised his sword to the sky. A hunger flashed in his eyes as he stared down at me. I wouldn't look away. I wouldn't give him the satisfaction.

An abrupt flicker of fear swam in his eyes when he met my gaze, and he replaced it with a sneer. Lendorr went to bring his sword down. It sang through the air, nearly drowned out by a raven calling in the distance. Panic tore through my lungs, panting while I watched.

A hand wrapped around Lendorr's weapon-wielding arm and the war around me froze; a blur of armored bodies.

Bones snapped as the gloved hand pulled Lendorr's arm back, sending the king's sword clattering to the ground. Lendorr howled in agony, and with no hesitation, Valor unsheathed his sword.

He grabbed Lendorr's hair in his gloved fist and yanked his head back. Valor's gaze locked with mine, the fury and fear burning in his eyes. There was no mask. No walls to hide him.

At that moment, he was every bit a horrified father.

He tore his focus away before his arm hardly even twitched.

The blade plunged through the king's chest.

Forty-Six

Lendorr's body fell to the ground in a heap of bloodied armor as Valor released his hair. The guard who held me screamed in disbelief, pulling their blade close to the edge of my cheek. It reflected the orange sunset that swept through the sky, glinting in the corner of my eye, mirroring a horrified scarlet gaze.

It never made contact.

A sickening crack resounded, and I dropped to the side as Galan nearly tore the guard's head from their shoulders. Bile rose in my throat, but I swallowed the disgust and stumbled to my feet, staring at him in disbelief.

Galan didn't give the guard another glance as he grabbed a fallen sword and offered it to me. "We must not linger," he said. His voice was quiet as the enemy's shock and horror at the king's fallen body erupted throughout the ruins.

My hands shook, but I took the short sword from him and gripped the hilt tight. Galan nodded and ran through the crowd. His armor disappeared in the havoc that ensued around us. In the sea of people, I hoped for a glimpse of Casimir or Sol. Neither of them were in the vicinity, and their absence unsettled me.

I brought my attention to where Valor stood near the king's body. His eyes locked with mine across the space, and I gulped.

Blood speckled his face, his anger blatant.

"Valor—" I didn't have time to say anything else when a horrible wail pierced through the chaos.

My head whipped around to see Talos charging our way, his face red with burning fury, blood crusted to his once pristine armor. His sword raised over his head as he went for Valor. The sunset colored his armor with flickers of orange; a flame as hunger warped his purple splotched face.

The thrum of the earth was gone, my abilities drained, and I remembered what Halburn said in the ruins. I used them recklessly, and now I'd face the consequences of my foolish decisions. I wouldn't reach them in time, but I still sprinted toward them as Valor raised his sword.

The two never got the chance to collide.

A horse charged through the crowd of soldiers, and I watched as the Iron Guard atop the horse grabbed Talos by his armor. He jerked back, and the horse stomped on the crumbling stones, unsettled by the movement.

"Release me!" Talos thundered. The guard didn't listen. He held onto him until another soldier brought forth a second horse.

I froze in place and watched as they forced him to retreat. He screamed curses and thrashed. His blonde hair drooped in his face while he snarled in Valor's direction.

A guard muttered something in his ear, and Talos halted his thrashing and gritted his teeth.

Alarm rang through me when he drew his attention my way. He stared with unbridled hunger, and I recoiled. My hands dampened with sweat as I gripped the hilt of the sword as tight as possible. I waited for them to charge, but they never did.

Talos sneered, then mounted his own horse.

Shock rippled through the battlefield as the Iron Guard and Talos began their retreat. Their king was dead, and a horrible realization overcame me—Talos would take his place. They wouldn't allow the king's only heir to die.

Somehow, we gained the upper hand, and the soldiers of the Iron Thorn ran in the opposite direction. Somewhere in the sea of enemies, a horn blew, and more bodies fell back.

To my dismay, I noted young soldiers from the Iron Thorn linger back. They stared after Talos and the Iron Guard, too wounded, and they slumped among the ruins and watched in disbelief while their soon-to-be king left them behind. I waited for some of them to fight. It broke something in me when the younger soldiers wept.

Cries echoed through the desolate kingdom. It whistled among the trees. Our soldiers and theirs—all grieving their losses.

As I looked at Valor, I saw animosity flicker across his features. He advanced toward Talos, even as the prince's horse took off in a gallop.

I went to stop him, but a rough hand jerked me back. A yelp of fear crawled up my throat, but when I turned, it was only Sol. She had a horse by her side and thrust the reins toward me.

"No," I said in disbelief. I took a step back. "The wounded—"

"You're no healer," Sol interrupted. "Go."

My lips pursed, and I pivoted away from her. Every turn of my head made me sick when I realized the carnage that remained as the dead king's army withdrew from the fight.

The young men and women from the Iron Thorn stumbled around in disorientation. Most of them appeared younger than Galan. They would be left to the mercy of Valor and Estelle. If they didn't die of their wounds, they'd die trying to find their way back to the Stone Border.

So many soldiers left behind. So many dead...

Worry flared in my head and I searched for any sign of Casimir in the crowd of the bewildered Mistvalle warriors who stood and watched Talos leave.

His petal-covered hair was nowhere in sight, even as the crowd thinned. Our numbers became decimated, and a knot formed in my stomach. The only familiar faces I could see were Galan, Myra, Estelle, and Valor. Many who remained were faces I hardly recognized.

No, no. Please.

"Sol, where is Casimir?" I whipped around and grabbed her forearm.

She bristled, and her serious demeanor shifted. "He was brawling with the prince," she said. Her tone did nothing to reassure me, and it was worse when I thought about how Talos remained intact.

I paled and released her arm to look around once more.

My gaze caught Estelle stopping Valor as he glared after the retreating enemies. The Mistvalle soldiers that remained also turned in circles where they paused. They stared at the enemy left behind, seeming unsure. The young enemies cowered.

I watched as healers started to go through the crowd of Mistvalle soldiers, searching the ground for the wounded. They ignored those from the Iron Thorn, and a young woman caught my eye. She held another soldier's body in her arms, tears coating her cheeks. Blood covered the side of her face.

They were too young, and Talos left them to die. Too wounded to ride out in a rush, he wouldn't fight for them. And our healers avoided them, offering no help.

Halburn was one of the many healers who dodged the Iron Thorn soldiers, and he sprinted through the frozen faces, trying to help anyone who marched with us from Mistvalle. As the thunderous sound of hooves on cobblestone faded, all I heard were sobs of shock and agony.

I took a step away from Sol and toward the lone young woman who wept for her dead companion.

Valor crossed the space without me realizing, and he grabbed my arm. "Return to camp, Fullan." His tone dripped with anger.

"They need help." I sounded as small as I felt. In my arrogance, I almost died by taking on an enemy much stronger than I was. Still, I didn't regret interrupting the king when he charged for Valor.

"You can't help them. Return to camp and have your wounds tended to. That's an order," Valor commanded.

I surveyed the mess of battered bodies and shook my head. "We have to help the ones Talos left behind. They're too young—"

"They are your enemy, and you will do well to remember that." Valor glowered at me, disbelief and fury equal in his expression.

His scolding threatened to make me retreat. But all I saw when I stared at the soldiers left behind were more people who the king lied to. Forced to give a sacrifice they weren't ready for. One they didn't even have to give. They suffered at the king's hand, just as we did.

I disregarded Valor and shook his hand off my arm. He shouted at me, but I tuned it out and shuffled over to the woman whose blood dripped from her temple to her chin. The dead soldier shook in her lap from the force of her sobs.

She didn't look up when I stopped in front of her. Stones scuffed under my boots, and I crouched. The wasted energy nearly made me topple over, the pain returning to my body all at once.

Another soldier rested in her lap, much too young to be there. His face appeared younger than Alba's, no more than sixteen. And he died for the selfish king. Like many Roses had before.

I hesitated before I reached out. The young woman flinched and her head snapped up. She stared at me, terror in her gaze. My hand paused, and shakily, I ran a hand over the boy's face, closing his eyes.

Tears fell as she stared at me.

Footsteps followed me, harsh on the rubble and destruction from the battle. I didn't turn. I suspected it was Valor, possibly Estelle.

For the first time since Ronin, I stared a stranger from the Iron Thorn in the eye without fear. Even as she flinched, staring at my red irises, I didn't recoil.

I kept my tone soft as I asked, "Are you hurt anywhere else?"

She jumped, and her attention went to whoever stood behind me. Her chest moved with rapid gasps until they became another swell of sobs. It made some of the tension leave my shoulders. She wouldn't try to fight us. Her resolve was gone, if it'd ever been present.

After a pause, I glanced over my shoulder. Estelle, Valor, and Sol stood behind me, their hands on their weapons. It took me a moment to gain the courage to stand and face them.

"Lady Estelle," I said, trying to avoid Valor's glare. "She needs a healer."

Estelle's eyes widened, and a hand loosened on her sword. "Elita, we shouldn't—"

"Please, my lady. They were following the decree of a cruel king. Is that not what the Roses sought to escape?"

It was foolish, and in the back of my mind, thoughts of betrayal shattered my peace. Estelle could heal the young woman, and just as quickly, she could pull her blade on us. Something told me she wouldn't.

Estelle searched my face, contemplating. I gave her the time to mull it over and tried to ignore the biting panic when I thought of Casimir's absence. He still hadn't found us, and Talos was long gone.

When the young woman coughed, spitting blood, Estelle made her choice. She dropped to a knee and outstretched her hand. "Will you allow me to heal you?"

The soldier stared at her, bewildered and afraid.

It surprised me when the soldier looked at me. I gave her a nod and hoped it would put her mind at ease. She had no reason to trust any of us. We were her enemy. Even so, she put her hand in Estelle's.

Tension caused a deep ache across my back when I thought of Estelle's other ability—to drain life. I hoped the young woman hadn't seen such a horrific display.

Estelle steadied herself, and the young soldier stared in confusion. I remembered how odd it was to me when Taryn first healed my wounds, her eyes darting side to side. Still, she didn't pull back. I watched relief fill her expression as Estelle eased some of her pain.

Someone tapped my shoulder, and I turned to see Sol waiting. Valor's fists were furled tight, and the two watched me rather than Estelle. Her abilities didn't give an enemy the chance to have the upper hand. She could switch from healing to killing the girl in an instant.

I straightened and met Sol's gaze as she said, "We should head to camp."

"But the others—"

Valor stepped closer. "Lady Estelle and I will see that the soldiers who were left behind get their wounds tended."

I glanced at the young woman, and she appeared to be speaking in a whisper to Estelle. Her gratitude was clear.

"You can't leave them all here, Valor. They'll die just as easily from the elements."

Exasperation crossed his face. "Fullan—"

"Please. Help them. Be better than Lendorr." The words caught in my throat. It felt wrong, especially after I made such a horrible mistake when I took up for Ronin—a norm from the Iron Thorn.

Valor didn't bring up my past folly. He glanced around us at the ruins, coated in the blood of Roses and norms alike. Mistvalle's army and King Lendorr's. None of those we called on were under the age of eighteen. Even Galan joined of his own accord. We didn't force anyone into a fight they didn't believe in.

Many of the young soldiers left behind by Talos appeared aimless. They trembled in fear each time a Rose passed them. They needed to see that we were better.

Finally, Valor sighed. "We will do what we can. But you must return to the camp. I don't want you on this battlefield."

Hope swelled, foreign to me. It dissipated just as quickly when I once again noted Casimir's absence. With one last survey of the area, I pressed my lips into a tight line and walked over to Sol.

I took the reins from Sol's hand and turned from Valor, getting on the saddle with a struggle, air hissing through my clenched teeth. My whole body ached from the effort, but it wasn't enough to erase the fear that crippled me with the absence of familiar red petals.

Regardless of how it would sound, I looked back at Valor before leaving. "Find Casimir, please," I said, voice low and pleading. His brow pulled together.

"We will return with any soldier that survived the fight."

"Valor—"

"And we will return for the dead once everyone is safe."

Icy horror wedged its way up my spine. I didn't get a moment to say another word. Sol hopped onto the saddle behind me and clicked her heels on the horses' sides.

Night devoured the sky by the time we made it back to the camp. It erupted in mayhem as wounded soldiers returned to the healers who stayed behind among the tents. I watched as the few healers struggled to handle the influx of bodies. They darted between tents with supplies in their arms, and overwhelm on their faces.

I thought about Taryn and how they made her stay back when she wanted to help. They could have used her hands, no matter how hard they tried to convince her that she was inadequate.

In the same breath, I was grateful she wasn't another friend to worry about in the fight. She was safe in Mistvalle with Ulrik, who needed his mother more than the soldiers needed her.

Sol and I dismounted, and a healer close by paused. "Is it over?" the healer asked.

Tears bit at my eyes, and I couldn't bring myself to answer. The horrors of the battle spilled over, and the worry for Casimir muddled my thoughts. Sol gave the healer a nod, and she sighed in relief.

Blood covered the healer's smock; her appearance disheveled. There must have been more injured tucked in the privacy of the tents.

After a pause, the healer surveyed the both of us. Her gaze stopped on me and she stepped forward. "Let's get you into a tent, miss." Her tone was soft, as if I would spook if she spoke too loud.

I glanced over at Sol, but none of the blood on her seemed to be her own. She made it out unscathed.

Sol gave a nod of reassurance, and I followed the healer to one of the large gray tents. When we entered the drapes, the sight made me falter. There were already over twenty of our soldiers cramped in the space, lying in cots or on the floor as healers moved between them.

The healer took my elbow and guided me over to an empty cot. I sat, and as soon as I did, exhaustion threatened to swallow me.

"Steady, miss. We'll get you healed up so you can rest," she said, patting my knee. "My name is Briar. Would you allow me to assess your wounds?"

I nodded, and before she asked, I pulled loose the armor over my chest. As I removed them, my shoulders ached with relief from the weight being lifted. I tried to ignore the dried blood on the breastplate. I discarded it to the side and removed my vambraces next. Each piece that came off couldn't erase the things I endured. I longed for the memories to lift with each item of armor, but they never did.

Once I removed all the armor pieces, only my black tunic and the leather trousers remained. Both had tears through them and cuts peeking out from beneath the fabric.

Briar brought over a divider and opened it. She used it to wrap around the cot for more privacy, and she turned back to me. "Apologies, miss, but I'll need to see the wounds to assess and heal them."

The awful things I experienced only hours before allowed no room for me to have a shred of embarrassment. I removed my tunic and allowed her to scan over my wounds and heal them. My right side was already purple with large bruises, and the other wounds were blackened by crusted blood.

Both the gash on my chest and thigh needed suturing, but I blocked it out and tried to listen for the sound of people returning from the battlefield. Horrible thoughts plagued me. What if Talos had turned around and caught them off guard, shorthanded on soldiers? What if the people I cared for never returned?

The fears overlapped until the nerves in my temples went numb. The panic had nowhere to go.

I sat through the healing until, eventually, Briar handed me a damp washcloth for my face, and pulled out the bandages to wrap my wounds. Time passed in a blur until the sensation of hoofbeats pounding the earth caught my attention.

With time to rest, a weak thrum filled my veins, and my head snapped up as the sounds of disarray increased. It wasn't just another soldier or two coming back for healing. There were too many hoofbeats, and their arrival sent tremors through the earth as they rode into camp.

My heart jumped into my throat and I glanced down as Briar finished wrapping my torso to secure the bandages over the wound the king left across my chest, the previous sutures redone.

Impatience surged as she wrapped it under and over my arms, and around my torso once more until it resembled a bodice.

When she tucked the last piece in, I went to stand, but she put a hand up. "Your leg, miss."

I pursed my lips and threw back on my tunic before tearing away more of the hole in my trousers. Briar didn't comment on it but made quick work of suturing the last remaining wound on my thigh. When she finished, she went to reach for the bandages. I stood.

"Thank you, Briar, that will be all," I said dismissively while I went to leave.

"But miss—"

I didn't stay to hear what she said.

The sour breeze hit my face when I left the drapes, and the torches illuminated the night. Their flames whipped in the wind, adding another layer to the chaos around me.

More people scrambled through the camp. Wounded soldiers lay on the ground outside of tents waiting to be seen. Those who appeared well enough to help secure the horses and took over running supplies for the healers. To my surprise, Valor kept his word. Some of the soldiers among the crowd weren't our own. While they were being guarded far from our people, I was grateful Estelle and Valor offered them more kindness than the king ever would.

The dim glow of the lanterns wasn't enough to help me quickly scan the crowd, and my stomach dropped as I tried to search for Casimir. His petals were obvious, and he was the only one in full bloom. It should've made it easy to spot him, but he remained out of eyesight.

I fought the grim thought that they left him behind in the carnage, or worse, that they took him to shear his bloom. Not for a moment had I thought Talos could've won in combat against Casimir, but I saw Talos leave alive.

As I stalked through the camp, the tents all passed in a haze, and it felt as if my tunic and trousers were barely holding onto me.

In a rush of unease, my hands reached out to anyone I crossed paths with, asking if they had seen Casimir. With each 'no' muttered in reply, the desperation increased tenfold. I tried not to let it get to me. Casimir was capable. He had to have made it out alive.

Yet my heart was in my throat as I walked by Galan, grabbing his arm. "Have you seen Casimir?" I asked breathlessly.

Galan's face pulled into concerned lines, and he glanced around us. "No, I have not. Are you well?" he asked.

I didn't have time for his question. I released his arm and my head whipped around in a frenzy as I searched the sea of bodies for the red petals littered among messy black hair.

Without replying to Galan, I jogged through the crowd and pushed past the people who stood in my way. Some grunts of annoyance erupted, but I didn't pause to apologize.

When Halburn ducked out of a tent, I ran straight for him. His eyes widened when I skidded to a stop in front of him.

"Captain Vanmore, have you seen him?" I rasped.

He wrung his bloody hand through a towel. "Two tents down that way. I left there not long ago—"

I didn't let him say anything else.

My feet carried me to the tent in a sprint. The drapes flapped in the acidic winds and I ran right for them, darting inside.

Scarlet eyes met mine from across the tent, full of surprise as they took in my appearance. "Are you alright?" Casimir asked, jolting up from where he'd been sitting. His gaze lingered on the bandages that peered from the top of my tunic.

My stride brought me inches from his chest. The tunic he wore similarly hung off his frame, half torn through. Dust and blood clung to the fabric. I searched his body for any other sign of injury, noting the red that stained the bandage on his shoulder.

"I didn't see you." The words caught. "After Talos, I didn't see you. And then Valor made me leave, I—" My hands trembled when I reached for his torn tunic, brushing a piece of it away to expose a sutured wound at the base of his neck. "Casimir…" I ran my fingertips close to the wound, brushing his skin. His breath hitched.

He's okay. He's safe.

"That coward ran off while I fought his guards. I'm offended that you'd think he won." It was meant to be lighthearted, but the weight of battle still hung in the air, and Casimir's heavy tone showed how worn down he was. Guilt wracked him, but he wasn't at fault for Talos's cowardice.

Tears burned in my eyes while I stared at his damaged skin. The cut wasn't deep enough to be lethal, it was just a skim from a blade. But if it had been any deeper…

He's alive. The battle is over, and he's okay.

My gaze flicked back to his. "You shouldn't have stepped in," I whispered, afraid if I spoke any louder, every awful fear I'd had over the last few months would pour out.

Casimir gently grabbed my wrist as my fingers twitched against his skin. His eyes trailed over my bandages. "I told you not to worry about me, El."

My pulse quickened when he shortened my name, in the way only he did. The familiarity burned over into something different, and the warmth pulled me closer to his chest. His jaw twitched, and I watched him tense.

Though I was aware of his feelings, nerves erupted in my chest. I wanted to reach forward and caress his cheek. I wanted his lips on mine. My skin lit up with heat and I inched closer with my gaze still locked on his bandages. I didn't look up at him. The thought of meeting his gaze threatened to steal my courage.

Casimir didn't move. I heard every shift in his breath and sensed him staring down at me, his hand still on my wrist.

"Cas…" I dared a glance at him, and it did nothing to ease the flutters beneath my rib cage.

This time, I knew it wasn't my imagination. I watched as he traced the curve of my lips with his eyes. His hand lifted, fingers brushing my messy curls behind my ear. He was hesitant, and the stroke of his hand left his palm cupping the curve of my neck.

The space between us suddenly felt too far, and I tilted my head upward, my gaze locked on his, pleading with my entire being for him to close the distance.

Footsteps thundered outside the tent, and I jumped. It broke the tension in the air, and I struggled to catch my breath. I gulped, and moved back just as the drapes whipped open.

Valor seethed on the other side of the opening and he stormed in, his glare fixed on me. "What were you thinking, Fullan?" he snapped.

I stammered and stared at him, bewildered. "Lendorr was closing in on your blindside—"

"The prophecy may mean little to you, yet that gives you no justification for putting yourself in harm's way. Companions were meant to be at your side at all times. Do you think yourself invincible?"

I flinched and my anger flared. "You have no clue what the prophecy means to me, Valor. I carry it around with me everywhere I go. A burden none of you have to bear," I countered.

Casimir stepped to my side, and a sense of comfort followed. "Sir, we may have lost the battle if not for Elita. Her abilities gave us the advantage we needed. Had she not been there, you and Estelle would have been dead before the battle even began." Casimir taking up for me gave me a boost of confidence.

I stood straighter, not backing down even as Valor glowered.

"That does not excuse her blatant disregard for her life," Valor said, looking at Casimir.

Casimir didn't back down. "And are you speaking as her general, or as her father? Because any decent soldier would step in to protect others over the concern for their own safety."

Valor's nostrils flared, and for a moment, I worried he would unleash his fury on Casimir.

The expression couldn't hide the fear of a father. It was something I had lost, and when I first met Valor, I believed he hated me. It wasn't new, and I had accepted that another parent didn't want me. But for all those years, Valor thought about coming back for me. He made sure I was safe. And I couldn't bring myself to be offended by his upset. I had a parent who cared for me, and that was something I thought I lost.

Without thinking, I stepped forward and embraced Valor.

He froze.

"Thank you for keeping me safe," I said.

I didn't expect him to embrace me, but he brought up a single arm and put it around my back. Some of the tension in his shoulders fell, and a grin tugged at my cheeks.

Valor cleared his throat, and I pulled back. His mask of indifference wasn't enough to disguise his concern.

"Yes, well, prepare for departure. We must get the wounded back to Mistvalle," Valor said, uncomfortable with the display of emotion. "We will discuss this when we're in the safety of Mistvalle." Valor ducked his head and departed without another word.

My lips pressed in a line and looked over at Casimir. A small smile tugged at his cheeks. "His parental skills could use some work," Casimir mused.

I hummed in agreement. An air of discomfort fell over us in the tent, and I couldn't bring myself to look at him again.

"I should go. I sent Nix back when the battle started, and I want to make sure she found her way back safely."

Casimir shifted on his feet and dipped his head. "Of course."

Wordlessly, I darted out of the tent.

The courage died in my throat, and a sting of disappointment followed me as I left Casimir behind.

Forty-Seven

Our numbers were too decimated to stay in Tyvolia. Even as they worried Talos may turn around to finish what his father started, we had no choice but to leave. Over twenty of the Iron Thorn soldiers lingered in the back of the line, guarded by a few of the Roses who could conjure vines, lest they try to attack during our retreat.

The wounded surpassed those who made it out unscathed. Between many of the horses, soldiers laid suspended on stretchers. We barely had enough to carry them back, and many of the wounded ended up in the carts meant to be used for supplies. We left behind the tents and only took what was necessary.

I remained near the back of the line along with those who could fight if it came to that. The healers stayed among the injured, and closer to the front of the line.

Estelle and Sol rode beside me, which made for a quiet ride through the mountain pass.

The company who survived the battle made it through the worst of the mountain pass, although we struggled. All the suspended soldiers had to take a different route, led by Casimir, Orin, and a few healers.

As the woods shifted into something recognizable, some of the tension released from my shoulders. The jarring sights of Tyvolia were far behind us, and I looked forward to bathing away the blood from the battle. It clung to my skin as a cruel reminder. Anytime I thought of the fight, the fallen soldiers flashed through my mind.

Sabian's death followed me the most, and I knew it would soon become another haunting face.

I hated to think of who else died in the fight. We didn't have much time to assess, and though Valor said they'd return for them, they never did. They left the dead among the ruins of Tyvolia.

There weren't enough horses or carts to carry their bodies. It seemed cruel to leave them after the sacrifice they gave. I reminded myself over and over there was no other way. It didn't make it any easier.

Once more, innocent blood was spilled over the whims of a selfish king. It painted the land of Tyvolia in their blood. Nothing but a dead king came from their bravery. And it wouldn't end with his death. Talos lived, and I worried what would come of it.

They knew where Mistvalle was. It wouldn't be wise to stay there long. We would either have to return to fight another pointless battle or try to flee.

I thought then of my friends back in Mistvalle. It brought me joy to think about seeing them again. To see them safe and unharmed. It didn't erase how painful our losses were, but their safety was why we marched in the first place.

Bitterness racked my body. We didn't win. Not truly. If Talos returned for more blood, we were doomed. We lost too many of our soldiers in the first battle. I wished for more time—for the chance to discuss what our plan was, or how Estelle intended to keep Mistvalle from falling. She stayed eerily silent since we left the battlefield. She led her people to Tyvolia, and it took more from her than I think she prepared herself for.

From what I saw, we maybe had half the people we left Mistvalle with. The rest would remain in Tyvolia, in the pool of bloodshed.

No one foresaw a different path. We bought ourselves time, and I only hoped it would be enough.

I tried to ignore the dread of what my return to Mistvalle meant. Although I despised being studied, it needed to be done. When we returned, I'd go back to mending, and having healers observe me. We needed to find a solution before the realm perished.

The losses couldn't be in vain. If we didn't find a purpose for my abilities, I worried that meant it was all for nothing.

Our descent of the mountain pass drew my attention from the daunting thoughts. As we moved through the path, I noticed how the leaves gave up their hold on the branches.

To the left of the party, I noticed Casimir and Orin emerge through the trees. The healers and stretchers followed them, and it appeared they all made it through unharmed.

It was a small relief, and it meant we were close to the gates of Mistvalle. The thought didn't ease the horrors that followed us back. So many innocent people were returning with blood on their hands, and the lives of loved ones lost.

Even in the face of so much death, I couldn't help but scoff at the voice that rang in my mind throughout the battle. We made it out. My presence did more for them than I ever thought possible.

And there was more blood on my hands than I could bear.

The pearlescent gates of Mistvalle brought a swell of relief. Four guards stood watch, and they straightened at our return, opening them for us to come through. Their faces fell when they took in our numbers. Silence followed us through the gates of Mistvalle. It remained untouched, and though it should have brought great relief, the loss we all felt was too heavy.

Hoofbeats clacked on the stonework paths. We moved at a controlled pace to prevent rattling the injured.

Estelle turned and glanced at me. It was the first time she had since I left the battlefield. "Rest tonight. Find me at the healing center in the morning. We have much to discuss." Estelle's words were grim, and I knew she shared the same fears that occurred to me on our journey back.

We may not have enough time to unravel the truth of my bloom before enemies pursued us again. And knowing Talos, he would recruit even more from the villages. Any able-bodied person. He wouldn't stop until they overpowered us.

The thought brought a shiver down my spine.

With a nod at Estelle, I departed from the crowd as they worked their way toward the healing center. Sol followed, as well as Galan.

I was grateful for their company. I wasn't ready to be alone with my thoughts yet. Though they couldn't erase the images of our people dead in Tyvolia, I at least didn't have to endure it alone.

The three of us rode to the stables, with only a few others following. I noted Myra in the crowd with a roughly sutured gash across her cheek, and beside her was Novian. I watched in shock when he leant over on his horse and put a hand under her chin, eyeing the cut.

It was tender and completely different from who I assumed him to be. I thought back to when Sabian thought I was Myra and mentioned Novian to me. It made sense then, and once more, Sabian's lifeless eyes haunted me.

I looked away and headed into the stables. Nix whinnied, and I dismounted with a thud. The soles of my boots hit the ground, heavy with exhaustion. My hands worked at releasing her bridle and the leather straps of her saddle. Nix bristled with relief as I took them off and sat them to the side.

Elrin walked behind me, leading her gray and white gelding. Her eyes met mine, though she didn't say a word. She was as battered as I was, if not more. She gave me a nod of recognition, trudging further into the stables. I had watched her cut down many soldiers, and though her abilities didn't offer much help on the battlefield, she held her own with a sword. I was grateful that whatever had made her dislike me before had blown over.

They disappeared down the stables, and I went to pour Nix some feed. Footsteps rushed through the dead silent stables, and I turned at the sound, just in time for a body to knock into mine. I groaned, the pain radiating through my torso.

"You made it back," Alba cried, her hair overwhelming the space.

I chuckled and hugged her back despite the discomfort. "Couldn't leave you here with just Taryn for company. You two would kill each other before long."

Alba pulled back and wiped at the tears on her face. "Sorry I stayed behind. I was scared—"

"Don't apologize. Galan would have lost his focus if you were there, honestly," I said, squeezing her shoulder.

Alba's eyes widened, and she spun around in the stables, looking around. "Galan is here?" Her voice broke.

I scanned through the stables, and the sight of Sol's emerald armor caught my eye, prompting me to point in that direction. "He came in after Sol, he should be—" I didn't get to finish speaking as she took off through the stables, her hair a wave of black tendrils behind her.

She reached where Sol stood as Galan ducked out of the stall where he put his horse. He didn't have a moment to ready himself before she collided with him, knocking him to the ground with a grunt.

Sol snickered at them and turned her attention back to her horse.

I chuckled at the two as she talked to him with a stream of tears pouring down her cheeks. She grinned through the tears, and didn't seem to care about the other soldiers who made their way through the stables. It brought me a sliver of joy to see the two reunited.

In a rush, I poured Nix some feed, and walked through the stables, back to the courtyard. I yearned to be rid of the clothes which reeked of war and bloodshed.

When I walked outside, the sun was already low. The rocky cliffs of Mistvalle provided a stunning backdrop as the sky transformed into a mesmerizing canvas of pink and blue during sunset.

The courtyard was full of the families who stayed behind. Parents charged through the crowd to hug their older children who fought in the battle. Partners reunited, and amid the merriment, I watched as Casimir and Orin directed other family members out of the crowd. The sense of peace depleted, knowing what news they were going to deliver to those people. In the crowd, I noticed those who shared many similarities with Sabian. Casimir pulled them to the side, and I couldn't bring myself to watch them go. Their faces were already grim as they stared back in confusion at the families being reunited.

When a familiar head of red hair appeared in the crowd, Taryn's grin and eager wave distracted me. Beside Taryn, Ulrik clung to her sleeve. His sideways smile was enough to allow me a chance to block out the grim thoughts.

"White bloom!" Taryn called.

I met them halfway through the courtyard, and let her pull me into a one armed embrace. She squeezed hard, and I grimaced.

"Oh, right, my bad." She chuckled. "Battle and all that. How are you holding up? Missing any teeth or limbs?" Her eyes surveyed me.

I shook my head. "All intact. At least, I hope."

"I'm just glad you made it back safe. Good to see you held your own. I only somewhat doubted you could."

Her bluntness never ceased to amuse me.

"Thanks, Taryn," I muttered.

Ulrik shuffled at her side, peering up at me beneath red curls. "I'm glad you're back." His soft voice made me smile.

Ulrik giggled when I ruffled his curls. I said, "Glad to be back."

Taryn clapped a hand to my shoulder. "You best get yourself washed up. You're looking a tad rough—covered in blood and whatnot." She paused, glancing down at Ulrik before she gave me a mischievous grin. "What do you say to all of us meeting at the tavern to celebrate?"

It took all my focus not to grimace when she implied there was something to celebrate. The king's heir lived, and many of our people laid behind, dead. And though I swore to never drink ale again, I nodded anyway. If it helped me forget—even for a moment—the horrors that haunted me, I'd take it.

Taryn grinned, showing teeth. "That's what I like to hear." For a moment, her expression fell. "Is Galan back?" It was clear she feared the answer.

"Yes, he's here. Although Alba may have knocked him out by accident."

"Perfect. I'll be sure to find him and drag him and Alba along."

"You should invite Sol," I said, and watched as apprehension crossed her face.

"That gal wouldn't know fun if it hit her in the teeth. But I guess it wouldn't hurt." She put her hands on her hips, and Ulrik rested a small hand at her wrist. He never did let go if she was around, and it was endearing. After she agreed to include Sol, I parted ways with the two.

The reality of the battle contrasted with life in Mistvalle. Peace felt wrong. Every sound in the courtyard swelled with joy rather than screams of agony and battle cries.

We had only been gone for five days, but every moment in Tyvolia seemed like it moved at a snail's pace. It was strange to be back, but I knew the area well.

Rather than go to my tent, I made my way to the bathhouse. They always kept spare clean linens, and I wasn't picky. I only wanted the blood-covered clothing off me.

The white stone resounded beneath my boots. Fallen leaves dusted over the ground, painting it in a sea of red and gray. All the flowers wilted many weeks before, and their bushes lay bare.

I tried to bask in the cleaner air and let it refresh me. The sun continued to disappear behind the cliffs, and darkness would soon engulf us. I noted the guards who walked throughout the area, lighting the lanterns that hung on stone posts. Their job was not one I envied.

Heavy footfalls echoed behind me, and I didn't have to turn to know who trailed close by. I became well acquainted with his presence after so many years, and it reverberated in the earth's thrum. Casimir appeared at my side, still wearing his torn tunic. I glanced over at him. He fixed his gaze forward, his jaw clenched.

It was a heavy task to inform families their loved ones didn't return. I imagined it made it harder to tell them there wasn't a body to bury, either. In the heaviness, we remained silent, and he continued to head toward the bathhouse along with me.

People swarmed the streets of Mistvalle as they crossed the bridge near the waterfalls. It was evident the entire group that stayed behind had vacated the hidden stronghold. Chatter filled the fleeting daylight, too eager and untouched by the dread following every soldier.

We approached the bathhouse, where the same shimmering white stone made up the structure. It comprised two different sides, separated by an archway. It broke off in the middle for the men and women, and Casimir and I found ourselves paused outside of the archway.

He stood with his arms crossed, looking up at the arch.

One of my arms wrapped around my waist, holding the sore ribs while I glanced at him. "Casimir?" I spoke with caution, timid despite us being alone. It was difficult to tell if he wanted the silence or if he needed to talk.

He glanced down at me but remained quiet.

"Are you okay?" I asked, afraid it would unearth more pain.

"Just a heavy day," he said. In stark contrast to before we left Tyvolia, his walls were back, and he buried any of his feelings deep down. It was painfully easy to relate to the desire to block it out.

If I thought too long on the lives I took, I'd drown in agony.

When I thought of Taryn's offer, I said, "I'm meeting Taryn and a few others at the tavern after this. Do you want to join me?" Somehow asking sparked my nerves.

Casimir raised a brow. "You intend to drink ale again?"

"I considered swearing it off after that first time, but I think I could use the warmth and the company." I shrugged and faced back to the bathhouse as a flicker of amusement crossed Casimir's face.

"I suppose I'll come along. Even if only to make sure no one challenges you to another drinking competition," he said, a halfhearted hint of mischief in his tone.

"See you there?" I asked as I walked backward, watching his reaction.

Casimir's smile never reached his eyes, and it hurt to think none of us would ever be the same again after what took place in Tyvolia.

He dipped his head at me. "It sounds entertaining. I'll meet you there."

Before tears could prickle in my eyes, the change in both of us too evident to ignore, I gave him a short wave and darted into the bathhouse.

Wet curls fell around my face and past my shoulders, longer as the months passed. They dripped water onto the clean, green linen top I wore. The deep emerald tone was beginning to be one of my favorites. It rested just below the waistband of cream linen trousers. The comfort was a nice contrast, and I walked out of the bathhouse refreshed and desperate to forget the events of the past few days.

In the morning, I'd have to talk to Estelle and resume mending, but for one night, I wanted to rest and be in the company of my companions.

Though it seemed wrong, I intended to bask in the peace we fought for. Even if it only lasted the day.

I walked through the stillness that settled over Mistvalle as the sunlight disappeared from the sky. Lanterns illuminated my path, casting a warm glow as the brown slippers I took from the bathhouse tapped on the stones. The center markets were empty, save for a few stragglers. Many people had already returned to their homes or their tents.

On my way to the tavern, I noticed a few of the other soldiers who returned with us. Some still wore their armor, and many of them appeared to have just got out of the healing center.

When the tavern appeared in front of me and I spotted Alba heading inside, the sight of her was a relief. She walked through the doors, which were propped open with white stones. A warm glow emanated from it, and I heard the patrons who gathered inside. It sounded cheery and joyous.

A breeze kicked up fallen leaves as I made it to the entrance. I paused on the threshold and stared inside. Soft music trilled, and the people laughed and celebrated. They didn't appear haunted, and I envied their ignorance of what befell our people in the battle.

My feet didn't carry me inside.

I stood there, my arms wrapped around my torso. My fists knotted in the linen, and it seemed less comfortable and more rough the more I rubbed my fingers over it.

"Not a drinker?"

I jumped and looked over my shoulder to see Sol walking toward me. She wore a red set of linens, and the color contrasted with her pale skin and hair. It appeared even Sol couldn't bear to wear the remnants of war any longer.

My lips pursed, and I looked back inside the tavern. "They're celebrating, Sol," I said in disbelief.

"Let them. A soldier carries the burden of war, not them."

I couldn't argue with her. It only felt wrong to join them.

Yet in the crowd of celebrating individuals, some patrons slumped into bar chairs, their eyes drowning in the drinks. There was no peace in their faces.

Finally, I took a step into the tavern. I reminded myself that it was just one night. It was okay to allow myself to enjoy a moment with my friends, even if death followed me like a dark cloud.

Because soon, I would have to go back to carrying the weight of the realm on my shoulders. For one night, I didn't want to feel anything but the warmth of the ale and the laughter of my companions.

Forty-Eight

The noise was worse inside the tavern. It made my head throb, but I moved through the crowd anyway, and found my way to the group of companions at the barstools.

Casimir sat at the very end next to Galan, who had Alba at his other side. Taryn already appeared two mugs of ale in and her laughter rang throughout the tavern.

Next to Casimir was an empty barstool, and my neck grew warm. Sol gave me a knowing look when I slowed my pace. She walked over to the farthest stool and plopped down next to Taryn. I watched as Taryn already started up a conversation with Sol and was glad Taryn was a few mugs in. Knowing her, she'd talk anyone's ear off, ale or not.

My slippers thudded over the wooden floorboards until I reached the empty stool. It scuffed the floor when I pulled it out, and Casimir glanced over at me. His grin was full of warmth, and he smelled of patchouli. Every flicker of the lanterns lit his features, and it made my heart flutter.

"I thought you backed out," he said.

I swallowed the hesitation and chuckled sheepishly. "Not in my nature to be shown up."

He gave me a look of amusement. "You've really come into your own here." His tone made my heart swell.

"Have you started yet?" I changed the subject and turned my gaze to the barkeeper.

As I asked, they brought over a mug and set it down in front of him. "One spiced cider," she said with a kind smile. "And what can I get you, dear?" she asked, facing me.

"One spiced ale, please," I said, feeling somewhat out of place as mugs lined up in front of my other companions.

"Coming right up." She winked, her thick wither dress twirling when she whirled back to the wall of various barrels.

I turned my attention to Casimir as he wrapped his hand around the dark oak mug. He raised it at me, then chugged it in one go. I watched with my lips pressed in a tight line to hold back a grin.

He set down the empty mug and grimaced. "Stuff is vulgar," he said, and wiped at his mouth with the back of his hand.

Galan leaned forward to look at me past Casimir and gave me a boyish grin. Three empty mugs sat in front of him, and I chuckled.

"Both of you need better taste," Galan stated. "This is delightful."

I hummed in amusement. "It's actually quite unpleasant. I'll be having one, but that's it."

Galan shook his head. "One? I'm already three in."

"Oh, I've made that mistake once. Estelle expects me in the morning. I wouldn't dare accept another drinking challenge with you, Galan."

Alba sat higher on her barstool and glanced over Galan's head. "Come on! I missed out last time since I wasn't invited." She gave Galan a pointed look, and he muttered an apology. "I want to see you joke about morbid things," she said, sounding giddy.

My face twisted. "Glad Taryn and Galan recounted it for you. I'll do two mugs, but that's it."

Alba smiled and sat down, drinking her own ale.

I ordered a second spiced ale, hoping it would help thaw some of the ice in my chest.

The room swirled with merry chatter and the gentle notes of musical instruments. It brought me a sense of peace I desperately needed. Regardless of how I expected to have nightmares of the battle, I at least had some reprieve first.

When the barkeep passed me two mugs, I chugged the first one. It burned as bad as the first time I tried it, and I sputtered some—but continued to gulp it, anyway. I saw Casimir, Galan and Taryn all giving me amused looks as I finished it off.

I sucked in a heavy breath and proceeded to cough.

"There it is," Taryn jeered.

I pointed at her. "Better than the first time."

She scoffed. "Hardly. I'll be impressed when you can drink without sputtering like a child."

I rolled my eyes and sipped at the second one rather than forcing another down too fast. The ale burned to the pit of my gut, and I dreaded the effort it would take to finish it. Everyone carried on in conversation that felt too light, but I tried to let myself relax as time ticked by. If anything, I chose to be grateful I was among friends.

Casimir drank another, seemingly in competition with Galan. The two chortled when they each slammed one down in unison. Casimir put up a finger to signal for another one, and I watched, entertained as they tried to outdrink each other.

Casimir caught up to Galan quicker than I thought possible, and where Galan started to sway, Casimir remained steady. He appeared proud of himself.

Galan sat straighter, even as he couldn't sit still. "Drinking with you is always unfortunate. I cannot believe I haven't learned," Galan grumbled.

From his right, Alba patted his hand and pressed a kiss to his cheek. Galan's face lit up. "Don't feel bad. No one has ever outdone Casimir."

That didn't seem to help Galan any, and he continued to pout in his seat. Taryn cleared her throat, and we all glanced to the end of the bar, where Sol sat with eight mugs drained in front of her.

I gaped at her, and my gaze bounced between the five mugs in front of Casimir and her impressive number. She didn't bat an eye, and I watched in disbelief when she ordered herself another one. Only an hour had passed since we walked through the doors.

Taryn chortled and clapped a hand to Sol's shoulder. "I was wrong about this one. Thought there wasn't a fun bone in her body."

Sol didn't appear bothered in the slightest at what Taryn said, and continued to drink her ninth mug. My two started to seem like admitting defeat, and I knew I would regret my next choice in the morning.

Nevertheless, I requested another mug.

The warmth sat in my stomach, and the tavern distorted some. Everyone's laughter and chatter blurred into one, and I found myself resting an elbow on the bar to set my chin on my fist.

I smiled and watched Alba teasing Galan. Though she didn't have much either, she didn't seem to worry herself about the competition. She finished her few drinks and kept an arm draped through Galan's. The sight brought me joy, and I sipped the last bit of my third mug and let it rest on the bar counter.

Casimir's shoulder brushed my cheek while the tavern swayed. He glanced down at me, and the flash of mirth in his gaze made my head swim.

"Do you intend to fall asleep there?" Casimir mused.

I stammered when I realized how much I leaned into his side and straightened. A warm blush crept over my face, and I hoped he would amount it to the ale, which caused me to totter.

Down the line of companions, I saw Taryn grab her last mug and raise it in the air. "For my brave friends, and to the dead royals," she cheered.

My stomach dropped as she chugged the ale. Galan, Casimir, and Sol all looked her way, and back at each other.

Sol bristled in her seat as she said, "The princeling lives."

A horrible silence settled over our group, and a rare look of horror filled Taryn's expression as she dropped her mug. Her jaw clenched, and her other hand curled into a fist on the bar counter.

In the background, the melodic song continued, and other patrons settled into quiet, friendly chatter. It made the expression on Taryn's face contrast even more. A few simple words drained her joy.

"You left him alive?" Taryn's voice caught. "You let him go, and said it was safe to leave the stronghold? Are you mad!"

My eyes widened, and I watched her scramble up from her stool. She shook with both anger and fear.

Casimir pushed back from the counter and faced her in his seat. "They retreated much too quickly for us to catch up. We lost too many soldiers, Taryn. We had no other choice." Casimir's voice was smooth, slipping into his Captain tone.

Taryn shook her head and fury took over her features. "I can't believe you all returned with him alive."

I stood from my stool. The ground warped beneath my feet, but I didn't let it stop me from walking over to Taryn.

She trembled, and I reached out to put a hand on her shoulder. "I'm sure Estelle wouldn't have let us return if it were too risky. She cares for her people. And Valor, too. I hate that Talos walked away, but there isn't anything else we can do right now."

Taryn shrugged my hand off. "You should know better than any of them. It isn't safe with him alive," she snapped.

The memories were never too far, and her words made me flinch. When I used to think about how I would handle seeing Talos again, I had imagined myself able to cut him down. But I froze, and in the process, got Casimir hurt. If I had only sent a few thorns his way, or taken a dagger to his throat, he wouldn't be the next king.

To my surprise, Taryn gasped, and she waved furiously over her head. She stalked out of the tavern with no warning.

I looked at Alba, who already left her seat behind. We exchanged concerned glances and followed Taryn out into the night. Taryn had her fists balled at her sides, and her boots pounded the stone, echoing. Her anger rang through the courtyard while we followed her.

I jogged in order to catch up to her, and I caught her arm. She turned and glared. "I need to get Ulrik."

I let go of her arm. "Let us come with you, Taryn," I said.

Taryn noted Alba following us, and she let go of a heavy sigh. "Only if you swear not to ask me questions," she muttered.

I nodded in reply, and I didn't have to see Alba to know she agreed. Taryn's unfamiliar distress alarmed us both.

We followed her on the path up the cliffs. None of us spoke, but her fear was palpable in the silence. It followed her, its presence casting a heavy shadow over her usual lighthearted demeanor.

The trees all stood bare, making it easier to see the mountain cliffs the higher we climbed. They appeared drained of life, with only gray and white trees left after all the leaves fell away. An icy breeze swept through the bare branches, and it rustled through my dried curls. It danced with the waves and made them sting with the bite of frost.

When we made our way to the top, the sight was jarring.

The familiar tents were as we left them, and a few people hung outside of them at bonfires. It thrummed with sadness and triumph in equal measure.

Scattered pieces of armor, belonging to those of Everbloom, were left stacked near the healing tent. It remained for emergencies, though I assumed many of those who made it back likely needed to be watched through the night.

Alba and I hung back while Taryn walked to the tent that her mother, Nora, stayed in. I watched her duck inside to retrieve Ulrik.

When her frame disappeared into the drapes, I faced Alba. "Is she okay?" I asked. The two had known each other for years before I showed up at Everbloom, and I hoped she could supply some answers.

Alba looked as confused as I was, and she lifted her arms in exasperation. "The only times I've heard her mention the prince has been around you. She doesn't talk about her life back in the kingdom at all."

That offered no comfort.

We both quieted down when Taryn left the tent with Ulrik wrapped around her torso, and her arms carrying his sleeping figure. With a jerk of her head in a different direction, we continued to follow.

The noise in the camp was more muted than that of the tavern. Fires crackled, and people talked in hushed voices while sitting around the enormous bonfires. It was more fitting than the cheer that erupted in the tavern. We achieved victory by a narrow margin, and the evil that sought to capture us all remained. I knew Talos wouldn't allow us the time to recover.

I wondered if they would even take the time to crown him before he set back out to finish what his father started. The look he gave me on the battlefield—the things he said to me—haunted me and assured me it wouldn't be long enough before he returned.

The thoughts faded into the night when we stopped at Taryn's tent. Alba opened the drapes for her and Ulrik, and we both followed them in. I watched as Taryn lowered Ulrik into a small bed to the left of the tent. She pulled his blankets over him, pecked his cheek, and stood. He remained undisturbed and slept through it all.

Taryn flopped down on the other bed with a huff and discarded her boots. They hit the chest in the corner with a loud thud, and I flinched. Ulrik didn't even twitch.

Alba went further into the tent and took off her boots. She bunched up her cloak and laid on the floor near Taryn's bed. She didn't ask, and Taryn stared at her in exasperation.

"I didn't invite you to stay. Bug off."

Alba crossed her arms over her chest and closed her eyes. "No can do. You're clearly in distress. What kind of friends would we be if we abandoned you?" Alba countered.

Taryn muttered a curse and fell back against her pillows. In complete silence, she flung a spare one at me. I caught it and slid off my slippers. The stone chilled my feet, and I shivered. There was no point in asking her for a blanket or cloak. Not in the state she was in.

Like Casimir had once before, I leaned against the frame of the bed and propped my head up with the pillow Taryn gave me. The wood dug into my back, and the stone already hurt my tailbone.

Alba peeked with one eye at the two of us and giggled. "I haven't had to share a tent with a bunch of girls since I lost my sisters."

Her words made my blood run cold.

I offered her a somber smile, and she faced back to the top of the tent. Her own sad smile adorned her face as she relaxed against the cloak she used as a pillow.

The flames from outside cast shadows on the deep blue fabric. It made it too bright, and I watched the strange shifting shapes. Every person who passed by made another distorted image on the drapes. I watched in a daze, waiting for the exhaustion to take over. Instead, more harrowing thoughts plagued me, and it made it seem impossible to close my eyes. I knew what would follow.

Taryn didn't speak, but she got out of her bed. She crept over to where Ulrik slept, and I watched as she rested her back to him. Her hands pulled through her hair several times.

She looked over at me and pointed at the bed. "Feel free to take it," she mumbled. My gaze fell to Alba, but within a matter of minutes, she was out cold. I envied her ability to fall asleep so fast.

Carefully, I climbed into the bed, the wound on my thigh tight and sore at the stitches, and let my attention focus back on the shifting shadows.

As the minutes ticked on without sleep, I couldn't take another moment of the quiet. I watched to make sure Taryn was still awake before I spoke and when I spotted her still messing with the strands of her hair; I faced her.

"I fought Talos." It came out shaky, and I ignored the twinge in my side, remembering the ease in which he tossed me around. "So many of us did. But my abilities were too drained, and he had too much help. His guards overwhelmed ours, and Talos fled."

Taryn met my stare as her hands paused their movement.

"I wanted nothing more than to make him pay for what he did to me. But gods…something was off. He was too much for us, and he retreated before we had a real chance to end it."

The noises from outside filled the tent. Taryn seemed to hesitate, and after some time passed, she sat on the edge of the bed. Her knuckles turned white as she gripped her hands around the frame.

"I've met him before, Elita."

I jolted upright and stared at her. The sudden admission made my heart sink. A rush of panic made me nearly sick, but I tried to hide my shock.

She sighed. "I worked in a small tavern on the outskirts of Eldravine. He visited it often. Turned on the charm, that one, believe it or not." Taryn ran a hand through her hair again and glanced at Ulrik. "I knew it was a mistake. I knew better, but gods, he was there, and I assumed a night wouldn't hurt anything."

"Did you know he was the prince?" I asked, my fists curled tightly as I struggled to understand.

Taryn scoffed, then rubbed at her neck as if embarrassed. "Yeah, well, lonely people tend to get desperate. I had lost so much. My father passed, and my mother couldn't bear to be around me for a while. Said I looked too much like him." She pursed her lips, ran her hands over her trousers and met my gaze. "I don't fault her for it. She was grieving. But I was lonely, and Talos was there. It didn't matter that he was the prince. In some ways, it felt like getting back at the royals. At the realm."

The way she spoke of her grief, it reminded me a lot of how I felt after my parents died. I had leaned on Ronin without questioning his intentions, desperate not to be alone. I had known better than to trust anyone in the kingdom, but I was in too much pain to care.

I pushed back the initial alarm. "When I lost my family, I let myself get too comfortable with Ronin. I wasn't thinking clearly at the time...it was a realm damning mistake, but I had been desperate. Don't think for one second that I'll look at you differently."

Taryn released a heavy exhale, her shoulders loosening. "You have my thanks, white bloom. There aren't many who know, and those who do didn't take it too well."

"Of course, Taryn. Now, a very wise healer once told me not to let the prince have a hold on me anymore. I'd like to share that same advice with you," I said, my tone a bit lighter.

She chuckled. "Yeah, yeah. I will when you do." She winked, though the sadness still lingered in her gaze. Exhaustion pulled at her features, and she yawned, leaning further into the bed with Ulrik.

The heaviness lingered, but eventually, I could tell Taryn didn't want to talk about it anymore, and stillness fell in the tent once more. The only interruption being the soft snoring that came from Alba.

My mind went to Ronin and how easily I fell for his false friendship. All it took for me to cave was a few well thought out lies, and to feel protected by him. The trauma of watching his personality split before me still caused deep pain.

I pondered what Taryn said, and the weight of it sank in. Ronin's betrayal didn't deserve to hold power over my life anymore. The idea of continuing to live in fear, unable to let my guard down and open up, no longer appealed to me.

What I yearned for was to feel total peace in the presence of my friends. And to succumb to the constant pull I felt to Casimir.

Eventually, I fell asleep, finding solace in the fact that my past no longer had the power to rob me of my present.

Forty-Nine

"**B**etter get up, white bloom." Taryn's voice startled me, and I sat, my body stiff with new aches. I rubbed at my eyes, trying to erase the visions of death and desolation that followed me in my sleep.

"What's happening?" I asked. The light poured in from outside the tent, and the drapes hung open. It displayed chaos as the camp moved about, carting stuff back and forth.

Taryn shrugged. "Something about the Lady and General. Also, according to a guard, the council is waiting for you."

"Oh!" I jumped out of the bed, regretting it when my wounds smarted, and slid my slippers on in a rush. "I should have told Casimir to get me when it was time to go."

Taryn's eyes narrowed, and she gave me a mischievous grin. "Have you managed to unwind that boy, then?"

I sputtered, pausing as I went to leave. "Don't you start with that. I've heard enough from Alba. We're friends."

She chortled. "You're piss poor at lying. Friends don't ogle each other the way you two do."

My cheeks ran hot, and I shook my head. "Not another word," I warned, though it was mostly in jest. Her laughter echoed, and she gave me a playful salute.

Still in my sleep linens, I dashed out of the drapes and tried to make a break for my tent, but a guard waited outside. He stared at me expectantly, and I recognized him as one of those who had accompanied us in the battle. There was no time to change, and I sighed in frustration.

We walked through the camp, which moved with the morning crowd. Many of them were returning from down the cliffs, likely from the first meal. I groaned at the realization I missed it.

I anticipated Estelle's disappointment in my tardiness, but there was little to be done about it. The fatigue that lingered after the fight made every inch of my body sore, and my skull pulsated with a deep headache.

The sole of my slippers scuffed the stone pathway. It took me a moment to realize how slick it was with frost, and I almost slipped several times as we made our way down the cliffs. I shivered and wished there was time to grab a cloak from my tent. The strange weather hadn't been too chilly the night before, and it changed to frigid that morning.

Clutching my torso, I attempted to match the hurried pace of the silent guard. He seemed displeased with his duty to retrieve me. Part of me wished he hadn't, and even if it meant more nightmares, I longed for more rest.

The ale didn't affect me anymore, and I was grateful it wore off at least. If I hadn't known Taryn so well, it would've surprised me at how well she functioned in the early hours.

The guard never stopped or let up his pace, and I resented how hurriedly we moved. Though, I understood how important it was for me to get back to mending and my other duties.

In the morning light, the palace shimmered too brightly and it blinded me as we made our way up the steep, white steps. They lacked the colors that used to contrast them, and I missed the hues that once brightened Mistvalle. With any hope, it wouldn't be the last harvest I got to see. The idea of experiencing the sprouting once more in the face of everything we endured brought a pep to my step.

My stomach twisted with hunger, I ignored it and jogged up the rest of the way, careful not to slip in my slippers. The guard attempted to keep up with me, and I nearly laughed as I returned his indifference.

Opening both massive doors wide, we rushed inside. It didn't offer much relief from the freezing temperature, but it was preferable to the breeze that cut through my thin clothing. I tried not to think about how my disheveled appearance would come off to them. It would have done me good to stay in Casimir's tent, but I no longer knew how to ask for space where he slept.

There were more people present in the palace than normal, and they carried around items from the main hall. I remembered a similar amount of disarray when we had to leave the shores of Orondal. They were preparing in case we needed to flee.

The pressure to figure out my abilities weighed heavier than armor on my shoulders. We didn't have much time to work with, and before we left for the battle, there wasn't much known about my abilities. The idea of mending again made my body protest, evident in the way my pulse quickened. I overused my abilities on the battlefield, and they didn't have the time to recover.

I knew the hall well after the nights spent sitting in on council meetings after Karion's attack. The library in the far left hall called for me, but I wasn't there for my pleasure.

The soft click of my slip shoes on the marble floors echoed in the empty hall we made our way through. For his lack of words, the guard made up in thunderous footfalls.

Estelle's council door appeared at the very end of it, and there was no need to announce our arrival. Another guard waited for us and ushered us inside with haste.

Heat crawled up my face when I entered.

Every council member sat at the table, appearing impatient. They all wore their armor and cloaks. Estelle wore a billowing dress, and it overflowed in her seat at the head of the table. The fabric shimmered in the light that poured in through the windows. Valor sat at the opposite end, wearing his usual choice of armor. On either side of Valor sat Orin and Casimir, both dressed as if they were returning to war.

I stood in the middle of the room, wearing nothing but my sleep clothes and slip shoes.

When Casimir caught sight of me, I saw amusement flash across his face. My hands curled into fists at my sides, and I fought the urge to turn around and run.

Estelle stood, and her dress moved as if made of water. "Elita, dear, thank you for joining us. I do hope you rested well." Her soft tone rang throughout the muted room. Each move she made appeared graceful and fluid, yet the images of her draining the life from soldiers were ones I wouldn't soon forget.

"I'm sorry to keep you all waiting," I stammered as I walked into the room.

When I saw that the only available seat was next to Orin, I contemplated whether it would be better to stand. After some hesitation, I sat in the empty seat. Orin snickered beside me, and my eyes nearly rolled out of my head. Across the table, Casimir covered his smirk with a gloved hand and brought his attention to Estelle.

She stood at the head of the table and didn't return to her seat. Her eyes focused on me, and it caused my palms to dampen in my lap.

"I assume we are all aware it is prudent we depart from Mistvalle as soon as possible." She began, her focus never shifting from me. "The prince will be crowned king, and he will return. We lack the ability to fight. Not with our current numbers."

The mood shifted in the room.

"Many families will depart the next two days. There is another enclave in the Emerald Mountain that we intend to seek aid from. Until then, these next few days, I need you close by, Elita."

I jumped when she said my name. It took me a moment to realize they all already knew. She likely briefed them while I overslept.

"Halburn is being sent with a group that is leaving tonight, so I will take over your healings and observation."

Despite my apprehension, I grew close to Halburn and considered him a friend. I deflated more when I realized that meant Sol would leave, too. Their relationship may have been strained, but she held her father in high regard, and she wouldn't stay behind.

I bristled in my seat, and my fingers toyed with the hem of my top. "Yes, my lady, whatever you think is best." I tried to hide the sadness that tainted my words. I would see them again. We simply had to figure out my abilities, and no one was as skilled at that as Estelle.

Estelle smiled and tipped her head at me.

Valor stood, and it drew my attention in his direction. "With all due respect, Halburn has warned against her overusing her ability to mend. He knows her abilities well, and I don't see how this is the best course of action," Valor said.

A hush fell over the room, and I forced myself to glance at Estelle. Her smile vanished, replaced with a look that made me recoil.

"General, you are a guest here. Do not forget that."

"Your hospitality does not go unnoticed, my lady. However, I will not allow you to ask more of my people than they can give."

Estelle shook her head in exasperation and one of her hands hit the top of the table, echoing throughout the room. "And all of your people will die if we cannot find a purpose in the white bloom's abilities," Estelle hissed.

I watched the two in shock. Despite having fought in a battle beyond anything I ever imagined, I felt a sudden urge to retreat from the council room.

Orin scoffed beside me. "There is no question whether the entire realm is worth more than one life. It is her destiny, written by the gods, and had it been anyone else in this room or realm, it would still be their duty," Orin said.

My hands stopped fiddling with the hem of my linen. They tingled from the friction of my incessant rubbing, and I furled them back into tight fists.

"He isn't wrong," I said with reluctance. Every head in the room turned to me. I made it a point to ignore Valor and Casimir's reaction. "If there is something I can do with my abilities, I think it's worth trying." I gulped down the fear as I spoke the next few words. "I trust Estelle to be sure I don't kill myself in the process."

I found Estelle's gaze across the table, and she gave me a nod of agreement. If I was sure of anything, I knew she wouldn't allow me to go too far with mending. Above Halburn, she was the best healer in Mistvalle. I trusted her need to save her people. If I died from overdoing it, there was no hope.

"Fullan—"

I turned and tried to give Valor a reassuring look. I hoped he didn't see my fear. "And I trust my general and captain to help me know my limits as well."

"Are you sure this is what you want?" Casimir asked.

It was the first time I looked in his direction.

In his mess of wavy black hair, I spotted his thirtieth bloom. It stood out compared to the rest and adorned the crown of his head. His expression was not one of doubt. He believed in my ability to assess how much I could handle before I reached my breaking point.

"Yes, I'm sure." The words quivered.

Estelle clapped her hands together, silencing anyone else who may have wanted to speak. I looked at her and watched as she beamed with delight.

"Then we must not wait. We leave from here to the mending grounds."

They gave me no time to change. It should have been the first sign I'd regret my decision to allow Estelle free rein over my schedule. We left the council room, and she led me straight to a private room for a quick healing, her abilities more intense than Halburn's. It eased the pain in my stiff limbs until it wasn't so overwhelming. When she finished, we went right for the mending gardens.

Valor and Casimir didn't have another moment to protest. To my dismay, Casimir took off elsewhere, and Valor accompanied us to begin training my abilities.

The field appeared more ominous without the leaves on the branches. The patch of circular dirt disrupted the group of trees near the waterfront. Waterfalls roared close behind us, and there were new planters filled with flowers that shouldn't have been able to exist in the harsh, cold conditions.

The three small trees remained in the very center of the circle. They reached to the tip of my shoulder, and their leaves still echoed with the remnants of life. I sensed the thrum of the earth in my pulse. It sang through my blood, and despite my hesitation, it was second nature to me.

Estelle's gown flowed through the grass behind her as she strode with eagerness in her step, foregoing a cloak herself. Her energy put me at ease.

She paused near the planters and tapped a finger on her lips.

I wrapped my arms around my torso and watched. A cool breeze blew in from the river nearby, and I shivered.

Valor stopped beside me. "You should not have folded so easily, Fullan," he whispered. "There was time to at least grab proper training clothes. By gods, even rest." He looked at me, likely noting the bruises that bloomed beneath my skin, the bandages that peered out of my tunic. "She's an excellent leader, however, she'll allow your fingers to freeze before she allows you to quit."

I shrugged, regretting it when it brought back some of the soreness in my shoulders. "Who knows when Talos will return? And if we have to sail again, that leaves little room for me to sharpen my skills. She's hardly prepared to sit in the cold, either. I trust her. I rested enough last night."

"You lie as poorly as your mother did," he pondered.

His response made me chuckle, even as my teeth chattered. He was the second to point that out since I woke up. Though I did trust Estelle, I simply resented the lack of time to change or rest. It wasn't a sacrifice I made alone as she shivered in her gown, preparing everything with less sleep carrying her feet.

Bumping Valor's shoulder, I said, "I'm also stubborn, like my father." He glanced down at me, eyes wide. "I mean you, of course. My other father didn't have a stubborn bone in his body. Except in his reluctance to bring me to the Temple."

Valor straightened his posture and cleared his throat. "I wish I could give him my thanks. I owe him a great deal."

Fondness stung at the rim of my eyes, and I faced Estelle as she grabbed a planter and brought it to the center of the field. She didn't have to instruct me. I was already walking to where she stood by the time she straightened from her kneel. Dirt dusted the ends of her extravagant gown, yet she held no regard for it.

The plants inside were the same three I grew accustomed to. Peonies, roses, and mint filled the planter.

Valor stayed back to observe, as he tended to. Most days I spent mending the plants, I had a larger crowd of curious onlookers. I assumed those missing were part of the group who needed to prepare for the departure. I didn't envy their task, and part of me despised the idea of leaving Mistvalle.

It felt more like home to me than anywhere ever had.

Estelle leaned over, and with a move of her palm, she drained the peonies of life. They crinkled in her wake. It created a heap of brown, shattered petals. She took a more simple route with the roses and snapped their stems. And for the mint, she pulled it from the soil and tore them to pieces. Spearmint swirled in the air. Crisp in the chill of wither. I inhaled and reached for the planter. Estelle put a hand out and stopped me.

"Heal them simultaneously," she instructed.

My brow furrowed. "I've only ever done one form of mending at a time—"

"We're going into the next phase of your abilities. It does the realm no good if you cannot heal more than one snapped stem. I've seen what you can do. And this," she gestured to the plants, "you can do. Trust in your abilities. Let them guide you."

Her encouragement gave me the push I needed. I rolled my shoulders and put my hand in the soil of the planter. Reaching out made my muscles smart with the leftover strain of fighting. Though I should have said something, I ignored the ache.

With a shaky inhale, the energy thrummed through my veins until it prickled in my fingertips. It pulsed through the soil, searching for every torn or drained fiber.

"Hope no one has started without me."

I jumped and my arm drew back from the soil. Halburn stood near Valor and offered a small wave with his free hand. The other cradled random items which seemed close to dropping.

Estelle didn't appear pleased with his interruption. "She had only just begun, Halburn. You have pulled her focus," she said.

"Apologies, my lady. I'm on orders from the Everbloom captain to bring her some items to help. Lest we forget, she's a person first and foremost." Halburn winked at me and strode over to where I sat.

"Vanmore..." Estelle sighed, a slight smile tugging at her lips.

"You're next, my lady. Mistvalle needs her leader in top shape." He gave her a soft look, offering one of the items to her. A fur cloak, by the look of it. Estelle gave him her thanks, and wrapped it around her shoulders.

I stood and dusted off my linen trousers, making my way to Halburn, my sights set on the rest of his things.

Halburn unraveled another fur cloak and offered it to me. Beneath the folded fabric, there was a cloth bag held between his fingers. "Nourishment and proper wither clothing. Both of which are helpful in keeping the white bloom strong."

I bit the inside of my cheek and grabbed both of the items from him. "If you see him again, give him my thanks," I said while I slipped on the cloak. The inside was wool lined, and the fabric did a wonderful job at blocking the harsh bite of wither. It was a few sizes too big, and the scent which clung to it made me think of Casimir's tent.

Halburn passed me the cloth bag, and I unraveled it in a hurry. A small sugary pastry was inside, along with some dried fruit. It perked me up, and I devoured it as the three waited.

Estelle chuckled as I finished it in a rush. "Ready, dear girl?"

I nodded.

"All three plants, please."

Fifty

Energy coursed through my hands and into the soil for what seemed like the thousandth time. Sweat dripped down the side of my temple despite the frigid temp as the sun set behind the cliffs. The sting of salt along the scrapes on my face made me flinch, stealing my focus.

The mending grounds occupied my entire day, with the exception of a break to dine with Estelle, Valor, and Halburn. It was a familiar group of people after my training and observation.

The two more stoic ones only scoffed at the jokes Halburn made to lighten the mood. I found it entertaining, though exhaustion gripped me more than it had in a long time.

A quick healing helped restore some of my energy when both Estelle and Halburn used their abilities at the same time. It carried me back to the mending garden more equipped to do what I needed to.

My bones seemed to protest not long after we returned to the mending circle. I only repaired two of the plants in unison, and it needed to be all three. The task appeared impossible.

Estelle sat to the side, arms ducked into her fur cloak, eyes heavy with the lack of sleep. I wondered if she'd even slept when we returned, but with the preparations to clear Mistvalle, I doubted it.

As the sun disappeared, the chill was unbearable. The soil was icy against my skin as I reached deeper into the planter and tuned out the three people who observed me. The very act of their breathing became a distraction for me.

The energy of the three plants tickled my skin, and I tried again to call to all three. I found the stems of the roses, and the torn mint. They both continued to echo with life, but the peonies Estelle drained had no pulse. My nostrils flared, and I shut my eyes to ground myself. Each shift in my mood made me lose the thrum, and I searched for it once more.

"Focus, Elita. You felt the ready of a hundred archers on the battlefield. You can find the life left in the peonies," Estelle said. Her tone filled with exhaustion.

Someone shifted behind me. "Speaking breaks her focus, my lady," Halburn whispered, as if I didn't hear him a few feet away.

I huffed in annoyance and added my other hand to the soil as well, careful not to disrupt the roots. Every piece left of the peonies remained withered, and without their energy to guide me, I couldn't figure out how to mend them. It brought me a sense of weakness. I grew accustomed to feeling capable, and my constant failure with the task vexed me.

None of them could offer any help other than quiet encouragement from the side. They couldn't sense what I did. Estelle had tried a few times before. Where her abilities let her drain the life and water from any living thing, mine were a stark contrast. She couldn't understand the missing piece that evaded me.

Pushing past the exhaustion in my limbs, I dug deeper into my own energy and directed it into my palms. I gasped when the fatigue almost made me topple over. In the dust from the petals, I focused less on finding life, and instead, creating it. If I found a way to use my pulse to give some back to the peonies, perhaps they would mend.

The effort tore through my veins and lit them ablaze. Colors warped the edge of my vision—visible waves in the air while my head swam. Underneath the sting, I sensed the peonies awaken. Their petals pinked up, and I watched in awe as they burst to life.

I left the roses and mint untouched, and couldn't form a connection between the three.

Without meaning to, I let go, and the peonies didn't have a chance to fully mend. My vision sharpened, the blur of black and crimson dissipated. I slumped back into the dirt as my head swam. A hand grasped my arm, but I struggled to turn and see who it was.

"She needs rest." Valor's voice was at my side, and from the corner of my eye, his gloved hand held me up.

Halburn stepped into my line of sight as Estelle stood.

"Did you not see? She tapped into the peonies. She *did it*. Creating life when there was none. And you want her to quit?" Estelle sounded desperate. Her eyes met mine, swimming with emotions I couldn't understand. The observation bounced from the peonies to me, hope and grief both in her gaze.

Halburn shook his head. "By Aeterna, Estelle, she'll keel over if you don't let her rest."

When my pulse faltered, my body swaying, I was grateful that, for whatever reason, Halburn decided not to leave Mistvalle. Though it was clear Valor agreed with Halburn's assessment.

Estelle sighed. "Fine. But she will return in the morning."

In spite of the circumstances, I chuckled nervously. "Sorry, my lady, but I think I need longer than that."

Her eyes widened. "Is the fate of the realm a joke to you?"

Valor helped me stand up. My hands were numb when I ran them over the cloak to dust it off. "Not at all. However, if I die while mending, that leaves no room for trying again. I meant no disrespect, Estelle."

Valor grabbed the planter from the ground and set it down on the table near Estelle.

"We all feel the pressure of time slipping away, Estelle. But she needs her rest." Valor dropped formalities, and I saw her features soften.

Estelle's fists uncurled when she exhaled. "As a healer, I can sense Elita's energy. I would never push her beyond her limits. However, if we aren't quick enough, all of our people will die, Valor. And every woman, man, and child in this realm. I implore you to set your blood aside and see reason."

Before Valor got the chance to reply, she put a hand up. "Elita will spend tomorrow in the healing center to help her regain her energy. I will have a round of healers on rotation. For now, she may rest."

The idea of a day stuck in the healing center made me grimace. But I took it. Perhaps if I begged them, Taryn, Sol, and Alba would take turns keeping me company.

Halburn and Valor exchanged heavy glances when I agreed to Estelle's terms, but all I wanted was to leave and get a full night's sleep for the first time in weeks. I hadn't slept a full night since I stopped staying in Casimir's tent, and it weighed me down.

Estelle assured me she would be at the camp in the morning to retrieve me, and I darted out of the mending grounds before any of them spoke another word. In my absence, I hoped they would figure out a better system.

Still in the slippers from the morning, the frosty stone path up the cliffs gave me more trouble than I was in the mood for. I grumbled curses and attempted to make it up without slipping.

With any luck, Casimir was in his tent, and I could ask for his help with sleep. I would need it before healer hands were on me for an entire day.

The Everbloom camp moved with the night time crowd. It was always the same few, but the numbers dwindled, with many of the people preparing to leave Mistvalle to find their way to the Emerald Mountain. Although I didn't want to leave Mistvalle, the prospect of seeing somewhere new sparked my curiosity. Much of the realm and the inner workings of the sanctuaries were unknown to me. Even after I scoured the Mistvalle libraries, there were many things I wanted to see for myself.

When I reached Casimir's tent, I hesitated at the drapes. Nerves pooled in my stomach, but I undid the tie. The drapes fell open, and to my disappointment, Casimir wasn't inside.

I glanced around his tent and noticed my sleeping mat was gone from the corner. The nerves twisted into dismay, and I backed out of his tent. When he retrieved things for me in the morning, he must've returned my bed mat.

Rather than wait for him, I turned and made haste for my tent.

No laughter or celebration echoed in the camp. Everyone was sobered by the looming departure and the loss. It made my frustrated footfalls sound louder than they should have. The sole of the slippers caused my feet to ache, and I nearly pitched them into the bonfire that roared in the middle of the camp.

I stopped in front of my tent and tore the drapes open. As expected, Casimir returned the mat to my bed frame and appeared to have tossed the blankets on top of it. I should've been grateful he returned my things. But the feeling never came. What I needed was rest, and it'd be a lie to think I didn't miss the sound of him sleeping close by. I didn't want the nightmares to return, the vision or the figure…and part of me couldn't resist the pull to him any longer. It should've terrified me, made me pause, but I was too exhausted to lie to myself.

Slowly, I backed out of the tent, closing the drapes before I scanned the area. Across the camp, I spotted a head of red petals heading in the direction of the guard tents.

Exhaustion and misplaced frustration propelled me toward him. He didn't see me heading his way, and I picked up my pace to catch him before he went inside. I watched him pause in front of his tent; attention on the ties I forgot to redo.

Wordlessly, I came up beside him and pulled him into the tent. He grunted in protest, but quickly stopped when he realized it was me.

"What are you doing?" he asked.

It made me more flustered. "Why did you move my sleeping mat?" I crossed my arms when I let go of him.

His brow creased in confusion. "Before we left for battle, you had returned to your own quarters. I knew you'd be tired after mending. I figured you wanted your mat—"

"I didn't want it back," I retorted.

He stared, bewildered. "You intended to sleep on the ground again?"

"No," I stammered. "I haven't slept well since the scouting mission, and I can't sleep in there." My lips pursed, and I glanced at his empty bed, which was adorned with the soft gray quilt I'd become familiar with.

"Do you need my help?" Casimir asked. His tone softened, and my shoulders fell in response.

"Please."

Casimir sighed, and I looked over to see him finish off the ties on the drapes. "I guess I'll take the floor again. Unless you'd like me to grab your mat? I didn't mean to assume. I didn't want to make you uncomfortable."

I observed as he floundered. It was endearing, and all of my misplaced frustration faded in an instant as the words he said before we left to fight the king's army echoed in my mind. The pull to him became impossible to ignore.

I chose to push back the fear that Casimir might one day hurt me the way Ronin did. Part of me knew he never would.

Timidly, I walked closer to him. He watched without speaking, and I paused when I was an arm's length from his chest.

"I'm sorry. My frustration was misplaced, I just—" The words got trapped in my throat.

The scent of patchouli followed him, and his hair appeared damp as if he'd just returned from the bathhouse. He wore gray linen trousers and a loose black tunic, and from the top of it, his bandages peered out of the fabric. I froze and swallowed the hesitation. My hand twitched at my side before I reached forward and brushed my fingertips over the exposed skin near his bandages. Casimir tensed, and I watched his skin prickle.

"What you said before we left Mistvalle…" I paused and allowed my gaze to flicker back to his. "It scared me."

Casimir shifted, apprehensive. "I didn't mean to put you in a position where you felt you had to respond. It wasn't my intention to make you uncomfortable," he said, concerned.

"It scared me because I don't know how—" The words felt trapped as panic tried to silence me. "I can't lose you, and it makes me afraid. My heart is foolish, and I think—" The pad of my thumb brushed over the slight dip in his tunic and his throat bobbed. The next words were barely a whisper. "I think I've fallen for you."

It tumbled out and lingered in the space between us. I ducked my head, afraid to see his reaction, but there was no way to take it back. It was a mix of terror and exhilaration.

In the deafening silence, Casimir's hand lifted, and his knuckle ran across my jaw, the touch shifting into something new. He tipped my chin until our gaze locked. He hesitated, searching my face before he took a step closer, our chests nearly brushing.

"You think you've fallen for me?" Despite the glow of mirth in his eyes and the soft stroke of his thumb across my jaw, the question held a hint of disbelief. I melted into his touch, only able to muster a shaky nod.

Moments ticked by, a visceral tug bringing us closer until it turned into a palpable thrum around us. Casimir took a shaky breath, his hand releasing my chin. There wasn't a moment to allow insecurity to creep in —flutters erupted in my chest when he ducked his head, using his lips to barely brush the edge of my cheek.

"Casimir," I breathed, waiting for him to say something. Anything. My fingers trembled against his tunic as heat swirled through my body, numbing me to the ache in my muscles.

He brought his lips close to mine, nearly brushing them. "You *think* you've fallen?" he whispered as he cupped the curve of my neck with his hands, his thumbs running over the edge of my jaw. The intimacy ravaged my pulse until I grew dizzy.

"I have, Casimir." The words forced their way out, breathless and uncertain.

One of his hands left my neck, and fell to the curve of my waist. He pulled me closer. "Mm, you said it first," he said, voice a low rumble.

More heat devoured my face, coloring me as dark as a rose. "Don't taunt me," I said, exasperated.

He lowered his face and pressed his lips to the edge of my jaw, pulling a soft gasp from my chest.

"But that's always been my favorite part," he muttered, his tone amorous.

"Casimir—"

In a tender caress, his warm lips met mine, swallowing my words. The realm outside vanished as his mouth softly opened against mine, brushing with a restrained need I couldn't replicate—not as a hum of delight crawled up my throat, my lips crashing with his as I pulled him closer by the front of his tunic.

It was desperate and hungry, as if one of us would vanish at any moment; a dream shattered by the rush of emotion.

Casimir's hands gripped my waist, careful for my wounds as he kissed me harder, returning the depth of pent-up longing. In turn, my palms ran over the expanse of his chest, and I felt his breath catch along with the stutter of his heartbeat. His body molded to mine, all the tension and hesitation gone.

After years of only seeing him in my sleep, for a split second, the moment felt too perfect to be real. Buried emotions found their way to the surface; feelings for a ghost. Every strange flutter beneath my rib cage from the time I was old enough to sense the undeniable pull to him—it overflowed. Every touch was new, yet how he knew me made it seem as if we'd been there a hundred times before.

Casimir's thigh brushed mine, and it pulled at the bandage beneath my trousers. A nerve above my eye twitched, my body tensing just a fraction at the friction. I breathed a chuckle against his lips when his hands found the bare skin under my tunic, easing the discomfort in my wounds. He smiled into the kiss as his icy fingers gripped me tighter.

Our knees bumped while we stumbled further into the tent, our breaths both ragged and needy. When my foot caught on the rug, his hands slipped out of my tunic, and grabbed my thighs. A gasp of surprise caught in my throat when he lifted me. I wrapped my legs around his torso, and let him carry me backward.

Years of yearning spilled over, a shared knowing. My fingers knotted into his hair, careful for the petals. I pulled us closer, our flushed chests brushing when he sat us down on the bed, my legs straddling his hips. A soft groan rolled past his lips and onto my tongue, igniting the spark in my chest until every inch of my body became an inferno. I gasped, dizzy with euphoria.

Casimir slowly broke the kiss, lingering inches away. His hands grasped my thighs. "You have no idea how long I've wanted to do that," he breathed.

I mustered a raspy chuckle and glanced at the top of the tent when he leaned forward until his mouth caressed the skin on my neck.

Casimir left a trail of feverish kisses across my skin and I forced us even closer. *Closer. Closer.*

My body trembled at his touch, the adoration evident in every press of his warm, soft lips. His hands found their way into my hair, knotting in the curls before he gently tugged, exposing more of my neck. My chest clenched with elation, a pleased sound escaping me.

I felt him grin in response against my skin. His hands loosened, and racked through the curls. He froze, his entire demeanor shifting in an instant. He pulled back from me, and my stomach sank.

All the color drained from Casimir's face. In a panic, his hands moved through my hair. It wasn't an embrace, but rather terror oozing with desperation. I watched his face and hated the way dread replaced the fluttering. A look of anguish flitted across his expression as he withdrew.

I wanted to go back to before he stared at me with such torment.

Although I didn't want to, I asked anyway, "What is it?"

His jaw tightened. After a moment of hesitation, he said, "There are buds in your hair."

"No." The word was a plea, disbelief shattering the bliss.

The tent swam in a whirl, abrupt and sickening. Dizzy with dread rather than elation. His words faded into the breeze that shook the fabric of the tent. I was just with Estelle and Halburn, and they would have said something. They sensed my abilities, my energy. How could they not sense a bloom?

There couldn't be buds. Ronin sheared my petals and damned the realm. The white bloom was no longer meant to be my destiny.

My hand shook when I reached for my hair.

Casimir grabbed my wrist. "I could be wrong," he said.

We both knew he wasn't.

The brief moment of ecstasy was ripped from me, and when Casimir released my wrist, I brushed a hand over my curls.

Memories rushed back to me from what felt like a different life—they belonged to a girl who no longer existed, yet it was visceral. Every dreadful moment in the cottage that I examined my first buds. The way my father spoke to me when he knew. Or how badly it hurt when the first petal adorned my head.

It all came back, and I gasped as my hand fell.

Without a word, Casimir ran his fingers through my hair again. Shock rippled through me when he kissed my forehead. It was tender, and his lips were warm against my skin as I ran cold with dread.

"Casimir." It came out like a plea, and his entire body tensed beneath mine. "What do I do?"

It should have been a relief. The realm wouldn't perish, and I could offer my bloom as the deities intended. Everything would be as it should. I waited for the solace, and it never came.

"You have time. There's still time to find another way, El," Casimir said softly, though I heard the catch in his voice.

It had been a fool's hope to believe mending was my purpose. That if I trained hard enough, the realm would be saved with ability alone. The gods laughed in my face and took joy in my suffering. I sensed it every moment of my life.

In the face of one bitter victory, my life remained the cost I was required to pay.

Fifty-One

Casimir rummaged through the trunk in his tent while he muttered under his breath. I stood in the middle of the space, my arms clutching my torso while I watched him. I couldn't sleep. Not with the weight of death heavy on my shoulders.

The overwhelming exhaustion over the past week made more sense, although it was easy to blame it on the battle. Back at the cottage, alone in my room, it had been easier to notice the difference and the odd sensations. Even so, the new buds couldn't be more than a day old. I had scrubbed the blood and dirt from my head upon returning to Mistvalle, and I didn't notice.

Casimir straightened, scratched his stubble, and went back to his panicked search. He hadn't said another word in almost an hour. Though, I couldn't bring myself to move, either.

When Casimir cursed once more, I finally released my hold on my tunic. I hadn't noticed how tight I clutched the fabric until my fingers unfurled and ached.

I walked to Casimir and put a hand on his back. He glanced over his shoulder, searching my face, and I knew he saw my fear. There was no way for me to hide it. He turned to me, a tunic and the book on abilities held in one hand. After a moment of hesitation, his free hand took mine. It was cautious, as if I would withdraw from him. Using his thumb, he brushed the inside of my palm. The change in how he touched me sparked warmth in my frozen veins.

I spent the last hour mulling over what I needed to do. The weight of the decision pressed on me, and I hesitated to utter the one option that appeared obvious.

Before I spoke, I squeezed Casimir's hand. It was warm in mine, and I started to wonder if I ran cold. "I have to go to Estelle." It tumbled out, and there was a buried hope he'd counter it with a solution.

His head snapped up. "No. Do not speak to anyone until we've talked to Valor first."

I deflated when he offered no further guidance.

"Casimir, please, I need to speak with someone who has no ties to me. There may be time, but don't pretend this doesn't change things."

Casimir stood chest to chest with me, and his hand gripped my elbow, pulling me close. "Any of the leaders here will let you die. They will drag you to the sacrificial gardens and watch you be sheared without flinching. Do not speak a word to Estelle or any of the others until we've had a chance to speak with Valor."

I bit at the skin on my lip. The warning in his words was clear. If I made my bloom known, it may be a terrible mistake. But Estelle had a distance from me that Casimir nor Valor did. I didn't expect Estelle to freeze and consider any other choice. I knew she would put the realm first, and it made her the sole person I trusted to be rational.

For now, I let Casimir believe I had faith in another path. Even as the deities haunted my sleep and showed me time and time again, they demanded my sacrifice. If it'd ease the agony in his expression, I would pretend for his sake.

The lantern in the tent's corner shuddered and cast sharp shadows across his features. His black lashes fluttered as he gazed at me, waiting for me to agree. I sensed his panic. The intensity disrupted the thrum of the earth, and guilt racked me.

In the cover of night, I tugged him closer and tucked my face into his chest. He shifted to the side, relieved his arm of the items, and held me. His embrace was familiar, yet there was an added tenderness that caused my pulse to quicken.

I felt him kiss the top of my head before he whispered against my hair, "You have time before a sacrifice would even be an option. A bloom takes months. You don't have to figure this out on your own. I'm here." Another gentle kiss. "I'm not going anywhere."

Tears stung at the corners of my eyes. Such dread wasn't new to me. Somewhere in the sinister part of myself, I had waited for it. Too much good fortune came to me in Mistvalle, and the scales finally tipped.

The gods demanded my debt be paid. And for the realm, for Casimir and all of those I held dear, I would pay it. I knew Valor and Casimir wouldn't understand. Their blooms never carried such weight.

Casimir held me there for a long time. His heart hammered against my ear as the light from the lantern dwindled until the wick dipped into the wax, and we were plunged into darkness.

Despite the protest from my heart, I shrugged out of his arms. My fingers found the clasp of my cloak, and I released it from my shoulders. It fell in a heap on the ground, and I shivered without its warmth.

Nerves erupted in my veins, but I forced it away.

"Will you lie down with me?" It came out unsure as my chin quivered and a blush began to bloom. The dark gave me cover, but I knew he heard the uncertainty. I felt it in the way he ran his fingers from my shoulder down to my wrist, squeezing softly.

"Of course," he said, voice strained. A lump of fabric pressed to my hand, and I grabbed it from him. "Here. What you have on is covered in soil."

I hummed in response, unfurling the clothes as Casimir went to the bed. I heard him shuffle around, and in the darkness, I turned my back to him and swapped my clothes for his. The tunic was oversized, the fabric cold after sitting in the chest. It fell to the midpoint of my thighs, leaving my bare skin covered in goosebumps.

"Done," I whispered, reaching out to touch the edge of his shoulder.

He turned, close enough that his sigh sprawled hairs from my face. He tugged on my arm and led me to the frame of the bed, which I suspected would be too small. It didn't concern me.

Casimir sat at the edge and removed his boots. Streaks of moonlight pooled in from the cracks of the drapes, offering a glimpse of his face. Silently, he moved across the bed and made room for me.

I clambered onto the cushion and allowed one of his arms to drape over my side, pulling me close. Butterflies changed the flutter of my heartbeat, and his quiet exhale ruffled the curls that attempted to fall across my face.

His hand rested on the curve of my waist. "Is this okay?" he asked. Though the room was thick with trepidation over my buds, I chuckled at his uncertainty.

"Yes," I whispered.

He pulled me even closer. "Are *you* okay?"

My chest twisted in knots. "For right now? Yes."

He hummed low in his throat and rested his chin at the top of my head. My lashes fluttered with exhaustion, the pull to sleep unbearable. Relief enveloped me while tucked close to his body.

I nestled my head into the safety of his chest, and our legs tangled. It'd be a mistake to be so close, but I didn't pull back. My hand rested between our bodies, feeling every breath he took.

Casimir's grip tightened, a comforting squeeze before he let go to pull the quilt over both of our bodies. He left a trail of goosebumps up my leg when his fingers brushed the bare skin.

Once the quilt was pulled higher, his arm rested back over my waist. I tried to stem the tide of dread, but it was already too late. Our spoken confessions changed things, and in a horrible realization, I knew it would only cause him more pain when I died.

Casimir couldn't change my destiny, and too many people I cared about died trying to do the same. I hated the way my heart sank while I rested there with him. Sleep tried to pull me under, but I fought the urge to close my eyes.

When Casimir fell into a deep enough sleep, I needed to find Estelle. Perhaps he was right and she would march me straight to the sacrificial gardens, and then I wouldn't have to experience another painful goodbye.

He would fall asleep next to me, and a first would turn into a last. But it'd be too painful to watch him search for another answer, knowing there was none. We didn't have time, and if I didn't bend to the will of the gods, I worried what else they would take from me in light of my defiance.

When Casimir's arm grew heavier atop my waist, and his breathing settled into a slow rhythm, I carefully inched away.

My pulse quickened when he stirred. He didn't even open his eyes when he spoke. "You okay?" Casimir's voice was thick with sleep. Disarming and full of concern for me.

"Yes," is all I said while I paused at the edge of the bed. A pang of guilt rippled through me, and tears bit at my eyes.

The feel of his hand brushing my waist sent sparks across my skin, and ignited the sense of regret before I even left his bed. He gripped me gently, and a thumb ran over the curve of my hip bone.

"What's wrong?" he asked, still half asleep.

"Just need something to drink." It was a poor lie, and I was grateful my back was to him. Tears settled on my lower lashes and made it difficult to see. I choked back the urge to cry. "You can sleep. I'm okay."

The fatigue from the battle still weighed him down, and his hand slipped off my waist. When the rhythm of his breath slowed, and his hand twitched beside me, I took it as my signal to go.

I found a pair of his trousers, and pulled them on while I watched him sleep. Messy petaled hair rested over his temple and forehead. His hand still laid near where I sat. My heart tore itself apart the longer I looked at him.

I wanted to stay and never leave.

That was never my fate.

The moon peered through wispy clouds, and cast a soft glow on the landscape. The light from it guided me back to my tent, distancing me from Casimir. If I were to see Estelle, I needed to be ready to leave.

It was doubtful she would drag me back to the Iron Thorn, though Casimir worried she would. My last buds took over two months to bloom, but I didn't think I could stay in Mistvalle another moment if it meant Casimir was close. His presence threatened to have me turn my back on the prophecy and give me the chance to laugh back at the deities.

The weight of the warning from my dream stayed with me, and I prayed there was still time to appease them.

Inside my tent was frigid, and I hated returning to it alone. A jolt ran through me when I remembered how different my concerns were hours before. The only thing I dreaded was a day spent with healers and their hands on me or sleeping alone. Those problems were miniscule.

The moon provided me with only a faint glimmer of light as I rummaged through my trunk blindly. I grabbed a pair of leather trousers, a tunic, an armor vest, and a thick cloak. The boots I wore before the battle rested at the foot of my bed, and I made haste, changing in the cold that swept through the slits in the tent.

It felt wrong to remove Casimir's clothes, but I tucked them neatly on top of my clothing chest, and made quick work of pulling the leather trousers on first, then the tunic—tucking the extra fabric into the waistband. The armor vest took more effort to tie behind my back, but when it was on, I added the cloak and boots.

The longer I stayed, the more my resolve waned.

I left my belongings behind and wondered if I would see them again. Estelle would either get me far from Mistvalle to keep me hidden or at least have me remain in the palace under her watchful eye.

It was an exchange I was finally willing to make, much too late, and with too much blood on my hands.

What seemed like a lifetime ago, I once told my father I would forsake my safety to die with innocent hands. It made sense to me at the time, and the very thought of taking a life never occurred to me. I was naive, and yet I wished to be that girl again, if for only a moment.

My boots padded softly on the stone path. No one lingered outside their tents, and the bonfires were out for the night. The silence was eerie, and I forced myself to keep walking through the camp.

It'd be too easy to take a turn and sneak back into Casimir's tent, and keep my buds a secret until they eventually bloomed. I scoffed at the thought, remembering how easy it was for my parents to spot them after they had time to grow.

To think my buds could remain hidden in a land full of Roses was foolish, and it'd bring me more torment to delay the inevitable. I dedicated a significant portion of my life to doing that already, and I wouldn't do it again.

When I passed the guard quarters, I paused and bit the inside of my cheek. My eyes locked onto the familiar tent, visible through the gaps in the trees. It pulled at me. My fists clenched at my sides and I turned from it.

I jumped when I noticed Taryn a few feet from me, her hands tucked into pockets in her trousers. Her red hair hung loosely over her shoulder in a braid, and she gave me a knowing look.

"Off to see the lady about your buds?" she inquired, taking a step closer. The scent of ale followed her, and I assumed she had left the tavern not long ago.

I stole another glance at the tents. "Were they there when I left your tent?"

Her shoe scuffed on the stone path as she kicked at a leaf. "It didn't feel right to be the one to say something. I assumed you were just hiding it."

I shook my head and faced her. "Even Estelle and Halburn didn't notice. I guess we can all see who the best healer is." Bitterness dripped from my tongue, and I hoped she wouldn't think my anger was for her. The burning hole of disdain for the gods pierced through me, leaving me hollow. I feared it would eat away at my soul.

Taryn rocked on her heels and walked closer. "Wanna talk about it? Or are you going back to being one of those 'wallow alone' gals?"

I pursed my lips and forced myself not to glance in Casimir's direction again. "I'm worried if I don't say something I might hide in Casimir's tent until I bloom here."

Taryn chuckled and came over to me, looping her arm with mine. "You finally let go of Rory's hold on you?"

I raised an eyebrow. "Ronin?"

"Ah, that's the one. Not like he deserves to be remembered for anything. Although he was pleasant to look at."

"Gross, Taryn," I grumbled.

She chortled, and I had half a mind to cover her mouth as we walked back through the camp.

No matter how much I needed to speak with Estelle, I let her lead me through the sea of tents which held our sleeping companions. Everbloom became nothing more than a few scattered canopies on a cliff side. Nevertheless, Taryn made light of the one who brought us there.

It softened some of the edge from Ronin's memory, and I had immense gratitude for every person who helped chip away at the shell of his betrayal.

Taryn didn't speak again until we settled on the stone benches at the furthest fire pit. Embers crackled in it as the flames continued to die out. It put me in a daze, and I watched as they flickered with light.

We sat shoulder to shoulder, and I sensed Taryn's nervous energy with every twitch of her foot. She bit at her nails, and I sighed.

"Are you the one that needs to talk?" I asked.

She avoided making eye contact with me; her pale orange gaze focused on something in the distance. Her shoulders hunched, weighed down by an invisible burden.

After a long pause, she looked at me. "Don't let your need to make amends walk you into a corner. White bloom or not, it's just plain stupid not to try something first before giving yourself up. You're young, but don't let that keep you ignorant."

I averted my gaze, afraid if one more person told me not to go, I would listen. "Ulrik deserves to grow up in a realm without the struggles we had to endure. And so does every generation to come. Don't you want that for him?"

She bristled next to me and bit at another nail. "Of course. But paying it in blood is plain wrong." She spat at the ground and went for another nail.

I flinched and stopped her. "I'll be fine, and I promise I won't let Estelle march me back to the kingdom."

"Is that why you were staring at pretty-boy's tent with longing?" She scoffed. "Don't be a martyr, white bloom. It's dramatic." She looked away as a light breeze swept up curls from both her hair and mine. The braid she wore offered little help with her stray coils.

I still found it in me to envy her ability to braid her hair with ease. I forcefully pushed my curls behind my ears, unable to ignore the peculiar feeling of the buds intertwined with my hair.

With a heavy sigh, I got up from the bench. Taryn looked at me and quirked a brow.

"Didn't think I could offend you that quick," she teased.

Grinning, I shook my head. "I try not to take anything you say to heart, Taryn. I appreciate the lack of coddling. Ulrik will be one strong kid, that's for sure."

Taryn scratched at her arm and glanced toward the tent where Ulrik stayed with his gran. "He's probably the only soul in this realm I coddle. And he deserves every last bit of it."

I pulled my cloak tighter over my shoulders. "Then stop stalling me, and let me do what I can so he has a long life ahead of him," I said, my tone lighthearted.

Taryn started to chortle.

The earth disrupted beneath my feet. It surged through my veins, and her laughter died in her throat.

Screams rang like an alarm bell through the camp as I ducked to catch Taryn's falling frame. An arrow speared through her neck, and she sputtered and fell into my arms. Her blood coated my skin and painted her tunic in a harsh display.

The screaming carried on. My throat burned raw, and a wall of vines flew up to block the other arrows as they soared through the trees.

"Please," I cried as I turned Taryn over and pressed my hands to the wound through her neck. Warm blood pooled over my skin, and I tried to apply more pressure.

The thrum of her life was gone before she even fell.

Confused shouting erupted in the camp, and I felt every individual body as they stumbled from their beds. It echoed through my head, and I begged the energy to go away before it shattered me.

I couldn't think.

My hands applied more pressure, and it only caused more blood to form around her shoulders in a puddle.

"Please, *please,* breathe," I begged.

Every person in the camp darted from their tents, and I sensed the footsteps as they ran for me. They shouted questions, but it all blurred in the horrible ringing in my ears.

The enemy approached from the woods, but I couldn't bring myself to care. Numbness filled my limbs. I moved my hands over the wound, trying to stop the bleeding.

Under the panic, the sensation of swords cutting through my vines was unmistakable. I stayed there, frozen.

Taryn's pale eyes had no life in them as they gazed at the sky. Stars echoed in their reflection, and I felt sick at the sight.

Weapons sang as they unsheathed. Thundering footsteps ran past me. I didn't look up to watch them; I didn't need to. Every pulse in their body echoed with mine, and it nauseated me.

Tears fell onto my hands, disrupting the blood in ripples of salty drops. I watched them fall and refused to move my hands. I begged the gods to allow me to mend her like I did the flowers.

Her braid laid in a mess on the stone, loose from how she had overlapped it lazily. Strands of red rested on her face, and without thinking, I brushed them away, leaving a trail of blood behind.

Sobs wracked my body, and I struggled to catch my breath.

Strong hands pulled at my arms, and I thrashed on instinct. "No!" My voice rang over the chaos, splitting my head as the sounds whirled.

"Are you hurt?!" Casimir yelled over my screams.

I whipped my head in his direction as he looked me over for injuries. His gaze flickered to my bloodied hands, and then he found Taryn's body dead against the stone. His grip faltered, and he stared at her in equal parts horror and disbelief.

"Help her!" I cried. My bloodied hands pulled at him, and torment flashed across his expression. I watched in shock as he shook his head.

"We have to go."

His words sent me scrambling away. I pressed my hands to her chest this time and pounded them against her ribs. Casimir once brought me back, and I begged the gods to allow me to do the same for her.

Please, Taryn, come back.

"Elita—"

A projectile soared through the air and landed with a resounding thud near the base of the fire pit, causing it to erupt in a dense cloud of smoke.

My skin prickled, and I jolted upright, grasping for Casimir.

The scent reminded me of the cell from so long ago. It was never too far from my mind, and terror flooded me as I tried to do something before the sensation hit me.

Stone met with my back and I writhed on the ground as the herbs rushed through my body, and just as quick, Casimir dropped beside me.

Fire licked up my skin, and I fought the familiar agony.

Through bleary eyes, ruby armor came into view.

I tried to scream.

A mistake I once learned to avoid.

Nothing came out as I watched members of the Iron Guard move through the camp, swords drawn as they went for the tents. My stomach turned, and I waited to see Talos appear, only to find more Iron Guards coming out of the trees.

"Find the boy!" one of the guards yelled over the chaos. "The king wants Prince Ulrik and the mother unharmed! When they're secured, find Blackthorne."

Tears fell down my temples as I stared back into Taryn's lifeless eyes across from me. The shock and fear couldn't even take root as grief shattered in my chest.

An Iron Guard nearly sprinted past us, but froze, their attention on Taryn's body. "Damn it...the king will have our heads." The guard pressed a boot to Taryn's cheek, and burning anger tore through me. In the next moment, the guard's eyes found mine, shining with recognition. "We just need the prince. I've found the Rose!" he shouted.

The guard kneeled beside me on the ground, and flipped me over while they pulled out what sounded like shackles. I groaned, the stone cold on the side of my cheek.

I squeezed my eyes shut, begging for my limbs to move so I could fight back. Something moved to my right, and I looked, horrified as Casimir staggered upright. My mouth wouldn't move, and the words were trapped in my throat.

"Get your fucking hands off her," he snapped, swaying on bare feet with no sword in sight.

A whimper left my lips and I wanted to reach out to him, to stop him from fighting a fruitless battle. But I couldn't move past it like he did, and Casimir went to charge for the guard that held me to the ground.

He didn't make it a full step before an arrow caught his right shoulder, tearing through his tunic and skin, sending spatters of blood through the air. Tears pooled down my face as I tried to use all the strength I had left, moving as much as I could.

Casimir straightened on shaking legs, and to my horror, another arrow soared through the air, catching him in the right side of his chest.

"*No!*" The scream tore through me as I tried to move, scrambling toward Casimir's falling body in agonizing inches. "Please!"

The guard shoved my face to the stone as I wept, watching Casimir hit the ground with a sickening thud.

My eyes were wide in disbelief as I watched blood seep through his tunic. "Casimir!" His name left my lips in a broken sob. I used every last bit of strength I had to reach out to him, my fingers brushing his ankle. He didn't groan or writhe on the ground. He laid horribly still, and I cried harder, trying to activate my abilities.

The guard wasted no time, and he tore my outstretched arm back, securing my wrists.

"Please. *Please!*" I sobbed, my face soaked with tears.

Somewhere in the distance, a child screamed.

The Iron Guard began to stand, tugging me along.

"No! Casimir!" I cried out his name as my heart shattered in my chest. My limbs wouldn't wake up, and I wailed into the night, unable to do anything but watch as they dragged me away, leaving Casimir and Taryn dead in the dirt.

Fifty-Two

Darkness engulfed me, and a strange rolling movement nearly made me vomit. The ground raced beneath me and I rattled around the space with my hands knotted behind my back. The moment I became conscious enough to form a thought, Casimir and Taryn's deaths plagued me. Their blood spilled among what was meant to be our sanctuary.

"Is someone there?" Galan's voice came from beside me, the body to my right. I didn't reply.

Someone else moved to the left in the dark carriage, at least, that's what it felt like we were in. I couldn't bring myself to care. Not as I stared into the blackness, hoping that, wherever it was we rode to, I would die soon after we got there.

Anything but the torment that settled deep in my soul.

My ghost was gone.

I'd lost everything.

Water dripped in the distance. It carried on a taunting tune, and brought me out of my daze. I curled in on myself, listening to the sound of chains scrape when I did. It didn't matter that my ankle was tethered. I folded my hands close to my chest, squeezing my eyes tightly.

Something solid knocked against my foot. I didn't move. Didn't look to see what it was.

Casimir…

The sting of tears built behind my eyes, and I tried to curl further into myself. Small enough for every bone to ache—small enough to disappear. When I inhaled, it burned through my entire chest, an inferno in my lungs. I shook with silent sobs as my nails dug into my palms.

"Steady, Fullan." *Valor*. His voice brought me more sorrow. I couldn't find relief. He would be dead soon, too.

"She was out for quite some time." Orin's voice came from nearby, raspy.

Another tap to my leg made my swollen eyes peer open. In front of me in a small cell sat Valor, one of his wrists chained to the iron bars. He was disheveled and wearing sleep clothes. Unharmed except for a new cut across his cheek.

Valor leaned forward, his boot still pressed to my shin. "Are you injured?" he asked, his gaze on my hands. The blood was long ago dried, buried beneath my nails, and crusted in the cracks of my skin.

My heart sank deeper in my chest. The hollow organ fell through me, and for a moment, it felt as if it vanished entirely. Every inch of my body echoed a grief too heavy, too wicked.

I opened my mouth, choking out a weak sob around the words. "Casimir is dead. They killed Taryn, too." I didn't sound like myself, and before Valor could reply past the horrified expression on his face, I curled into a ball once more, letting out panicked, hot breaths against my knees. "They're dead. The Iron Guards killed them. They're gone…" I swallowed past the sensation of something stuck in my throat.

I failed them. The gods warned me, and I didn't listen.

My eyes shut, and the questions that filled the cell became nothing but a buzz in my ears. Orin's broken shouts echoed, the words meaningless. I didn't owe them answers. I wouldn't comfort them through their grief. Not when I had been ruined by mine.

In the darkness, the torment swallowed me whole.

The scent of cloves brought me out of a listless state. Herbs swirled in my blood, and it was as if I was floating outside of my body. Anchored only by a soul damned to pay for the sins of a goddess.

Down the hall, I heard the same voice that filled many of my nightmares. Talos's hysteric shouts echoed in the stone cells, carrying emotions unfit for a king who captured the people he'd been hunting.

Panic filtered through the bars as guards scrambled to settle him. He spat curses, muttering over and over again: *"Where is she?"* The first few times, I thought he meant me. It didn't take long to sink in that he meant Taryn.

"You fools!" Talos's shout reverberated off the stones. It would've made me recoil if I was able to feel anything. All I could allow room for was the sting of tinctures in my blood.

Casimir is dead.

A shallow inhale pulled between my dry lips, burning my raw throat. *How long had I been screaming?*

"We brought her body, Your Majesty. A proper burial may bring you peace—"

"Who is responsible? Who fired the arrow?" Grief didn't suit Talos, and the fact he ever trusted guards from the Iron Thorn with a Rose's life, it proved he wasn't as clever as he thought.

But he had no right to grieve Taryn. No right to punish someone for doing what he would have accomplished by shearing her.

More sounds erupted through the cells. A struggle? I couldn't place it. Beneath the tinctures, a soft thrum began to return to my veins, and I sensed the despair. The kind that belonged to the companions around me. The kind that was carried by a king who brought about his own misfortune.

A blade cut through flesh. I heard a dagger retract before a body fell to the stones somewhere down the hall. The aftermath of a king undone by loss that didn't belong to him. Taryn wasn't his to grieve.

Tears trailed over the bridge of my nose, and beneath the sound of Talos losing his temper, I heard the shuffle of boots and chains. Then, a hand rested on my shoulder, the weight familiar enough.

Under it all, I heard Valor whisper, "I'm sorry, Fullan. I know what he meant to you." I wondered then if he had felt the full weight of losing my mother, regardless of the years they spent apart, had he experienced the same crushing pain?

After the sounds settled down the hall, disappearing with the panicked rush of Talos's pulse, I opened my heavy eyes to look at my father. "It's okay. Soon, I won't have to feel it." It came out weak, riddled with defeat.

Valor's brow furrowed, and his hand squeezed my shoulder. "It's too early to give up. Steady your heart."

I released a shaky sigh. "I can't." The simple statement couldn't begin to explain the despair. It didn't tell him that I had nothing left. That watching my father and friends die on top of all the other deaths was unfathomable. I couldn't cling to hope when I watched mine bleed out in the dirt back at Mistvalle.

Another gentle squeeze, and I tilted my head up at Valor.

"I nearly wallowed in my grief when your mother died. I'd been in Mistvalle when the news reached me…the pain lingers, but I find myself grateful that I didn't stay there. That I didn't let it stop me from coming back. Had I let it bury me, I would have never had the chance to meet my daughter."

Tears welled in my eyes, and my chin quivered. "I'm so afraid. I can't watch you die too." The words came out broken, but as I stared at him, at the face of my father, I couldn't bear to accept such a cruel fate. I wouldn't let them kill him, nor the others they captured.

Valor shifted closer and moved his hand to my hair, pushing back the ragged curls. "The realm is not finished with us yet. This isn't the end."

I swallowed the grief, even if only for a moment. I wouldn't let them die. Not as I carried buds in my hair. Not as I carried the weight of the prophecy. If I had to, I would buy them their freedom in exchange for willingness to sacrifice my bloom.

A lull of silence brought me back to the last moments of peace with Casimir, and though it only increased the sorrow, I pushed past it, never taking my eyes off Valor.

Outside of Casimir and Taryn, no one else knew about my bloom.

Softly, I said, "There are buds in my hair. If we escape, there is still hope for the realm. We can end the hiding. The bloodshed. Our people can finally have rest."

Valor's eyes widened, and his hand lingered on my hair. There was no time for him to reply. A slow increase of incense filled the cells. A release of herbs.

It numbed the thrum of abilities that tried to return.

The pain in my body distracted me from the hole in my chest.

Fifty-Three

Stabbing pain radiated from my head, down my neck and through my shoulders. Through cloudy vision, I tried to take in my surroundings. The room blinded me with swirls of white and silver marble. Stained glass windows stretched high to the ceiling, though no sun poured through them.

In the dark of night, lanterns cast a display of bending light, illuminating the throne room. Though I had never been in that exact room, the scenery was familiar.

Six months passed since I was the king's prisoner there.

They brought us to the Temple.

Across the room, a few Roses knelt, still chained together. They all blurred in my vision, nothing more than splotches of spilled ink.

Two guards held me up on my knees in the middle of the room as I swayed, my head not yet steady. My hands were bound with chains rather than rope. Cold metal eased some of the rawness left from the rough fiber. My head lolled back, my eyelids heavy when I blinked.

The scent of cloves swept through the throne room, and a nerve in my face twitched when an icy hand ran over the back of my neck.

"A rose is a beautiful flower, is it not?" Talos's voice was smooth, hiding the pain that echoed in every footfall on the marble. I felt the suffocating grief he left in his wake. He walked in front of me, wearing his father's black crown in his wavy golden hair. Pale green eyes stared down at me, clouded with unfitting sadness. His face was adorned with blooming bruises, and his right hand was wrapped in bandages. He looked undone, and nothing like the polished prince he once was.

Talos stopped, his head tilting to the side as he stared at me. "What, you don't agree?" He frowned and let a rose drop to the floor in front of me, his foot crushing it. "I find their beauty quite delightful. A flower so special, Aeterna dedicated a whole race to them."

He grabbed my chin, forcing me to look over at the Roses chained, their faces pale and their resolve gone as they came into focus.

"Do they appear favored by the gods to you?" Talos sneered in my ear. "What a wicked race to leave this realm to die, and rob me of a father and family." Talos's words made my skin crawl. As if he had any claim on Taryn and Ulrik.

I clenched my teeth and tried to pry my face out of his hand, but he gripped my jaw tighter. "I once asked you a simple question, one that could've spared unnecessary bloodshed. Do you not see what your arrogance has cost me?" he seethed.

My will to fight back dwindled with every flash of Casimir's body falling to the ground that swam through my mind.

The gods tried to warn me. If only I'd listened.

Tears trailed my cheeks, and Talos scoffed, releasing my face. Hair fell across my cheek, catching in a raw cut I hadn't noticed before. I barely glanced up at the line of Roses. It was the first time I took in the faces staring back at me. They were all Roses who fought in the battle, and I understood what was happening.

Valor, Galan, Moria, and Orin were the only Roses they gathered. I wondered if that meant everyone back in Mistvalle died on the cliffside along with Taryn and Casimir. To my dismay, none of them appeared able to fight. They stared back at me, hands bound, their features weighed down by tinctures. Orin wore a bloodied tunic, his lip split, and the rim of his eyes red. I felt sick when I realized one of Valor's arms looked dislocated. Moria could barely stay upright, her hair in a mess of gray and black knots, and Galan had dried blood from his nose to his chin. Whatever the guards had done, it left them a shell of their former selves.

Talos straightened, his hands shaking as he adjusted his crown with a manic look in his eye. "Now, this Rose…" My heart dropped as Talos pointed to Valor, taking a step toward him. "He killed my father and hundreds of my best soldiers. It seems unfitting to give him a quick death."

The room spun with dread as I watched Talos close in on my father, malice in every shift of his body. "Perhaps I should repay him for the damage he's done." Talos stopped before Valor, and pulled out a dagger with his good hand.

My panicked breaths filled the room as he pressed the steel to Valor's throat. "*No!*" The scream reverberated through the throne room, heavy with desperation.

Talos's head snapped in my direction, a crease in his brow. He looked me over, the dagger still touching Valor's skin. It was only a flick from draining his life.

Tears streamed down my face as I raised higher on my knees. "Don't hurt him. Please."

Talos's expression told me that I made a horrible mistake. Every inch of my body turned to stone as he faced Valor, observing him.

"How poetic…" Talos glanced at me over his shoulder, then to Valor once more. "Your father killed mine, am I correct?" He didn't need me to answer. The sobs that poured out of me proved his assumption right. "How fitting that I be the one to kill yours."

"Don't touch him!" Anger bled from my tongue as I pulled against the chains, attempting to stand. One of the guards shoved me back to the floor, but I didn't take my eyes off Talos—not as he toyed with Valor's life.

"I am the final bloom. Please, if you—"

The blade flicked across Valor's cheek, reopening the scar from years long past.

"Please!" It tore out of me, echoing the hysteria that clawed through my veins. Another cut to his other cheek, leaving two bloody trails down his face. Valor didn't even flinch.

"*Stop!*" My entire body trembled, itching with unnatural heat. Red and black stirred at the edge of my vision.

Talos whipped around, the bloodied dagger in his hand as he stalked over to me, his cape billowing behind him. When he reached me, he bent down until we were eye-to-eye. "You assume I'm ignorant to your bloom? As if I wasn't given that information before your people led me right to you?"

The inferno in my blood turned cold, and I winced, pulling back.

Talos straightened but never broke eye contact. "You have nothing to offer me. No bargaining pieces. Your desperation is not enough to save them."

I pushed past the confusion, pleading, "I will go willingly. I'll remain here, be sheared at your hand, if you at least allow him a painless death."

He scoffed. "I already have you, White Bloom. Your words mean nothing," he taunted. When he went to turn back toward Valor, something sparked in my veins. Heat like I hadn't experienced before. It overpowered the herbs in my blood, and the smoke at the edge of my vision seemed to manifest.

Talos froze, his head turned to me. Over his shoulder, I saw a glint of gold in the center of his green eyes.

"Do not touch him." It came out like a command, my voice not my own.

Despite the way the Roses behind him cowered at the sound, Talos appeared enthralled. He walked back to me, returned the dagger to its hilt, and ran a hand over the vines that curled through the air, struggling to manifest. He didn't show any fear even as I managed to conjure past the herbs.

He knelt before me and gripped my chin. "How interesting," he mused, turning my head to the side. My skin prickled, and I tried to jerk away, but he wouldn't release me. "Much more resilient than I expected."

As soon as he said it, the scent of herbs slithered up my nose. I hadn't noticed the guard that came to my side until the numbness crept through me, devouring the dark tendrils. I gasped at the sensation as my body drooped, slack in Talos's hand.

He held me there as if the weight was nothing. "Lock her in my chamber to prepare for the ceremony. She is who Esen spoke of," he said, his gaze roving over me.

Across the throne room, Valor's eyes widened. I couldn't bear to look at the others as their expressions displayed their fear. I held Valor's stare, knowing it would be some of the last moments I ever got to look into the eyes of my father.

"And the others?" the guard inquired.

Talos paused and hardly offered a glance at the people I cared for, deciding their fate in a matter of seconds. "The gardens to await their execution will do."

I thought I had cried all I could. That there was nothing left. But a mixture of a sob and a scream tore out of my chest as the guards lifted me by my arms and dragged me further from the Roses and the throne room as I thrashed.

Valor watched me go, agony distorting his features.

The doors shut, and I wailed, shattered and burning with fury at the realm, the deities, and a destiny I never wanted.

Fifty-Four

Flames licked up my body, and I welcomed them. They crawled through my veins until gasps fell from my lips, the only exit for such torment. I allowed it to take over, and relished in how the pain drowned out anything else. Until it wasn't enough, and visions of Casimir and Taryn made me recoil. No torture compared, and the walls swirled with images of their faces.

Velvet scratched my bare hands and feet as I scrambled away from the visions of death. Never before was I able to cry past the herbs. They failed to silence me then as I wailed.

More liquid poured down my throat, and the sensation of Talos's hand on my chin made me recoil. The herbs were preferable over the feel of his slender fingers while they caressed my jaw.

Heat erupted in my throat, and I kicked at the air, wishing for my feet to make contact with something.

Talos huffed and moved back. The room swirled in colors of red, silver, and white. Such evil shouldn't have extravagant things, yet the gods offered him everything he wanted with no regard for his cruelty.

A guard near the door came over to where I flailed and poured a different tincture down my throat. It numbed and filled me with ice until my lashing turned into shaking.

Talos sighed as if exhausted. "I'll have to make a stronger tincture. Have my things ready for later."

The guard nodded in reply and hurried out the door.

Talos crossed the room as my movement settled.

I wished for tears, but I stayed there frozen. Talos's green gaze flickered over me, and eventually, he released a heavy exhale.

"Try not to hurt my maids when they prepare you for the ceremony. After everything you've stolen from me, you'll watch them die." One of his pale fingers grazed my cheek, and I tried to move away, but my limbs protested. The connection from my brain to my body grew disconnected. Whatever he thought I was at fault for made little sense, and I could do nothing but remain rigid from the tincture.

He left my side, and it should have given me relief, but I accepted nothing would ever again.

I was going to witness my friends and family die once more. Ripped from me by evil rulers and gods who laughed at my torment. In the depths of my being, I cursed Aeterna. I screamed in the confines of my mind, wishing for her to appear before me for the chance to slit her throat. In the madness, snickering reverberated in my thoughts. I brought the gods nothing but amusement.

Now, they came to claim the sacrifice I owed.

I barely noticed the women who entered the room. They disrupted the silence and woke me from a state of nothingness. Everything around me drowned in the color red, and with each inhale, my chest grew heavier. Their disruption reminded me of too many awful things.

With nimble hands, they shoved me into a feather-light black gown, reminiscent of the one I wore long ago. Long sleeves reached my wrists, encircling them with lace. The bodice was fitted with a neckline that wrapped around the lower part of my neck. It left enough room for the sacrificial scar to show.

I tried to take comfort in the fact that the sacrifices ended with me. Roses wouldn't have to live in fear of being sheared. I wondered if there'd be any Roses after Talos hunted them through the realm.

There was no time to ponder it.

The maids finished putting me in the gown and left my hair and face in a mess of sweat and blood. They brought out a thin black lace veil and covered my hair and face. The edge of it fell to my chin and fluttered with each breath. It left only a portion of my neck exposed, and the purpose was clear.

Everyone moved in a blur as they pulled me out of the bedchamber. My legs were ready to crumble beneath me, but I followed them with no other choice. A guard held onto my chains and tugged me along. I didn't remember them putting the restraints on. They left a strange sensation around my wrists and cut into my skin with every pull.

The halls of white didn't interest me. I numbed myself to everything, and my gaze fell to my feet—still bare. They peeked past the billowing black fabric, and I felt more shadow than human. Void of life. Darkness that walked the earth, nothing more than a smidge of ink on the land. It was fitting.

With my eyes low, I missed the moment Talos joined the crowd of bodies that walked beside me. His scent was unmistakable, and it filled my senses, threatening to knock me to my knees. My muscles coiled, and the only evidence of pain echoed beneath my eye as a nerve jumped. It was uncomfortable, and if I cared more, I may have tried to rub the sensation away.

The hall narrowed, and though I wanted to block it out, I watched Talos through the thin veil while he took the chain linked to my shackles in a gloved hand. He wore long scarlet robes with silver roses embroidered into the silk fabric. It swept across the floor, and if he were any closer, I would've stepped on it.

Large doors at the end of the hall stole my attention from the marble floors. Each door had a large silver rose on them. They shimmered in the lantern lights, and the milky shade of the wood made it sear my eyes. The handles were twisting vines covered in thorns, and I wished then for the ability to conjure thousands of them.

We reached the doors, and two guards yanked them open for us. Talos glanced over his shoulder, dark circles beneath his pale gaze.

It sent a jolt through me when I realized Ulrik had the same color eyes as his father.

He led me outside, and the garden before me sent sweat trailing down my spine. We were on a platform high above the sacrificial gardens, and below us, the people I cared for were all chained and on their knees. They stared up at us with resolute expressions. They refused to give the new king the satisfaction of begging for their lives.

Sweat drenched my body, and I thought I may be sick again at the sight of my father among the line of Roses. Valor's scarlet stare brought me nothing but dread and more pain.

Talos brought me to the edge of the platform, and I glanced at the garden below, taking in the decay of the plants. It wasn't the typical death of wither, but something more malevolent. Everything turned black with rot, and the trees twisted and bent as if they were born from the Drought Lands. White moss grew over the dirt, and it painted the knees of every

Rose with the appearance of ash. In the center, the black agate stone platform reflected the burning fire of the torches.

The center was void of any Roses to be sacrificed. Talos had no need for them when my hair was filled with buds.

Before Talos sentenced them to die, he came closer to me. I tried to move away, but there was nowhere to go. He tilted my head, exposing the side of my neck. The veil slipped with the tilt of my head, and he brushed it out of the way of the old scar.

He pulled out a thin blade dipped in ink, and carved into my neck. The twitch beneath my eye threatened to close it. I didn't move from his grasp. I stood and endured it, unwilling to fold in his presence.

Rather than shutting my eyes, I stared through the veil, my gaze locked onto the face of every Rose beneath me. A heavy weight settled over me when I realized I would never see the flicker of life in their eyes again. I wanted to remember the deep set shape of Galan's almond eyes. The way Valor gazed back with unwavering resolve; pieces of his features mirroring my own—the face of my father.

When Talos finished, the skin he carved throbbed. He adjusted the veil over my face, tugging it back to my chin.

I finally received my true sacrificial marking. I half expected the gods to erupt in sickening cheers throughout the realm. No sounds thundered through the night sky. In the crisp wither air, the usual chirp of fleeing birds fell silent. The wind didn't howl. An eerie silence swept through the garden. It'd make it so much worse to hear them all die in unison.

I wondered if I would sense their lives drain against the earth, as I had the soldiers in Tyvolia.

Whatever tincture Talos gave me weakened my abilities. Even so, I reached for the power and begged it to ripple through my veins. My heart ached with insurmountable sorrow, longing to grant them freedom from their fate. I'd let Talos shear my head a thousand times over. Cover me in sacrificial markings. Drown me in the torturous herbs. Anything other than what came next.

Talos walked to the very edge of the platform and glowered over the railing at those below us. If I had the physical strength, I'd kick him over the edge. My limbs trembled with the desire to reach out and throw him off the platform and listen as he hit the dirt.

Again, I called to my abilities, but they slipped through my grasp.

Talos jutted his chin and squared his shoulders. He stood like a king, all pride and arrogance, and no soul.

Even when my father used to tell me about the evils of the realm or of our king, I never believed it possible for someone to harbor such cruelty in their heart. Talos proved me wrong at every turn. No matter how far the Roses ran, or how well they hid, his need for vengeance doomed every last one of them.

He'd rid the world of our race until we were nothing more than legends in children's books. Reduced to what he made us out to be—villains of the realm, who left the people to suffer from drought—the truth buried with us.

Talos tightened his grip on the railing, and some of his blonde hair fell from beneath his crown. "By order of your new king, I sentence you all to death. By my hand, and by the blessing of Esen." Talos's voice echoed in the dead garden.

Not a single Rose flinched, and he grew irate when they appeared unaffected. They were prepared to die without giving him the terror he hungered for.

Their lack of fear did nothing to steel my own resolve. Every inch of my body shuddered with calamity. Sweat coated my skin, and my pulse thundered until the hair on my neck stood on end. A tangible, horrible sensation. From my feet to my head, the blood rushed so loud it made me dizzy. Heat slithered beneath my skin.

Breathe. Breathe. Breathe.

Energy buzzed in the back of my skull until my vision warped. Waves rippled around me, there and not. It twisted like smoke while I panted. Desperation tore me apart with every attempt to summon my power.

Talos took a scepter from a nearby guard and raised it at his side, preparing to slam it down and signal the end of their lives.

Time slowed, and my pulse erupted with fiery pain. It sucked the air from my lungs, and in a rush of familiarity, the thrum of the earth echoed through my entire being.

The sensation ravaged my veins.

Shrieks of agony clawed out of my throat as I dropped to the floor of the platform, the veil torn away. My palms found the marble beneath our feet, and I disrupted the earth.

It broke apart in pieces of dirt and stone as the ground exploded between the platform and the Roses. Their screams of shock rang in my ears, and I felt every heartbeat flutter with panic.

I only have to give them enough time to get out.

Roots stretched and grew through the gardens, shielding them from the king and the guards.

Energy tore through me like molten stone. It ignited every vein in my arms, and I forced myself to push past the block. The herbs fought against me, but I pressed further until my fingers bled. The sleeves tore open, revealing horrible streaks through my skin as they ripped up my arms like twisting vines.

My abilities waged war with every nerve in my body, and my shrieks turned into guttural sobs.

A guard reached for me and yelped when he touched my skin. I felt his life drain, and a surge of energy burst through me as his life force fueled my own. The atmosphere became charged as the waves in the air heightened, turning a deep, dark combination of black and crimson.

I gasped and pressed further into the rush of energy. His death brought me nothing but strength, and the wall of roots continued their reach until they surpassed the top of the Temple.

Talos's presence echoed in the thrum, and I tried to reach for the pulse in his body. But with every shift of my focus, I nearly lost the roots. As they faltered, I pushed aside the desire for Talos's blood and embraced the torment that clawed at my flesh. My arms became a canvas of bloody streaks, reminiscent of bleeding vines.

Another guard reached for me and regretted it the same. His life poured into me, and I sucked in a hot breath through gritted teeth. The waves twisted and blurred the edge of my vision.

Through the pain, I sensed the shift in the Roses. They moved with the energy they had left, and I hoped I bought them enough time.

In another burst of power, I tore roots and vines through the earth outside of the Temple. If I disrupted the path enough, the Iron Guard had no chance to reach the Roses by horse as they ran from the sacrificial garden.

The anguish ripped through my fingers to my shoulders, and salt covered my face, leaking into my mouth, as I tried to keep air in my lungs.

Silver glinted at my side, and wet heat spread through my right cheek bone when a blade cut across my skin.

The thrum died, and before I had the chance to bury thorns into anyone around me, smoke burst on the platform, and the aroma of the herbs slithered down my throat and up my nose. I sputtered and gagged as my abilities evaporated.

The torn skin on my arms and face mirrored the anguish that coursed through my body, leaving me in a state of misery. Even so, a horrible chuckle rattled my chest, and I fell back onto the marble floor, oblivious to the way it smacked my skull.

Talos's eyes swirled with horror and rage when he met my gaze.

I devoured the expression, committing it to memory.

Before the herbs lulled me into the endless black, I spat blood at him, grinning when he recoiled.

The cold marble surface cradled me.

I surrendered to the herbs.

"Foolish girl. You will pay with your blood."

Acknowledgments

First and foremost, sorry for the emotional damage. But I want to thank my readers, because they genuinely bring me so much joy. I've made incredible connections since publishing this series, and it has been the best part of this journey.

Now, I would like to get a little selfish and thank myself. I wrote this in a dark place in my life while I navigated my own trauma. It has been so healing for me to explore human emotion through the eyes of my characters. This book was a labor of love, but it also took many tears and late nights. There were times I considered shelving it or hiding out, but I continued despite the self-doubt, and here we are! Book one got me here, but book two is very special to me.

Onto the people who gave me their endless support, unhinged reactions, and the feedback that helped me shape the story: Sarah, Lorraine, Ashley. R, Kallie, Ashley. C, Katelyn, Sara, Kelly, Samantha, and Meg. Yes, that is a lot of people, and YES, these incredible women all played a vital role in my journey with this book. I appreciate them dearly, and they have all become close friends.

Another special mention for my husband. He was the first eyes on this story and read as I drafted. It was messy and didn't make much sense, but he was locked in, and I will forever have it ingrained in my brain when he finished it. I had fallen asleep while he read the last few chapters, and when I woke up, the first thing he said to me was, "I can't believe you did that."

And to my parents, who have supported me endlessly, it has meant the world to me. There's nothing quite like hearing your parents having sat down and read your book, love it, and believe in you. I am lucky to have a supportive family, brothers, and sisters who have read my books and cheered me on (without trying to swipe a free copy).

All of that said, I once again come back to the readers who continue to give my series a chance. I hope you still trust me enough after this book to read the next one. I'll unfortunately continue the theme of emotional damage, but I promise it'll pay off, eventually!

Content Warnings

Strangulation.
Graphic descriptions of death.
Sleep paralysis.
Explicit language.
Violence, mild gore.

And as always, this series contains themes of navigating loss, grief, and PTSD.

*This list does not cover every possible trigger, and if you find more that you think need to be mentioned, don't hesitate to reach out to me!